# And Quiet Flows the don

## (Book One)

Mikhail Sholokhov

## Alpha Editions

This edition published in 2019

ISBN : 9789353299378

Design and Setting By
**Alpha Editions**
email - alphaedis@gmail.com

# KEY TO
# PRINCIPAL CHARACTERS

ASTAKHOV, STEPAN. A Cossack.

ASTAKHOVA, AKSINYA. Wife of Stepan.

BUNCHUK, ILYA. A Cossack revolutionary.

FOMIN, YAKOV YEFIMOVICH. A Cossack commander, at first a Red, then leader of a White bandit group.

KALMYKOV. White Guard officer.

KAPARIN. Captain. Red officer. Afterwards Fomin's chief of staff.

KOPYLOV, MIKHAIL GRIGORYEVICH. Captain. Chief of staff to Grigory Melekhov.

KORSHUNOV, GRISHAKA. An old Cossack.

KORSHUNOV, MIRON GRIGORYEVICH. His son, father of Natalya Melekhova.

KORSHUNOVA, MARYA LUKINICHNA. Wife of Miron.

KORSHUNOV, DIMITRY MIRONOVICH (Mitka). Son of Miron and Marya Korshunov.

KORSHUNOVA, AGRIPPINA MIRONOVNA. Daughter of Miron and Marya.

KOSHEVOI, MIKHAIL (Misha). A Red Cossack.

KOTLYAROV, IVAN ALEXEYEVICH. A Red Cossack.

KRIVOSHLYKOV. A Cossack revolutionary.

KUDINOV. Commander of Don Cossack insurgent forces.

LISTNITSKY, NIKOLAI ALEXEYEVICH. A landowner.

LISTNITSKY, YEVGENY NIKOLAYEVICH. Son of Nikolai Listnitsky, a White officer.

MELEKHOV, PANTELEI PROKOFYEVICH. An elderly Cossack.

MELEKHOVA, ILYINICHNA. Wife of Pantelei.

MELEKHOV, PYOTR PANTELEYEVICH. Pantelei's elder son, a Cossack officer.

MELEKHOV, GRIGORY PANTELEYEVICH (Grisha). Pantelei's younger son, a Cossack officer, commander of Cossack insurgent division.

MELEKHOVA, YEVDOKIYA PANTELEYEVNA (Dunya). Pantelei's daughter.

MELEKHOVA, DARYA. Wife of Pyotr Melekhov.

MELEKHOVA, NATALYA. Wife of Grigory Melekhov.

MELEKHOVA, POLYA (Polyushka). Daughter of Grigory and Natalya.

MELEKHOV, MISHATKA. Son of Grigory and Natalya.

MOKHOV, SERGEI PLATONOVICH. Shopkeeper and mill-owner in the village of Tatarsky.

MOKHOVA, YELIZAVETA SERGEYEVNA (Liza). Sergei's daughter.

PODTYOLKOV. A Cossack revolutionary. Commander of Red Cossack forces.

POGUDKO, ANNA. Machine-gunner in Bunchuk's detachment

SHAMIL, MARTIN, ALEXEI and PROKHOR. Cossacks, brothers.

STOCKMAN, OSIP DAVYDOVICH. A Communist organizer.

TIMOFEI, "Knave." Scalesman at Mokhov's mill.

TOKIN, CHRISTONYA. A Cossack.

ZYKOV, PROKHOR. A Cossack, orderly to Grigory Melekhov.

# МИХАИЛ ШОЛОХОВ

*Tikhii Don*

# ТИХИЙ ДОН

РОМАН В ЧЕТЫРЕХ КНИГАХ

✳

КНИГА ПЕРВАЯ

ИЗДАТЕЛЬСТВО ЛИТЕРАТУРЫ НА ИНОСТРАННЫХ ЯЗЫКАХ

МОСКВА

# MIKHAIL SHOLOKHOV

# AND QUIET FLOWS THE DON

A NOVEL IN FOUR BOOKS

✳

BOOK ONE

FOREIGN LANGUAGES PUBLISHING HOUSE
MOSCOW

A TRANSLATION FROM THE RUSSIAN
BY STEPHEN GARRY

REVISED AND COMPLETED
BY ROBERT DAGLISH

DESIGNED
BY O. VEREISKY AND Y. KOPYLOV

**BOOK ONE**

Not by the plough is our glorious earth furrowed. . . .
Our earth is furrowed by horses' hoofs,
And sown is our earth with the heads of Cossacks.
Fair is our quiet Don with young widows,
Our father, the quiet Don, blossoms with orphans,
And the waves of the quiet Don are filled
                        with fathers' and mothers' tears.


Oh thou, our father, the quiet Don!
Oh why dost thou, our quiet Don, so sludgy flow?
How should I, the quiet Don, but sludgy flow!
From my depths the cold springs beat,
Amid me, the quiet Don, the white fish leap.

Old Cossack Songs

# PART ONE

## I

The Melekhov farm was at the very end of the village. The gate of the cattle-yard opened northward towards the Don. A steep, fifty-foot slope between chalky, moss-grown banks, and there was the shore. A pearly drift of mussel-shells, a grey, broken edging of wave-kissed shingle, and then—the steel-blue, rippling surface of the Don, seething in the wind. To the east, beyond the willow-wattle fences of threshing-floors—the Hetman's highway, grizzled wormwood scrub, the hardy greyish-brown, hoof-trodden plantain, a cross standing at the fork of the road, and then the steppe, enveloped in a shifting haze. To the south, a chalky ridge of hills. To the west, the street, crossing the square and running towards the leas.

The Cossack Prokofy Melekhov returned to the village during the last war but one with

Turkey. He brought back a wife—a little woman wrapped from head to foot in a shawl. She kept her face covered, and rarely revealed her wild, yearning eyes. The silken shawl bore the scent of strange, aromatic perfumes; its rainbow-hued patterns aroused the envy of the Cossack women. The captive Turkish woman kept aloof from Prokofy's relations, and before long old Melekhov gave his son his portion. All his life the old man refused to set foot inside his son's house; he never got over the disgrace.

Prokofy speedily made shift for himself; carpenters built him a house, he himself fenced in the cattle-yard, and in the early autumn he took his bowed foreign wife to her new home. He walked with her through the village, behind the cart laden with their worldly goods. Everybody, from the oldest to the youngest, rushed into the street. The men laughed discreetly into their beards, the women passed vociferous remarks to one another, a swarm of unwashed Cossack children shouted catcalls after Prokofy. But, with overcoat unbuttoned, he walked slowly along, as though following a freshly-ploughed furrow, squeezing his wife's fragile wrist in his own enormous, black palm, and holding his head with its straw-white mat of curls high in defiance. Only the wens below his cheek-bones

swelled and quivered, and the sweat stood out
between his stony brows.

Thenceforth he was rarely seen in the village,
and never even attended the Cossack gatherings. He lived a secluded life in his solitary
house by the Don. Strange stories were told of
him in the village. The boys who pastured the
calves beyond the meadow-road declared that
of an evening, as the light was dying, they had
seen Prokofy carrying his wife in his arms
right as far as the Tatar burial mound. He
would set her down, with her back to an ancient, weather-beaten, porous rock, on the crest
of the mound, sit down at her side, and they
would gaze fixedly across the steppe. They
would gaze until the sunset had faded, and
then Prokofy would wrap his wife in his sheepskin and carry her back home. The village was
lost in conjecture, seeking an explanation for
such astonishing behaviour. The women gossiped so much that they had not even time to
search each other's heads for lice. Rumour was
rife about Prokofy's wife also; some declared
that she was of entrancing beauty; others main-
tained the contrary. The matter was settled when
one of the most venturesome of the women, the
soldier's wife Mavra, ran along to Prokofy's
house on the pretext of getting some leaven;
Prokofy went down into the cellar for the

leaven, and Mavra had time to discover that Prokofy's Turkish conquest was a perfect fright.

A few minutes later Mavra, her face flushed and her kerchief awry, was entertaining a crowd of women in a by-lane:

"And what could he have seen in her, my dears? If she'd only been a woman now, but a creature like her! Our girls are far better covered! Why, you could pull her apart like a wasp. And those great big black eyes, she flashes them like Satan, God forgive me. She must be near her time, God's truth."

"Near her time?" the women marvelled.

"I wasn't born yesterday! I've reared three myself."

"But what's her face like?"

"Her face? Yellow. No light in her eyes—doesn't find life in a strange land to her fancy, I should say. And what's more, girls, she wears ... Prokofy's trousers!"

"No!" the women drew in their breath together.

"I saw them myself; she wears trousers, only without stripes. It must be his everyday trousers she has. She wears a long shift, and underneath you can see the trousers stuffed into socks. When I saw them my blood ran cold."

The whisper went round the village that Prokofy's wife was a witch. Astakhov's daughter-in-law (the Astakhovs were Prokofy's nearest neighbours) swore that on the second day of Trinity, before dawn, she had seen Prokofy's wife, barefoot, her hair uncovered, milking the Astakhovs' cow. Since then its udder had withered to the size of a child's fist, the cow had lost its milk and died soon after.

That year there was an unusual dying-off of cattle. By the shallows of the Don fresh carcasses of cows and young bulls appeared on the sandy shore every day. Then the horses were affected. The droves grazing on the village pasture-lands melted away. And through the lanes and streets of the village crept an evil rumour.

The Cossacks held a meeting and went to Prokofy. He came out on the steps of his house and bowed.

"What can I do for you, worthy elders?"

Dumbly silent, the crowd drew nearer to the steps. One drunken old man was the first to cry:

"Drag your witch out here! We're going to try her. . . ."

Prokofy flung himself back into the house, but they caught him in the passage. A burly Cossack, nicknamed Lushnya, knocked his head against the wall and told him:

"Don't make a row, there's no need for you to shout. We shan't touch you, but we're going to trample your wife into the ground. Better to de-

stroy her than have all the village die for want
of cattle. But don't you make a row, or I'll
smash the wall in with your head!"

"Drag the bitch out into the yard!" came a
roar from the steps. A regimental comrade of
Prokofy's wound the Turkish woman's hair
around one hand, clamped his other hand over
her screaming mouth, dragged her at a run across
the porch and flung her under the feet of the
crowd. A thin shriek rose above the howl of
voices. Prokofy flung off half a dozen Cossacks,
burst into the house, and snatched a sabre from
the wall. Jostling against one another, the Cossacks rushed out of the house. Swinging the
gleaming, whistling sabre around his head,
Prokofy ran down the steps. The crowd drew
back and scattered over the yard.

Lushnya was heavy on his feet, and by the
threshing-floor Prokofy caught up with him;
with a diagonal sweep down across the left
shoulder from behind, he clave the Cossack's
body to the belt. The crowd, who had been tearing stakes out of the fence, fell back, across the
threshing-floor into the steppe.

Half an hour later the Cossacks ventured to
approach Prokofy's farm again. Two of them
stepped cautiously into the passage. On the
kitchen threshold, in a pool of blood, her head
flung back awkwardly, lay Prokofy wife; her

lips were writhing tormentedly, her gnawed tongue protruded. Prokofy, with shaking head and glassy stare, was wrapping a squealing little ball—the prematurely-born infant—in a sheepskin.

Prokofy's wife died the same evening. His old mother had compassion on the child and took charge of it. They plastered it with bran-mash, fed it with mare's milk, and, after a month, assured that the swarthy, Turkish-looking boy would survive, they carried him to church and christened him. They named him Pantelei after his grandfather. Prokofy came back from penal servitude twelve years later. With his clipped, ruddy beard streaked with grey and his Russian clothing, he did not look like a Cossack. He took his son and returned to his farm.

Pantelei grew up swarthy, and ungovernable. In face and figure he was like his mother. Prokofy married him to the daughter of a Cossack neighbour.

From then on Turkish blood began to mingle with that of the Cossack. And that was how the hook-nosed, savagely handsome Cossack family of Melekhovs, nicknamed "Turks," came into the village.

When his father died Pantelei took over the farm; he had the house rethatched, added an acre of common land to the farmyard, built new sheds, and a barn with a sheet-iron roof. He ordered the tinsmith to cut a couple of weather-cocks out of the scrap iron, and when these were set up on the roof of the barn they brightened the Melekhov farmyard with their carefree air, giving it a self-satisfied and prosperous appearance.

Under the weight of the passing years Pantelei Prokofyevich grew gnarled and craggy; he broadened and acquired a stoop, but still looked a well-built old man. He was dry of bone, and lame (in his youth he had broken his leg while hurdling at an Imperial Review of troops), he wore a silver half-moon ear-ring in his left ear, and his beard and hair retained their vivid raven hue until old age. When angry, he completely lost control of himself and undoubtedly this had prematurely aged his buxom wife, whose face, once beautiful, was now a perfect spider-web of furrows.

Pyotr, his elder, married son, took after his mother: stocky and snub-nosed, a luxuriant shock of corn-coloured hair, hazel eyes. But the younger, Grigory, was like his father: half a head taller than Pyotr, some six years younger, the same pendulous hawk nose as his father's, the whites of his burning eyes bluish in their slightly oblique slits; brown, ruddy skin drawn tight over angular cheek-bones. Grigory stooped

slightly, just like his father; even in his smile
there was a similar, rather savage quality.

Dunya—her father's favourite—a lanky large-
eyed lass, and Pyotr's wife, Darya, with her
small child, completed the Melekhov household.

## II

Here and there stars still hovered in the
ashen, early morning sky. The wind blew from
under a bank of cloud. A mist rolled high over
the Don, piling against the slope of a chalky
hill, and creeping into the gullies like a grey,
headless serpent. The left bank of the river, the
sands, the wooded backwaters, the reedy
marshes, the dewy trees, flamed in the cold,
ecstatic light of dawn. Below the horizon the
sun smouldered, and rose not.

In the Melekhov house Pantelei Prokofyevich
was the first to awake. Buttoning the collar of
his embroidered shirt, he walked out on to the
steps. The grassy yard was spread with a dewy
silver. He let the cattle out into the street. Darya
ran past in her shift to milk the cows. The dew
sprinkled over the calves of her bare white legs,
and she left a smoking, flattened trail behind
her over the grass of the yard. Pantelei Prokofyevich stood for a moment watching the grass

rise from the pressure of Darya's feet, then turned back into the best room.

On the sill of the wide-open window lay the dead rose petals of the cherry-trees blossoming in the front garden. Grigory lay asleep face downward, one arm flung out sideways.

"Grigory, coming fishing?"

"What?" Grigory asked in a whisper, dropping his legs off the bed.

"Come out and fish till sunrise."

Breathing heavily through his nose, Grigory pulled his everyday trousers down from a peg, drew them on, tucked the legs into his white woollen socks, and slowly put on his sandals, straightening out the trodden-down heel.

"But has Mother boiled the bait?" he asked hoarsely, as he followed his father into the porch.

"Yes. Go to the boat. I'll come in a minute."

The old man poured the strong-smelling, boiled rye into a jug, carefully swept up the fallen grains into his palm, and limped down to the beach. He found his son sitting hunched in the boat.

"Where shall we go?"

"To the Black Bank. We'll try around the log where we were sitting the other day."

Its stern scraping the ground, the boat broke away from the shore and settled into the water.

The current carried it off, rocking it and trying to turn it broadside on. Grigory steered with the oar, but did not row.

"Why aren't you rowing?"

"Let's get out into midstream first."

Cutting across the swift mainstream current, the boat moved towards the left bank. The crowing of the village cocks rang out after them across the water. Its side scraping the black, craggy bank rising high above the river, the boat slid into the pool below. Some forty feet from the bank the twisted branches of a sunken elm emerged from the water. Around it turbulent flecks of foam eddied and swirled.

"Get the line ready while I scatter the bait," Pantelei whispered. He thrust his hand into the steaming mouth of the jug. The rye scattered audibly over the water, like a whispered "Sh-sh." Grigory threaded swollen grains on a hook, and smiled.

"Come on, you fish! Little ones and big ones too."

The line fell in spirals into the water and tautened, then slackened again. Grigory set his foot on the end of the rod and fumbled cautiously for his pouch.

"We'll have no luck today, Father. The moon is on the wane."

"Bring any matches?"

"Uh-huh."

"Give me a light."

The old man began to smoke, and glanced at the sun, stranded beyond the elm.

"You can't tell when a carp will bite," he replied. "Sometimes he will when the moon is waning."

"Looks as if the small fish are nipping the bait," Grigory sighed.

The water slapped noisily against the sides of the boat, and a four-foot carp, gleaming as though cast from ruddy copper, leaped upward with a groan, threshing the water with its broad, curving tail. Big drops of spray scattered over the boat.

"Wait now!" Pantelei wiped his wet beard with his sleeve.

Near the sunken tree, among the branching, naked boughs, two carp leaped simultaneously; a third, smaller, writhed in the air, and flapped stubbornly close to the bank.

Grigory impatiently chewed the wet end of his cigarette. The misty sun was half up. Pantelei scattered the rest of the bait, and, glumly pursing his lips, gazed stolidly at the motionless end of the rod.

Grigory spat out the stub of his cigarette, watching its rapid flight angrily. Inwardly he was cursing his father for waking him so early.

Smoking on an empty stomach had made his mouth reek like burnt bristles. He was about to bend and scoop up some water in his palm, but at that moment the end of the rod jerked feebly and began to sink.

"Hook him!" the old man breathed.

Grigory started up and grabbed the rod, but it bent in an arc from his hand, and the end plunged into the water.

"Hold him!" Pantelei groaned, as he pushed the boat off from the bank.

Grigory attempted to lift the rod, but the fish was too strong and the stout line snapped with a dry crack. Grigory staggered and almost fell.

"Strong as a bull!" his father whispered, trying to jab a hook into some fresh bait but missing it. With an excited laugh Grigory fastened a new line to the rod, and made a cast. Hardly had the lead touched the bottom when the end of the rod bent.

"That's him, the devil," Grigory grunted, with difficulty holding in the fish, which was making for midstream.

The line cut the water with a loud swish, raising a sloping, greenish rampart behind it. Pantelei fumbled with the bailer handle in his stumpy fingers.

"Take care he doesn't snap the line."

"Don't worry."

A great red and yellow carp rose to the surface, lashed the water into foam, and dived back into the depths.

"He's pulling my arm off! No, you don't!"

"Hold him, Grisha!"

"I am holding him!"

"Don't let him get under the boat!"

Taking breath, Grigory drew the played-out carp towards the boat. The old man thrust out the bailer, but with its last strength the carp again plunged into the depths.

"Get his head up! Make him swallow some air, that'll quiet him!" Pantelei ordered.

Once more Grigory drew the exhausted fish towards the boat. It floated open-mouthed with its nose against the rough gunwale, its orange-golden fins flickering.

"He's finished!" Pantelei croaked, lifting the fish in the bailer.

They sat on for another half hour. The carp stopped leaping.

"Wind in the line. We've had our catch for today!" the old man said at last.

Grigory pushed off from the bank. As he rowed he saw from his father's face that he wanted to say something, but Pantelei sat silently gazing at the houses of the village scattered under the hill.

"Look here, Grigory . . ." he began uncertainly, pulling at the knot of the sack under his feet. "I've noticed that you and Aksinya Astakhova. . . ."

Grigory flushed violently, and turned away. His shirt collar cut into his muscular, sunburnt neck, pressing out a white band in the flesh.

"You watch out, young fellow," the old man continued, now roughly and angrily, "or I'll be having another kind of talk with you. Stepan's our neighbour, and I won't have any mucking about with his woman. That kind of thing can lead to mischief, and I warn you beforehand, if I see you at it I'll flay the hide off you!"

Pantelei clenched his gnarled fist, and with narrowed eyes watched the blood ebbing from his son's face.

"It's all lies!" Grigory muttered, and gazed straight at the bluish bridge of his father's nose.

"You keep quiet."

"People like to talk—"

"Hold your tongue, you son of a bitch!"

Grigory bent to the oars. The boat leapt forward. The bubbling water danced away from the stern in little scrolls.

They remained silent until, as they were approaching the shore, his father reminded him:

"Mind what I've said, or from now on I'll

25

stop your going out at night. You won't stir a step outside the yard!"

Grigory made no answer. As he beached the boat he asked:

"Shall I give the fish to the women?"

"Go and sell it," the old man said more gently. "You can have the money for tobacco."

Biting his lips, Grigory followed his father. "Try it, Dad! I'm going out tonight even if you hobble my feet!" he thought, his eyes boring fiercely into the back of the old man's head.

When he got home Grigory carefully washed the sand off the fish and fixed a twig through its gills.

At the farm gate he ran into his old friend Mitka Korshunov. Mitka was strolling along, toying with the end of his silver-studded belt. His round, yellow eyes glistened impudently in their narrow slits. Mitka's pupils were long, like a cat's, making his glance swift and elusive.

"Where are you off to with the fish?"

"We caught it today. I'm going to sell it."

"To Mokhov?"

"Uh-huh."

Mitka estimated the weight of the fish with a glance.

"Fifteen pounds?"

"Fifteen and a half. We weighed it on the scales."

"Take me with you. I'll do the bargaining."

"Come on."

"And what do I get?"

"You needn't fear. We shan't quarrel over that."

Church was over, and the villagers were filling the streets. The three Shamil brothers came striding down the road side by side. The eldest, one-armed Alexei, was in the middle. The tight collar of his army tunic held his sinewy neck erect, his thin, curly, pointed little beard twisted provokingly sideways, his left eye winked nervously. His carbine had exploded in his hands at the shooting range many years previously, and a piece of the flying iron had ploughed into his cheek. Now his left eye winked in season and out of season, and a blue scar ran across his cheek, burying itself in his tow-like hair. His left arm had been torn off at the elbow, but Alexei was a past master at rolling a cigarette with one hand. He would press his pouch against his chest, tear off the right quantity of paper with his teeth, bend it into a trough-shape, rake up the tobacco, roll the cigarette and almost before you realized what he was doing, he would be asking you for a light.

Although he was one-armed he was the finest fighter in the village. His fist was not particularly large as fists go—about the size of a calabash

—but he had once happened to get annoyed with his bullock when ploughing, and being without his whip, gave it a blow with his fist that stretched the bullock out over the furrows, blood streaming from its ears. And it hardly recovered. The other brothers, Martin and Prokhor, resembled Alexei down to the last detail. They were just as stocky and broad-shouldered, only each had two arms.

Grigory greeted the Shamils, but Mitka walked on, turning his head aside sharply. At the fisticuffs during Shrovetide, Alexei Shamil had shown no regard for Mitka's youthful teeth. With a powerful swing, he had struck him in the mouth, and Mitka had spat out two good teeth on the grey-blue ice, scarred by the trampling of iron-shod heels.

As he came up to them, Alexei winked five times.

"Selling your load?"

"Want to buy it?"

"How much?"

"A couple of bullocks, and a wife thrown in."

Screwing up his eyes, Alexei jerked the stump of his arm.

"You're a card! Haw-haw! A wife thrown in! Will you take the brats, too?"

"Leave yourself some for breeding, or the Shamils will die out!" Grigory grinned.

In the square the villagers were gathered around the fence of the church. The church warden was holding a goose above his head and shouting: "Going for fifty kopecks. Any more offers?"

The goose craned its neck and peered round, its beady eye squinting contemptuously.

In the middle of a ring of people a grizzled old man, his chest covered with crosses and medals, stood brandishing his arms.

"Old Grishaka is telling one of his tales about the Turkish war," Mitka said, nodding towards the ring. "Let's go and listen."

"While we're listening to him the carp will start stinking and swell."

"If it swells it'll weigh more."

In the square beyond the firecart shed rose the green roof of the Mokhov's house. Passing the outhouse, Grigory spat and held his nose. From behind a barrel, an old man emerged, buttoning up his trousers, and holding his belt in his teeth.

"Hard pressed?" asked Mitka ironically.

The old man buttoned up the last button, and took the belt out of his mouth.

"What's it got to do with you?"

"Your nose ought to be stuck in it, or your beard; so that your old woman wouldn't be able to wash it off in a week."

"I'll stick you in it," said the old man, offended.

Mitka screwed up his cat's eyes in the sun's
glare.

"Aren't you touchy!"

"Get out, you son of a bitch. Why are you
bothering me? Do you want a taste of my belt?"

Laughing quietly Grigory approached the
steps. The balustrade was richly fretted with
wild vine. The steps were speckled with lazy
shadows.

"See how some folk live, Mitka!"

"Even the door-handle's got gold on it!"
Mitka sniffed as he opened the door leading to
the verandah. "Imagine that old fellow getting
in here. . . ."

"Who's there?" someone called from the other
side of the door.

Grigory entered shyly. The carp's tail trailed
over the painted floor-boards.

"Whom do you want?"

A girl was sitting in a wicker rocking-chair,
a dish of strawberries in her hand. Grigory
stared silently at the full, rosy, heart-shaped
lips embracing a berry. With her head on one
side the girl looked the lads up and down.

Mitka came to Grigory's rescue. He coughed.

"Want to buy some fish?"

"Fish? I'll go and ask."

She rocked the chair upright, and rising padded away in her embroidered slippers. The sun shone through her white dress, and Mitka saw the dim outline of full legs and the broad, billowing lace of her underskirt. He was astonished at the satiny whiteness of her bare calves; only on the small round heels was the skin milkily yellow.

"Look, Grisha, what a dress! Like glass! You can see everything through it," he said, nudging Grigory.

The girl came back through the door leading to the corridor, and sat down gently on the chair.

"Go into the kitchen!"

Grigory tiptoed into the house. When he had gone Mitka stood blinking at the white thread of the parting that divided the girl's hair into two golden half-circles. She studied him with mischievous, restless eyes.

"Are you from the village?"

"Yes."

"Whose son are you?"

"Korshunov's."

"And what's your name?"

"Mitry!"

She examined her rosy nails attentively, and with a swift movement tucked up her legs.

"Which of you caught the fish?"

"My friend Grigory."

"And do you fish, too?"

"When I feel like it."

"With hook and line?"

"Yes."

"I'd like to go fishing some time," she said, after a pause.

"All right, I'll take you if you want to."

"Really? How can we arrange it?"

"You'll have to get up very early."

"I'll get up, only you'll have to wake me."

"I can do that. But how about your father?"

"What about my father?"

Mitka laughed. "He might take me for a thief and set the dogs on me."

"Nonsense! I sleep alone in the corner room. That's the window." She pointed. "If you come for me, knock at the window and I'll get up."

The sound of Grigory's timid voice, and the thick, oily tones of the cook came intermittently from the kitchen. Mitka was silent, fingering the tarnished silver of his belt.

"Are you married?" she asked hiding a smile.

"Why?"

"Oh, I'm just curious."

"No, I'm single."

Mitka suddenly blushed, and she, smiling coquettishly and playing with a twig from the hot-house strawberries scattered over the floor, asked:

"And do the girls like you, Mitka?"

"Some do, some don't."

"Really. ... And why have you got eyes like a cat?"

"A cat?" Mitka was now completely abashed.

"Yes, that's just it, they're cat's eyes."

"Must have got them from my mother. I can't help it."

"And why don't they marry you off, Mitka?"

Mitka recovered from his momentary confusion, and sensing the hidden sneer in her words, let a glitter appear in the yellow of his eyes.

"The cock must grow before it finds a hen."

She raised her eyebrows in astonishment, flushed, and rose from her seat. There was a sound of footsteps ascending the steps from the street. Her fleeting smile lashed Mitka like a nettle.

Shuffling softly in his capacious kid boots, the master of the house, Sergei Platonovich Mokhov, carried his corpulent body with dignity past Mitka.

"Want me?" he asked as he passed, without turning his head.

"They've brought some fish, Papa."

Grigory appeared without his carp,

## III

The first cock had crowed when Grigory returned from his evening out. From the porch came the scent of sour hops, and the spicy perfume of stitchwort.

He tiptoed into the room, undressed, carefully hung up his Sunday trousers, crossed himself and lay down. There was a golden pool of moonlight on the floor, criss-crossed by the shadow of the window-frame. In the corner the silver of the icons gleamed dully under embroidered towels, from the shelf over the bed came the droning hum of agitated flies.

He would have fallen asleep, but in the kitchen his brother's child started to cry. The cradle creaked like an ungreased cartwheel. He heard his brother's wife Darya mutter in a sleepy voice: "Go to sleep, you little brat! You don't give me a moment's peace!" And she began crooning softly to the child:

> *Oh, where have you been?*
> *I've been watching the horses.*
> *And what did you see?*
> *A horse with a saddle*
> *All fringed with gold. . . .*

As he dozed off with the steady, soothing creak in his ears, Grigory remembered: "Tomorrow Pyotr goes off to the camp. Darya will be

left with the baby. . . . We'll have to do the mowing without him."

He buried his head in his hot pillow, but the
chant seeped persistently into his ears:

> *And where is your horse?*
> *Outside the gate.*
> *And where is the gate?*
> *Swept away by the flood.*

He was aroused from sleep by lusty neighing. By its tone he recognized Pyotr's army
horse. His sleep-numbed fingers were slow in
buttoning up his shirt, and he almost dropped
off again under the flowing rhythm of Darya's
song.

> *And where are the geese?*
> *They've gone into the reeds.*
> *And where are the reeds?*
> *The girls have mown them.*
> *And where are the girls?*
> *The girls have taken husbands.*
> *And where are the Cossacks?*
> *They've gone to the war.*

Rubbing his eyes, Grigory made his way to
the stable and led Pyotr's horse out into the
street. A floating cobweb tickled his face, and
his drowsiness unexpectedly left him.

Slanting across the Don lay the wavy never-
ridden track of the moonlight. Over the river

hung a mist, and above it, the stars, like sprinkled grain. The horse set its hoofs down cautiously. The slope to the water was hard going. From the farther side of the river came the quacking of ducks. A sheat-fish jumped with a splash in the muddy shallows by the bank, hunting at random for smaller fry.

Grigory stood a long time by the river. The bank exuded a dank and musty rottenness. A tiny drop of water fell from the horse's lips. There was a light, pleasant void in Grigory's heart, he felt good and free from thought. As he walked back, he glanced towards the east, where the blue murk was already clearing.

By the stable he ran into his mother.

"Is that you, Grisha?"

"And who do you think it is?"

"Watered the horse?"

"Yes," he answered shortly.

His mother waddled away with an apronful of dried dung fuel, her bare withered feet slapping on the ground.

"You might go and wake up the Astakhovs. Stepan said he would go with our Pyotr."

The morning rawness set a spring stiffly quivering in Grigory. His body tingled with prickles. He ran up the three echoing steps leading to the Astakhovs' house. The door was unlatched. Stepan was asleep on an outspread rug in the kitchen, his wife's head resting on his arm.

In the greying dawn light Grigory saw Aksinya's shift rumpled above her knees, and her unashamedly parted legs white as birch bark. For a moment he stood gazing, feeling his mouth going dry and his head bursting with an iron clangour.

He shifted his eyes stealthily. In a strange, hoarse voice he called:

"Hey! Anyone here? Get up."

Aksinya gave a sob of waking.

"Oh, who's that?" She hurriedly began to fumble with her shift, drawing it over her legs. A little drop of spittle was left on her pillow; a woman's sleep is sound at dawn.

"It's me. Mother sent me to wake you up."

"We'll be up in a minute. We're sleeping on the floor because of the fleas. Stepan, get up, d'you hear?" By her voice Grigory guessed that she felt embarrassed and he hastened to leave.

Thirty Cossacks were going from the village to the May training camp. Just before seven o'clock wagons with tarpaulin covers, Cossacks on foot and on horseback, in homespun shirts and carrying their equipment, began to stream towards the square.

Pyotr was standing on the steps, hurriedly stitching a broken rein.

Pantelei stamped about round Pyotr's horse, pouring oats into the trough. Every now and then he shouted:

"Dunya, have you put the rusks in the sack yet? Have you salted the bacon?"

Dunya, rosy and blooming, flew to and fro like a swallow and answered her father's shouts with a laugh:

"You look after your own affairs, Father, and I'll pack for Brother so well that nothing will budge till he reaches Cherkassk."*

"Not finished eating yet?" Pyotr asked, nodding towards the horse.

"Not yet," his father replied deliberately, testing the saddle-cloth with his rough palm. One little crumb sticking to the cloth can chafe a horse's back into a sore in a single march.

"When he's done eating, water him, Father."

"Grisha will take him down to the Don."

Grigory took the tall, rawboned Don horse with a white blaze on its forehead, led it out through the gate, and resting his left hand lightly on its withers, vaulted on to its back and went off at a swinging trot. He tried to rein the horse in at the descent to the river, but the animal stumbled, quickened its pace, and flew down the slope. Leaning back until he

* Novocherkassk.

38

almost lay along the animal's spine, Grigory saw a woman with pails going down the hill. He turned sharply off the path and dashed into the water, leaving a cloud of dust behind him.

Aksinya came swinging down the slope. When still some distance away she shouted to him:

"You mad devil! You almost rode me down. You wait, I'll tell your father how you ride."

"Now, neighbour, don't get angry. When you've seen your husband off to camp maybe I'll be useful on your farm."

"How the devil could you be useful to me?"

"You'll be asking me when mowing time comes," Grigory laughed.

Aksinya dexterously drew a full pail of water from the river, and pressed her skirt between her knees away from the wind.

"Is your Stepan ready yet?" Grigory asked.

"What's that to do with you?"

"What a spitfire! Can't I ask?"

"He is, what of it?"

"So you'll be left a grass-widow?"

"Yes."

The horse raised its lips from the water, and stood gazing across the Don, its fore-feet treading the stream. Aksinya filled her second pail, hoisted the yoke across her shoulders, and with a swinging stride set off up the slope.

Grigory turned the horse and followed her. The wind fluttered her skirt and played with the fine, fluffy curls on her swarthy neck. Her flat, embroidered cap flamed on her heavy knot of hair, her rose-coloured shift, gathered into her skirt at the waist, clung smoothly to her steep back and compact shoulders. As she climbed the slope she bent forward, and the hollow between her shoulders showed clearly beneath her shift. He saw the brownish rings under her arms, where her shift was stained with sweat. Grigory watched her every movement. He wanted to renew the talk with her.

"You'll be missing your husband, won't you?"

Without halting Aksinya turned her head and smiled.

"Of course I shall. Get married yourself," she caught her breath and went on jerkily, "then you'll know whether you miss your darling or not."

Grigory brought the horse level with her and looked into her eyes.

"But other wives are glad when their husbands go. Our Darya will grow fat without her Pyotr."

Aksinya's nostrils quivered and she breathed hard.

"A husband's not a leech, but he sucks your

blood all the same." She pushed her hair straight. "Shall we be seeing you married soon?"

"I don't know, it depends on Father. After my army service, I suppose."

"You're still young; don't get married."

"Why not?"

"It dries you up." She looked up from under her brows, and smiled cheerlessly without parting her lips. For the first time Grigory noticed that her lips were shamelessly greedy and rather swollen. Stranding the horse's mane with his fingers, he replied:

"I don't want to get married. Someone will love me without that."

"Have you noticed anyone, then?"

"What should I notice? Now you're seeing your Stepan off. . .?"

"Don't try to play about with me!"

"What will you do about it?"

"I'll tell Stepan."

"I'll show your Stepan. . . ."

"You're so cocksure, mind you don't cry first."

"Don't try to scare me, Aksinya!"

"I'm not trying to scare you. You hang around with the girls, let them hem your hankies for you, but keep your eyes off me."

"I'll look at you all the more now."

"Well, look then."

Aksinya gave him a conciliatory smile and left the path, trying to pass the horse. Grigory turned the animal sideways and blocked the way.

"Let me pass, Grisha."

"I won't."

"Don't be a fool. I must see to my husband."

Grigory smilingly teased the horse, and it edged Aksinya towards the bank.

"Let me pass, you devil! There are some people over there. If they see us what will they think?" she muttered.

She swept a frightened glance around and passed by, frowning and without a backward glance.

Pyotr was saying good-bye to his family on the steps. Grigory saddled the horse. His brother, holding his sabre to his side, hurried down the steps and took the reins. Scenting the road, the horse fretted and chewed the bit. With one foot in the stirrup, Pyotr said to his father:

"Don't overwork the baldheads, Father. In the autumn we'll sell them. Grigory will need a horse for the army, you know. And don't sell the steppe grass; you know yourself what hay we're likely to get in the meadow this year."

"Well, God be with you. Good luck," the old man replied, crossing himself.

Pyotr swung his firm body into the saddle, and adjusted the folds of his shirt in his belt at the back. The horse moved towards the gate. The sabre swung rhythmically, its pommel glittering dully in the sun.

Darya followed with the child on her arm. Wiping her eyes with her sleeve and her nose with the corner of her apron, his mother, Ilyinichna, stood in the middle of the yard.

"Brother! The pasties! You've forgotten the pasties! The potato pasties!" Dunya dashed to the gate.

"What are you bawling for, you fool!" Grigory snapped irritably.

"He's left his pasties behind," she moaned, leaning against the gate-post, and tears ran down her burning cheeks on to her blouse.

Darya stood gazing under her hand after her husband's white shirt through the screen of dust. Old Pantelei jerked the rotting gate-post and looked at Grigory:

"Mend the gate, and put a new post in." He stood in thought for a moment, then announced as if it were news:

"Pyotr's gone."

Over the wattle fence, Grigory saw Stepan getting ready. Aksinya, dressed up in a green

woollen skirt, led out his horse. Stepan smilingly said something to her. Unhurriedly, posses-
sively, he kissed his wife, and his arm lingered
long around her shoulder. His hand, darkened
by sun and toil, looked coal-black against her
white blouse. He stood with his back to Grigory; his firm, clean-shaven neck, his broad,
rather sloping shoulders, and (whenever he bent
towards his wife) the twisted ends of his light-
brown moustache were visible across the fence.

Aksinya laughed at something and shook her
head. The big black stallion lurched slightly as
Stepan swung his great weight into the saddle.
Sitting as though planted in the saddle, Stepan
rode his black horse at a brisk trot through
the gate, and Aksinya walked at his side, holding the stirrup and looking up lovingly and
hungrily, like a dog, into his eyes.

Grigory watched them to the turn of the
road with a long unblinking gaze.

IV

Towards evening a thunderstorm gathered.
A mass of heavy cloud lay over the village.
Lashed into fury by the wind, the Don sent
foaming breakers against its banks. The sky
flamed with dry lightning, occasional peals of
thunder shook the earth. A kite circled with

44

outspread wings just below the clouds and was pursued by croaking ravens. Spreading its cool breath, the cloud passed down the Don from the west. Beyond the meadows the heavens blackened menacingly, the steppe lay in expectant silence. In the village there was a rattle of closing shutters, the old people hurried home from vespers crossing themselves. A grey pillar of dust whirled over the square, and the heat-burdened earth was already beginning to be scattered with the first seeds of rain.

Shaking her braided tresses, Dunya flew across the yard, slammed the door of the chickenhouse, and stood in the middle of the yard with nostrils distended like a horse at a hurdle. In the street the children were prancing about. Eight-year-old Mishka, his father's absurdly large peaked cap drawn over his eyes, was spinning round and chirruping shrilly:

> Rain, rain, rain away,
> We're going off for the day,
> To pay God our vow,
> And to Christ to bow.

Dunya enviously watched Mishka's chapped bare feet stamping the ground. She, too, wanted to dance in the rain and to get her head wet, so that her hair might grow thick and curly; she, too, wanted to stand on her hands like

45

Mishka's friend in the roadside dust, at the risk of falling into the nettles. But her mother was watching and angrily moving her lips at the window. With a sigh she ran into the house. The rain was now falling heavily. A peal of thunder broke right over the roof and went rolling away across the Don.

In the porch Pantelei and the perspiring Grigory were hauling a folded drag-net out of the side-room.

"Raw thread and a pack-needle, quick!" Grigory called to Dunya. Darya sat down to mend the net. Her mother-in-law grumbled as she rocked the baby:

"What else will you take into your head, man! Let's go to bed. Kerosene costs more and more. What do you think you'll catch now? Where the plague are you going? And you'll get drowned into the bargain, the terror of the Lord is upon us. Just look at the lightning! Lord Jesus Christ, Mother of Heaven. . . ."

For an instant it was dazzlingly blue and silent in the kitchen; the rain could be heard drumming on the shutters. A clap of thunder followed. Dunya whimpered and buried her face in the net. Darya made the sign of the cross towards the windows and door. The old woman stared with terrible eyes at the cat rubbing itself against her legs:

"Dunya, chase this d–, Mother of Heaven, forgive me my sins. . . . Dunya, put the cat out into the yard! Shoo, evil spirit! May you. . . ."

Dropping the net, Grigory shook with silent laughter.

"Well, what are you fussing about? Enough of that!" shouted Pantelei. "Get on with your mending, women. I told you the other day to see to the net."

"There's no fish now," his wife ventured.

"If you don't understand, hold your tongue! The sterlet will make for the bank now, they're afraid of storms. The water must be muddy by now. Dunya, go out and see whether you can hear the stream running."

Dunya edged unwillingly towards the door.

Old Ilyinichna would not be repressed. "Who's going to wade with you? Darya mustn't, she'll catch cold in her chest," she persisted.

"Me and Grigory, and for the other net . . . we'll call Aksinya and another of the women."

Dunya ran in breathlessly. Drops of rain hung trembling on her lashes. She smelt of the dank, black earth.

"The stream's roaring like anything," she panted.

"You coming too?"

"Who else is going?"

"We'll get some of the women."

"All right."

"Put on your coat and run to Aksinya," her father told her. "If she'll go, ask her to fetch Malashka Frolova, too."

"That one won't freeze," Grigory said with a grin, "she's fat as a hog."

"Why don't you take some hay, Grisha dear," his mother advised. "Stuff some under your heart or you'll take a chill inside."

"Yes, go for some hay, Grigory. The old woman's quite right."

Dunya quickly returned with the women. Aksinya, in a blue skirt and a ragged jacket belted with rope, looked shorter and thinner. Exchanging laughs with Darya, she took off her kerchief, wound her hair into a tighter knot, and throwing back her head, stared coldly at Grigory. As the stout Malashka tied up her stockings, she said hoarsely:

"Have you got your sacks? We're sure to haul up the fish today."

They all went into the yard. The rain was still falling heavily on the sodden earth, frothing the puddles and trickling in streams down to the Don.

Grigory led the way down to the river.

For no reason he suddenly felt very gay.

"Mind the ditch, Dad."

"How dark it is!"

"Hang on to me, Aksinya," Malashka laughed hoarsely.

"Isn't that the landing stage, Grigory?"

"That's it."

"Begin from here," Pantelei shouted above the roar of the wind.

"Can't hear you, uncle," Malashka called throatily.

"Start wading, I'll take the deep side. . . . The deep . . . I say. Malashka, you deaf devil, where are you dragging to? I'll go out into the deeps. . . . Grigory, Grisha, let Aksinya take the bank!"

A groaning roar from the Don. The wind was tearing the slanting sheet of rain to shreds. Feeling the bottom with his feet, Grigory waded up to his waist into the water. A clammy cold crept into his chest, drawing tightly in a ring round his heart. The waves lashed his face and tightly screwed-up eyes like a knout. The net bellied out and was carried off into the deeps. Grigory's feet, in woollen socks, slipped over the sandy bottom. The net was being dragged out of his hand. Deeper, deeper. A sudden drop. His legs were carried away. The current snatched him up and bore him into midstream. With his right hand he vigorously paddled back to the bank. The black, swirling depths frightened him as never before. His feet joyously found the muddy bottom. A fish knocked against his knee.

"Take it deep!" his father's voice came from the clinging darkness.

Again the net heeled over and pulled down into the depths. Again the current carried the ground away from under his feet, and Grigory swam, spitting out water.

"Aksinya, you all right?"

"All right, so far."

"Isn't the rain stopping?"

"The fine rain is, now we'll get the heavy stuff."

"Talk quietly. If my father hears he'll go for me."

"Afraid of your father, huh?"

For a moment they hauled in silence.

"Grisha, there's a sunken tree by the bank, I think! We must get the net round it."

A terrible buffet flung Grigory far away from her.

"Ah-ah!" Aksinya screamed somewhere near the bank. Terrified, he swam in the direction of her call.

"Aksinya!"

Wind, and the flowing roar of the water.

"Aksinya!" Grigory shouted again, going cold with fear.

"Hey, Grigory," he heard his father's voice from afar.

He struck out wildly. He felt something sticky under his feet, and caught it with his hand—it was the net.

"Grisha, where are you?" he heard Aksinya's tearful voice.

"Why didn't you answer my shout?" he bawled angrily, crawling on hands and knees up the bank.

Squatting down on their heels, they disentangled the net. The moon broke through the cracked shell of a cloud. There was a restrained mutter of thunder beyond the meadows. The earth gleamed with moisture. Washed clean by the rain, the sky was stern and clear.

As he disentangled the net Grigory stared at Aksinya. Her face was a chalky white, but her red, slightly upturned lips were smiling.

"The way I was knocked against the bank! I nearly went out of my mind. I was scared to death. I thought you were drowned."

Their hands touched. Aksinya tried to push hers into the sleeve of his shirt.

"How warm your arm is," she said plaintively, "and I'm frozen!"

"Look where that bastard got away," Grigory showed her a hole about five feet across in the middle of the net.

Someone came running along the bank. Grigory guessed it was Dunya. He shouted to her:

"Got the thread?"

"Yes. What are you sitting here for? Father sent me for you to come at once to the point. We've caught a sackful of sterlet." Unconcealed triumph sounded in her voice.

With teeth chattering, Aksinya sewed up the hole in the net. Then, to get warm, they raced to the point.

Pantelei was rolling a cigarette with scarred fingers swollen by the water; jigging about, he boasted:

"The first time, eight fish; but the second time . . ." he paused and silently pointed with his foot to the sack. Aksinya peeped curiously inside: from it came the slithery scraping sound of stirring fish.

"Where were you?"

"A sheat-fish broke our net."

"Did you mend it?"

"Yes, somehow."

"Well, we'll wade in once more up to our knees, and then home. In you go, Grisha; what are you waiting for?"

Grigory stepped out with numbed legs. Aksinya was shivering so much that he felt the net trembling.

"Stop shaking!"

"I wish I could, but I can't catch my breath."

"Listen! Let's get out, and damn the fish!"

At that moment a great carp leaped over the net. Grigory dragged the net into a tighter circle. Aksinya toiled up the bank. The water splashed on the sands and slopped back. Fish lay quivering in the net.

"Back through the meadow?"

"It's nearer through the wood."

"Hey there, are you coming?"

"Go on ahead. We'll catch you up. We're cleaning the net."

Frowning, Aksinya wrung out her skirt, hoisted the sack of fish over her shoulder and set off almost at a trot. Grigory picked up the net. They had covered some two hundred yards when Aksinya began to groan:

"I can't go on. My legs are numb."

"Look, there's an old haystack. Why don't you have a warm there."

"Good! I'll never get home otherwise."

Grigory turned back the top of the stack and dug out a hole. The long-lying hay smelt warm and rotten.

"Crawl into the middle. It's like a stove here."

She threw down the sack and buried herself up to the neck in hay. Shivering with cold, Grigory lay down at her side. A tender agitating scent came from her damp hair. She lay with head thrown back, breathing regularly through her half-open mouth.

"Your hair smells like henbane. Do you know that white flower?" Grigory whispered, bending towards her. She was silent. Her gaze was misty and distant, fixed on the waning, crescent moon.

Taking his hand out of his pocket, Grigory suddenly drew her head towards him. She tore herself away fiercely, and raised herself from the hay.

"Let me go!"

"Keep quiet!"

"Let go, or I'll shout!"

"Wait, Aksinya!"

"Uncle Pantelei!"

"Have you got lost?" Pantelei's voice sounded quite close, from behind a clump of hawthorn bushes. Clenching his teeth, Grigory jumped out of the stack.

"What are you shouting for? Are you lost?" the old man questioned as he approached.

Aksinya stood by the haystack adjusting her kerchief, steam rising from her clothes.

"We're not lost, but I'm nearly frozen."

"Look, woman, there's a haystack, warm yourself," the old man told her.

Aksinya smiled as she stopped to pick up the sack.

# V

It was some sixty versts to the training camp at Setrakov. Pyotr Melekhov and Stepan Astakhov rode in the same wagon. With them were three others from their village: Fedot Bodovskov, a young Cossack with a pock-marked Kalmyk face, Christonya Tokin, a second-draft reservist in the Ataman's Regiment of Lifeguards, and the artilleryman Ivan Tomilin. After the first halt for food they harnessed Christonya's and Astakhov's horses to the wagon, and the other horses were tethered behind. Christonya, burly and a bit queer in the head like all the men of the Ataman's Regiment, took the reins. He sat in front with his back, curved like a wheel, blocking out the light from the interior of the wagon, and urged on the horses in his deep, rumbling bass voice. Pyotr, Stepan and Tomilin lay smoking under the tightly-stretched tarpaulin cover. Bodovskov walked behind, his bandy Kalmyk legs making light of the dusty road.

Christonya's wagon led the way. Behind trailed seven or eight others, leading saddled and unsaddled horses. The road was noisy with laughter, shouts, songs, the snorting of horses, and the jingling of empty stirrups.

Pyotr's head rested on a bag of rusks. He lay still, twirling his tawny whiskers.

"Stepan!"

"Huh?"

"Let's have a song."

"It's too hot. My throat's dry as a bone!"

"You won't find any drink round here. So don't wait for that!"

"Well, sing up. Only you're no good at it. Your Grisha now, he can sing. His isn't a voice, it's a pure silver thread."

Stepan threw back his head, coughed, and began in a low, tuneful voice:

> *Oh, a fine glowing sunrise*
> *Came up early in the sky.*

Tomilin rested his cheek on his palm like a woman and picked up the refrain in a thin, wailing voice. Smiling, Pyotr watched the little knotted veins on his temples turning blue with the effort.

> *Young was she, the little woman*
> *That went tripping to the stream.*

Stepan, who was lying with his head towards Christonya, turned round on his elbow:

"Come on, Christonya, join in!"

> *And the lad, he guessed her purpose,*
> *Saddled up his chestnut mare.*

Stepan turned his smiling glance towards Pyotr, and Pyotr, flicking the tip of his moustache out of his mouth, added his voice. Opening wide his heavily-bearded jaws, Christonya roared in a voice that shook the tarpaulin cover:

> Saddled up his chestnut mare
> To catch the little woman.

Christonya tucked his bare foot under him and waited for Stepan to begin again. Closing his eyes, his perspiring face in shadow, Stepan sang on gently, now dropping his voice to a whisper, now making it ring out metallically.

> Let me, let me, little woman,
> Bring my chestnut to the stream.

And again Christonya's deep booming tones drowned the others. Voices from the neighbouring wagons took up the song. The wheels clanked on their iron rims, the horses snorted with the dust and the song floated on, strong and deep. A white-winged peewit flew up from the brown wilted steppe. It flew with a cry towards a hollow, turning an emerald eye to watch the chain of white-covered wagons, the horses kicking up clouds of dust with their hoofs, the men in white, dusty shirts, walking at the edge of the road. And as the peewit dropped into the hollow and its black breast nestled into the damp grass pressed flat by roaming animals, it missed the scene that was taking place on the road. The wagons were trundling along as before, the sweating horses were still loping unwillingly through the dust, but now the Cossacks in their dust-grey shirts were running from their wagons to the leader, milling round it and roaring with laughter.

Stepan was poised at full height on the wagon, holding the tarpaulin with one hand, beating time with the other, and roaring out a catchy tune in double-quick time:

> *Oh, don't sit by me,*
> *Oh, don't sit by me,*
> *Folk will say you're in love with me,*
> *In love with me*
> *And coming to me,*
> *In love with me*
> *And coming to me,*
> *But I'm not one of the common run. . . .*

Dozens of rough voices took up the chorus with a roar that flattened the roadside dust:

> *But I'm not one of the common run,*
> *I'm not one of the common run.*
> *I'm brigand born,*
> *And brigand bred—*
> *Not one of the common run,*
> *And I'm in love with a prince's son. . . .*

58

Fedot Bodovskov whistled; the horses strained at the traces; leaning out of the wagon, Pyotr laughed and waved his cap; Stepan, with a dazzling smile on his face, impudently swung his shoulders; along the road the dust rolled in a cloud. Christonya jumped out of the wagon in his great long unbelted shirt, his hair matted, his face streaming with sweat, and did the Cossack dance, whirling round like a fly-wheel, frowning and groaning, and leaving the huge splayed imprints of his bare feet in the silky-grey dust.

## VI

They stopped for the night by a mound with a sandy summit. Clouds gathered in the west. Rain dripped from their black wings. The horses were watered at a pond. Above the dyke dismal willows bowed before the wind. In the water, covered with stagnant duckweed and scaled with miserable little ripples, the lightning was distortedly reflected. The wind crumbled the raindrops sparingly as though scattering alms into the earth's swarthy palms.

The hobbled horses were turned out to graze, three men being appointed as guards. The other men lit fires and hung pots on the wagon shafts.

Christonya was cooking millet. As he stirred it with a spoon, he told a story to the Cossacks sitting around:

"The mound was high, like this one. And I says to my now deceased father: 'Won't the ataman* give it us for digging up the mound without permission'?"

"What's he blathering about?" asked Stepan, as he came back from the horses. He squatted down by the fire and flicked an ember on to his palm, juggling it about for a long time while he lighted a cigarette.

"I'm telling how I and my father, may his soul rest in peace, looked for treasure. It was the Merkulov mound. Well, and Father says: 'Come on, Christonya, we'll dig up the Merkulov mound.' He'd heard from his father that treasure was buried in it. You see, Father promised God: 'Give me the treasure, and I'll build a fine church.' So we agreed and off we

---

* *Atamans* were elected by the Cossacks of tsarist Russia for posts of leadership at various levels. The chief of the Don Army was called the army ataman, the chief of a stanitsa, a Cossack district or district centre, the stanitsa ataman. When a Cossack detachment went out on a campaign it elected its own "campaign ataman." In a broad sense the word meant "chief." When the Don Cossacks finally lost their independence, the title of Ataman of all Cossack Forces became a hereditary title of the tsar and, in effect, all Cossack troops were commanded by appointed atamans.

went. It was on common land, so only the ataman could stop us. We arrived late in the afternoon. So we waited until nightfall and then
climbed up on top with shovels. We began to
dig straight down from its top-knot. We'd dug
a hole six feet deep; the earth was like stone.
I was wet through. Father kept on muttering
prayers, but believe me, brothers, my belly was
grumbling so much. . . . You know what we eat
in summer: sour milk and kvass. My father, he
says: 'Pfooh!' he says, 'Christonya, you're a
heathen. Here am I praying, and you can't
hold your food. I can't breathe for the stink.
Get off the mound, you ... or I'll split your
head open with the shovel. Your stink's enough
to make the treasure sink into the ground.' So
I lay down by the mound, fit to die with my
belly-ache, and my father—a strong man he
was—goes on digging alone. And he digs down
to a stone slab. He calls me. I push a crow-bar
under it, and lift it up. Believe me, brothers, it
was a moonlight night, and under this slab was
such a glitter. . . ."

"Now you're lying, Christonya," Pyotr broke
in, smiling and tugging at his whiskers.

"Who's lying? Go to the devil, and to the
devil's dam!" Christonya hitched up his *sharovari* and glanced round at his audience. "No,
I'm not lying. It's God's truth! There it shone.

I look, and it's charcoal. Some forty bushels of it. Father says: 'Crawl in, Christonya, and dig it up.' So I dug out this rubbish. I went on digging till daylight. And in the morning there he was."

"Who?" asked Tomilin.

"Why, the ataman, who else? He happens to come driving by. 'Who gave you permission?' and all the rest of it. He lays hold of us and hauls us off to the stanitsa. We were called before the court at Kamenskaya the year before last, but Father, he guessed what was coming, and managed to die beforehand. We wrote back saying he was not among the living."

Christonya took his pot of boiling millet and went to the wagon for spoons.

"Well, what about your father? He promised to build a church; didn't he do it?" Stepan asked, when he returned.

"You're a fool, Stepan. What could he build for charcoal?"

"Once he promised he ought to have done it."

"There was no agreement whatever about charcoal, and the treasure. . . ." The guffaw that went up made the flames of the fire tremble. Christonya raised his head from the pot, and not understanding what the laughter was about, drowned all the rest with his heavy roar.

# VII

Aksinya was seventeen when she was given in marriage to Stepan Astakhov. She came from the village of Dubrovka, from the sands on the other side of the Don.

About a year before her marriage she was ploughing in the steppe eight versts or so from the village. In the night her father, a man of some fifty years, tied her hands and raped her.

"I'll kill you if you breathe a word, but if you keep quiet I'll buy you a plush jacket and gaiters with goloshes. Remember, I'll kill you if you . . ." he promised her.

Aksinya ran back through the night in her torn petticoat to the village. She flung herself at her mother's feet and sobbed out the whole story. Her mother and elder brother harnessed horses to the wagon, made Aksinya get in with them, and drove to the father. Her brother almost drove the horses to death over the eight versts. They found the old man close to the field camp. He was lying on his overcoat in a drunken sleep with an empty vodka bottle by his side. Before Aksinya's eyes her brother unhooked the swingle-tree from the wagon, brought him to his feet with a kick, curtly asked him a question or two and struck him a blow between the eyes with the iron-shod swingle-tree. He and his mother went on beating him steadily for an hour and a half. The ageing mother, who had always been an obedient wife, frenziedly tore at her unconscious husband's hair, the brother used his feet. Aksinya lay under the wagon, her head covered, shaking silently. They carried her father home just before dawn. He lay moaning pitifully, his eyes wandering around the room, seeking for Aksinya, who had hidden herself away. Blood and puss ran from his torn ear on to the pillow. Towards evening he died. They told the neighbours he had fallen from the wagon.

Within a year match-makers arrived on a gaily bedecked wagonette to ask for Aksinya's hand. The tall Stepan with his clean-cut neck and well-proportioned figure appealed to his future bride, and the wedding was fixed for the autumn.

The day was frosty and the ice rang merrily on the roads when Aksinya was installed as young mistress of the Astakhov household. The morning after the festivities her mother-in-law, a tall old woman doubled up with some painful woman's disease, woke Aksinya, led her into the kitchen, and aimlessly shifting things about, said to her:

"Now, dear daughter, we didn't take you for making love, nor for you to lie abed. Go and milk the cows, and then get some food ready. I'm old and sick. You must take over the household, it will all fall on you."

The same day Stepan took his young wife into the barn and beat her deliberately and terribly. He beat her on the belly, the breasts and the back, taking care that the marks should not be visible to others. After that he neglected her, kept company with flighty grass-widows and went out almost every night, leaving Aksinya locked in the barn or the best room.

For eighteen months, until there was a child, he would not forgive her his disgrace. Then he was quieter, but was grudging with caresses and rarely spent the night at home.

The large farm with its numerous cattle burdened Aksinya with work. Stepan worked halfheartedly, and went off to smoke, to play cards, to learn the latest news, and Aksinya had to do everything. Her mother-in-law was a poor help. After bustling around a little she would drop on to the bed, and with lips tightdrawn and eyes gazing agonizedly at the ceiling, would lie groaning, rolled into a bundle. At such times her face, which was dotted all over with great ugly moles, broke out in perspiration and tears slithered one by one down her cheeks. Throwing down her work, Aksinya would hide in a corner and stare at her mother-in-law's face in fear and pity.

The old woman died just before the child was born. In the morning Aksinya's labour pains began, and about noon, an hour or so before the child came into the world, the grandmother dropped dead by the stable door. The midwife ran out to warn the tipsy Stepan not to go into the bedroom, and saw the old woman lying with her legs tucked under her. After the birth of the child, Aksinya devoted herself to her husband, but she had no feeling for him, only a bitter womanly pity and force of habit remained. The child died within a year. The old life returned. And when Grisha Melekhov crossed Aksinya's path, she realized with terror that she was attracted to the gentle, swarthy young fellow. He waited on her with a persistent expectant love, and it was this persistence that Aksinya feared in him. She saw that he was not afraid of Stepan, she felt that he would not hold back because of him, and without consciously desiring it, resisting the feeling with all her might, she noticed that on Sundays and weekdays she was attiring herself more carefully. Making up excuses for her conscience, she tried to place herself more frequently in his path. It made her happy to feel Grigory's black eyes caressing her heavily and rapturously. When she awoke of a morning and went to milk the cows she would smile, and without realizing why, think to herself: "Today's a happy day. But why...? Oh, Grigory.... Grisha." She was frightened by the new feeling which filled her, and in her thoughts she felt her way gropingly, cautiously, as though crossing the Don over the melting ice of March.

After seeing Stepan off to camp she decided to see Grigory as little as possible. After the fishing, her decision was still further strengthened.

## VIII

Some two days before Trinity the distribution of the village meadowland took place. Pantelei attended the allotment. He came back at dinner-time, kicked off his boots with a groan, and noisily scratching his weary feet, announced:

"We've got the stretch near the Red Bank. Not very good grass as grass goes. The upper part runs up to the forest, it's just scrub in places. And a bit of quitch coming through."

"When shall we do the mowing?" Grigory asked.

"After the holidays."

"Are you going to take Darya along?" the old woman frowned. Pantelei Prokofyevich brushed her aside.

"Let me alone! We'll take her if we need her. Get lunch ready. Why do you stand around gaping?"

The old wife opened the oven door with a clatter, and drew out the warmed-up cabbage soup. Pantelei sat over the meal a long time, telling of the day's events, and of the tricky ataman, who had all but swindled the whole assembly of Cossacks.

"He was up to his tricks last year," Darya put in. "The way he tried to swindle Malashka when they were sharing out the plots."

"He's always been a son of a bitch," Pantelei muttered.

"But who's going to do the raking and stacking, Dad?" Dunya asked timidly.

"What about you?"

"I can't do it all by myself."

"We'll ask Aksinya Astakhova. Stepan asked us to mow for him."

The next morning Mitka Korshunov rode up to the Melekhov yard on his white-legged stallion. A fine rain was falling. Thick mist hung over the village. Mitka leaned out of his saddle, opened the wicket and rode in. The old wife hailed him from the steps.

"Hey, you rapscallion, what do you want?"
she asked with evident dissatisfaction in her
voice, for she had no love for the reckless and
quarrelsome Mitka.

"What's that to you, Ilyinichna?" Mitka
said in surprise, as he tied his horse to the railing. "I want Grisha. Where is he?"

"He's asleep in the shed. But have you had
a stroke? Have you lost the use of your legs
that you must ride?"

"You're always poking your nose in, old lady!" Mitka retorted huffily. Smacking an elegant whip against the legs of his glossy leather
boots, he went to look for Grigory, and found
him asleep in a cart. Screwing up his left eye,
Mitka lashed Grigory with his whip.

"Get up, muzhik!"

"Muzhik" was the most abusive word Mitka
could think of using. Grigory jumped up as
though on springs.

"What do you want?"

"You've been in bed long enough."

"Stop fooling around, Mitka, before I get
angry."

"Get up, I've got to talk to you."

"Well?"

Mitka sat down on the side of the cart, and
scraping the dried mud off his boots with a
stick, he said:

"I've been insulted, Grisha."

"Well?"

"You see, it's ..." Mitka cursed heavily. "He's a lieutenant, so he likes to show off." He snapped out the words angrily, without opening his mouth, his legs were trembling. Grigory got up.

"What lieutenant?"

Seizing him by the sleeve, Mitka said more quietly:

"Saddle your horse at once, and come to the meadows. I'll show him! I said to him: 'Come on, Your Honour, and we'll see.' 'Bring all your friends and comrades,' he said, 'I'll beat the lot of you. My mare's dam took prizes at the officers' hurdle-races at St. Petersburg.' What is his mare or her dam to me? Curse them! I won't let them outrace my stallion!"

Grigory hastily dressed. Choking with rage Mitka hurried him up.

"He's come to visit the merchant Mokhov. Wait, what's his name? Listnitsky, I think. Big, serious-looking fellow, wears glasses. Well, and let him! His glasses won't help him: I won't let him catch my stallion!"

With a laugh, Grigory saddled the old mare and, to avoid meeting his father, rode out to the steppe through the threshing-floor gate. They rode to the meadow at the foot of the hill.

Close to a withered poplar, horsemen were awaiting them: the officer Listnitsky on a handsome, clean-limbed mare, and seven of the village lads mounted bareback.

"Where shall we start from?" the officer turned to Mitka, adjusting his pince-nez and admiring the stallion's powerful chest muscles.

"From the poplar to the Tsar's Pond."

"Where's the Tsar's Pond?" Listnitsky screwed up his eyes short-sightedly.

"There, Your Honour, on the edge of the wood."

They lined up the horses. The officer raised his whip above his head.

"When I say 'three.' All right? One ... two ... three!"

Listnitsky got away first, pressing close to the saddle-bow, holding his cap on with his hand. For a second he led all the rest. Mitka, his face desperately pale, rose in his stirrups—to Grigory he seemed unbearably slow in bringing the whip down on the croup of his stallion.

It was some three versts to the Tsar's Pond. Stretched out straight as an arrow, Mitka's stallion caught up with Listnitsky's mare when half the course had been covered. Left behind from the very beginning, Grigory trotted along, watching the straggling chain of riders.

By the Tsar's Pond was a sandy hillock, washed up by the spring floods. Its yellow camel-hump was overgrown with sandwort. Grigory saw the officer and Mitka gallop up the hillock and disappear over the brow together, the others following. When he reached the pond the horses were already standing in a group around Listnitsky. Mitka was sleek with restrained delight, every movement expressing his triumph. Contrary to his expectations, the officer did not seem at all disconcerted. He stood with his back against a tree, smoking a cigarette, and said, pointing to his foam-flecked horse:

"I've ridden a hundred and fifty versts on her already. I rode over from the stanitsa only yesterday. If she were fresh, you'd never have caught me, Korshunov."

"Maybe," Mitka said magnanimously.

"His stallion's the best in the district," a freckled lad, who had come up last, remarked enviously.

"He's a good horse," said Mitka and stroked the stallion's neck, his hand trembling with emotion. He glanced at Grigory and grinned foolishly.

Grigory and Mitka left the others and rode home, skirting the village. The lieutenant took a chilly leave of them, thrust two fingers under the peak of his cap and turned away.

As they were approaching home, Grigory saw Aksinya coming towards them. She was stripping a twig as she walked. When she noticed him she bent her head lower.

"What are you blushing for, are we naked?" shouted Mitka and winked.

Gazing straight before him, Grigory almost rode by her, then suddenly struck the ambling mare with his whip. She sat back on her hind-legs and sent a shower of mud over Aksinya.

"Oh, you mad devil!"

Wheeling sharply and riding his excited mount at her, Grigory demanded:

"Why don't you say hullo?"

"You're not worth it!"

"And that's why I sent the mud over you. Don't think so much of yourself."

"Let me pass!" Aksinya shouted, waving her arms in front of the horse's nose. "What are you trampling me with your horse for?"

"She's a mare, not a horse."

"I don't care; let me pass."

"What are you getting angry for, Aksinya? Surely not because of the other day, in the meadow?"

Grigory gazed into her eyes. Aksinya tried to say something, but a little tear started from the

73

corner of her dark eye, and her lips quivered
pitifully. Swallowing hard, she whispered:

"Go away, Grigory. . . . I'm not angry. . . .
I. . . ." And she went.

The astonished Grigory overtook Mitka
at the gate.

"Coming out for the evening?" Mitka asked.

"No."

"Why, what's on? Or did she invite you to
spend the night with her?"

Grigory rubbed his forehead with his palm
and made no reply.

## IX

All that was left of Trinity in the village
houses was the dry thyme scattered over the
floors, the dust of crumpled leaves, and the
shrivelled, withered green of broken oak and
ash branches fastened to the gates and stairs.

The haymaking began immediately after
Trinity. From early morning the meadow blossomed with women's holiday skirts, the bright
embroidery of aprons, and coloured kerchiefs.
The whole village turned out for the mowing.
The mowers and rakers attired themselves as
though for an annual holiday. So it had been
from of old. From the Don to the distant alder

thickets the ravaged meadowland stirred and sighed.

The Melekhovs were late in starting. They set out when nearly half the village were already in the meadow.

"You sleep late, Pantelei Prokofyevich," the perspiring haymakers greeted him.

"Not my fault . . . the women again!" the old man laughed, and urged on the bullocks with his knout of raw hide.

"Good-day to you, neighbour! You're a bit late, aren't you?" a tall Cossack in a straw hat said, shaking his head as he stood sharpening his scythe at the side of the road.

"You reckon the grass will be dry?"

"If you don't get a move on, it soon will be."

At the back of the cart sat Aksinya, her face completely covered to protect it from the sun. From the narrow slits left for her eyes she stared calmly and severely at Grigory seated opposite her. Darya, also wrapped up and dressed in her Sunday best, her legs dangling between the rungs of the wagon-side, was giving her long blue-veined breast to the child dozing in her arms. Dunya fidgeted on the box, her happy eyes scanning the meadow and the people walking along the road. Her face, cheerful and sunburnt, with a sprinkling of freckles across her nose, seemed to say, "I feel gay and happy, because the day, with its blue and cloudless sky, is also happy; because my soul is filled with the same cloudless blue calm. I'm happy, I have everything I want."

Drawing the sleeve of his cotton shirt over his fists, Pantelei wiped away the sweat running down from under the peak of his cap. The shirt stretched tightly across his bent back, darkened with moist patches. The sun pierced slantingly through a grey fleecy cloud, and dropped a fan of misty, refracted rays over the meadow, the village, and the distant, silvery hills of the Don.

The day was sultry. The little clouds crept along drowsily, not even overtaking Pantelei's bullocks as they plodded along the road. The old man himself lifted and waved the knout languidly, as though in doubt whether to strike their bony flanks or not. Evidently realizing this, the bullocks did not hasten their pace, and slowly, gropingly set forward their cloven hoofs and swished their tails. A dusty gold-and-orange-tingled horsefly circled above them. The meadowland that had been scythed near the threshing-floors glowed with pale-green patches; where the grass had not yet been cut, the grassy silk, green with a gleam of black in it, rustled in the breeze.

"There's our strip," Pantelei waved his knout.

Grigory unharnessed the weary bullocks. The

old man, his ear-ring glittering, went to look for the mark he had made at the end of the strip.

"Bring the scythes," he called out after a moment, waving his hand.

Grigory went to him, treading down the grass, and leaving an undulating trail behind him. Pantelei faced the distant bell-tower and crossed himself. His hook-nose shone as though freshly varnished, the sweat clung to the hollows of his swarthy cheeks. He smiled, baring a close-set row of white, gleaming teeth in his raven beard, and, with his wrinkled neck bent to the right, swept the scythe through the grass. A seven-foot semicircle of mown grass lay at his feet.

Eyes half closed, Grigory followed in his steps, laying the grass low with the scythe. The women's aprons blossomed in a scattered rainbow before him, but his eyes sought only one, a white one with an embroidered border; he glanced at Aksinya and started mowing again, keeping pace with his father.

Aksinya was continually in his thoughts. Half closing his eyes, in imagination he kissed her and spoke to her in burning tender words that came to his tongue from he knew not where. Then he dropped such thoughts and stepped out again methodically, one ... two ... three; and his memory slipped in fragments of the

past. Sitting under the damp hayrick ... the
moon over the meadow ... now and then a drop
falling from the bush into the puddle ... one
... two ... three.... Good! Ah, that had been
good!

He heard laughter behind him. He looked
back: Darya lay under the cart and Aksinya
was bending over her, telling her something.
Darya waved her arms, and again they both
laughed. Dunya was sitting on the shaft and
singing in a shrill voice.

"I'll get to that bush, then I'll sharpen my
scythe," Grigory thought. At that moment he
felt the scythe pass through something soft and
yielding. He bent down. A little wild duckling
went scurrying into the grass with a squawk.
By the hole where the nest had been another
was huddled, cut in two by the scythe, the rest
of the brood scattered twittering in the grass.
He lay the dead bird on his palm. It had evidently come from the egg only a few days previously; there was still a living warmth in the
down.

On the flat, half-open beak there was a pink-
ish bubble of blood, the beady eyes were
puckered slyly, the little legs were still warm
and quivering. With a sudden keen feeling of
compassion he stared at the inert little ball lying in his hand.

"What have you found, Grisha?"

Dunya came dancing along the mown alley, her pigtails tossing on her breast. Frowning, Grigory threw away the duckling and angrily wielded his scythe.

Dinner was eaten in haste. Bacon-fat and the Cossacks' stand-by, sour skimmed milk, brought from home in a bag, were the entire meal.

After dinner the women began to rake the hay. The cut grass wilted and dried, giving off a heavy, stupefying scent.

"No point in going home!" Pantelei said during dinner. "We'll turn the bullocks out to graze in the forest, and tomorrow as soon as the dew is off the grass we'll finish the mowing."

Dusk had fallen when they stopped for the day. Aksinya raked the last rows together, and went to the cart to cook some millet mash. All day she had maliciously made fun of Grigory, gazing at him with eyes full of hatred, as though in revenge for some great, unforgettable injury. Grigory, gloomy and faded somehow, drove the bullocks down to the Don for water. His father had watched him and Aksinya all day. Eyeing Grigory unpleasantly he said:

"Have your supper, and then guard the bullocks. See that they don't get into the grass! Take my sheepskin."

Darya laid her child under the cart and went into the forest with Dunya for brushwood.

Over the meadow the waning moon mounted the dark, inaccessible heaven. A snowstorm of moths whirled around the flames. Near the fire supper was laid on a piece of coarse cloth. The millet boiled in the smoky field-pot. Wiping a spoon with the edge of her underskirt, Darya called to Grigory:

"Come and have your supper."

His father's sheepskin draped over his shoulders, Grigory emerged from the darkness and approached the fire.

"What's made you so moody?" Darya smiled.

"Got the back-ache. Must be going to rain," he countered lightly.

"He doesn't want to watch the bullocks," Dunya laughed, and, sitting down by her brother, she tried to start a conversation. But somehow her efforts were unsuccessful. Pantelei supped his porridge, crunching the undercooked millet with his teeth. Aksinya ate without lifting her eyes, smiling half-heartedly at Darya's jokes. A troubled flush burned in her cheeks.

Grigory got up first and went off to the bullocks.

"Take care the bullocks don't trample somebody else's grass," his father shouted after him, then a crumb of millet stuck in his throat and for a long time he coughed raspingly. Dunya's cheeks swelled as she tried to suppress her laughter.

The fire burned low. The smouldering brushwood wrapped the little group in the honey scent of burning leaves.

At midnight Grigory stole up to the camp, and halted some ten paces away. His father was snoring tunefully on the cart. The unquenched embers stared out from the ash with golden peacock's eyes.

A grey, shrouded figure broke away from the cart and came slowly towards Grigory. Two or three paces away, it halted. Aksinya! Grigory's heart thumped fast and heavily; he stepped forward crouchingly, flinging back the edge of his sheepskin, and pressed her compliant, burning body to his own. Her legs bowed at the knees; she trembled, her teeth chattering. Grigory suddenly flung her over his arm as a wolf throws a slaughtered sheep across its back, and, stumbling over the trailing edges of his open coat, and panting hard, made off.

"Oh, Grisha, Grisha! Your father. . . ."

"Quiet!"

Tearing herself away, gasping for breath in the sour sheep's wool, choking with the bitterness of regret, Aksinya cried in a low moaning voice that was almost a shout:

"Let go, what does it matter now...? I'll go of my own accord."

## X

Not azure and poppy-red, but rabid as the wayside henbane is a woman's belated love.

After the mowing Aksinya was a changed woman: as though someone had set a mark on her face, branded her. When other women met her they smiled slyly, and nodded their heads after her. The girls were envious, but she held her happy, shameful head proud and high.

Soon everybody knew of her affair with Grigory Melekhov. At first it was talked about in whispers—only half-believed—but after the village shepherd had seen them in the early dawn by the windmill, lying under the moon in the young rye, the rumour spread like a wave breaking turbidly on the shore.

It reached Pantelei's ears also. One Sunday he happened to go along to Mokhov's shop. The throng was so great that no more could have crowded through the door. He entered, and everybody seemed to be making way for him, smiling at him. He pushed towards the counter where the draperies were sold. The master, Sergei Platonovich Mokhov, took it upon himself to attend to the old man.

"Where have you been all this long while, Prokofyevich?" he asked.

"Too much to do. Troubles with the farm."

"What? Sons like yours, and troubles?"

"What of my sons? I've seen Pyotr off to camp, there's only me and Grisha to do everything."

Mokhov divided his stiff, ruddy beard into two with his fingers and glanced significantly out of the corner of his eye at the crowd of Cossacks.

"Oh, yes, old man, and why haven't you told us anything about it?"

"About what?"

"How d'you mean, what? Thinking of marrying your son, and not a word to anybody!"

"Which son?"

"Why, your son Grigory isn't married."

"And I'm not thinking of marrying him yet."

"But I've heard that you're getting yourself a daughter-in-law ... Stepan Astakhov's Aksinya."

"What? With her husband alive.... Why, Platonovich, you must be joking! Aren't you?"

"Joking? But I've had it from others."

Pantelei smoothed out the piece of material spread over the counter, then, turning sharply, limped towards the door. He made straight for home. He walked with his head lowered like a bull, his fingers knotted in his fist, hobbling more noticeably on his lame leg. As he passed the Astakhovs' house he glanced over the wattle fence: Aksinya, looking young and smart, with a lithe swing in her hips, was going into the house with an empty bucket.

"Hey, wait!" he called, and stumped in at the gate. Aksinya halted and waited for him. They went into the house. The cleanly-swept earthen floor was sprinkled with red sand; on the bench in the corner were pasties fresh from the oven. A smell of musty clothes and sweet apples came from the best room.

A tabby cat with a huge head purred round Pantelei's legs. It arched its back and pressed itself against his boots. With a fierce kick he sent it flying against the bench.

"What's all this I hear? Eh?" he shouted looking Aksinya straight in the eyes. "Your husband hardly out of sight, and you already setting your cap at other men! I'll make Grisha's blood flow for this, and I'll write to your Stepan! Let him hear of it! You whore, haven't you been beaten enough! Don't set your foot inside my yard from this day on. Carrying on with a young man, and when Stepan comes, I'll have to. . . ."

Aksinya listened with narrowed eyes. And suddenly she shamelessly swung the hem of her skirt, enveloped Pantelei in the smell of woman's clothes, and came breasting at him with writhing lips and bared teeth.

"What are you, my father-in-law? Eh? Who are you to teach me? Go and teach your own fat-bottomed woman! Keep order in your own yard! You limping, stump-footed devil! Clear out of here, you won't frighten me!"

"Wait, you daft hussy!"

"There's nothing to wait for! Get back where you came from! And if I want your Grisha, I'll eat him, bones and all, and answer for it myself! Chew that over! What if I love Grisha? Beat me, will you? Write to my husband? Write to the ataman if you like, but Grisha belongs to me! He's mine! Mine! I have him and I shall keep him!"

Aksinya pressed against the quailing Pantelei with her breast (it beat against her thin blouse like a bustard in a noose), seared him with the flame of her black eyes, overwhelmed him with more and more terrible and shameless words. His eyebrows quivering, the old man backed to the door, groped for the stick he had left in the corner, and waving his hand, pushed open the door with his bottom. Aksinya pressed him out of the passage, pantingly, frenziedly shouting:

"I'll have my love, I'll make up for all the wrongs I've suffered! And then kill me if you like! He's my Grisha! Mine!"

Muttering something into his beard, Pantelei limped off to his house.

He found Grigory in the room. Without saying a word, he brought his stick down over his son's back. Doubling up, Grigory hung on his father's arm.

"What's that for, Father?"

"For your goings-on, you son of a bitch!"

"What goings-on?"

"Don't wrong your neighbour! Don't shame your father! Don't run after women, you young buck!" Pantelei snorted, dragging Grigory, who had grabbed the stick, around the room trying to wrest it from him.

"I'm not going to let you beat me!" Grigory cried hoarsely, and setting his teeth, he tore the stick out of his father's hand. Across his knee it went, and—snap!

Pantelei Prokofyevich struck him on the neck with his hard fist.

"I'll whip you in public. You accursed son of the devil! I'll marry you to the village idiot! I'll geld you!" his father roared.

The noise brought the old mother running into the room.

"Pantelei, Pantelei! Cool down a little! Wait!"

But the old man had lost his temper in real earnest. He sent his wife flying, overturned the table with the sewing-machine on it, and victoriously flew out into the yard. Grigory, whose shirt had been torn in the struggle, had not had time to take it off when the door banged open again, and his father appeared once more like a storm-cloud on the threshold.

"I'll marry him off, the son of a bitch!" He stamped his foot like a horse and fixed his gaze on Grigory's muscular back. "I'll drive off tomorrow and arrange the match. To think that I should live to see people laugh in my face about my son."

"Let me get my shirt on first, then you can marry me off."

"I'll marry you to the village idiot!" The door slammed, and the old man clattered away down the steps.

## XI

Beyond the village of Setrakov the carts with tarpaulin covers stretched in rows across the steppe. At unbelievable speed a neat, white-roofed little town had grown up, with straight streets and a small square in the centre, where a sentry stood guard.

The men lived the usual monotonous life of a training camp. In the morning the detachment of Cossacks guarding the grazing horses drove them into the camp. Then followed cleaning, grooming, saddling, the roll-call, and muster. The staff officer in command of the camp, Lieutenant-Colonel Popov, bawled stentoriously; the sergeants training the young Cossacks shouted their orders. They staged mock attacks on a hill, they cunningly encircled the "enemy." They fired at targets. The younger Cossacks eagerly vied with one another in the sabre exercises, and the old hands dodged as much of the training as they could.

While voices grew hoarse with the heat and the vodka, a fragrant exciting wind blew over the long lines of covered wagons, the susliks whistled in the distance, and the steppe beckoned away from the stuffiness and smoke of the whitewashed huts.

About a week before the break-up of the camp Andrei Tomilin's wife came to visit him. She brought him some home-made cracknel, an assortment of dainties and a sheaf of village news.

She left again very early in the morning, taking the Cossacks' greetings and instructions to their families and relations in the village. Only Stepan Astakhov sent no message back by her.

He had fallen ill the evening before, drunk vodka to cure himself and was incapable of seeing anything in the whole wide world, including Tomilin's wife. He did not turn up on parade; at his own request the doctor's assistant let his blood, setting a dozen leeches on his chest. Stepan sat in his undershirt against the wheel of his cart (making the white linen cover of his cap oily with cart grease) and stared sulkily at the leeches sucking at his barrel-like chest and swelling with dark blood.

The regiment medical orderly stood by smoking and letting the smoke filter through the wide gaps between his teeth.

"Feel any better?"

"They're drawing well. Easier for the heart somehow."

"Leeches are a great thing!"

Tomilin came up and gave Stepan a wink.

"Stepan, I'd like a word with you."

Stepan rose with a grunt and took Tomilin aside.

"My woman's been here on a visit. She left this morning."

"Well?"

"There's a lot of talk about your wife in the village."

"What?"

"Not pleasant talk, either."

"Well?"

"She's carrying on with Grigory Melekhov. Quite openly."

Turning pale, Stepan tore the leeches from his chest and crushed them underfoot. When he had crushed the last one, he buttoned up his shirt, and then, as though suddenly afraid, unbuttoned it again. His chalky lips moved incessantly. They trembled, slipped into an awkward smile, then shrivelled and gathered into a livid pucker. Tomilin thought Stepan must be chewing something hard and solid. Gradually the colour returned to his face, the lips, caught by his teeth, froze into immobility. He took off his cap, smeared the grease over the white cover with his sleeve, and said aloud: "Thanks for the news."

"I just wanted to warn you.... You won't hold it against me."

Tomilin clapped his hands against his trousers in a gesture of sympathy, and went off to his horse. A sound of voices and shouting was heard from the camp, the Cossacks had returned from the sabre exercises. Stepan stood for a moment staring fixedly and sternly at the black smear on his cap.

A half-crushed, dying leech crawled up his boot.

# XII

In ten more days the Cossacks would be returning from camp. Aksinya lived in a frenzy of belated bitter love. Despite his father's threats, Grigory slipped out and went to her at night, coming home at dawn.

In two weeks he had drained his strength, like a horse striving beyond its powers. From lack of sleep his brown face was suffused under the high cheek-bones with a blue tinge, his tired eyes gazed wearily out of their sunken sockets. Aksinya went about with her face completely uncovered, the deep hollows under her eyes darkened funereally; her swollen, avid lips smiled with a restless challenge.

So extraordinary and open was their mad association, so ecstatically did they burn with a single, shameless flame, neither conscience-stricken nor hiding their love from the world, becoming gaunt and dark before its very eyes, that people began to be ashamed to meet them in the street. Grigory's comrades, who previously had chaffed him about Aksinya, now kept silent and felt awkward and constrained in his company. In their hearts the women envied Aksinya, yet they condemned her, gloating at the prospect of Stepan's return, and pining with curiosity as to how it would all end.

If Grigory had made some show of hiding from the world his affair with this grass-widow, and if the grass-widow Aksinya had kept her relations with Grigory comparatively secret, without shunning others, the world would have seen nothing unusual in it. The village would have gossiped a little and then forgotten. But they lived together almost openly, they were bound by something greater, which had no likeness to any temporary association, and for that reason the villagers decided it was immoral and held their breath in peeping expectation. Stepan would return and cut the knot.

Over the bed in the Astakhovs' bedroom ran a string threaded with empty white and black cotton-reels. They hung there for decoration. The flies spent their nights on the reels, and spiders' webs stretched from them to the ceiling. Grigory was lying on Aksinya's bare, cool arm and gazing up at the chain of reels. With the toil-roughened fingers of her other hand Aksinya was playing with the thick strands of hair on his head. Her fingers smelt of warm milk; when Grigory turned his head, pressing his nose into Aksinya's armpit, the pungent, sweetish scent of woman's sweat flooded his nostrils.

In addition to the wooden, painted bedstead with pointed pine cones at the corners, the room contained a capacious iron-bound chest that stood close to the door, holding Aksinya's dowry and all her finery. In the corner was a table, an oleograph of General Skobelev riding towards a row of flapping banners dipped before him, two chairs, and above them icons in gawdy paper aureoles. Along the side wall hung fly-blown photographs. One was a group of Cossacks, with curly forelocks, swelling chests decorated with watch chains, and drawn swords—Stepan and his comrades on active service. On a hook hung Stepan's uniform, it had not been put away. The moon stared through the window and uncertainly fingered the two white sergeant's straps on the shoulder.

With a sigh Aksinya kissed Grigory on the bridge of his nose, between his eyebrows.

"Grisha, my love."

"What?"

"Only nine days left."

"That's not so soon."

"What am I to do, Grisha?"

"How should I know?"

Aksinya restrained a sigh and again smoothed and parted Grigory's matted hair.

"Stepan will kill me," she half-asked, half-declared.

Grigory was silent. He wanted to sleep. With difficulty he forced open his clinging eyelids and saw above him the glittering bluish blackness of Aksinya's eyes.

"When my husband comes back, you'll give me up, won't you? You'll be afraid?"

"Why should I be afraid of him? You're his wife, it's for you to be afraid."

"When I'm with you I'm not afraid, but when I think about it in the daytime I am."

Grigory yawned and said: "It doesn't matter so much about Stepan coming back. My father's talking of getting me married off."

He smiled and was going to add something, but he felt Aksinya's hand under his head suddenly wilt and soften, bury itself in the pillow, and after a moment harden again.

"Who has he got in mind?" she asked in a stifled voice.

"He's only talking about it. Mother says he's thinking of Korshunov's Natalya."

"Natalya . . . she's a good-looking girl. Very good-looking. . . . Well, go ahead and marry her. I saw her in church the other day. Dressed up she was. . . ." Aksinya spoke rapidly, but he could scarcely hear her, her voice was so lifeless and dull.

"I don't care two pins about her good looks. I'd like to marry you."

Aksinya sharply pulled her arm from under Grigory's head and stared with dry eyes at the window. A frosty, yellow mist was in the yard. The shed cast a heavy shadow. The crickets were chirruping. Down by the Don the bitterns boomed; their deep sullen tones floated through the bedroom window.

"Grisha!"

"Thought of something?"

Aksinya seized Grigory's rough, unyielding hands, pressed them to her breast, and to her cold, almost lifeless cheeks, and cried:

"What did you take up with me for, curse you! What shall I do? Grisha! I'm finished. . . . Stepan is coming back, and what shall I tell him. . .? Who is there to help me?"

Grigory was silent. Aksinya gazed mournfully at his handsome eagle nose, his shadowed eyes, his dumb lips. . . . And suddenly a flood of feeling swept away the dam of restraint. Madly she kissed his face, his neck, his arms, the rough, curly black hair on his chest, and Grigory felt her body trembling as, gasping for breath, she whispered:

"Grisha . . . my dearest . . . beloved . . . let's go away. My darling! We'll throw up everything and go. I'll leave my husband and everything, so long as you're with me. . . . We'll go far away,

to the mines. I'll love you and care for you. I've
got an uncle who is a watchman at the Paramo-
nov mines: he'll help us. . . . Grisha! Oh, say
something!"

Grigory lay thinking, then unexpectedly
opened his burning foreign-looking eyes. They
were laughing, gleaming derision.

"You're a fool, Aksinya, a fool! You talk
away, but you say nothing worth listening to.
How can I leave the farm? I've got to do my
military service next year. . . . I'll never stir anywhere away from the land. Here there is the
steppe, and something to breathe—but there?
Last summer I went with Father to the station.
I nearly died. Engines roaring, the air all thick
and heavy with burning coal. How people live
there, I don't know; perhaps they're used to
it!" Grigory spat and said again: "I'll never
leave the village."

The night grew darker outside the window, a
cloud passed over the moon. The frosty, yellow
mist vanished from the yard, the shadows were
washed away, and now there was no telling
whether it was last year's faggots or some old
bush that loomed darkly beyond the fence outside the window.

The room, too, grew darker. The stripes on
Stepan's uniform faded, and in the grey, stagnant murk Grigory did not see the fine shiver that

shook Aksinya's shoulders, or her head pressed between her hands and silently shaking on the pillow.

## XIII

After the visit of Tomilin's wife Stepan's features became distinctly less handsome. His brows drooped over his eyes, a deep and harsh frown puckered his forehead. He spoke little with his comrades, began to quarrel over trifles, had a cross with the sergeant-major and would hardly look at Pyotr Melekhov. The threads of friendship which had previously united them were snapped. In his sullen, seething rage Stepan plunged downhill like a bolting horse. They returned home enemies.

Of course something had to happen that brought the vague hostility of their relations to a head. They set out for their village in the same group as before. Pyotr's and Stepan's horses were harnessed to the wagon. Christonya rode behind on his own horse. Tomilin, who was suffering from fever, lay covered with his greatcoat in the wagon. Fedot Bodovskov was too lazy to drive, so Pyotr took the reins. Stepan walked along at the side of the wagon, lashing off the purple heads of the roadside thistles with his whip. Rain was falling. The rich black earth stuck to the wheels like tar. The sky was an autumnal blue, ashy with cloud. Night fell. No lights of any village were to be seen. Pyotr belaboured the horses liberally with the knout. And suddenly Stepan shouted in the darkness:

"You, what the... you...! You spare your own horse, but keep the knout on mine all the time."

"Keep your eyes open! I whip the one that doesn't pull."

"Mind I don't put you in the shafts. That's what Turks are good for."

Pyotr threw the reins down.

"What do you want?"

"Oh, stay where you are."

"Shut up."

"What are you flaring up at him for?" asked Christonya, riding up to Stepan.

Stepan did not reply. They rode on for another half hour in silence. The mud squelched under the wheels. The rain pattered drowsily on the tarpaulin. Pyotr dropped the reins and smoked, running over in his mind all the insulting words he would use in the next quarrel with Stepan.

"Out of the way. I want to get under cover." Stepan pushed Pyotr aside and jumped on the step of the cart.

The wagon suddenly jolted and stopped. Slipping in the mud, the horses pawed the earth.

Sparks showered from their hoofs and the shaft groaned.

"Whoa!" Pyotr shouted and leaped to the ground.

"What's the matter?" Stepan snapped anxiously.

"Show a light," Pyotr demanded.

In front a horse was struggling and snorting. Someone struck a match. A tiny orange ring of light, then darkness again. With trembling hands Pyotr felt the spine of the fallen horse, then pulled at the bridle.

The horse sighed and rolled over, the centre-shaft snapped in half. Stepan struck a bunch of matches. His horse lay craning her neck with one foreleg buried to the knee in a marmot's hole.

Christonya unfastened the traces.

"Unharness Pyotr's horse, look snappy," he ordered.

"Whoa! Easy there! Easy!"

At last Stepan's horse was lifted with difficulty to its feet. While Pyotr held it by the bridle, Christonya crawled on his knees in the mud, feeling the helplessly-hanging leg.

"Seems to be broken," he boomed.

"See if he can walk."

Pyotr pulled at the bridle. The horse hopped a step or two, not putting its left foreleg to the ground, and whinnied. Drawing on his great-coat, Tomilin stamped about bitterly.

"Broken, damn it! A horse lost!"

Stepan, who all this time had not spoken a word, almost seemed to have been awaiting such a remark. Thrusting Christonya aside he flung himself on Pyotr. He aimed at his head, but missed and struck his shoulder. They grappled together and fell into the mud. There was the sound of a tearing shirt. Stepan got Pyotr under him, and holding his head down with one knee, pounded away with his fists. Christonya dragged him off cursing.

"What's that for?" Pyotr shouted, spitting blood.

"Look where you drive, you snake!"

Pyotr tried to tear himself out of Christonya's hands.

"Now then! You try fighting me!" Christonya roared, holding Pyotr with one hand against the wagon.

They harnessed Bodovskov's small but sturdy horse with Pyotr's. Christonya gave his horse to Stepan to ride, and himself crawled into the cart with Pyotr. It was midnight when they arrived at a village. They stopped at the first house, and Christonya asked for a night's shelter.

Ignoring the dog snapping at the skirts of his coat, he squelched through the mud to the window, opened the shutter, and scratched at the pane with a horny fingernail.

"Master!"

Only the whisper of the rain and a peal of barking.

"Master! Good folk, hi! Let us in for the night, for Christ's sake. Eh? From the training camp. How many? Five of us. Well, Christ save you."

"Drive in!" he shouted turning to the gate.

Bodovskov led the horses in. He stumbled over a pig's trough thrown down in the middle of the yard, and cursed vigorously. They led the horses into a shed. Tomilin, his teeth chattering, went into the house, Pyotr and Christonya remained in the cart.

At dawn they made ready to set out again. Stepan came out of the house, an old hunchbacked woman hobbling after him. Christonya, who was harnessing the horses, shouted sympathetically:

"Ho, granny, what a hump they've given you! Bet you're all right at bowing down in church. You don't have far to bend to reach the floor!"

"If I'm good for bowing down, you're good for hanging dogs on, my lad. There's something for all of us," the old woman smiled severely, surprising Christonya with a full row of small sound teeth.

"And what teeth you've got, like a pike! Won't you give me a few? Here am I, a young man, and nothing to chew with."

"What shall I have left for myself, my dear?"

"We'll give you a horse's set, gran. You've got to die one day and they don't look at your teeth in the next world. The saints aren't horse-dealers, you know."

"Keep it up, Christonya," Tomilin grinned as he climbed into the cart.

The old woman followed Stepan into the shed. "Which one is it?"

"The black," sighed Stepan.

The woman laid her stick on the ground, and with an unexpectedly strong, masculine movement raised the horse's damaged leg. She felt the knee-cap carefully with her thin, crooked fingers. The horse set back its ears and reared on to its hindlegs with the pain.

"No, there's no break there, Cossack. Leave him and I'll heal him."

Stepan waved his hand and went to the cart.

"Will you leave him or not?" the old woman watched him narrowly.

"Let him stay," he replied.

"She'll heal him for you. He won't have any legs left when you come back. The vet's a hunchback herself," Christonya said booming with laughter.

## XIV

"Oh how I long for him, granny dear! I'm withering away before my own eyes. I can't put tucks into my skirt fast enough. Every time he goes past the house my heart burns. I'd fall to the ground and kiss his footprints. Help me! They're going to marry him off. . . . Help me, dear. . . . Whatever it costs, I'll give you. . . . I'll give you my last shirt, only help me!"

With luminous eyes set in a lacework of furrows the old crone Drozdikha looked at Aksinya, shaking her head at the bitter story.

"Which lad is it?"

"Pantelei Melekhov's."

"That's the Turk, isn't it?"

"Yes."

The old woman chewed away with her toothless gums, and hesitated with her answer.

"Come to me very early tomorrow, child, as soon as day is dawning. We'll go down to the Don, to the water. We'll wash away your yearning. Bring a pinch of salt with you."

Aksinya wrapped herself in her yellow shawl and with drooping shoulders walked out through the gate. Her dark figure was swallowed up in the night, and the only sound was of her sandals scraping dryly on the earth. Then her steps died away. From somewhere at the end

of the village came sounds of brawling and
singing.

At dawn, Aksinya, who had not slept all
night, was at Drozdikha's window.

"Granny!"

"Who's there?"

"It's me, Aksinya! Get up!"

They made their way by back lanes down
to the river. The abandoned shafts of a wagon
lay water-logged near the landing stage. At the
water's edge the sand stung their bare feet icily.
A damp, chilly mist crept up from the Don.

Drozdikha took Aksinya's hand in her own
bony hand and drew her to the water.

"Give me the salt. Cross yourself to the
sunrise."

Aksinya crossed herself, staring fiercely at
the happy rosiness of the east.

"Take up some water in your palm and
drink."

Aksinya drank, wetting the sleeves of her
blouse. Like a black spider the old woman
straddled the lapping waves, squatted down,
and began to whisper.

"Icy streams from the deep.... Sorrowing
flesh.... A beast in the heart.... Yearning and
fever.... By the holy cross, by the pure and
holy Mother.... The slave of God, Grigory ..." reached Aksinya's ears.

Drozdikha sprinkled some salt over the damp sand at her feet and some more into the water, then put the rest in Aksinya's bosom.

"Sprinkle some water over your shoulder. Quickly!"

Aksinya did so. She stared moodily and angrily at Drozdikha's russet cheeks.

"Is that all?"

"Yes, that's all. Go and sleep."

Aksinya ran breathlessly home. The cows were lowing in the yard. Darya, sleepy-eyed and flushed, was driving her cows off to join the village herd. She smiled as she saw Aksinya run past.

"Slept well, neighbour?"

"Praise be!"

"And where have you been so early?"

"I had a call to make in the village."

The church bells were ringing for matins. The copper-tongued clapping broke apart in splashes of sound. The village herdsman cracked his stockwhip in the side-street. Aksinya hurriedly drove out the cows, then carried the milk into the porch to strain it. She wiped her hands on her apron, and, lost in thought, poured the milk into the strainer.

A heavy rattle of wheels and snorting of horses in the street. Aksinya set down the pail and went to look out of the front window.

Holding his sabre pommel, Stepan was coming through the wicket-gate. The other Cossacks were galloping away towards the village square. Aksinya crumpled her apron in her fingers and sat down on the bench. Steps in the porch.... Steps in the passage.... Steps at the very door....

Stepan stood on the threshold, gaunt and estranged.

"Well?"

Aksinya, all her full, buxom body reeling, went to meet him.

"Beat me," she said slowly, and turned sideways towards him.

"Well, Aksinya?"

"I shan't hide. I have sinned. Beat me, Stepan!"

Her head drawn into her shoulders, crouching down and protecting only her belly with her arms, she faced him. Her eyes stared unblinkingly from their dark sockets, out of her dumb, fear-distorted face. Stepan swayed and walked past her. His unwashed shirt smelled of male sweat and bitter roadside scents. He dropped on to the bed without removing his cap. He lay for a moment, then jerked his shoulders, and threw off his sword-belt. His blond usually crisp moustache drooped limply. Not turning her head, Aksinya glanced sidelong at him. Now and then she shuddered. Stepan put his feet on the foot of the bed. The mud slowly oozed from his boots. He stared at the ceiling and toyed with the leather tassel of his sword.

"Breakfast ready?"

"No. . . ."

"Get me something to eat."

He sipped some milk, wetting his moustache. He chewed slowly at the bread. Aksinya stood by the stove. In burning terror she watched her husband's little gristly ears rising and falling as he ate.

Stepan rose from the table and crossed himself.

"Come on, m'dear, tell me about it," he curtly demanded.

With bowed head Aksinya cleared the table. She was silent.

"Tell me how you waited for your husband, how you guarded his honour. Well?"

A terrible blow on the head tore the ground from under Aksinya's feet and flung her towards the door. Her back struck against the door-post, and she groaned dully.

Women are weak and soft in the body, but Stepan could send lusty and sturdy guardsmen flying with a well-aimed blow on the head. It may have been fear that lifted Aksinya, or perhaps it was a woman's will to live—she came to her senses, lay a moment, resting, then scrambled on to all fours.

Stepan was lighting a cigarette in the middle of the room and did not see her rising to her feet. He threw his tobacco pouch on the table, but Aksinya had already slammed the door behind her. He chased after her.

Her head streaming with blood, Aksinya ran towards the fence separating their yard from the Melekhovs'. Stepan overtook her at the fence. His black hand fell like a hawk on her head. His fingers wound into her hair. He tore at it and threw her to the ground, into the cinders that Aksinya dumped by the fence every day.

What if a husband does trample his wife with his boots, his hands behind his back? One-armed Alexei Shamil walked past the gate, looked in, blinked and parted his bushy little beard with a smile; after all it was quite understandable why Stepan should be punishing his lawfully-wedded wife. Shamil was tempted to stop to see whether he would beat her to death or not, but his conscience would not allow him. After all, he wasn't a woman.

Watching Stepan from afar, you would have thought he was doing the Cossack dance. And so Grigory thought, as through the window he saw Stepan jumping up and down. But he looked again, and flew out of the house. Pressing his heavy fists against his chest, he ran on his toes to the fence. Pyotr pounded after him.

Over the high fence Grigory flew like a bird. He charged Stepan from behind at full speed. Stepan staggered and turning round came at Grigory like a bear.

The Melekhov brothers fought desperately. They pecked at Stepan like carrion-crows at a carcass. Grigory went down several times under Stepan's rock-like fist. He was not quite a match for a hardened brawler like Stepan, but the stocky agile Pyotr, although he bent under the blows like a reed before the wind, stood firmly on his feet.

Stepan, one eye flashing (the other was turning the colour of an underripe plum) retreated to the steps.

Christonya happened to come along to borrow some harness from Pyotr, and he separated them.

"Stop that!" He waved his arms. "Break away, or I'll report it to the ataman."

Pyotr carefully spat blood and half a tooth into his palm, and said hoarsely:

"Come on, Grigory. We'll get him some other time."

"Mind I don't get you!" Stepan threatened from the steps.

"All right, all right!"

"And no 'all right' about it, I'll tear your guts out."

"Is that serious or joking?"

Stepan came swiftly down the steps. Grigory broke forward to meet him, but pushing him towards the gate, Christonya promised:

"Only dare, and I'll give you a good hiding."

From that day onward the hatred between the Melekhovs and Stepan Astakhov drew itself into a tight knot. Grigory Melekhov was fated to untie that knot two years later in East Prussia, near the town of Stolypin.

## XV

"Tell Pyotr to harness the mare and his own horse."

Grigory went out into the yard. Pyotr was pushing a wagonette out of the lean-to shed by the barn.

"Dad says you've got to harness the mare and your own horse."

"I know that without him telling me. Tell him to mind his own business," Pyotr responded, fixing the shaft-bow. Pantelei, solemn as a churchwarden at mass, although sweating like a bull, sat finishing his soup. Dunya was watching Grigory alertly, hiding a girlish twinkle somewhere in the shadowy cool of her long upturned lashes. Ilyinichna, large and portly in her lemon-yellow Sunday shawl, a motherly anxiety lurking at the corners of her lips, said to the old man:

"Stop stuffing yourself, Prokofyevich. One would think you were starving."

"Won't even let me eat. What a nagger you are, woman."

Pyotr's long, wheaten-yellow moustache appeared at the door.

"Your carriage is ready, if you please!"

Dunya burst into a laugh, and hid her face in her sleeve. Darya passed through the kitchen and looked the future bridegroom over with a flutter of her fine lashes.

Ilyinichna's shrewd widow cousin, Auntie Vasilisa, was to go with them as match-maker. She was the first to perch herself on the wagonette, twisting and turning her head, laughing, and displaying her crooked black teeth beneath the pucker of her lips.

"Don't show your teeth, Vasilisa," Pantelei warned her. "You'll ruin everything. Those teeth of yours look as if they had been on a night out, there's not one that can stand up straight."

"Ah, Cousin, I'm not the bridegroom-to-be. . . ."

"Maybe you're not, but don't laugh all the same. What teeth . . . the colour's enough to make you sick."

Vasilisa took umbrage, but meanwhile Pyotr had opened the gate. Grigory sorted out the good-smelling leather reins and jumped into the driver's seat. Pantelei and Ilyinichna sat side by side at the back just like newlyweds.

"Whip 'em up!" shouted Pyotr, letting go the halter.

Grigory bit his lips and lashed the horses. They pulled at the traces and started off without warning.

"Look out! You'll catch your wheel!" Darya shrilled, but the wagonette swerved sharply and, bouncing over the roadside hummocks, rattled down the street.

Leaning to one side, Grigory touched up Pyotr's lagging horse with the whip. His father held his beard in his hand, as though afraid that the wind would snatch it away.

"Whip up the mare!" he cried hoarsely, leaning over Grigory's shoulder. With the lace sleeve of her blouse Ilyinichna wiped away the tear that the wind had brought to her eye, and blinked at Grigory's blue satin shirt fluttering and billowing on his back. The Cossacks along the road stepped aside and stood staring after them. The dogs came running out of the yards and yelped under the horses' feet. Their barking was drowned in the rumble of the freshly-shod wheels.

Grigory spared neither whip nor horses, and within ten minutes the village was left behind. Korshunov's large house with its plank fence soon came into view. Grigory pulled on the reins, and the wagonette, breaking off its iron song right in the middle, suddenly drew up at the painted finely-carved gates.

Grigory remained with the horses; Pantelei limped towards the steps. Ilyinichna and Vasilisa sailed after him with rustling skirts. The old man hurried, afraid of losing the courage he had summoned up during the ride. He stumbled over the high threshold, knocked his lame leg, and frowning with pain stamped furiously up the well-swept steps.

He and Ilyinichna entered the kitchen almost together. He disliked standing at his wife's side, as she was taller by a good six inches; so he stepped a pace forward, and removing his cap, crossed himself before the blackened icon.

"Good health to you!"

"Praise be!" the master of the house, a stocky, freckled old man replied, rising from the bench.

"Some guests for you, Miron Grigoryevich," Pantelei continued.

"Guests are always welcome. Marya, give the visitors something to sit on."

His elderly, flat-chested wife wiped non-existent dust from three stools, and pushed them towards the guests. Pantelei sat down on the very edge of one, and mopped his perspiring brow with his handkerchief.

"We've come on business," he began without beating about the bush. At this point Ilyinichna and Vasilisa, pulling up their skirts, also sat down.

"By all means. On what business?" the master smiled.

Grigory entered, stared around him and greeted the Korshunovs. A deep russet spread across Miron's freckled face. Only now did he guess the object of the visit. "Have the horses brought into the yard. Get some hay put down for them," he ordered his wife.

"We've just a little matter to talk over," Pantelei went on, twisting his curly beard and tugging at his ear-ring in his agitation. "You have a girl unmarried, we have a son. Couldn't we come to some arrangement? We'd like to know. Will you give her away now, or not? Mebbe we might become relations?"

"Who knows?" Miron scratched his bald spot. "I must say, we weren't thinking of giving her in marriage this autumn. We've our hands full with work here, and she's not so very old. She's only just past her eighteenth spring. That's right, isn't it, Marya?"

"That's it."

"She's the very age for marriage," Vasilisa put in. "A girl soon gets too old!" She fidgeted on her stool, prickled by the besom she had stolen from the porch and thrust under her jacket. Tradition had it that match-makers who stole the girl's besom were never refused.

"We had proposals for our girl way back in early spring. Our girl won't be left on the shelf. We can't grumble to the good God.... She can do everything, in the field or at home..." Korshunov's wife replied.

"If a good man were to come along, you wouldn't say no," Pantelei broke into the women's chatter.

"It isn't a question of saying no," the master scratched his head. "We can give her away at any time."

Pantelei thought he was going to be refused and got ruffled.

"Well, it's your own business, of course. A man's got his choice, he can ask where he likes. If you're keen on finding some merchant's son,

or someone of that kind, it's a different matter
and we beg your pardon."

The negotiations were on the point of breaking down. Pantelei began to get agitated, and
his face flushed a beetroot red, while the girl's
mother clucked like a sitting hen shadowed by
a kite. But Vasilisa intervened in the nick of
time. She poured out a flood of quiet, soothing
words, like salt on a burn, and healed the
breach.

"Now, now, my dears! Once a matter like
this is raised, it needs to be settled decently
and for the happiness of your child. Natalya
now—why, you might search far in broad daylight and not find another like her! Work burns
in her hands! What a clever young woman!
What a housewife! And as for her looks, you
see for yourselves, good folk . . ." she opened
her plump arms in a generous sweep, turning
to Pantelei and the sulky Ilyinichna. "And he's
a husband worthy of any. As I look at him my
heart beats with yearning, he's so like my late
husband, and his family are great workers. Ask
anyone in these parts about Prokofyevich. In all
the world he's known as an honest man and a
kind one. . . . In good faith, do we wish evil to
our children?"

Her chiding little voice flowed into Pantelei's
ears like syrup. He listened and thought admir-

ingly to himself: "Ah, the smooth-tongued devil, how she talks! Just try to keep up with
her! Some women can even dumbfound a Cossack with their words. . . . And this from a petticoat!" He was lost in admiration of Vasilisa,
who was now oozing praise for the girl and her
family as far back as the fifth generation.

"Of course, we don't wish evil to our child."

"The point is it's early to give her in
marriage," the master said pacifically, with
a smile.

"It's not early! Honest to God it's not early,"
Pantelei rejoined.

"Sooner or later, we have to part with her,"
the mistress sobbed, half-hypocritically, half in
earnest.

"Call your daughter, Miron Grigoryevich,
and let's look at her."

"Natalya!"

A girl appeared timidly at the door, her dark
fingers fidgeting with the frill of her apron.

"Come in! Come in! She's shy," the mother
encouraged her, smiling through her tears.

Grigory looked at her.

Bold grey eyes under a black lace scarf. A
small, rosy dimple in the supple cheek. Grigory turned his eyes to her hands: they were
large and marred with hard work. Under the
short green jacket embracing the strong body,

117

the small, maidenly firm breasts rose outwards
naïvely and pitifully, and their sharp little nip-
ples showed like buttons.

In a moment Grigory's eyes had taken her
all in, from the head to the long, beautiful legs.
He looked her over as a horse-dealer surveys
a mare before purchase, thought: "She'll do,"
then let his eyes meet hers. The simple, sin-
cere, slightly embarrassed gaze seemed to be
saying: "Here am I all, as I am. Judge of me
as you wish." "Splendid!" Grigory replied with
his eyes and smile.

"Well, that's all." Her father waved her
out.

As she closed the door behind her, Natalya
looked at Grigory without attempting to conceal her smile and her curiosity.

"Listen, Pantelei Prokofyevich," Korshunov
began, after exchanging glances with his wife.
"You talk it over, and we'll talk it over among
the family. And then we'll decide whether we'll
call it a match or not."

As he went down the steps Pantelei slipped
in a last word:

"We'll call again next Sunday."

Korshunov remained deliberately silent, pretending he had not heard.

Only after he learned of Aksinya's conduct from
Tomilin did Stepan, nursing his pain and hatred
in his soul, realize that despite his poor sort of
life with her he loved her with a dreary, hate-
ful love. He had lain in the wagon at night, covered with his greatcoat, his arms locked behind his head, and thought of how his wife
would greet him on his return home. It was
as if he had a scorpion in his breast in place
of a heart. As he lay thinking over a thousand
details of his revenge his teeth felt as if they
were clogged with heavy grains of sand. The
fight with Pyotr had spilled his anger. When
he arrived home he had been tired out and Aksinya had got off lightly.

From the day of his homecoming an unseen
spectre dwelt in the Astakhovs' house. Aksinya
went about on tiptoe and spoke in whispers,
but in her eyes, sprinkled with the ash of fear,
lurked a small spark, left from the flame Grigory had kindled.

As he watched her, Stepan felt rather than
saw this. He tormented himself. At night, when
the drove of flies had fallen asleep on the cross-
beam, and Aksinya, her lips trembling, had
made the bed, he pressed his horny palm
over her mouth and beat her. He demanded

shameless details of her relations with Grigory. Aksinya tossed about and gasped for breath on the hard bed smelling of sheepskin. Tired of torturing her dough-soft body, he passed his hand over her face, seeking for tears. But her cheeks were burningly dry, and only her jaws worked under his fingers.

"Will you tell?"

"No!"

"I'll kill you!"

"Kill me, kill me, for the love of Christ! This isn't life. . . ."

Grinding his teeth, Stepan twisted the fine skin, all damp with sweat, on her breast. Aksinya shuddered and groaned.

"Does it hurt?" Stepan said jocularly.

"Yes, it hurts."

"Do you think it didn't hurt me?"

It would be late before he fell asleep. In his sleep he clenched his fists. Rising on her elbow, Aksinya would gaze at her husband's face, handsome and changed in slumber, then let her head fall back on the pillow, and whisper to herself.

She hardly saw Grigory now. Once she happened to meet him down by the Don. Grigory had been watering the bullocks and was coming up the slope, waving a switch and staring at his feet. Aksinya was going down to the

Don. She saw him, and felt the yoke of the buckets turn cold in her hands and the hot blood beat at her temples.

Afterwards, when she recalled the meeting, she found it difficult to convince herself that it had really happened. Grigory noticed her when she had all but passed him. At the insistent creaking of the buckets he raised his head, his eyebrows quivered and he smiled stupidly. Aksinya gazed straight over his head at the green waves of the Don, and beyond at the ridge of the sandy headland. A burning flush wrung tears from her eyes.

"Aksinya!"

She walked on several paces and stood with her head bent as though before a blow. Angrily whipping a lagging bullock, he said without turning his head:

"When is Stepan going out to cut the rye?"

"He's getting ready now."

"See him off, then go to our sunflower patch and I'll come along after."

Her pails creaking, Aksinya went down to the Don. The foam snaked along the shore, a yellow flare of lace on the green hem of the wave. White sea-gulls were hovering and mewing above the river. Over the surface of the water, tiny fish sprinkled in a silver rain. On the other side, beyond the white of the sandy headland, the grey tops of ancient poplars rose haughtily and sternly. As Aksinya was drawing water she dropped her pail. She pulled up her skirt and waded in up to her knees. The water tickled her calves, and for the first time since Stepan's return she laughed quietly and uncertainly.

She glanced back at Grigory. Still waving his switch, he was slowly climbing the slope. With eyes that were misty with tears Aksinya caressed his strong legs as they confidently trod the ground. His broad *sharovari* tucked into white woollen stockings were gay with crimson stripes. On his back, over his shoulder-blade, fluttered a strip of freshly-torn shirt, and a triangle of swarthy flesh showed through the hole. With her eyes Aksinya kissed this tiny scrap of the beloved body which once had been hers; and tears fell on her pallid, smiling lips.

She set her pails down on the sand to hook them on to the yoke, and noticed the imprints of Grigory's shoes. She looked stealthily around: no one in sight except some boys bathing from the distant jetty. She squatted down and covered the footprint with her palm; then rose, swung the yoke across her shoulders, and hastened home, smiling to herself.

Caught in a muslin mistiness, the sun was passing over the village. Beyond the curly flock of small white clouds spread a deep, cool, azure pasture. Over the burning iron roofs, over the deserted dusty streets, over the farmyards with their parched, yellow grass, hung a deathly sultriness.

When Aksinya approached the steps Stepan, in a broad-brimmed straw hat, was harnessing the horses to the reaping machine. "Pour some water into the pitcher."

Aksinya poured a pail of water into the pitcher and burned her fingers on the hot iron rim.

"You ought to have some ice or the water will get warm soon," she said, looking at her husband's perspiring back.

"Go and borrow some from the Melekhovs. No, don't go," Stepan shouted, remembering.

Aksinya went to shut the wicket-gate. Stepan lowered his eyes and snatched up the knout.

"Where are you going?"

"To shut the gate."

"Come back, you bitch. I told you not to go."

She hurriedly returned to the steps and tried to hang her yoke on the rails, but her hands were trembling too much. The yoke clattered down the steps.

Stepan flung his tarpaulin coat over the front seat, and took up the reins.

"Open the gate."

As she did so, she ventured to ask: "When will you be back?"

"By evening. I've agreed to reap with Anikushka. Take the food along to him. He'll be coming out to the fields when he's finished at the smith's."

The wheels of the reaper squeaked as they carved into the grey plush of the dust. Aksinya went into the house and stood a moment with her hand pressed to her head, then, flinging a kerchief over her hair, ran down to the river.

"But suppose he comes back? What then?" the thought suddenly burned into her mind. She stopped as though she saw a deep pit at her feet, glanced back, and sped almost at a run along the river bank to the meadows.

Fences. Vegetable patches. A yellow sea of sunflowers outstaring the sun. The pale green of potato plants. There were the Shamil women hoeing their potato patch; bowed backs in pink shifts, hoes rising and falling sharply on the grey earth. Reaching the Melekhovs' garden Aksinya glanced around, then lifted the wattle hasp and opened the gate. She followed the path to the green stockade of sunflower stems. Stooping, she pressed into the midst of them,

smothering her face with golden pollen, then
gathered her skirt and sat down on the weed-
woven ground.

She listened: the silence rang in her ears.
From somewhere above her came the lonely
drone of a bee. For perhaps half an hour she
sat thus, torturing herself with doubt. Would
he come? She was about to go, and was adjusting her kerchief, when the gate scraped
heavily.

"Aksinya!"

"This way."

"So you've come!" Rustling the leaves, Grigory approached and sat down at her side.

"What's that on your cheek?"

Aksinya smeared the fragrant golden dust
with her sleeve.

"Must be from the sunflowers."

"There too, under your eye."

She brushed it off.

Their eyes met. And in reply to Grigory's
mute inquiry, she broke into weeping.

"I can't stand it.... I'm lost, Grisha."

"What does he do?"

Fiercely she tore open the collar of her
blouse. The pink, girlishly swelling breasts were
covered with cherry-blue bruises.

"Don't you know? He beats me every day.
He's sucking my blood.... And you're a fine

125

one. . . . Soiled me like a dog, and off you go. . . . You're all. . . ." She buttoned her blouse with trembling fingers, and, frightened that he might be offended, glanced at his averted face.

"So you're trying to put the blame on me?" he said slowly, biting a blade of grass.

"And aren't you to blame?" she cried fiercely.

"A dog doesn't worry an unwilling bitch."

Aksinya hid her face in her hands. The insult struck home like a hard, calculated blow.

Grigory frowned and glanced sidelong at her. A tear was trickling between her first and middle fingers. A broken dusty sunray gleamed on the transparent drop, and dried its damp trace on her skin.

Grigory could not endure tears. He fidgeted impatiently, ruthlessly brushed a brown ant from his trousers, and glanced again at Aksinya. She hadn't moved; but three runnels of tears were now chasing down the back of her hand.

"What's the matter? Have I offended you? Aksinya! Now, wait! Stop, I want to say something."

She tore her hands from her face. "I came here to get advice. What did you do it for? It's bitter enough as it is. And you. . . ."

Grigory flushed with remorse. "Aksinya...
I didn't mean to say that, don't take on."

"I haven't come to fasten myself on you.
You needn't be afraid."

At that moment she really believed that she
had not come to fasten herself on Grigory, but
as she had run along by the Don she had
vaguely thought: "I'll talk him round! He won't
get married. Who else am I to live with?" Then
she had remembered Stepan and had obstinately
shaken her head to drive away the trou-
blesome thought.

"So our love is over?" Grigory asked, and
turned on to his stomach, resting on one elbow
and spitting out the rosy petals of the bindweed
flower he had been chewing.

"What do you mean—over?" Aksinya took
alarm. "What do you mean?" she insisted, trying to look into his eyes. There was a gleam of
bluish white as he turned them away.

The dry, exhausted earth smelled of dust and
sun. The wind rustled among the big green
leaves. For a moment the sun was darkened,
overcast with a fleeting cloud; and over the
steppe, over the village, over Aksinya's moody
head, over the pink cup of the bindweed flower,
there fell a smoky shadow.

Grigory sighed abruptly and lay on his back,
pressing his shoulder-blades into the hot soil.

"Listen, Aksinya!" he began slowly. "This is rotten somehow. . . . I've been thinking. . . ."

From the vegetable patch came the creaking sound of a cart, and a woman's voice: "Gee up, baldhead!"

To Aksinya the call seemed so close that she dropped flat on the ground. Raising his head, Grigory whispered:

"Take your kerchief off. It shows up. . . . They might see us."

She removed her kerchief. The burning breeze wandering among the sunflowers played with wisps of golden down on her neck. The noise of the cart slowly died away.

"Well, this is what I've been thinking," Grigory began again. Then, more animatedly: "What's done can't be undone. Why try to fix the blame? Somehow we've got to go on living."

Aksinya listened anxiously, breaking a stalk in her hand as she waited. She looked into Grigory's face and caught the dry and sober glitter of his eyes.

"I've been thinking, let us put an end to . . ."

Aksinya swayed. Her fingers clawed into the tough bindweed as she waited for the end of the sentence. A fire of terror and impatience avidly licked her face, her mouth went dry. She thought he was about to say, "put an end to Stepan," but impatiently he licked his dry lips (they were working fiercely) and said:

". . . put an end to this affair. Eh?"

Aksinya stood up, and pressing through the swaying, yellow heads of the sunflowers, went towards the gate.

"Aksinya!" Grigory called chokingly.

The gate creaked heavily in reply.

### XVII

Immediately after the rye was cut, and before it could be carried to the barns, the wheat ripened. In the clayey fields and on the slopes the parched leaves turned yellow and curled up into tubes, and the stalks, having served their purpose, withered.

Everybody boasted of the good harvest. The ears were full, the grain heavy and large.

After talking the matter over with Ilyinichna, Pantelei decided that if the Korshunovs agreed to the match, the wedding could not take place before the 6th of August. He had not yet called on the Korshunovs for an answer: first the harvesting had to be done, and then he had waited for a holiday.

The Melekhovs began reaping on a Friday. Pantelei stripped the wagon and prepared the underframe for carrying the sheaves. Pyotr and Grigory went to the fields to reap. Pyotr rode and Grigory walked alongside. Grigory was moody, and the muscles worked between his lower jaw and his cheek-bones. Pyotr knew this to be a sure sign that his brother was seething and ready for a quarrel, but smiling under his wheaten moustache, he set to work to tease Grigory.

"God's truth, she told me herself!"

"Well, what if she did?" Grigory muttered, chewing a hair of his moustache.

"'As I'm on my way back from town,' she says, 'I hear voices in the Melekhovs' sunflower patch.' "

"Pyotr, stop it!"

"Yes, voices. 'And I glance through the fence. . . .' "

Grigory's eyelids quivered. "Will you stop it, or won't you?"

"You're a queer lad! Let me finish!"

"I warn you, Pyotr, we'll be fighting each other in a minute," Grigory threatened, falling behind.

Pyotr raised his eyebrows and turned round in his seat to face Grigory.

"'. . .I glance through the fence, and there I see them, the two lovers, lying in each other's arms!' she says. 'Who?' I asked, and she an-

swers: 'Why, Aksinya and your brother.' I
say. . . ."

Seizing the handle of a pitchfork lying at the
back of the reaper, Grigory flung himself at his
brother. Pyotr dropped the reins, leapt from
his seat, and dodged in front of the horses.

"Pah, the devil!" he exclaimed. "He's gone
mad! Pah! Just look at him. . . ."

Baring his teeth like a wolf, Grigory threw
the pitchfork at his brother. Pyotr dropped to
his hands and knees, and flying over him the
pitchfork buried its points a couple of inches
into the earth and stuck upright, whanging and
quivering.

Scowling, Pyotr caught at the bridles of the
startled horses and swore lustily: "You might
have killed me, you swine!"

"Yes, and I would have killed you!"

"You're a fool, a mad devil. You're your
father's son all right, a true Turk."

Grigory pulled the pitchfork out of the
ground and followed after the reaping machine. Pyotr beckoned to him with his finger.

"Come here! Give me that pitchfork."

He passed the reins into his left hand, and
took the pitchfork by the prongs. Then with
the handle he struck Grigory across the back.

"Ought to have taken a better swing," he
grumbled, keeping his eyes on Grigory, who

had leaped away. After a moment or two they lit cigarettes, stared into each other's eyes and burst out laughing.

Christonya's wife, who was driving home along another road, had seen Grigory attack his brother. She stood up in her wagon but could not see what happened, for the Melekhovs' reaping machine and horses were between her and the brothers. Hardly had she reached the village street when she cried to a neighbour:

"Klimovna! Run and tell Prokofyevich the Turk that his boys have been fighting with pitchforks close to the Tatar mound. Grigory jabbed Pyotr in the side with the fork, and then Pyotr gave him. . . . The blood poured out. It was horrible!"

Pyotr had grown hoarse with bawling at the tired horses and was whistling instead. Grigory, his dust-blackened foot resting on the transom, was pitchforking the swathes off the reaper. The horses, bitten raw by the flies, swished their tails and pulled unwillingly. Reaping was in progress all over the steppe. The blades of the machines rattled and groaned, the steppe was dotted with swathes of corn. Mimicking the drivers, the marmots whistled on the hillocks.

"Two more lengths, and we'll stop for a smoke!" Pyotr shouted above the noise of the machine. Grigory nodded. He could hardly open his parched lips. He gripped his pitchfork closer to the prongs in order to get a better leverage on the heavy swathes, and breathed spasmodically. His dripping chest itched from sweat. From under his hat it poured down his face and stung his eyes like soap. Halting the horses, they had a drink and a smoke.

"There's someone riding a horse pretty hard along the road," Pyotr remarked, shading his eyes with his palm.

Grigory stared, and raised his eyebrows in astonishment.

"It looks like Father."

"You're mad! What could he be riding? We've got both horses here."

"It's him! God's truth, it's Father."

The rider drew nearer, and after a moment he could be seen clearly. "Yes, it's Father!" Pyotr stamped about in anxious surprise.

"Something's happened at home," Grigory gave expression to the thought troubling them both.

When still a hundred yards away, Pantelei reined his horse in. "I'll thrash you, you sons of a bitch!" he yelled, waving his leather whip above his head.

"What on earth. . .!" Pyotr was completely

flabbergasted, and thrust half his moustache into his mouth.

"Get on the other side of the reaper! By God, he'll lash us with that knout. While we're getting to the bottom of this business, he'll whip our guts out," Grigory said with a grin, putting the machine between himself and his father.

The foaming horse came over the swathes of corn at a lumbering trot. His feet knocking against the horse's sides (for he was riding bareback), Pantelei shook his whip: "What have you been up to out here, you children of the devil?"

"We've been reaping," Pyotr swept his arms around, nervously eyeing the whip.

"Who's been sticking who with the fork? What have you been fighting about?"

Turning his back on his father, Grigory began counting the clouds in a whisper.

"What fork? Who's been fighting?" Pyotr looked his father up and down.

"Why, she came running to me, the daughter of a hen, shrieking: 'Your boys have stuck each other with pitchforks.' What do you say to that?" Pantelei shook his head excitedly and, dropping the reins, jumped off his horse. "I grabbed a horse and came out at a gallop. Well?"

"Who told you all this?"

"A woman!"

"She was lying, Father. She must have been asleep in her wagon and dreamed it."

"Women!" Pantelei half-shouted, half-whistled, slobbering down his beard. "That whore of Klimov's! My God! I'll whip the bitch!" he danced with rage.

Shaking with silent laughter, Grigory stared at the ground. Pyotr, keeping his eyes fixed on his father, stroked his perspiring brow.

Pantelei danced to his heart's content, and then calmed down. He took the seat of the reaping machine and reaped a couple of lengths, then mounted his horse and rode back to the village, leaving his whip forgotten on the ground. Pyotr picked it up and swung it appraisingly remarking to his brother:

"We'd have had a bad time, young man. This isn't a whip! It would have maimed you, Brother. It could cut your head clean off."

## XVIII

The Korshunovs had the reputation of being the richest family in the village of Tatarsky. They had fourteen pairs of bullocks, as well as horses, mares from the Provalsk stud farm, fifteen cows, innumerable other cattle, and a flock of several hundred sheep. Their house with its six rooms and iron roof was as good as that of Mokhov the merchant. The outhouses were roofed with new and handsome tiles. The garden and meadow covered a good three acres. What more could a man want?

So it was rather timidly and with secret reluctance that Pantelei had paid his first visit to the Korshunovs to propose the match. The Korshunovs could find a much richer husband than Grigory for their daughter. Pantelei knew this and was afraid of a refusal. He did not like to go begging to Korshunov, but Ilyinichna gnawed into him like rust into iron, and at last she overcame the old man's obstinacy. So finally he had visited the Korshunovs, heartily cursing Grigory and Ilyinichna and the whole wide world. Now it was time to go for an answer. They were only waiting for Sunday.

Meanwhile, under the painted iron roof of the Korshunovs' house burning dissension had arisen. After the Melekhovs' departure Natalya declared to her mother:

"I like Grigory, I'll never wed another."

"She's found herself a bridegroom, the idiot," her father replied. "The only good thing about him is that he's as black as a gypsy. My little berry, I could find you a much better husband."

"I don't want any other, Father." The girl

flushed and began to weep. "You can take me to the convent otherwise."

"He's a woman-chaser, he runs after soldiers' wives. The whole village knows it," her father played his last card.

"Well, and let him!"

"Well, if it's 'let him' for you, then it's all the same to me."

Natalya, the eldest daughter, was her father's favourite, and he had not pressed her into a marriage. Proposals for her hand had been plentiful, some coming from distant villages, from rich, old-believer Cossacks. But Natalya had not taken to any of the prospective bridegrooms, and nothing had come of their efforts.

In his heart, Miron liked Grigory for his Cossack ardour, his love of farming and hard work. He had picked him out among the crowd of village youths when Grigory had won the first prize in the horse races, but he thought it a little humiliating to give his daughter to a man who was not rich, especially one who had a bad reputation.

"A hard-working lad and good-looking," his wife would whisper to him at night, stroking his freckled, hairy hand. "And Natalya is really gone on him. . . ."

Miron turned his back on his wife's cold, withered breast, and shouted angrily:

"Get off, you burr! Marry her off to an idiot, what do I care? God has taken away your reason. Good-looking!" he mimicked. "Will you reap a harvest off his face?"

"Harvests aren't everything. . . ."

"What does it matter about his looks? If only he had some standing. I must admit it's a bit of a come-down for me to give my daughter to the Turks."

"They're a hard-working family and comfortably off," his wife whispered, and moving closer to her husband's broad back, stroked his hand soothingly.

"Hey, the devil! Get away, can't you? Leave me a little room! Why are you stroking me as if I were a cow with calf? And do as you please with Natalya. Marry her to a close-cropped girl if that suits you."

"You should have some feeling for your child," she murmured into his ear. But Miron kicked, pressed himself against the wall and began to snore as though he had fallen asleep.

The Melekhovs' arrival for an answer took the Korshunovs by surprise. They came just after matins. As Ilyinichna set her foot on the step of the wagonette she nearly overturned it, but Pantelei jumped down from the seat like a young cockerel.

"There they are! What devil brought them here today?" Miron groaned, as he looked out of the window.

"Oh dear, here I am just out of the kitchen. Haven't even had a chance to change my every-day skirt."

"You'll do as you are. Nobody's thinking of marrying you, who wants you, you horse mange!"

"You're a born ruffian and you've completely lost your senses in your old age."

"Hold your tongue, woman!"

"You might put on a clean shirt, your back-bone's showing through that one. Aren't you ashamed, you old devil?" his wife scolded, sur-veying her husband as the visitors walked across the yard.

"Don't worry, they'll recognize me in what I'm wearing. They wouldn't refuse if I put on sackcloth."

"Good health!" Pantelei crowed, stumbling over the door-step. He was at once abashed by the loudness of his own voice, and tried to mend matters by crossing himself twice over before the icon.

"Good-day," Miron replied, staring at them grimly.

"God is giving us good weather."

"Praise be, and it's lasting."

"The people will be a little better off for it."

"That's so."

"Ye-e-es."

"Ahem."

"And so we've come, Miron Grigoryevich, to find out what you have decided among yourselves—whether we are to make a match of it or not."

"Come in, please. Sit down, please," the mistress of the house welcomed them, bowing and sweeping the floor with the edge of her long, pleated skirt.

Ilyinichna sat down, her poplin dress rustling. Miron Grigoryevich rested his elbows on the new oilcloth on the table, and was silent. An unpleasant smell of damp rubber and something else came from the oilcloth. Its corners were adorned with pictures of the last tsar and tsaritsa, while in the centre were the august imperial princesses in white hats, and the fly-blown Tsar Nicholas II.

Miron broke the silence.

"Well... we've decided to give our daughter. So we shall be kinsmen if we can agree on the dowry."

At this point, from somewhere in the mysterious depths of her glossy, puff-sleeved jacket, as if from behind her back, Ilyinichna drew out a great loaf of white bread and placed it on the table. For some unknown reason Pantelei wanted to cross himself, but his gnarled claw-like fingers, though set to the appropriate sign and raised half the requisite distance, suddenly changed their form. Against its master's will the great black thumb slipped unexpectedly between the index and middle fingers, and this shameless bunch of fingers stealthily slipped behind the open edge of his blue overcoat and drew out a red-topped bottle.

Blinking excitedly, Pantelei glanced at Miron's freckled face and caressingly slapped the bottom of the bottle with his broad, hoof-like palm.

"And now, dear friends, we'll offer up a prayer to God and drink and talk of our children and the marriage agreement," he proposed.

Within an hour the two men were sitting so close together that the tar-black rings of Melekhov's beard were mingled with the straight red strands of Korshunov's. Pantelei's breath smelt of pickled cucumbers as he argued over the amount of the marriage settlement.

"My dear kinsman," he began in a hoarse whisper. "My dearest kinsman," he repeated, raising his voice to a shout. "Kinsman," he roared, baring his great, blunt teeth. "Your demands are far too heavy for me to stand.

Think, dear kinsman, think how you are trying to rob me. Gaiters and goloshes, one; a fur coat, two; two woollen dresses, three; a silk kerchief, four. Why, it's ruination!"

Pantelei stretched his arms wide till the seams of his tunic split. Miron lowered his head and stared at the oilcloth, flooded with spilt vodka and pickle. He read the inscription on the flowery scroll at the top. "The Russian Royal Family." He brought his eyes lower. "His Imperial Majesty and Sire, Emperor Nicholas. . . ." A potato-skin lay over the rest. He stared at the picture. The emperor's features were invisible under an empty vodka bottle. Blinking reverently, Miron attempted to make out the style of the rich uniform with its white belt, but it was thickly covered with slippery cucumber seeds. The empress in a broad-brimmed hat stared up at him complacently, surrounded by the circle of insipid daughters. Miron felt so affronted that tears almost came to his eyes. "You look very proud now, like a goose staring out of a basket, but wait till you have to give your daughters away to be married, then I shall stare, and you'll flutter," he thought.

Pantelei droned on into his ear like a great black bumble-bee. Korshunov raised his tearfully misty eyes, and listened.

"In order to make such a gift in exchange for your, and now we can say our, daughter—these gaiters and goloshes and fur coats—we shall have to drive a cow to the market and sell it."

"And do you begrudge it?" Miron struck the table with his fist.

"It isn't that I begrudge it. . . ."

"Do you begrudge it?"

"Wait, kinsman!"

"And if you do begrudge it . . . the devil take you!" Miron swept his perspiring hand over the table and sent the glasses to the floor.

"It will be your daughter who'll work for it."

"Let her! But you must give the proper presents, otherwise there'll be no marriage!"

"A cow sold from the yard!" Pantelei shook his head.

"There has to be a gift. She's got plenty of clothes of her own, it's me you've got to show respect for if you've taken a fancy to her. That's our Cossack custom. That's how it was of old, and we stick to the old ways."

"I will show my respect!"

"Show your respect!"

"I will show it!"

"And let the youngsters work. We've worked, and we live as well as anybody. Let them do the same!"

The two men's beards wove together colour-
fully. They kissed and Pantelei began to eat a
juiceless, shrivelled cucumber and wept with
mixed, conflicting feelings.

The women were sitting locked in an embrace
on the chest, deafening each other with the
cackle of their voices. Ilyinichna glowed with a
cherry-coloured flush, Marya had turned green
from the vodka, like a winter pear nipped by
the frost.

"You won't find a child like her anywhere
else in the world. She'll be dutiful and obedient,
and will never say a word to contradict you,"
said Marya.

"My dear," Ilyinichna interrupted her, supporting her cheek with her left hand and holding her left elbow in her right hand, "so I've
told him, I don't know how many times, the
son of a bitch. He was getting ready to go out
the other Sunday evening, putting some
tobacco in his pouch, and I said to him, 'When
will you throw her over, you accursed heathen?
How long have I got to go on standing this
shame in my old age? That Stepan will stop
your little game one fine day!' "

Mitka stared into the room through the
door crack, and below him Natalya's two
younger sisters whispered to each other.
Natalya herself was sitting in the farther room,

wiping her tears on the tight sleeve of her
blouse. She was afraid of the new life opening
before her, oppressed by the unknown.

In the front room the third bottle of vodka
was finished; it was decided to bring the bride
and bridegroom together on the first of August.


## XIX


The Korshunovs' house hummed like a bee-
hive with the bustle of preparations for the
wedding. Underclothes were hurriedly sewn
for the bride. Natalya sat every evening knitting her bridegroom the traditional gloves and
scarf of goat's wool. Her mother sat till dusk
bent over a sewing-machine, helping the hired
seamstress. When Mitka returned with his
father and the farm-hands from the fields he
did not stop to wash or pull off his heavy farming boots, but went to keep Natalya company. He found great satisfaction in teasing his
sister.

"Knitting?" he would ask briefly, nodding
at the scarf.

"Yes, what of it?"

"Knit away, you idiot. Instead of being
grateful to you, he'll break your jaw."

"What for?"

"Oh, I know Grisha, he's a friend of mine. He's that sort, he'll bite and not say what it's for."

"Don't tell lies. You think I don't know him."

"But I know him better. We went to school together." Mitka would simulate a deep sigh, look at his scratched hands and bend his long back.

"You'll be lost, Natalya, if you marry him. Better stay an old maid. What do you see in him anyhow? He's ugly enough to scare a horse. Stupid too. Just look at him a bit closer: he's a lousy fellow."

Natalya would grow angry, choke back her tears, and bend a miserable face over the scarf.

"But worst of all he's in love," Mitka went on mercilessly. "What are you grizzling for? You're a fool, Natalya! Throw him over! I'll saddle the horse and ride over and tell them...."

Natalya was rescued from Mitka by Grandfather Grishaka, who would come into the room, groping over the floor with his knobbly stick and stroking his hempen-yellow beard. Poking his stick into Mitka's side, he would ask:

"What are you doing here, you good-for-nothing, huh?"

"I came to pay a visit, Grandad," Mitka would reply apologetically.

"To pay a visit? Well, I tell you to get out of here. Quick march!" The old man would lift his stick and approach Mitka on his shaky withered legs.

Grandad Grishaka had walked the earth for sixty-nine years. He had taken part in the Turkish campaign of 1877, had been orderly to General Gurko, but had fallen into disfavour and been sent back to his regiment. He had been awarded two crosses and the medal of St. George for distinction under fire at Plevna and Rossitz. And now, living with his son, enjoying the universal respect of the village for his lucidity of mind, his incorruptible honesty and his hospitable ways, he was spending his few remaining years in reminiscences.

In the summer he sat from dawn till dusk on the earthen bank round the house, his head bowed, drawing his stick over the ground, while vague images and scraps of thought floated through his mind, dull gleams of memory amid the shadows of forgetfulness. The broken peak of his cap threw a dark shade over his closed eyes. The black blood flowed sluggishly through the fingers curved over his stick, through the swollen veins on his hands.

His blood seemed to grow colder every year. He would complain to Natalya, his favourite grand-daughter:

"These socks are woollen, but they're not warm enough. You'd better crochet a pair for me, child."

"But it's summer, Grandad!" Natalya would laugh, and, seating herself on the bank by his side, would look at his big wrinkled yellow ear.

"What of it, child? It's summer, but my blood is as cold as the earth deep below."

Natalya looked at the network of veins on his hand and her mind flashed back to a day in her childhood. A well was being sunk in their yard, and she—still only a little girl—was taking clay out of the bucket and making heavy dolls, and cows with crumbling horns. She vividly recalled the feel of the lifeless icy earth, lifted up from a depth of thirty-five feet. And now, frightened, she stared at her grandfather's hands, covered with the brown clay-coloured freckles of old age. It seemed to her that dark, clayey earth was flowing in his veins instead of bright scarlet blood.

"Are you afraid to die, Grandad?" Natalya would ask.

The old man twisted his withered neck as though working it free of the stiff collar of his uniform coat, and shook his greenish-grey whiskers.

"I wait for death as I would for a dear guest. It's time—I've lived my days, I've served my tsars, and drunk vodka enough in my day," he replied showing his white teeth in a smile, his withered lids quivering.

Natalya would stroke her grandfather's hand and leave him, still bowed, sitting hunched on the bank in his patched grey uniform, scraping the earth with his stick, while the bright red tabs twinkled gaily and youthfully in his stiff upright collar.

He took the news of Natalya's approaching marriage with outward calm, but inwardly he grieved and was furious. At table Natalya always gave him the choicest pieces; she washed his linen, mended and knitted his stockings, his *sharovari* and shirts. And so, when the old man heard the news he gave her harsh, stern looks for a couple of days.

"The Melekhovs are good Cossacks. The late Prokofy, a fine Cossack he was. But what are his grandsons like? Huh?" he asked Miron.

"They're not so bad," Miron replied evasively.

"That Grigory's a disrespectful lad. I was coming from church the other day and he passed me without a word of greeting. The old men don't get much respect these days. . . ."

"He's a nice lad," Lukinichna put in a word for her future son-in-law.

"Nice, you say? Oh well, so long as Natalya likes him. . . ."

He took almost no part in the negotiations; he came out of the kitchen and sat down at the table for a moment or two, drank a glass of vodka, and then, feeling himself getting drunk, went off again. For two days he silently watched the happy Natalya, then seemed to soften in his attitude.

"Natalya!" he called to her. "Well, my little grand-daughter, so you're very happy, huh?"

"I don't rightly know myself, Grandad," Natalya confided.

"Well, well! Christ be with you. God grant. . . ." And then he bitterly upbraided her. "Couldn't you have waited till I was dead, you little brat . . . my life will be bitter without you."

Mitka was listening to their talk, and he remarked:

"You're likely to live another hundred years, Grandfather. Is she to wait all that time? You're a fine one!"

The old man turned almost purple with anger. He rapped on the ground with his stick and feet:

"Clear off, you son of a bitch! Clear off, I say! You devil's demon! Who told you to listen?"

Mitka ran out into the yard laughing.

Old Grishaka raged for a long time after, cursing Mitka; his legs in their short woollen stockings trembled at the knees.

Natalya's two little sisters—Marisha, a girl of twelve, and Grippa, an eight-year-old imp—waited impatiently for the wedding.

The farm-hands employed by Korshunov were also quite pleased. They expected a lavish treat from their master and several days off.

One of them—tall as a crane—a Ukrainian with the outlandish name of Het-Baba—went on a drinking spree about once every six months. He would drink away all his clothes as well as his wages. Although he had felt the familiar urge for a long time already, he had forced himself to delay the start of the drinking bout until the wedding.

The second farm-hand—a thin swarthy Cossack, named Mikhei, had been with the Korshunovs only a short time. Ruined by a fire, he had become a labourer. Having struck up a friendship with Het-Baba he gradually took to drink. He was a great lover of horses. When he was drunk he would weep, his angular, browless face smeared with tears, and pester Miron Grigoryevich:

"Master! Dear master! When you give your daughter away let me drive her horses. I'll show them some driving! I'll drive her through fire, and not a single hair on the horses will be burned. I myself once had horses. Oh. . . ."

The grim, unsociable Het-Baba for some reason or other became attached to Mikhei and constantly tormented him with the same old joke about the name of his native village. He would always laugh hoarsely at his own stale joke and slap his long, dry shanks. Mikhei would look disgustedly at Het-Baba's clean-shaven face and quivering Adam's apple, and curse him.

The wedding was to take place on the first day after Lent. Three weeks remained. On the Day of the Assumption Grigory came to visit his future bride. He sat at the round table in the best room, eating sunflower seeds and nuts with the bride's girl-friends, then drove away again. Natalya saw him off. In the lean-to shed, where his horse was standing saddled with a smart new saddle, she slipped her hand into her breast, and blushing, gazing at him with eyes that expressed her love, she thrust a soft little bundle, warm from her breast, into his hand. As he took the gift Grigory dazzled her with the whiteness of his wolfish teeth, and asked:

"What is it?"

"You'll see.... I've embroidered you a tobacco pouch."

Grigory irresolutely drew her towards him, wanting to kiss her; but she held him off forcibly with her hands against his chest, leaned away from him, and turned her eyes apprehensively towards the window of the house.

"They'll see us!"

"Let them!"

"I'm ashamed to!"

"That's only at first," Grigory explained.

Natalya held the reins while he mounted. Frowning, Grigory caught the stirrup with his foot, seated himself comfortably in the saddle and rode out of the yard. She opened the gate, and stood gazing after him. Grigory leaned over to the left in his saddle, Kalmyk fashion, waving his whip with a flourish.

"Eleven more days," Natalya thought to herself and sighed and smiled.

## XX

The green, sharp-leafed wheat breaks through the ground and grows; within a few weeks a rook can fly into its midst and not be seen. The corn sucks the juices from the earth and comes to ear, then it flowers and the ears are powdered with a golden dust; the grain swells with sweet and scented milk. The farmer goes out into the steppe and stands gazing and is filled with joy. But then a herd of cattle stray into the corn; they tread the laden grain into the glebe. Round patches of crushed wheat are left where the cattle have lain; the farmer grows bitter and desperate at the sight.

So with Aksinya. Grigory had trampled her feelings that had ripened to golden flower with his heavy, raw-hide sandals. He had sullied them, burned them to ash—and that was all.

As she came back from the Melekhovs' sunflower patch Aksinya's spirit grew empty and wild, like a deserted farmyard overgrown with goose-grass and scrub. She walked along chewing the ends of her kerchief, and a cry swelled her throat. She entered the house and fell to the floor, choking with tears, with torment, with the dreary emptiness that lashed through her head. But then it passed. The piercing anguish was drawn down and exhausted at the bottom of her heart.

The grain trampled by the cattle stands again. With the dew and the sun the trodden stalks arise; at first, bowed like a man under a too heavy burden, then erect, lifting their heads; and the day is day again and the wind still blows.

At night, as she passionately caressed her husband, Aksinya thought of another, and hatred was mingled with a great love in her heart. The woman was planning fresh dishonour, fresh shame; she had made up her mind to take Grigory from the happy Natalya, who had known neither the bitterness nor the joy of love. She lay thinking over her plans at night, her dry eyes blinking in the darkness. Stepan's handsome head lay heavily on her right arm, his long wavy forelock awry. He breathed through his half-opened lips, his black, toil-roughened fingers caressing his wife's breast in forgetfulness. Aksinya lay thinking and planning, but only one thing could she resolve firmly: she would take Grigory from everybody else, she would flood him with love, she would possess him as before she had possessed him. But at the bottom of her heart a deep pain, like the sting left by a bee, remained.

During the day Aksinya drowned her thoughts in household duties and cares. She met Grigory occasionally, and would turn pale, proudly carrying her beautiful body that yearned so much for him, gazing shamelessly, challengingly into the black wilderness of his eyes.

After each meeting Grigory was seized with yearning for her. He grew angry without cause, and poured out his wrath on Dunya and his mother, but most frequently he took his sabre, went out into the backyard and slashed away at stout twigs planted in the ground until he was bathed in perspiration. It made Pantelei curse:

"The lousy devil, he's chopped up enough for a couple of fences. Go into the woods, if you must chop away. You wait, my lad! When you're called up for service, you'll have the chance to do it. That'll soon take it out of you!"

## XXI

Four gaily-decorated two-horse wagonettes were to drive to fetch the bride. A crowd of village folk in holiday attire thronged around them as they stood in the Melekhovs' yard.

Pyotr was the best man. He was dressed in a black frock-coat and blue striped trousers, his left arm was bound with two white kerchiefs, and he wore a fixed scornful smile under his wheaten whiskers.

"Don't be shy, Grigory!" he said to his brother. "Hold your head up like a young cock, don't get sulky!"

Darya, as slender and supple as a willow branch, attired in a woollen, raspberry-coloured skirt, twitched the pencilled arches of her brows and gave Pyotr a nudge:

"Tell Father it's time we were off. They're waiting for us."

"Take your places," Pyotr ordered, after a whispered consultation with his father. "On my wagon, five and the bridegroom." They climbed into the wagonettes. Flushed and triumphant, Ilyinichna opened the gates. The four wagonettes chased after one another along the street.

Pyotr sat at Grigory's side. Opposite them Darya waved a lace handkerchief. The ruts and bumps interrupted the voices that had struck up a song. The crimson bands of the Cossack caps, the blue and black uniforms and frock-coats, the sleeves bound with white kerchiefs, the scattered rainbow of the women's kerchiefs, the gay skirts, and muslin trains of dust behind each wagonette made a colourful picture.

Grigory's second cousin, Anikei, drove the bridegroom's wagonette. Leaning forward over the tails of the horses, almost falling off his seat, he cracked his whip and whistled, and the perspiring horses pulled harder at the tautened traces.

"Give it to 'em," roared Pyotr.

The moustacheless hawk-like Anikei winked at Grigory, wrinkled his hairless womanish face into a thin smile, gave a whistle and belaboured the horses with his whip.

"Make way!" Ilya Ozhogin, the bridegroom's uncle on his mother's side, roared as he tried to overtake them with the second wagonette. Grigory recognized Dunya's sunburnt face behind his uncle's back.

"No, you don't!" Anikei shouted, jumping to his feet and emitting a piercing whistle. He whipped up the horses into a frenzied gallop. "You'll fall!" Darya exclaimed, encircling Anikei's patent leather top-boots with her arms. "Hold on!" Uncle Ilya called at their side, but his voice was lost in the continual groan and rattle of the wheels.

The two other wagonettes, tightly packed with whooping men and women, drove along side by side. The horses with red, blue, and pink cloths on their backs, paper flowers and ribbons woven into their manes and forelocks, and bells on their harness, tore over the bumpy road, scattering flakes of soapy foam, and the cloths on their wet, lathered backs flapped and billowed in the wind.

At the Korshunovs' gate a horde of village lads was on the look-out for the cavalcade.

They saw the dust rising from the road and ran into the yard bawling:

"They're coming!" "Here they are!" They surrounded Het-Baba who had just come out.

"Why the crowd? Get away, you little devils. What a noise you make! I can't hear myself speak."

The children jumped around Het-Baba's wide baggy *sharovari*, shouting and poking fun at the Ukrainian. Het-Baba, his head bent as if he were peeping into a deep well, looked down at the frenzied children and scratched his firm long belly with an indulgent smile.

The wagonettes came rattling up to the gate. Pyotr led Grigory to the steps, the others followed behind.

The door from the porch to the kitchen was shut fast. Pyotr knocked.

"Lord Jesus Christ, have mercy on us!" he intoned.

"Amen!" came from the other side of the door.

Pyotr repeated the words and the knock three times, each time receiving the same answer.

"May we come in?"

"You are welcome."

The door was thrown open. The parents' representative, Natalya's godmother, a good-looking widow, greeted Pyotr with a curtsey and a thin raspberry-lipped smile. "Take this for your health's sake, best man!" she said, handing him a glass of cloudy, over-fresh kvass. Pyotr smoothed his whiskers, drank it down, and spluttered amid a general restrained laugh: "Well, you've made me welcome! You wait, my blackberry, wait till I treat you. I'll make you pay for it."

While the best man and Natalya's godmother were competing in a duel of wits, the relatives of the bridegroom were brought three glasses of vodka each, in accordance with the marriage agreement.

Natalya, already attired in her wedding dress and veil, sat at the table, guarded by her two sisters. Marishka held a rolling pin in her outstretched hand, and Grippa, a challenging fervour in her eyes, brandished a mixing spoon. Sweating, and slightly tipsy with vodka, Pyotr bowed and offered them a fifty-kopeck piece in his glass. But Marishka struck the table with her rolling pin.

"Not enough! We shan't sell the bride!"

Once more Pyotr offered them some small silver in the glass:

"We won't let you have her!" the sisters raged, elbowing the downcast Natalya.

"Here, what's all this? We've already paid and overpaid."

"Give way, girls!" Miron ordered, and smilingly pressed towards the table. His ruddy hair, smeared with melted butter, smelt of sweat and dung. At this signal the bride's relatives and friends seated round the table stood up and made room for the newcomers.

Pyotr thrust the end of a handkerchief into Grigory's hand, jumped on to a bench, and led him to the bride, who had seated herself under the icons. Natalya took the other end of the handkerchief in her moist and agitated hand.

There was a champing of teeth around the table. The guests tore the boiled chicken apart with their hands, afterwards wiping them on their hair. As Anikei chewed at a breast bone the yellow fat ran down his bare chin on to his collar.

Feeling sorry for himself, Grigory stared first at his own and Natalya's spoons tied together in the handkerchief, then at the noodles steaming in a bowl. He badly wanted to eat; his stomach was rolling over with hunger.

Darya was helping herself. Uncle Ilya who sat next to her, nibbling at a rib of mutton with his large teeth, was evidently whispering improprieties to her, for she screwed up her eyes and lifted her brows, blushing and giggling.

The guests ate long and heartily. The reek of resinous masculine sweat mingled with the more caustic and spicy scent of the women. The skirts, frock-coats and shawls that had for long been packed away in chests, smelled of moth-balls and something else, heavy and cloying, like an old woman's much-used honey pot.

Grigory glanced sidelong at Natalya. And for the first time he noticed that her upper lip was swollen, and hung like the peak of a cap over her underlip. He also noticed that on the right cheek, below the cheek-bone, was a brown mole, and that two golden hairs were growing out of the mole; and for some reason this irritated him. He recalled Aksinya's slender neck with its curly, fluffy locks, and he had the feeling that someone had dropped a handful of prickly hay down his sweating back. He bristled, and with a suppressed feeling of wretchedness watched the others munching, chewing and smacking their lips.

When they got up from the table someone, breathing stewed fruit-juice and the sour scent of wheaten bread over him, poured a handful of millet down the leg of his boot in order to protect him against the evil eye. All the way back to his own house the millet hurt his feet; the tight collar band of his shirt choked him, and under the depressing influence of the marriage rites, in a cold, desperate fury Grigory muttered curses to himself.

## XXII

By the time they reached the Melekhovs' yard, the horses, though they had rested a bit at the Korshunovs, were exhausted. Their harnesses were spattered with foam. But the drunken drivers urged them on ruthlessly.

The procession was met by the old Melekhovs. Pantelei, his silver-inlaid black beard glistening, held the icon, and his wife stood at his side, her thin lips set stonily.

Amid a shower of hops and wheat grain Grigory and Natalya approached them to receive their blessing. As he blessed them a tear ran down Pantelei's face, and he frowned and fidgeted, annoyed that anyone should be witness of his frailty.

The bride and bridegroom went into the house. Darya, red from the vodka, the ride, and the sun, dashed out on to the steps and pounced on Dunya.

"Where's Pyotr?"

"I haven't seen him!"

"He ought to go for the priest, and he's nowhere to be found, curse him!"

She found Pyotr, who had drunk more vodka than was good for him, lying in a cart, groaning. She swooped on him like a kite. "You've had too much, you heathen! Get up and run for the priest!"

"Clear off! I don't know you. Who are you ordering about?" Pyotr protested, scrabbling about in the straw and fowls' dung.

With tears in her eyes Darya thrust two fingers into his mouth, gripped his lolling tongue, and helped him to ease himself. Then she poured a pitcher of cold well-water over his head, wiped him dry with the horse blanket and took him to the priest.

Less than an hour later Grigory was standing at Natalya's side in the church, clutching a wax candle in his hand, his eyes wandering over the wall of whispering people round him, and repeating to himself four words that would not leave his head: "You've had your fling!" Behind him the puffy-faced Pyotr coughed. Somewhere in the crowd he saw Dunya's eyes twinkling; he thought he recognized other faces. He heard the dissonant chorus of voices and the droning responses of the deacon. He was fettered with apathy. He followed Father Vissarion round the lectern, treading on the heels of the priest's battered boots; he halted when Pyotr gave a gentle tug at his frock-coat.

He stared at the flickering little tongues of candleflame, and struggled with the sleepy torpor which had taken possession of him.

"Exchange rings!" said Father Vissarion, giving Grigory a lukewarm smile.

They obeyed. "Will it be over soon?" Grigory mutely asked, as he caught Pyotr's glance. And the corners of Pyotr's lips twitched, stifling a smile. "Soon now." Then Grigory kissed his wife's moist, insipid lips three times, the church began to smell foully of extinguished candles, and the crowd pressed towards the door.

Holding Natalya's large, rough hand in his, Grigory went out into the porch. Someone clapped his hat on his head. A warm breeze from the east brought the scent of wormwood to his nostrils. The cool of evening came from the steppe. Lightning flickered beyond the Don, rain was coming; outside the white church fence, above the hum of voices he heard the gentle inviting tinkle of the bells on the restive horses.

## XXIII

The Korshunovs did not arrive at the Melekhovs' house until after the bride and bridegroom had gone to the church. Several times Pantelei went to the gate to see whether they were coming, but the grey road, lined with a growth of prickly thorns, was completely deserted. He shifted his eyes towards the Don. The forest was turning a golden yellow. The ripened reeds bent wearily over the Don-side marshes. Blending with the dusk, the sad blue drowsiness of early autumn enwrapped the village, the Don, the chalky ridge of hills, the forest lurking in a lilac mist beyond the river, and the steppe. At the cross-roads the sharp outline of the wayside cross was silhouetted against the sky.

Pantelei's ears caught the scarcely audible sound of wheels and the yapping of dogs. Two wagonettes turned out of the square into the street. In the first sat Miron with his wife at his side; opposite them was Grandad Grishaka in a new uniform, wearing his Cross of St. George and his medals. Mitka drove, sitting carelessly on the box, and not troubling to show the foaming horses his whip. In the second wagonette, Mikhei, leaning backward, tugged at the reins, trying to reduce the horses' gallop to a trot. His angular browless face was scarlet, sweat was streaming down from under the broken peak of his cap.

Pantelei threw open the gate, and the two wagonettes drove into the yard. Ilyinichna sailed down from the porch, the hem of her dress trailing in the dust.

"Welcome, dear friends! Do our poor house the honour of entering." She bent her corpulent waist in a bow.

His head on one side, Pantelei flung open his arms and welcomed them: "We humbly invite you to come in!"

He called for the horses to be unharnessed and went up to the father of his daughter-in-law. Miron brushed his *sharovari* with his hand to get the dust off them. Old Grishaka, shaken up by the wild ride, lagged behind.

"Come in, come in, my dears!" Ilyinichna insisted.

"Thank you, we're just coming."

"We've been waiting for you, do come in. I'll bring a besom for you to brush your uniform with. There's so much dust about at this time of the year, it's hard to breathe."

"Yes, indeed, it's very dry.... That's what makes the dust.... Don't trouble yourself, my dear, I'll just...." Bowing to his slow-witted hostess, old Grishaka backed away towards the barn and took refuge behind a painted winnowing machine.

"Can't you leave the old man alone, you fool!" Pantelei snorted, intercepting his wife on the steps. "He wants to do something, and you keep.... Where are your brains, woman!"

"How should I know?" Ilyinichna protested blushing. "You ought to guess. Never mind, take the guests to table."

The bride's family were taken into the best room, where a crowd of already half-intoxicated guests was sitting round the table. Soon after their arrival the newly-married couple returned from the church. As they entered Pantelei filled the glasses from a half-gallon bottle, tears standing in his eyes.

"Well, Miron Grigoryevich, here's to our children! May their life be filled with good, as ours has been. May they live happily, and enjoy the best of health."

They poured Grandfather Grishaka a large glass of vodka, and succeeded in sending half of it into his beard-mildewed mouth and half down the stiff collar of his uniform. Glasses were clinked together. The company drank and drank. The hubbub was like the noise of a market. A distant relation of the Korshunovs, Nikifor Koloveidin, who was sitting at the far end of the table, raised his glass and roared the traditional words:

"It's bitter!"

"Bitter! Bitter!" the guests seated around the table clamoured after him.

"Oh, bitter!" came the response from the crowded kitchen.

Scowling, Grigory kissed his wife's insipid lips and sent a hunted glance round the room. A crimson fever of faces. Coarse, drunkenly muddy glances and smiles. Mouths chewing greedily, slobbering on the embroidered tablecloth. A howl of voices.

Koloveidin opened wide his gap-toothed mouth.

"It's bitter!" the long-service badges on the sleeve of his blue Guards uniform wrinkled as he raised his glass.

"Bitter!" the cry was taken up once more.

Grigory stared with hatred into Koloveidin's mouth and noticed the livid tongue between his teeth as he cried, "Bitter!"

"Kiss, little chicks!" Pyotr spluttered, twitching his vodka-soaked moustache.

In the kitchen Darya, flushed and intoxicated, began a song. It was taken up by the others and passed into the best room. The voices blended, but above all the rest rose Christonya's rumble, shaking the window-panes.

The song ended and eating was resumed.

"Here's to a good time, good people...!"

"Try this mutton!"

"Take your paw away, my husband's looking!"

"Bitter! Bitter!"

"No, I don't want any of your mutton. Maybe I like sterlet better. Yes, I do ... it's juicy."

"Cousin Proshka, let's have another one."

"Ah, that warms the cockles of your heart. ..."

In the kitchen the floor groaned and shook, heels clattered, and a glass fell to the floor, but the crash was lost in the general uproar. Across the heads of those sitting at the table Grigory glanced into the kitchen. The women were dancing now, to the accompaniment of shouts and whistles. They shook their ample bottoms (there was not a thin one there, for each was wearing five or six skirts), waved lace handkerchiefs, and worked their elbows in the dance.

The grating notes of the accordion sounded imperatively. The player began the tune of the Cossack dance. A shout went up:

"A circle! Form a circle!"

"Squeeze up a bit!" Pyotr begged, pushing the perspiring women aside.

Grigory roused himself and winked at Natalya:

"Pyotr's going to dance the 'Cossack'! You watch him!"

"Who with?"

"Don't you see? With your mother."

Marya Lukinichna set her arms akimbo, her handkerchief in her left hand. Pyotr went up to her with mincing steps, cut a fine caper and retreated to his place. Lukinichna picked up her skirt as though about to step over a puddle, picked out the rhythm with her toe, and danced amid a roar of approbation, kicking out her legs like a man.

The accordion player rushed out a volley of low notes that swept Pyotr into action, and with a shout he dropped to a squatting position and danced round, smacking the palms of his hands against the legs of his boots and biting the tip of his moustache in the corner of his mouth. He swung his feet in and out at great speed; his damp forelock tossed wildly on his head, but could not keep up with his feet.

Grigory's view was blocked by the crowd at the door. He heard only the shouts of the drunken guests and the drumming of iron-shod heels, like the crackle of a burning pine-board.

Then Miron danced with Ilyinichna; he stepped out seriously and with his accustomed businesslike air. Pantelei stood on a stool to watch them, dangling his lame leg and clicking his tongue. Instead of his legs his lips and ear-ring danced.

The dance was taken up by experts and by

others who could not even bend a leg properly. All of them were shouted at:

"Go it!"

"Smaller steps! Oh, you. . . !"

"His legs are light enough, but his bottom
gets in his way."

"Oh, get on with it!"

"Our side's winning."

"Come on!"

"Tired, are you? I'll crack a bottle over your
head if you don't dance."

Grandfather Grishaka was completely drunk.
He embraced the bony back of his neighbour
on the bench, and buzzed like a mosquito in
his ear:

"What year did you first see service?"

His neighbour, an old man bent like an
ancient oak, replied:

"1839, my son!"

"When?" Grishaka stuck out his ear.

"1839, I told you."

"What's your name? What regiment did you
serve in?"

"Maxim Bogatiryov. I was corporal in
Baklanov's regiment."

"Are you related to the Melekhovs?"

"What?"

"I asked, are you related?"

"Uh-huh! I'm the bridegroom's grandfather on his mother's side."

"In Baklanov's regiment, did you say?"

The old man, vainly munching a piece of bread with his toothless gums, gazed at Grishaka with faded eyes, and nodded.

"So you must have been through the Caucasian campaign?"

"I served under Baklanov himself, may he rest in heaven, helped to conquer the Caucasus. We had some rare Cossacks in our regiment. They were as tall as the guards, though they weren't so straight. Great, long-armed, broad-shouldered fellows, not like the ones nowadays. That's the men we had, my son! His excellency the late general was good enough to give me the cat for stealing a carpet. . . ."

"And I was in the Turkish campaign. Eh? Yes, I was there."

Old Grishaka puffed out his sunken chest jingling with medals.

"We took a village at dawn, and at mid-day the bugler sounded the alarm."

"We were fighting around Rossitz and our regiment, the Twelfth Don Cossack, was engaged with the janissaries."

"The bugler sounded that alarm. . . ."

"Yes," Grishaka went on, beginning to get annoyed and angrily waving his hand. "The

*173*

Turkish janissaries serve their tsar and wear white sacks on their heads. Huh? White sacks on their heads."

"... The bugler sounded the alarm, and I said to my comrade: 'We'll have to retreat, Timofei, but first we'll have that carpet off the wall.' "

"I have been decorated with two Georges, awarded for heroism under fire. I took a Turkish major alive." Grandfather Grishaka began to weep and to bang his withered fist on his neighbour's spine. But the latter, dipping a piece of chicken in the cherry jelly, lifelessly stared at the soiled tablecloth and mumbled:

"And just listen to what sin the evil spirit led me into, my son!" The old man's eyes stared fixedly at the white creases of the tablecloth as if they saw not a tablecloth soaked in vodka and soup but the dazzling snowy folds of the Caucasian mountains. "I'd never before taken anything that wasn't mine, but now I happened to see that carpet, and I thought, 'That would make a good horsecloth.' "

"I've seen those parts myself. I've been in lands across the sea as well," Grishaka tried to look his neighbour in the eyes, but the deep sockets were overgrown with shaggy thickets of eyebrows and beard. So he resorted to craft. He wanted to win his neighbour's attention for the climax of his story, and he plunged into the middle of it without any preliminaries: "And the captain gives the order: 'In troop columns at the gallop! Forward!'"

But the old Baklanov regiment Cossack threw back his head like a charger at the sound of the trumpet and, dropping his fist on the table, whispered:

"Lances at the ready! Draw sabres, Baklanov's men!" His voice suddenly grew stronger, his faded eyes glittered and blazed. "Baklanov's boys!" he roared, opening wide his toothless yellow jaws. "Into attack—forward!"

And he gazed at Grishaka with a youthful and intelligent look, and let the tears trickling over his beard fall unwiped.

Grishaka also grew excited:

"He gave us this command, and waved his sword. We galloped forward, and the janissaries were drawn up like this," he drew a square on the tablecloth with a shaky finger, "and firing at us. Twice we charged them. Each time they beat us back. Whenever we tried, their cavalry came out of a little wood on their flank. So our troop commander gave the order and we turned and went at them. We smashed them. Rode them down. What cavalry in the world can stand up against Cossacks? They fled into the wood. I saw their officer just in front of me, riding on a bay. A good-looking officer, black whiskers he had. He looked back at me and drew his pistol. Bang! But he missed me. I spurred my horse and caught up with him. I was going to cut him down, but then I thought better of it. After all, he was a man too. So I grabbed him round the waist with my right arm, and he flew out of the saddle. He bit my arm, but I took him all the same. . . ."

Grishaka glanced triumphantly at his neighbour, but the old man's great angular head had fallen on to his chest, and he was snoring contentedly.

# PART TWO

## I

Sergei Platonovich Mokhov could trace his ancestry a long way back.

During the reign of Peter the First a state barge had been travelling down the Don to Azov with a cargo of biscuit and gunpowder. The Cossacks of the little rebel town of Chigonaki, nestling on the bank of the upper Don, fell on the barge by night, destroyed the sleepy guards, pillaged the biscuit and gunpowder and sank the vessel.

The tsar ordered out soldiers from Voronezh, and they burned down the town of Chigonaki, ruthlessly put the guilty Cossacks to the sword, and hanged forty of them on a floating gallows, which, as warning to the unruly villages, was sent sailing down the Don.

Some ten years later the spot where the hearths of the Chigonaki huts had smoked began again to be inhabited by Cossack settlers and those who had survived the sacking. The stanitsa grew up again with defensive ramparts round it. At the same time, a secret agent of the tsar, a Russian peasant named Mokhov, was sent to Chigonaki from Voronezh. He traded in knife-hafts, tobacco, flints, and the other odds and ends necessary to the Cossacks' everyday life. He bought up and resold stolen goods, and twice a year journeyed to Voronezh, ostensibly to replenish his stocks, but in reality to report to the authorities that the stanitsa was for the time being quiet and the Cossacks were not contemplating any fresh mischief.

It was from this Russian peasant Nikita Mokhov that the merchant family of Mokhovs was descended. They took deep root in the Cossack earth; they multiplied and grew into the district like sturdy roadside weeds, reverently preserving the half-rotten credentials given to their ancestor by the governor of Voronezh. The credentials might have been preserved until this day had they not been burned in their wooden box behind the icon during a great fire which occurred in the lifetime of Sergei Mokhov's grandfather. This

Mokhov had already ruined himself once by card-playing, but was getting on to his feet again when the fire engulfed everything. After burying his paralytic father, Sergei had to begin afresh, starting by buying bristles and feathers. For five years he lived miserably, swindling and squeezing the Cossacks of the district out of every kopeck, then he suddenly jumped from "peddler Seryozhka" to "Sergei Platonovich," opened a little drapery shop, married the daughter of a half-demented priest, from whom he got a sizeable dowry, and set up as a linen draper. Sergei Platonovich began to trade in textiles at just the right moment. On the instructions of the army authorities, about this time the Cossacks were migrating in entire villages from the left bank of the Don, where the ground was unproductive and sandy, to the right bank. Buildings sprang up round the young stanitsa of Krasnokutskaya; new villages hatched out on the edge of former estates, on the banks of the rivers Chir, Chornaya and Frolovka, and over valleys and ravines in the steppe, side by side with Ukrainian settlements. And instead of having to journey fifty versts or more for goods they found Sergei Mokhov's shop, its fresh deal shelves packed with attractive commodities, right on the spot. Sergei flung his business wide, like a full-size accordion, and traded in everything requisite to simple village life—hides, salt, kerosene, haberdashery. He even began to supply agricultural machinery. Reapers, seeders, ploughs, winnowers from the Aksaisk factory were drawn up in neat order outside the shop, whose cool green shutters kept it well protected from the summer's heat. It is hard to count the money in another's purse, but it seems that the quick-witted Sergei's trading yielded him considerable profit, for within three years he had opened a grain elevator, and the following year after the death of his first wife he began the construction of a steam flour-mill.

He squeezed Tatarsky and the neighbouring villages tightly in his swarthy fist with its sparse covering of glossy black hairs. There was not a home that was not in debt to Sergei Mokhov: a green slip with an orange border saying that a reaper had been given on credit to so-and-so, a bride's outfit for the daughter to someone else (time to marry the girl off and the Paramonovo elevator was cutting its prices on wheat—"Put it on my account, Mokhov"), and so it went on. Nine hands were employed at the mill, seven in the shop, and four labourers: altogether twenty mouths dependent on the merchant's pleasure for their daily bread.

He had two children by his first wife: the girl
Liza and a boy two years younger, the sluggish,
scrofulous Vladimir. His second wife, Anna, a
dry, sharp-nosed creature, was childless. All
her belated mother-love and accumulated spleen
(she had not married until the age of thirty-
four) were poured out on the children. Her nervous temperament had a bad influence on
them, and their father paid them no more
attention than he gave his stable-hand or cook.
His business activities occupied all his time.
The children grew up uncontrolled. His insen-
sitive wife made no attempt to penetrate into
the secrets of the child mind, the affairs of her
large household took too much of her time, and
the brother and sister grew up alien to each
other, different in character, as though they
were not related. Vladimir was sullen, sluggish,
with a sly look and unchildish seriousness.
Liza, who lived in the society of the maid and
the cook (the latter a dissolute, much too experienced woman), early saw the seamy side of
life. The women aroused an unhealthy curiosity in her, and while still an angular and bash-
ful adolescent, left to her own devices, she had
grown as wild as the true-love flower in the
forest.
　　The unhurrying years flowed by. The old
grew older and the young grew green of leaf,

One evening Sergei Platonovich glanced at his daughter across the tea-table, and was startled. Liza, who had just left high school, had grown into a slender good-looking girl. He looked at her and the saucer filled with amber-coloured tea trembled in his hand. How like her mother she was! God, her very image! "Liza, turn your head sideways!" He had never before noticed how amazingly his daughter resembled her mother.

Vladimir Mokhov, a narrow-chested, sickly-yellow lad now in the fifth form at school, was walking through the mill yard. He and his sister had recently returned home for the summer vacation, and, as usual, he had gone along to look at the mill, jostle among the flour-sprinkled crowd and listen to the steady rumble of cog-wheels and rollers, and the hiss of whirling belts. It ministered to his vanity to hear the respectful murmur of the Cossack customers: "The master's heir. . . ."

Carefully picking his way among the wagons and the heaps of dung, Vladimir reached the gate. Then he remembered he had not been to see the engine room, and turned back.

Close to the red oil-tank, at the entrance to the engine room, the mill-hand Timofei, a scalesman nicknamed "Knave," and Timofei's assistant David were kneading a great ring of clay with bare feet, their trousers rolled up above their knees.

"Ah! The master!" the scalesman greeted him jokingly.

"Good-afternoon. What are you doing?"

"Mixing clay," David said with an unpleasant smile, dragging his feet out of the clinging mass, which smelled of dung. "Your father's careful of the rubles, and won't hire women to do it. Your father's a screw, that he is," he added, making a squelching noise with his feet.

Vladimir flushed. He felt an unconquerable dislike for the ever-smiling David and his contemptuous tone, even for his white teeth.

"What do you mean, 'a screw'?"

"He's terribly mean, he'd eat his own dirt if it paid him," David explained with a smile.

The others laughed approvingly. Vladimir felt all the smart of the insult. He stared coldly at David.

"So you're ... dissatisfied?"

"Come into this mess and mix it yourself, and then you'll know. What fool would be satisfied? It would do your father good to do some of this. Take some of the fat off his belly," David replied. He trod heavily around the ring of clay, kneading it with his feet, now smiling gaily. Foretasting a sweet revenge,

Vladimir turned over a fitting reply in his mind.

"Good!" he said slowly. "I'll tell Papa you're not satisfied with your work."

He glanced sidelong at the man's face, and was startled by the impression he had caused. David's lips were twisted in a forced pitiful smile, and the faces of the others were clouded over. All three went on kneading the clay for a moment in silence. Then David tore his eyes away from his muddy feet, and said in a wheedling, bitter tone: "I was only joking, Volodya."

"I'll tell Papa what you said." With tears of injury in his eyes for his father and himself, and for David's miserable smile, Vladimir walked away.

"Volodya! Vladimir Sergeyevich!" David called after him in alarm, and stepped out of the clay, letting his trousers fall over his bespattered legs.

Vladimir halted. David ran to him breathing heavily.

"Don't tell your father! Forgive me, fool that I am. Honest to God, I just said it to tease you."

"All right, I won't tell him," Vladimir replied with a grimace, and walked on towards the gate. Pity for David had won. He walked along by the white fence with a feeling of relief. From the forge in the corner of the mill-yard, the cheerful tapping of a hammer could be heard, now soft and muffled as it struck the iron, now a hard and ringing double tap on the anvil.

"What did you want to say that for?" Knave's deep voice reached his ears. "Don't stir dung, and it won't stink."

"The swine!" Vladimir thought indignantly. "So he answers back.... Shall I tell Father or not?" Glancing back, he saw David wearing his everlasting smile, and decided: "I'll tell!"

A horse and wagon stood hitched to a post outside the shop. Children were chasing a twittering grey cloud of sparrows off the roof of the fire-house. From the verandah came the sonorous baritone of the student Boyarishkin, and another voice—cracked and husky.

Vladimir went up the steps of the house. The leaves of the wild vine grew thickly over the porch and verandah and hung in foaming green bunches from the carved blue-painted eaves.

Boyarishkin was shaking his blue-shaven head and addressing the teacher Balanda, a young man but already bearded.

"When I read him, despite the fact that I'm the son of a toiling Cossack and naturally hate all privileged classes, just imagine it, I feel an acute pity for that moribund section of society. I nearly turn into a nobleman and landlord myself, I study their ideal woman with rapture. I even take their interests to heart, damn it! Yes, my friend, that's what a genius can do. He can even make you change your creed."

Balanda toyed with the tassel of his silk sash and examined the red embroidery on the hem of his shirt, smiling ironically. Liza lay back in the armchair. The conversation evidently did not interest her in the least. With eyes that always seemed to be looking for something they had lost she was staring aimlessly at Boyarishkin's blue, razor-scratched head.

Bowing to them, Vladimir went to his father's private room and knocked. Sergei Platonovich was sitting on a cool leather couch, turning over the pages of the June issue of *Russkoye Bogatstvo*. A yellowed bone paper-knife lay at his feet.

"Well, what do you want?"

Vladimir hunched his shoulders slightly and straightened the folds of his shirt.

"As I was coming back from the mill," Vladimir began uncertainly. But then he recalled David's dazzling smile, and gazing at his father's corpulent belly in its tussore waistcoat, he resolutely continued: "I heard David, the mill-hand, say. . . ."

Sergei Platonovich listened attentively to his son's story, and said: "I'll sack him. You may go." Then he bent with a groan to pick up the paper-knife.

In the evenings the intelligentsia of the village were in the habit of gathering at Sergei Mokhov's house. There was Boyarishkin, a student of the Moscow Technical School; the puny teacher Balanda, eaten up with conceit and tuberculosis; his cohabitant the teacher Marfa, a shapely girl whose petticoat always showed indecently, and who never seemed to grow any older; and the postmaster, an eccentric, rather musty bachelor smelling of sealing-wax and cheap scent. Occasionally the young lieutenant, Yevgeny Listnitsky, rode over from his father's estate. The company would sit drinking tea on the verandah, carrying on a pointless conversation, and when there was a lull in the talk one of the guests would get up and set going the host's expensive inlaid gramophone.

On rare occasions, during the great holidays, Sergei Platonovich liked to cut a dash: he invited guests and regaled them with expensive wines, fresh caviare, ordered from Bataisk for the occasion, and the finest of *hors-d'oeuvres*. At other times he lived frugally. The one thing in regard to which he exercised no self-restraint was the purchase of books. He loved reading, and liked to get to the bottom of things with his own mind, which was tenacious as bindweed.

His partner, Yemelyan Konstantinovich Atyopin, a fair-haired man with a pointed beard and hidden slits of eyes, rarely visited Mokhov. He was married to a former nun, had had eight children by her in fifteen years of married life, and stayed at home most of the time. He had begun his career as a regimental clerk, and the fusty spirit of cringing and ingratiation brought from there permeated his family also. His children walked on tiptoe in his presence, and talked in whispers. Every morning after washing, they lined up in the dining-room under the black hanging coffin of the huge clock. Their mother stood behind them, and as soon as the dry cough was heard from the bedroom, they would begin discordantly "Our Father" and other prayers.

Yemelyan Konstantinovich would be dressed and emerge from the bedroom by the time the prayers were ended. Screwing up his tiny green eyes, he would extend his fleshy hand as though he were a bishop, while the children approached him in single file to kiss it. Then Yemelyan Konstantinovich would kiss his wife on the cheek and ask, lisping:

"Polya, is the tea ready?"

"It is, Yemelyan Konstantinovich."

"Pour me some strong tea."

He was the shop's accountant. He covered the pages under their bold-faced headings, "Debit" and "Credit," with his flowery clerk's handwriting. He read the *Stock Exchange News*, adorning his lumpy nose with a gold-rimmed pince-nez for which he had no need. He treated his employees politely.

"Ivan Petrovich, please show the Taurida calico to the customer."

His wife called him Yemelyan Konstantinovich, his children—Papa, his shop assistants—blah-blah.

The two village priests, Father Vissarion and the pious Father Pankraty, were not on friendly terms with Sergei Platonovich. They had a long-standing quarrel with him. Nor were they on very amicable terms with each other. The fractious, intriguing Father Pankraty was clever at making trouble for his neighbours, and the widower Father Vissarion with a syphilitic twang in his voice that belied his affable nature, who lived with a Ukrainian housekeeper, held himself aloof, and had no love for Father

Pankraty because of his inordinate pride and intriguing character.

All except the teacher Balanda owned their own houses. Mokhov's big house, faced with match-board and painted blue, stood in the square; right opposite, in the centre of the square squatted his shop with its glass door and faded signboard. Attached to the shop was a long, low shed with a cellar, and a hundred paces farther on rose the brick wall of the church yard and the church itself with a cupola that looked like a ripe green onion. Beyond the church were the whitewashed, officially severe walls of the school, and two smart-looking houses, one blue, with blue-painted fences, belonging to Father Pankraty; the other brown (to avoid any resemblance) with carved fencing and a broad balcony, belonging to Father Vissarion. Then came Atyopin's strangely narrow two-storied house, the post office, the thatched and iron-roofed houses of the Cossacks and finally the sloping back of the mill, with rusty tin cocks on its roof.

The inhabitants of the village lived behind their barred and bolted double shutters, cut off from all the rest of the world. Every evening, unless they were paying a visit to a neighbour, each family shot the bolts of their doors, unchained their dogs in the yards, and only the sound of the wooden tongue of the night watchman's clapper disturbed the silence.

## II

One day towards the end of August Mitka Korshunov happened to meet Liza Mokhova down by the river. He had just rowed across from the other side, and as he was fastening up his boat he saw a light gaily-painted skiff skimming the stream. It was being rowed by the student Boyarishkin. His shaven head glistened with perspiration, and the veins stood out on his forehead.

Mitka did not recognize Liza in the skiff at first, for her straw hat threw her face into shadow. Her sunburnt hands were pressing a bunch of yellow water-lilies to her breast.

"Korshunov!" she called, shaking her head at Mitka. "You've deceived me."

"Deceived you?"

"Don't you remember, you promised to take me fishing?"

Boyarishkin dropped the oars and straightened his back. The skiff thrust its nose into the shore with a scrunch.

"Do you remember?" Liza laughed, as she jumped out.

"I haven't had the time. Too much work to do," Mitka said apologetically, catching his breath as the girl approached him.

"No, it's impossible," Boyarishkin interrupted. "I've had enough, Yelizaveta. You have had all the service you will get from me! The distance we have covered over this confounded water! My hands are all blisters. Give me dry land."

Boyarishkin planted a long bare foot on the gravelly shore and mopped his forehead with the top of his crumpled student's cap. Without replying, Liza went up to Mitka. He clumsily shook the hand she offered him.

"Well, then, when shall we go fishing?" she asked with a toss of her head, narrowing her eyes.

"Tomorrow if you like. We've done the threshing and I've got more time now."

"You're not deceiving me this time?"

"No, I'm not!"

"Will you come early?"

"At dawn."

"I'll be waiting for you."

"I'll come, honestly I will."

"You haven't forgotten the window?"

"I'll find it."

"I am going away soon, I expect. And I'd like to go fishing first."

Mitka toyed silently with the rusty key for locking up the boat, and looked straight at her lips.

"Will you be through soon?" asked Boyarishkin, examining a shell lying in his palm.

"In a minute."

She was silent a moment, then, smiling to herself, she asked:

"You've had a wedding in your family, haven't you?"

"Yes, my sister's."

"Whom did she marry?" Then, without waiting for an answer, she smiled again mysteriously and fleetingly. "Do come, won't you?" Once again, as it had on the verandah of Mokhov's house her smile stung Mitka like a nettle.

He watched her to the boat. Boyarishkin pushed off clumsily and rowed away, while Liza smiled over his head at Mitka, who was still toying with the key, and nodded farewell.

When the boat was well out, Mitka heard Boyarishkin quietly ask: "Who is that fellow?"

"Just an acquaintance."

"Not an affair of the heart?"

Mitka did not catch her answer above the creak of the rowlocks. He saw Boyarishkin throw himself back with a laugh, but could not see Liza's face. The lilac ribbon on her hat, stirring gently in the breeze, caressed the slope of her bare shoulder with a melting softness that teased Mitka's misty glance.

Mitka, who rarely went fishing with rod and line, had never prepared for the occasion with such zeal as on that evening. He chopped some dung straw and boiled up the millet over a fire on the vegetable patch, then sorted out his hooks, renewing the lines that were rotten.

Mikhei, who was watching his preparations, asked: "Take me with you, Mitka. You won't be able to manage alone."

"I'll manage."

Mikhei sighed.

"It's a long time since we went out together. I'd just like the feel of a twenty-pounder pulling on the line."

Mitka frowned into the hot column of steam rising from the pot and said nothing. When he had finished he went into the back room. Grandfather Grishaka was sitting by the window, with round, copper-rimmed spectacles on his nose, studying the Gospels.

"Grandad!" Mitka said, leaning his back against the door-frame.

The old man looked at him over his spectacles.

"Eh?"

"Wake me up at the first cock."

"Where are you off to so early?"

"Fishing."

The old man had a weakness for fish but he made a pretence of opposing Mitka's designs.

"Your father said the hemp must be beaten tomorrow. There's no time to laze about."

Mitka stirred from the door and tried strategy.

"Oh, all right then. I wanted to give you a treat but as there's the hemp to be done, I won't go."

"Stop, where are you off to?" the old man took alarm and pulled off his spectacles. "I'll speak to your father about it, you can go. Tomorrow's Wednesday, I could just do with a bit of fish. All right, I'll wake you up. Go on, you young ass, what are you grinning at?"

At midnight the old man, holding up his linen trousers with one hand and gripping his stick in the other, floated like a trembling white shadow across the yard to the barn, entered the barn and jabbed his crutch into Mitka's sleeping body. In the barn the smell of newly-threshed grain and mice droppings mingled with the stale cobweb-choked air of a place that is never lived in.

Mitka was sleeping on a rug by the corn-bin. Grishaka poked at him with his stick, but could not rouse him for some time. At first he poked lightly, whispering:

"Mitka! Mitka! Hey, Mitka!"

But Mitka only sighed and drew his legs up. Grishaka grew more ruthless and began to bore the stick into Mitka's stomach. With a gasp Mitka seized the end of the stick and woke up suddenly.

"How you sleep!" grumbled the old man.

"Quiet, Grandad. Don't bumble," Mitka muttered sleepily, groping for his boots.

The lad made his way to the square. The village cocks were already crowing for the second time. As he passed Father Vissarion's house he heard a cock flap its wings in the hen-coop and give a mighty bellow worthy of the head deacon, while the hens clucked in alarm.

A night watchman was asleep on the steps of the shop, his nose tucked into the sheepskin warmth of his collar.

Mitka reached Mokhov's fence, set down his fishing tackle, and on tiptoe, so as not to disturb the dogs, crept into the porch. He tried the cold iron latch. The door was shut fast. He clambered across the banister of the verandah and went up to the window. It was half-closed. Through the black gap came the sweet scent of a girl's warm, sleeping body and the mysteriously sweet smell of perfume.

"Yelizaveta Sergeyevna!"

Mitka thought he had called very loudly. He

waited. Silence. "Suppose I'm at the wrong window! Suppose Mokhov's asleep in there! I'll be for it then. He'll use a gun!"

"Yelizaveta Sergeyevna, coming fishing?"

If he'd mistaken the window there'd be some fish caught all right!

"Are you getting up?" he said in irritation, and thrust his head through the window opening.

"Who's there?" a low startled voice sounded in the darkness.

"It's me, Korshunov. Coming fishing?"

"Oh! Just a minute."

There was a sound of movement inside. Her warm, sleepy voice seemed to smell of mint. Mitka saw something white and rustling moving about the room.

"I'd rather sleep with her than get cold fishing," he thought vaguely with the smell of the bedroom in his nostrils.

After a while her smiling face, framed in a white kerchief, appeared at the window.

"I'm coming out this way. Give me your hand." As he helped her down, she looked closely into his eyes.

"I didn't take long, did I?"

"It's all right, we'll be in time."

They went down to the Don. She rubbed her sleep-swollen eyes with a pink hand.

"I was sleeping so sweetly. I could have slept on. It's too early to go yet."

"We'll be just in time."

They followed the first lane from the square leading down to the river. During the night the river had risen, and the boat, which had been left high and dry the evening before, was now rocking on the water a little way out.

"I'll have to take off my shoes," she sighed, measuring the distance to the boat with her eyes.

"Let me carry you," Mitka proposed.

"No, I'd better take my shoes off."

"Carrying you would be easier."

"I'd rather not," she said, with embarrassment in her voice.

Mitka embraced her legs above the knees with his left arm, and, lifting her easily, splashed through the water. She clutched involuntarily at the firm, dark column of his neck and laughed with a cooing softness.

If Mitka had not stumbled over a stone used by the village women when washing clothes, there would not have been a brief, accidental kiss. She gasped and pressed her face against Mitka's hard cracked lips, and he came to a halt two paces away from the boat. The water swirled over the tops of his boots and chilled his feet.

Unfastening the boat, he pushed it off and jumped in. He rowed standing. The water rustled and wept under the stern. The boat gently breasted the stream, making for the opposite bank. The fishing rods jumped and clattered at the bottom of the boat.

"Where are you taking me?" she asked, glancing back.

"To the other side."

The keel grated on the sandy shore. Without asking permission he picked the girl up in his arms, and carried her into a clump of hawthorn. She bit at his face, scratched, gave one or two stifled screams, and feeling her strength ebbing, she wept angrily, but without tears.

They returned about nine o'clock. The sky was wrapped in a ruddy yellow haze. A strong breeze danced over the river, maning the waves. The boat danced over the waves, and the cold frothy spray sprinkled on Liza's pallid face and clung to her lashes and the strands of her hair. She wearily closed her vacant eyes, twisting in her fingers a flower that had fallen into the boat. Mitka rowed without looking at her. A small carp and a bream lay goggle-eyed at his feet, their mouths twisted in death; Mitka's face wore an expression of mingled guilt, content and anxiety.

"I'll take you to Semyonov's landing stage.

*199*

It will be nearer for you," he told her, as he turned the boat into the stream.

"All right," she whispered.

Along the deserted shore the dusty wattle fences pined in the hot wind, drenching the air with the smell of burnt brushwood. The heavy over-ripe caps of the sunflowers, pecked by sparrows, drooped low, scattering fluffy seeds over the ground. The meadowland was emerald with the young aftermath. Colts were frisking about in the distance; and the hot southerly wind wafted up the echoing laughter of the bells tied round their necks.

As Liza was getting out of the boat Mitka picked up a fish and held it out to her.

"Here, take the catch."

Her lashes flickered in alarm, but she took the fish.

"Well, I'm going."

Holding the fish by the willow twig Mitka had fixed through their gills, she turned miserably away. Gone were her recent assurance and gaiety, left behind in the hawthorn bushes.

"Liza!"

She turned round, surprise and irritation in her frown.

"Come back a minute."

And when she came closer he said, annoyed at his own embarrassment, "We were a bit careless. Your dress at the back . . . there's a stain on it. It's only a little one. . . ."

A hot flush spread over her face and neck. After a moment's silence, Mitka advised: "Go by the back ways."

"I'll have to pass through the square in any case. . . . I meant to put my black skirt on," she whispered, looking at Mitka with regret and sudden hatred.

"Let me green it a bit with a leaf," Mitka suggested simply, and was surprised to see the tears come into her eyes.

Like the rustling whisper of a summer breeze the news flew round the village. "Mitka Korshunov's been out all night with Sergei Platonovich's daughter." The women talked about it as they drove out the cattle to join the village herd in the morning, as they stood in the narrow shade of the well-sweeps with the grey dust swirling round them and water dripping from their buckets, or as they beat out their washing on the flat stones down by the river.

"Her own mother's dead you know."

"Her father never has a minute to spare, and her stepmother just doesn't trouble."

"The watchman says he saw a man tapping at the end window at midnight. He thought at first it was someone trying to break in. He ran to see who it was, and found it was Mitka."

"The girls these days, I don't know what they're coming to."

"Mitka told my Nikita he's going to marry her."

"He'd better wipe his nose first."

"He forced her, they say."

"Don't you believe it. . . ."

The rumours flowed round main street and back street, smearing the girl's good name, as a clean gate is smeared with thick tar.

Finally they descended on the greying head of Mokhov himself and crushed him to the ground. For two days he went neither to the shop nor to the mill. His servants, who lived downstairs, came to him only at dinner.

On the third day Sergei Platonovich had his dapple-grey stallion harnessed to his droshki, and drove to the stanitsa, bowing remotely to the Cossacks he met on the way. The droshki was followed by a highly-varnished carriage, which swished out of the yard, drawn by a pair of prancing black horses. Yemelyan the coachman, sucking his pipe, which had become permanently attached to his greying beard, shook out the blue silk of the reins and the two black horses went prancing down the street. Liza could be seen sitting pale-faced behind Yemelyan's craggy back. She held a light valise on her knees and was smiling sadly. At the gate she waved her glove to Vladimir and her stepmother.

Pantelei Prokofyevich happened to be limping out of the shop at the moment, and he stopped to ask the yardman Nikita: "Where's the master's daughter going?"

And Nikita, condescending to the simple human weakness, replied: "To Moscow, to study."

The next day an incident occurred which was long the subject of talk down by the river, under the shadow of the well-sweeps, and when the cattle were being driven out to graze. Just before nightfall (the village herd had already returned from the steppe) Mitka went to see Sergei Platonovich. He had waited until evening in order to avoid meeting anyone, for he came not merely to make a friendly call, but to ask for the hand of Mokhov's daughter, Liza.

He had met her perhaps four times, not more. At the last meeting the conversation had taken the following course:

"Liza, will you marry me?"

"Nonsense!"

"I shall care for you, I'll love you. We have people to work for us, you shall sit at the window and read your books."

"You're a fool!"

Mitka took offence, and said no more. That evening he went home early, and in the morning he announced to his astonished father:

"Father, arrange for my marriage."

"Don't be a fool."

"Honestly, Father, I'm not joking."

"In a hurry, aren't you? Who're you smitten on—crazy Marfa?"

"Send the match-makers to Sergei Platonovich."

Miron Grigoryevich carefully set down the cobbling tools with which he was mending harness, and roared with laughter.

"You're in a funny vein today, my son."

But Mitka stuck to his guns, and his father flared up.

"You fool! Sergei Platonovich has a capital of over a hundred thousand rubles. He's a merchant, and what are you? Clear off, or I'll leather you with this strap."

"We've got fourteen pairs of bullocks, and look at the land we own. Besides he's a muzhik, and we're Cossacks."

"Clear off!" Miron said curtly. He did not like long discussions.

Mitka found a sympathetic listener only in his grandfather. The old man attempted to persuade Miron in favour of his son's suit.

"Miron!" old Grishaka said. "Why don't you agree? As the boy's taken it into his head. . . ."

"Father, you're a great baby, God's truth you are! Mitka's silly enough, but you're...."

"Hold your tongue!" Grishaka rapped his stick on the floor. "Aren't we good enough for them? He ought to take it as an honour for a Cossack's son to wed his daughter. He'll give up, and gladly too. We're known all over the countryside. We're not farm-hands, we're masters. Go and ask him, Miron. What's stopping you? Let him give his mill as the dowry."

Miron snorted and went out into the yard. So Mitka decided to wait until evening and then go to Mokhov himself. He knew that his father's obstinacy was like a well-rooted elm: you might bend it, but you could never break it. It was not worth trying.

He went whistling as far as Mokhov's front door, then grew timid. He hesitated a moment, and finally went through the yard to the side door. On the steps he asked the maid in her crackling starched apron: "Master at home?"

"He's drinking his tea. Wait!"

Mitka sat down and waited, lit a cigarette, smoked it, and crushed the end on the floor. Mokhov came out, brushing crumbs off his waistcoat. When he saw Mitka he frowned, but said: "Come in."

Mitka entered Mokhov's cool private room that smelled of books and tobacco, feeling that

the courage with which he had been charged
so far had been sufficient to last only to the
merchant's threshold. The merchant went to his
table, and swung round on his heels: "Well?"
Behind his back his fingers scratched at the top
of the table.

"I've come to find out ..." Mitka plunged
into the cold slime of Mokhov's piercing eyes
and shuddered. "Perhaps you'll give me Liza?"
Despair, anger, fear, all combined to bring his
face out in perspiration, fine as dew during a
drought.

Mokhov's left eyebrow quivered, and his upper lip writhed back from the gums. He stretched
out his neck and leaned all his body forward:

"What? Wha-a-at? You scoundrel! Get out!
I'll have you before the ataman! You son of a
bitch!"

Encouraged by this shout, Mitka watched the
grey-blue blood flooding into Mokhov's cheeks.

"Don't take it as an insult. I only wanted to
make up for what I've done."

Mokhov rolled his bloodshot eyes and threw
a massive iron ash-tray at Mitka's feet. It re-
bounded and struck him on the knee. But he
stoically bore the pain, and jerking open the
door, shouted, baring his teeth with resentment
and pain:

"As you like, Sergei Platonovich, just as you

like, but I meant it. . . . Who would want her now? I thought I'd cover her shame. But now . . . even a dog won't touch a gnawed bone."

Pressing a crumpled handkerchief to his lips, Mokhov followed on Mitka's heels. He barred the way to the main door, and Mitka ran out into the yard. Here the master had only to wink to Yemelyan the coachman, and as Mitka was struggling with the stout latch at the wicket-gate, four unleashed hounds tore round the corner of the barn. Seeing a stranger, they bounded across the clean-swept yard straight at him.

In 1910, Sergei Platonovich had brought back a pair of black curly-haired pups from the fair at Nizhny Novgorod. In a year those black, curly, big-mouthed pups shot up like yearling calves. At first they snapped at the skirts of the women who passed Mokhov's yard, then they learned to pull the women to the ground and bite their legs, and it was only when they had killed Father Pankraty's calf and a pair of Atyopin's hogs that Sergei Platonovich ordered them to be chained up. Now the dogs were let loose only at night, and once every spring for the mating.

Before Mitka could turn round the foremost dog was up at his shoulders with its teeth fastened into his jacket. The writhing black bodies bit and tore at him. Mitka fought them off

and tried to keep his balance. He saw Yemelyan, his pipe scattering sparks, disappear into
the kitchen, and heard the door slam behind
him.

By the steps, leaning against a drain-pipe,
stood Sergei Platonovich, his hairy white fists
clenched. Swaying and staggering, Mitka tore
open the gate and dragged the bunch of snarl-
ing, hot-breathed dogs after him on his bleeding legs. He seized one by the throat and choked
it, and passing Cossacks with difficulty beat
off the others.

### III

Natalya fitted well into the Melekhov household. Although he was rich and employed labourers, her father had brought up his children to work. Hard-working Natalya won the
hearts of her husband's parents. Ilyinichna, who
secretly did not like her elder clothes-loving
daughter-in-law Darya, took to Natalya from
the very first.

"Sleep on, sleep on, little one! What are you
out so early for?" she would protest kindly,
bustling about the kitchen on her stout legs.
"Go back to bed, we'll manage without you."

And Natalya who had got up at dawn to help
in the kitchen would go back to the best room
to complete her rest.

Even Pantelei, who was usually strict in regard to household matters, said to his wife:

"Listen, wife, don't wake Natalya. She works hard enough as it is. She's going out with Grisha to plough today. But whip up that Darya. She's a lazy woman, and bad. She paints her face and blackens her brows, the bitch."

"Let her take it a bit easy, the first year," sighed Ilyinichna, remembering her own back-breaking life.

Grigory had begun to get used to his newly-married state; but after two or three weeks he realized with fear and chagrin that he had not completely broken with Aksinya. Something was left like a thorn in his heart, and the pain would not go soon. The feeling which, in the excitement of marriage, he had dismissed with a careless wave of the hand was deep-rooted. He thought he could forget, but it refused to be forgotten, and the wound bled. Even before the wedding Pyotr had asked him when they were threshing together:

"Grisha, but what about Aksinya?"

"Well, what about her?"

"Won't you feel sorry to throw her over?"

"Someone else will pick her up," Grigory had said with a laugh.

"Well, you know best," Pyotr said, biting at

the chewed tip of his moustache, "but don't
make a hash of your marriage."

"Love grows old and the body cold," **Grigory**
replied lightly.

But it had not worked out like that. As he
dutifully caressed his wife, trying to inflame
her with his own youthful zest, he met with
only coldness and an embarrassed submission
from her. Natalya shrank from bodily delights;
she had inherited something of her mother's
slow, unresponsive blood, and as he recalled
Aksinya's passionate fervour Grigory sighed:
"Your father must have made you on ice, Natalya. You're too chilly by half."

And when he met Aksinya she would smile
with a vague darkening of the pupils and her
words clung like the mud at the bottom of a
stream.

"Hullo, Grisha! How's love with your young
wife?"

"All right," Grigory would reply evasively,
and escape as quickly as possible from her caressing glance.

Stepan had evidently made up his quarrel
with his wife. He visited the tavern less frequently, and one evening, as he was winnowing
grain on the threshing-floor, he suggested, for
the first time since the beginning of the trouble: "Let's sing a song, Aksinya!"

They sat down, their backs against a heap of threshed, dusty wheat. Stepan began an army song, Aksinya joined in with her full, throaty voice. They sang well together, as they had in the first years of their married life, when they used to jog back from the fields under the crimson hem of the sunset glow and Stepan would sit on the load and sing an old song, as long and sad as the wild and desolate road across the steppe. Aksinya with her head resting on the bulging hoops of her husband's chest would take up the tune. The horses would pull the creaking wagon and the shaft-bow would bob up and down. And from afar the old men of the village would listen to the song.

"She's got a fine voice, that wife of Stepan's."

"Aye, nice singing."

"And what a voice Stepan has got, clear as a bell."

And as they sat on the earthen banks round their cottages watching the dusty purple of the sunset, the old men would exchange remarks across the street, about the song, where it came from, and about those who had loved it.

Grigory heard the Astakhovs singing, and while he was threshing (the two threshing-floors adjoined) he could see Aksinya as self-assured as before, and apparently happy. Or so it seemed to him.

Stepan was not on speaking terms with the Melekhovs. He worked on the threshing-floor, swinging his great sloping shoulders, occasionally making a jesting remark to Aksinya. And she would respond with a smile, her black eyes flashing. Her green skirt hovered constantly before Grigory's eyes. His neck was continually being twisted by a strange force which turned his head in the direction of Stepan's yard. He did not notice that Natalya, who was helping Pantelei spread out the sheaves for threshing, intercepted every involuntary glance with her own yearning, jealous gaze; he did not see Pyotr, who was driving the horses round the threshing circle, wrinkling his nose with a faint grin as he watched his brother.

The earth groaned under the crushing weight of the stone rollers and with the muffled rumble in his ears Grigory groped hazily in his mind and failed to catch the scraps of thought that slipped elusively out of range of his consciousness.

From near and distant threshing-floors came the sound of threshing: the shouts of drivers, the whistle of knouts, the rattle of the winnowing drums. The village, fat with the harvest, basked in the September warmth, stretching along the Don like a beaded snake across a road. In every farmyard with its wattle fence,

under every Cossack roof, each brimming bit-
ter-sweet life whirled on, separate and apart
from the rest. Old Grishaka had taken a chill
and was suffering with his teeth; Mokhov,
crushed by his shame, clawed his beard, weeping
and grinding his teeth in solitude; Stepan
nursed his hatred for Grigory in his heart and his
iron fingers tore at the patchwork quilt in his
sleep; Natalya would run to the shed and threw
herself on the heap of cowdung fuel, shaking
and huddling into a ball as she wept over her
desecrated happiness; Christonya, who had sold
a calf at the fair, then spent the money on drink,
was tortured by pangs of conscience; Grigory
sighed with insatiable longing and renewed
pain; Aksinya, as she caressed her husband,
flooded her undying hatred for him with tears.
David had been discharged from the mill, and
sat night after night with Knave in the carters'
shed, while Knave, his angry eyes flashing,
would declare:

"Just wait! They'll have their throats cut before long. One revolution wasn't enough for
them. Wait till we have another 1905, then we'll
settle scores. We'll settle scores!" he shook his
scarred finger threateningly, and with a shrug
adjusted the jacket flung across his shoulders.

And over the village slipped the days, passing into the nights; the weeks flowed by, the

months crept on, the wind howled over the hill, warning of bad weather to come, and, glazed with the clear greenish-blue of autumn, the Don flowed on indifferently to the sea.

## IV

One Sunday at the end of October Fedot Bodovskov drove to the stanitsa on business. He took with him four braces of fattened ducks and sold them at the market; he bought his wife some cotton print, and was on the point of driving home (with one foot on the wheel he was tightening the hame strap), when a stranger, obviously not of those parts, came up to him.

"Good-afternoon," he greeted Fedot, putting a sunburnt hand to the edge of his black hat.

"'Afternoon," said Fedot and paused inquiringly, narrowing his Kalmyk eyes.

"Where are you from?"

"One of the villages."

"And which village may that be?"

"Tatarsky."

The stranger drew a silver cigarette-case out of his pocket and offered Fedot a cigarette.

"Is yours a large village?"

"No thanks, just had one. Our village? Pretty big. Three hundred families or thereabouts."

"Is there a church there?"

"Of course."

"Any blacksmiths there?"

"Aye, there's a smithy."

"Is there a workshop at the mill?"

Fedot fastened the rein to his horse's bit, and looked distrustfully at the man's black hat and the furrows in the broad white face, fringed with a black beard.

"What do you want to know for?"

"I'm coming to live at your village. I've just been to the district ataman. Are you going back empty?"

"Aye."

"Will you take me back with you? I'm not alone. I have my wife with me and a couple of boxes."

"I can take you."

Having agreed about the price, they drove to Froska the bun-maker's where his passenger was lodging, collected the man's thin, blond wife, put the boxes in the back and set out on the return journey. Clicking his tongue and flicking the plaited reins over the horse's backs, Fedot twisted his angular head round from time to time; he was eaten up with curiosity. His passengers sat quietly behind him. Fedot first asked for a cigarette, then he inquired:

"Where are you from?"

"From Rostov."

"One o' them?"

"What did you say?"

"Were you born there?"

"Er, yes."

Fedot wrinkled his bronzed cheeks and peered at the distant clumps of steppe grass. The road began to climb and half a verst from the road, in the grey-brown brushwood on top of the ridge Fedot's practised eye spotted the scarcely visible movements of bustards' heads.

"Pity I haven't got a gun, or I'd be out after the bustards. There they go," he sighed, pointing with his thumb.

"I don't see anything," his passenger replied, blinking shortsightedly.

Fedot watched the bustards flutter into a gully and twisted himself round to study his passengers more closely. The man was of average height, but thin; his close-set eyes had a sly twinkle in them. He smiled frequently as he talked. His wife, wrapped in a knitted shawl, was dozing and Fedot couldn't see her face.

"What are you coming to live in our village for?"

"I'm a mechanic. I'm thinking of starting a workshop. I can do carpentry too."

Fedot stared suspiciously at the man's big hands, and catching his gaze, the stranger added: "I'm also an agent for the Singer Sewing-Machine Company."

"What's your name?" Fedot asked.

"Stockman."

"So you're not Russian, then?"

"Yes, I'm a Russian. But my grandfather was a Lett by birth."

In a short while Fedot had learned that Osip Davydovich Stockman had formerly worked at a factory, then somewhere in the Kuban, then in the South-Eastern Railway workshops. And a great number of other facts the inquisitive Fedot elicited concerning the stranger's life.

After a while the conversation flagged. Fedot watered his sweating horse at a wayside spring, and drowsy with the journey and the jolting of the cart, he began to doze. It was another five versts to the village. He fastened the reins to the wagon and lay back comfortably. But he was not allowed to go to sleep.

"How's life in your parts?" Stockman asked him bouncing and swaying with the motion of the cart.

"Not so bad, we get our bread."

"And the Cossacks generally, are they satisfied with life?"

"Some are, some aren't. You can't please everybody."

"That's true," the man assented, and went on asking his tricky probing questions.

"You live pretty well, you say?"

"Pretty well."

"The annual army training must be a nuisance? Eh?"

"Army training? We're used to it. Nothing to worry about when you're in the army."

"But it's hard on you Cossacks to have to supply all the equipment."

"Yes, the sons of swine!" Fedot said with sudden animation and glanced sidelong at the woman. She averted her eyes.

"Our authorities are a bad lot.... When I went to do my service I sold my bullocks and bought a horse and they rejected him."

"Rejected him?" Stockman said with assumed amazement.

"Right out. His legs were no good, they said. I argued with them, I tried everything. 'He's got legs like a prize stallion,' I said, 'it's just his funny way of stepping, that's all.' But no, they wouldn't pass him. It's enough to ruin you!"

The conversation went on briskly. Fedot jumped off the wagon and began to talk freely of the village life. He cursed the village ataman for his unjust division of the meadowland, and praised the way things were run in Poland, where his regiment had been stationed. Stockman, casting sharp glances at Fedot from his narrowed eyes, smoked mild cigarettes in a ringed bone holder and smiled frequently, but the frown furrow in his white sloping forehead stirred slowly and heavily, as though driven from within by hidden thoughts.

They reached the village in the early evening. On Fedot's advice Stockman went to the widow Lukeshka and rented two rooms from her.

"Who is that you brought back with you?" Fedot's neighbours asked him as he drove past their gates.

"An agent."

"What kind of angel?"

"You're fools, that's what you are. An agent, I said. He sells machines. He gives them away free to the handsome ones, but to such as you, Auntie Marya, he sells them."

"Look at yourself, you devil. Your Kalmyk snout is ugly enough to frighten a horse!"

"Kalmyks and Tatars come first in the steppe, so don't you joke about them," Fedot parried.

Mechanic Stockman lodged at the cross-eyed, long-tongued Lukeshka's. And the night had scarcely passed before all the women's tongues in the village were wagging.

"Have you heard the news, neighbour?"

"What news?"

"Fedot the Kalmyk has brought a foreigner down."

"Really?"

"So help me God. He wears a hat and his name is Shtopel or Shtokal...."

"He's not from the police?"

"No, he's an exciseman."

"It's all lies, my dears. He's a book-keeper, they say, just like Father Pankraty's son."

"Pashka, my dove, run to Lukeshka and ask her quietly: 'Who's that living with you, auntie?'"

"Run quickly, child!"

Next day Stockman reported to the village ataman.

Fyodor Manitskov, who was in his third year as ataman, turned the newcomer's passport over and over, then handed it to the clerk, who also turned it over and over. They exchanged glances, and the ataman, once a sergeant-major, authoritatively waved his hand.

"You can stay."

The newcomer bowed and left the room. For a week he did not put his nose outside Lukeshka's house keeping like a suslik to his burrow. He could be heard tapping with an axe, preparing a workshop in the tumble-down outdoor kitchen. The women's interest in him died away; only the children spent all day peeping over the fence and watching the stranger with unabashed curiosity.

## V

Three days before Intercession Grigory and his wife drove out to the steppe to plough. Pantelei was unwell; he leaned heavily on his stick and wheezed with pain as he stood in the yard seeing them off.

"Plough up the two strips on the other side of the common, by Red Dell, Grisha."

"All right. What about the one up by Willow Bank?" Grigory asked in a hoarse whisper; he had caught a cold while fishing and had a cloth round his throat.

"That can wait till after the holiday. You'll have enough to do as it is, so don't be greedy. There must be fifteen acres up there."

"Will Pyotr be coming to help?"

"He's going to the mill with Darya. We want to get our milling done before the crowds begin."

As Ilyinichna put some freshly-baked buns in Natalya's jacket she whispered: "Perhaps you'll take Dunya with you, to lead the bullocks?"

"Two people are enough."

"All right, my dear. Christ be with you."

Arching her slender figure under the weight of a load of damp washing, Dunya went past on her way to the Don to rinse the clothes. As she went by she called to Natalya:

"Natalya, there's lots of sorrel in Red Dell. Pull some up and bring it home."

"Now then, be off with you, chatterbox!" Pantelei said shaking his stick at Dunya.

The three pairs of bullocks dragged the upturned plough out of the yard, gouging the drought-hardened earth. Grigory kept adjusting the kerchief bound round his neck as he walked along at the roadside, coughing. Natalya walked at his side, a bag with their food in it swinging on her back.

A crystal stillness enveloped the steppe. Beyond the common, on the other side of the humpbacked hill the earth was being combed with ploughs, and the drivers were whistling; but here along the high-road there was only the blue-grey of stunted wormwood, the roadside clover nibbled by sheep, and the ringing glassy cool of the sky above, criss-crossed with flying threads of jewelled gossamer.

After seeing the ploughmen on their way, Pyotr and Darya made ready to drive to the mill. Pyotr winnowed the wheat in the granary, Darya sacked it and carried it to the cart.

Pantelei harnessed the horses carefully adjusting the traces.

"Going to be long?"

"Coming," Pyotr answered from the granary.

When they arrived at the mill they found the yard crowded with wagons. The scales were surrounded by a dense throng. Pyotr threw the reins to Darya and jumped down from the cart.

"My turn soon?" he asked Knave the scalesman.

"You'll get there."

"Who's being served now?"

"Number thirty-eight."

Pyotr turned to fetch his sacks. As he did so he heard cursing behind him. A hoarse, ill-tempered voice barked: "You oversleep yourself, and then you want to go out of your turn. Get away, khokhol*, or I'll give you one."

Pyotr recognized the voice of Horseshoe Yakov. He stopped to listen. The sound of shouting swelled in the weighing-room. Then came the sharp smack of a blow and an elderly, bearded Ukrainian with his cap crushed on the back of his head came tumbling out through the doorway.

"What's that for?" he shouted, holding his cheek.

_____

* Khokhol—a derogatory term for a Ukrainian.

223

"I'll wring your neck!"

"But look here...."

"Mikifor, help!"

Horseshoe Yakov, a spirited, stocky artilleryman, who had earned his nickname because of the horseshoe marks left on his face by the kick of a horse, came running out of the weighing-room, rolling up his sleeves. A tall Ukrainian in a pink shirt struck hard at him from behind. But Yakov stayed on his feet.

"Brothers, they're beating up the Cossacks!" he cried.

Cossacks and Ukrainians, who were at the mill in large numbers, came running from all sides into the wagon-filled yard. A fight began round the main entrance. The door gave way under the pressure of the struggling bodies. Pyotr threw down his sack and with a grunt ran lightly towards the melee. Standing up on the cart, Darya saw him press into the middle of the crowd, knocking the others aside. She groaned as she saw him carried to the mill wall, flung down and trampled underfoot.

Mitka Korshunov came skipping round the corner from the machine-room, brandishing an iron bar. The same Ukrainian who had struck at Yakov from behind burst out of the struggling crowd, a torn pink sleeve fluttering out behind him like a bird's broken wing. Bent double, his hands touching the ground, he ran to the nearest cart and pulled out a shaft as if it were a match-stick. Hoarse cries rang out over the yard. A crunching sound. Blows. Groaning. A steady roar of shouting. The three Shamil brothers came running out of their house. One-armed Alexei caught his feet in a pair of reins left lying on the ground and sprawled at the gate. He jumped up and went bounding across the lined-up cart-shafts, pressing his armless left sleeve to his stomach. His brother Martin bent down to tuck in the trouser leg, which had come out of his white sock. The shouting at the mill rose to a crescendo. Somebody let out a cry that floated high over the mill roof like a wind-blown thread of cobweb, and Martin straightened up and dashed after his brothers.

Darya stood watching from the cart, panting and wringing her hands. Around her, women were squealing and wailing, horses pricked up their ears restlessly, bullocks bellowed and pressed against the carts. Pursing his lips Mokhov stalked past pale-faced, his belly bobbing up and down like an egg under his waistcoat. Darya saw the Ukrainian with the tattered shirt cut Mitka Korshunov down with the shaft, the next moment he himself was sent headlong by one-armed Alexei's iron fist. Scenes from the fight passed before Darya's eyes like scraps of coloured rag. Without surprise she saw Mitka, on his knees, sweep Mokhov's legs from under him with the iron bar. Mokhov threw out his arms and crawled like a crab to the weighing-shed, there to be kicked and trodden underfoot. Darya laughed hysterically, the black arches of her painted brows cracked with her laughter. But she stopped abruptly as she saw Pyotr; swaying, he had made his way out of the heaving, yelling mob, and was lying under a cart, spitting blood. Darya ran to him with a shriek. Cossacks came hurrying from the village with stakes; one of them flourished a crowbar. The fighting was taking on fantastic proportions. It was no mere tavern brawl or Shrovetide fisticuffs between villages. At the door of the weighing-shed a young Ukrainian lay with a broken head in a pool of blood; bloody strands of hair fell over his face. It looked as though he was departing his pleasant life.

Herded together like sheep, the Ukrainians were slowly being driven towards the unloading-shed. Things would have taken a bad turn, had not an old Ukrainian had an inspiration. Darting into the shed, he pulled a flaming brand out of the furnace and ran towards the shed where the milled grain was stored: a thousand poods and more of flour. Smoke streamed over his shoulder like muslin and sparks, daylight-dimmed, scattered about.

"I'll set it afire!" he screamed, raising the crackling brand towards the thatched roof.

The Cossacks wavered and came to a halt. A dry, blustering wind was blowing from the east, carrying the smoke away from the roof of the shed towards the group of Ukrainians. One goodly spark in the dry rush thatch, and the whole village would go up in flames.

A low murmur arose from the Cossacks. Some of them began to back away towards the mill, while the Ukrainian, waving the brand above his head and scattering fiery rain, shouted:

"I'll burn it! I'll burn it! Out of the yard!"

With fresh red-blue bruises on his scarred face Horseshoe Yakov, the man who had started the fight, was the first to leave the yard. The other Cossacks streamed hurriedly after him. Throwing their sacks hastily on to their wagons, the Ukrainians harnessed their horses, then, standing up in their wagons, waving the ends of the leather reins around their heads, and whipping up their horses frantically, they tore out of the yard and away from the village.

One-armed Alexei stood in the middle of the yard, his empty knotted sleeve jerking on his hard flat belly, his eye and cheek twitching as usual.

"To horse, Cossacks!"

"After them!"

"They'll not go far."

Mitka Korshunov, the worse for wear, made as if to dash out of the yard. A fresh ripple of disturbance passed over the crowd of Cossacks round the mill. But at that moment an unfamil·iar figure in a black hat appeared from the engine room and approached the group with hasty steps; his piercing eyes narrowed into slits darted over the crowd as he raised his hand and shouted:

"Stop!"

"Who are you?" Yakov demanded, scowling. "Where'd you spring from?"

"Bash him!"

"Stop, villagers!"

"Who are you calling villagers, you bob-tail?"

"Muzhik. Give him one, Yakov!"

"The dirty bumpkin!"

"That's right, black his eyes for him!"

The man smiled diffidently, but without a sign of fear. He took off his hat and wiped his brow with a gesture of complete simplicity; his smile was utterly disarming.

"What's the matter?" he asked, waving his hat at the blood by the door of the weighing-shed.

"We've been beating up the khokhols," one-armed Alexei replied peaceably, eye and cheek twitching.

"But what for?"

"They wanted to go out of turn," Yakov explained, stepping forward and wiping a clot of blood from his nose with a sweep of the arm.

"We gave 'em something to remember us by."

"Pity we didn't go after them. . . . Nothing to burn in the steppe."

"We got scared, he wouldn't have dared set fire to it."

"He'd have done it all right, he was desperate."

"The khokhols are a mighty bad-tempered lot," Afonka Ozerov said with a grin.

The man waved his hat in Ozerov's direction. "And who are you?"

Ozerov spat contemptuously through his widely-spaced teeth, and, watching the flight of the spittle, planted his feet apart.

"I'm Cossack. But you . . . what are you, a gypsy?"

"You and I are both Russians."

"You're lying," Afonka declared deliberately.

"The Cossacks are descended from the Russians. Do you know that?"

"And I tell you the Cossacks are the sons of Cossacks."

"Long ago," the man explained, "serfs ran away from the landowners and settled along the Don. They came to be known as Cossacks."

"Go your own way, man!" Alexei said with restrained anger, clenching his heavy fist and blinking hard.

"The swine wants to make muzhiks out of us! Who is he?"

"He's the new fellow living with cross-eyed Lukeshka," another explained.

But the moment for pursuit of the Ukrainians was past. The Cossacks dispersed, animatedly discussing the fight.

That night, in the steppe some eight versts from the village, as Grigory wrapped himself in his thick prickly sheepskin, he said wistfully to Natalya:

"You're a stranger, somehow! You're like that moon, you neither chill a man, nor warm him. I don't love you, Natalya; you mustn't be angry. I didn't want to say anything about it, but there it is; we can't go on like this. I'm sorry for you; it looked as if we were coming closer lately, but I can't feel anything in my heart. It's just empty. Like the steppe tonight."

Natalya stared up at the inaccessible starry pastures, at the shadowy, ghost-like cloak of the clouds floating above her, and was silent.

From somewhere in the bluish-black wilderness above a belated flight of cranes called to each other with voices like little silver bells.

The withered grass had a sad, dead smell about it. On a hillock flickered the ruddy glow of a ploughman's camp-fire.

Grigory awoke just before dawn. A three-inch layer of snow covered his sheepskin. The steppe was hidden beneath the shimmering, virginal blue of the fresh fall; the clearly-marked tracks of a hare that had lost its way on the first snow ran close by the spot where he lay.

## VI

For many years past, if a Cossack travelled alone along the road to Millerovo and fell in with Ukrainians (the Ukrainian villages began at Lower Yablonovsky and stretched for seventy-five versts, as far as Millerovo), he had been obliged to yield them the road, or they would set about him. So the Cossacks were in the habit of driving to the railway station in groups, and then they were not afraid of falling in with Ukrainians out in the steppe and exchanging invective:

"Hey, khokhol! Give us the road! Think you can live on the Cossacks' land, you swine, and not let them pass!"

The Ukrainians, who had to cart their grain to the elevator at Paramonovo on the Don, were not to be envied either. Fights would break out without cause, simply because they were "khokhols," and once a man was a "khokhol," he had to be beaten up.

Many centuries ago a diligent hand had sown the seeds of caste hatred in the Cossack land and cultivated them with care, and the seed had yielded rich fruit. The earth flowed with the blood shed in these brawls between Cossack and newcomer from the Ukraine and Russia.

Some two weeks after the battle of the mill a district police officer and an inspector arrived in the village. Stockman was the first to be examined. Rummaging in his brief case, the inspector, a young official from the Cossack nobility, asked him: "Where were you living before you came here?"

"At Rostov."

"What were you imprisoned for in 1907?"

Stockman's eyes glided over the inspector's brief case and his bowed head with its scurfy side parting.

"For disturbances."

"Hm! Where were you working then?"

"At the railway workshops."

"What as?"

"Mechanic."

"You're not a Jew, are you? Or a converted one?"

"No. I think. . . ."

"I'm not interested in what you think. Have you been in exile?"

"Yes, I have."

The inspector raised his head, and bit his clean-shaven, pimply lips.

"I advise you to clear out of this district," he said, adding to himself, "and I'll see to it that you do."

"Why, inspector?"

The answer was another question.

"What did you talk to the Cossacks about on the day of the fight at the mill?"

"Well. . . ."

"All right, you can go."

Stockman went out on to the verandah of Mokhov's house (the authorities always made the merchant's house their headquarters) and glanced back at the painted double doors with a shrug.

## VII

Winter came on slowly. After Intercession the snow melted and the herds were driven out to pasture again. For a week a south wind blew, warming the earth; a late stunted green gave a last bright gleam in the steppe. The thaw lasted until St. Michael's Day, then the frost returned and heavy snow fell, and the vegetable patches by the Don, where the snow had drifted to the top of the fences, were criss-crossed with the marks of hares' feet. The streets were deserted.

The smoke of dung fuel hung low over the village, and rooks pecked about on the heaps of ash scattered by the roadside. The smooth sledge-track wound in a faded grey-blue ribbon through the village.

A village assembly was to be held to arrange for the allotment and cutting of brushwood. The Cossacks crowded round the steps of the village administration in their sheepskins and greatcoats, until the cold drove them inside. Behind a table, beside the ataman and clerk, the respected village elders with their silvery beards were gathered; the younger Cossacks with beards of various colours and those with no beard at all stood round in groups and muttered to one another out of the warmth of their coat collars. The clerk covered sheet after sheet of paper with close writing, while the ataman watched over his shoulder, and a restrained hum filled the chilly room.

"The hay this year. . . ."

"Aye, the meadow hay is good, but the steppe hay is all clover."

"In the old days they'd be grazing in the steppe till Christmas."

"That was all right for the Kalmyks."

A throaty cough.

"The ataman's getting a neck like a wolf's on him. So fat he can't turn his head."

"Fed himself up like a pig, the devil!"

"Hullo, Grandpa, trying to scare the winter away? What a sheepskin you've got on!"

"Time for the gypsy to sell his coat soon."

"Did ye hear of the gypsy lad who spent the night in the steppe and hadn't anything to cover himself with except a fishing net? When the cold started creeping round his guts, he wakes up, pushes his finger through a loop in the net and says to his mother: 'So that's where the draught's coming from. I thought it was chilly.'"

"I fear we'll have some slippery days soon."

"Better get the oxen shod."

"I've been cutting the willows down in Devil's gully. Good stuff there."

"Button your fly, Zakhar. If you get frostbite, your woman'll turn you out of the house."

"What's this I hear about you taking over one of the common bulls, Avdeyich?"

"I decided not to. That Parasha woman's going to take care of it. I'm a widow, she says, the more the merrier. All right, I says, it may give you an addition to the family...."

"Haw-haw-haw!"

"Now, elders! What about the wood-cutting? Quiet there!"

"Yes, I says, if you get an addition, you'll need a godfather."

"A little quieter, please."

The meeting began. Toying with his rod of office, the ataman called out the names, plucking icicles out of his beard with his little finger. Now and then the door slammed at the back of the room and people squeezed in amid clouds of cold air.

"You can't fix the wood-cutting for Thursday!" Ivan Tomilin attempted to shout down the ataman and rubbed his purple ears, cocking his head in its blue artillery cap on one side.

"Why not?"

"You'll rub your ears off, gunner!" somebody called out.

"We'll sew on a pair of bull's ears for him."

"On Thursday half the village will be going out to bring in hay. A fine way to arrange things. . . ."

"You can leave that till Sunday!"

"Elders!"

"What now!"

"Good luck to him!"

A howl of derision arose from the assembly.

Old Matvei Kashulin leaned across the rickety table and, pointing his smooth ash stick at Tomilin, croaked furiously.

"The hay can wait! It's for the community to say. Ye're always agin everybody else. Ye're a young fool, my lad! And that's that!"

"You've got no brains to boast about, anyway..." one-armed Alexei joined in, his disfigured cheek twitching. For six years he had been quarreling with old Kashulin over a strip of land. Alexei beat up the old man every spring, although the strip that Kashulin had grabbed was not big enough to swing a cat in anyway.

"Shut up, jelly-face!"

"Pity you're out of my reach, or I'd bloody your nose for you," Alexei threatened.

"Why, you one-armed twitcher...!"

"Now then, enough of this bickering...."

"Go outside if you want to try your strength."

"Chuck it, Alexei, look how the old fellow's bristling up, he'll lose his hat in a minute."

"Put 'em in the cooler if they won't behave."

The table groaned as the ataman brought his heavy fist down on it with a crash.

"I'll call the watchman in in a moment, if there isn't silence." When order was restored, he added: "Wood-cutting will begin on Thursday at dawn."

"Well, what do you say, elders?"

"Good luck to it!"

"God grant it!"

"They don't listen much to the old folk nowadays!"

"They'll listen all right. Do they think they can do what they like? My Alexander, when I gave him his portion, he wanted to start a fight over it, laid hands on me, he did. I put him in his place though. 'I'll go to the ataman this minute,' I says, 'and have you thrashed. . . .' That cooled him off all right. . . ."

"And one other thing, elders. I've received an order from the district ataman." The village ataman raised his voice and twisted his neck; the stiff collar of his uniform was cutting into his chin. "Next Saturday the youngsters are to go to be sworn in at the district ataman's office. They are to be there by the afternoon."

Pantelei Prokofyevich was standing by the window nearest the door, holding up his lame leg like a crane. At his side Miron Grigoryevich was sitting on the window-sill, smiling into his ruddy beard. His short fair eye-lashes were fluffed with hoar-frost, his big brown freckles had turned grey in the cold. The younger Cossacks were crowded close by, winking and smiling at one another. In the middle of their group, his blue-topped quardsman's cap thrust back on his smooth bald head, his unageing face everlastingly blushing like a ruddy winter apple, stood Avdeyich Sinilin.

Avdeyich had served in the Ataman's Life-guards, and had come back with the nick-name "Braggart." He had been one of the first in the village to be assigned to the Ataman's Regiment. He had always been a little queer in the head, but on active service something very strange had happened to him. From the very first day of his return he had begun to tell astonishing stories of service at the court and his extraordinary adventures in St. Petersburg. His astounded listeners at first believed him, drinking it all in with gaping mouths, but then they discovered that Avdeyich was the biggest liar the village had ever produced, and they openly laughed at him. But he was not to be abashed (although he was always so red in the face you could never tell if he was blushing), and did not give up his lying. As he grew older he began to get annoyed when caught out in a lie, and would resort to his fists; but if his listeners only laughed and said nothing he grew more and more expansive in his story-telling.

As far as his farming was concerned he was a practical and hard-working Cossack, in everything he acted sensibly, sometimes cunningly, but when the subject turned to his service in the Lifeguards—everyone simply threw up their hands and doubled up with laughter.

Avdeyich stood in the middle of the room, rocking on his heels. Glancing round the assembled Cossacks, he observed in his ponderous, bass voice:

"Speaking of service, these days the Cossacks aren't at all what they were. They're just shrimps, no size at all. You could crack any one of 'em in half just by sneezing at him. But . . ." and he smiled contemptuously, "I saw some Cossack skeletons once! Ah! They were Cossacks in those days!"

"Where did you dig the skeletons up, Avdeyich?" smooth-faced Anikushka asked, nudging his neighbour.

"Don't start telling any of your lies, Avdeyich, with the Holy Day so near," Pantelei said, wrinkling up his nose and tugging his ear-ring. He did not like Avdeyich's bragging habits.

"It isn't in my nature to lie, brother," Avdeyich replied firmly, and stared in astonishment at Anikushka, who was shaking as though with fever. "I saw these skeletons when we were building a house for my brother-in-law. As we were digging the foundation we came to a grave. So down here by the Don, next the church there must have been a cemetery in the old days."

"Well, what about the skeletons?" Pantelei asked impatiently, getting ready to go.

"Arms—that long." Avdeyich said extending both his rake-like arms. "Head as big as a cauldron—true as I live!"

"You'd better tell the youngsters how you caught a robber in St. Petersburg," Miron suggested, as he rose from the window-sill.

"There's nothing really to tell," Avdeyich replied, affected by a sudden attack of modesty.

"Tell us, tell us, Avdeyich!"

"Well, it was like this," Avdeyich cleared his throat and drew his tobacco pouch out of his trouser pocket. He replaced the two copper coins that had dropped out of the pouch, poured a pinch of tobacco on to his palm, and ran a beaming eye over his audience. "Some villain had escaped from prison. They looked for him all over the place, but do you think they could find him? They just couldn't. All the authorities were beaten.

"Well, one night the officer of the guard calls me to him: 'Go into the imperial palace,' he says. 'His Imperial Majesty wants to see you.' So in I went. I stood to attention, but he claps me on the shoulder and says: 'Listen!' he says, 'Ivan Avdeyich, the biggest villain in our kingdom has done a bunk. Find him, even if you have to stand on your head to do it. And don't let me see you till you have!' 'Very good, Your Imperial Majesty!' I says. Yes, lads, that was a facer. . . . So I took three of the best horses in the tsar's stables and set out."

Lighting a cigarette, Avdeyich surveyed the bowed heads of his listeners and, warming to his subject, boomed out of the cloud of smoke enveloping his face:

"I rode all day, and I rode all night, until on the third day I came up with the villain near Moscow. I clapped the bird into my coach, and hauled him back to St. Petersburg. I arrived at midnight, all covered with mud, and went straight to His Imperial Majesty himself. All sorts of counts and princes tried to stop me, but in I marched. Hm. . . . Well, I knocks at the door. 'May I come in, Your Imperial Majesty?' 'Who is it?' 'It's me,' I says, 'Ivan Avdeyich Sinilin.' I heard a noise in the room, and heard His Majesty himself cry out: 'Maria Fyodorovna, Maria Fyodorovna! Get up quick and get a samovar going. Ivan Avdeyich has arrived.' "

There was a roar of laughter from the Cossacks at the back of the crowd. The clerk, who had been reading a notice about stray cattle, stopped in the middle of a sentence, and the ataman stretched out his neck like a goose and stared hard at the guffawing crowd.

Avdeyich's face clouded and his eyes wandered uncertainly over the faces before him.

"Wait a bit!"

"Ha-ha-ha!"

"Oh, he'll be the death of us!"

" 'Get a samovar going! Avdeyich has arrived!' Ha-ha-ha!"

The assembly began to break up. A constant steady creaking rose from the frozen steps of the administration house. On the trampled snow outside Stepan Astakhov and a tall, long-shanked Cossack, the owner of the windmill, were wrestling to get themselves warm.

The Cossacks gathered round shouting advice.

"Throw him, the heathen!"

"Knock the stuffing out of him, Stepan!"

"Don't grab him there! Think you're clever!" old Kashulin shouted, hopping about like a sparrow; and in his excitement he failed to notice a large bright dewdrop hanging shyly from the tip of his bluish nose.

## VIII

When Pantelei returned from the meeting he went at once to the room which he and his wife occupied. Ilyinichna had been unwell for some days, and her puffy face reflected her weariness and pain. She lay propped up high on a plump feather bed with a pillow at her back. At the sound of Pantelei's footsteps she turned her head; her eyes rested on his breath-dampened beard and matted whiskers with the look of severity that had become a habit with her, and her nostrils twitched. But the old man smelled only of frost and sour sheepskin. "Sober today," she thought, and contentedly laid down her knitting-needles.

"Well, what about the wood-cutting?"

"They've decided to begin on Thursday." Pantelei stroked his moustache. "Thursday morning," he added, sitting down on a chest at the side of the bed. "Well, feeling any better?"

"Just the same. Shooting pains in all my joints."

"I told you not to go into the water, you fool. And in autumn too! You knew what would happen," Pantelei fumed, tracing broad circles on the floor with his stick. "There were plenty of other women to ret that hemp, curse the stuff . . . curse it all!"

"I couldn't let the hemp be wasted. There weren't any women. Grisha was out ploughing with his. Pyotr and Darya had gone off somewhere."

The old man blew into his cupped hands and bent towards the bed.

"And how's Natalya?"

There was a note of anxiety in Ilyinichna's voice as she replied:

"I don't know what to do. She was crying again the other day. I went out in the yard and found someone had left the barn door wide open. I went up to shut it, and there she was standing by the millet bin. I asked her what was the matter, but she said she only had a headache. I can't get the truth out of her."

"Maybe she's poorly?"

"I don't think so. Either someone's given her the evil eye, or else it's Grisha. . . ."

"He hasn't taken up again with that woman, by any chance?"

"Goodness, no! What a thing to say!" Ilyinichna exclaimed in alarm. "What do you take Stepan for—a fool? No, I haven't heard anything."

Pantelei sat with his wife a little longer, then went out. Grigory was in his room sharpening fishing hooks with a file. Natalya was smearing them with lard, and carefully wrapping each in a separate rag. As Pantelei limped by he stared at her inquisitively. Her sallow cheeks were flushed like an autumn leaf. She had grown noticeably thinner during the past month, and there was a new, wretched look in her eyes. The old man paused at the door.

"He's killing the girl!" he thought, as he glanced back at Natalya's smooth head bowed over the bench. Grigory sat near the window. His black tousled forelock jerked with every stroke of the file.

"Drop that, devil take you!" the old man shouted, turning livid in a sudden frenzy. Grigory looked up startled.

"I've got two more points to sharpen, Dad."

"Drop it, I tell you! Get ready for the wood-cutting. The sledges aren't ready at all, and you sit there sharpening hooks," he added more quietly, and lingered at the door, evidently wanting to say something else. But he went out. Grigory heard him giving vent to the rest of his anger on Pyotr.

As Grigory pulled on his coat, he heard his father shouting in the yard:

"Haven't you watered the cattle yet, you young lounger? And who's been meddling with that stack by the fence? Didn't I say it wasn't to be touched? You'll use up all the best hay, damn you, then what will you feed the bullocks on in spring?"

A good two hours before dawn on Thursday, Ilyinichna woke Darya: "Get up! Time to light the fire!"

Darya ran in her shift to the stove, found some matches and struck a light.

"Get a move on!" Pyotr nagged his wife, coughing as he lit a cigarette.

"They don't go and wake that Natalya up! Am I to tear myself in two?" Darya grumbled crossly, still only half-awake.

"Go and wake her up yourself," Pyotr advised her. But the advice was unnecessary, for Natalya was already up. Pulling on her blouse, she went out to get fuel for the fire.

"Fetch some kindling," her sister-in-law commanded.

"Tell Dunya to fetch the water, Darya, do you hear?" Ilyinichna called hoarsely, moving about the kitchen with difficulty.

The kitchen smelled of fresh hops, harness, and the warmth of human bodies. Darya shuffled about in her felt boots, rattling the pots; under her pink shift her small breasts quivered. Married life had not soured or withered her. Tall and slender, supple as a willow switch, she looked like a girl.

She walked with a twisting movement of the shoulders; she laughed at the shouts of her husband; a firm row of small close-set teeth showed under the fine rim of her shrewish lips.

"You ought to have brought some fuel-bricks in overnight. They would have dried in the stove," Ilyinichna grumbled.

"I forgot, Mother. It can't be helped," Darya answered.

Dawn broke before the meal was ready. Pantelei hurried over his breakfast,. blowing on the thin porridge. Grigory ate slowly and moodily, his jaw muscles working up and down, and Pyotr, unnoticed by his father, amused himself with teasing Dunya, who was suffering with toothache and had her face bound up.

The sound of sledge-runners was heard from the street. Bullock sledges were moving down to the river in the grey dawn. Grigory and Pyotr went out to harness their sledges. As he went Grigory wound a soft scarf, his wife's gift, around his neck, and gulped in the dry frosty air. A raven flew overhead with a full, throaty cry. The swish of its slowly flapping wings could be heard distinctly in the frosty stillness. Pyotr watched its flight and remarked:

"Flying south, to the warm."

Behind a rosy little cloud, as gay as a girlish smile, a tiny slip of moon gleamed dimly. The smoke from the chimneys rose in columns, reaching towards the inaccessibly distant, golden pointed blade of the waning moon:

The river was not quite frozen over opposite the Melekhovs' house. Along the edges of the stream the ice was firm and green under drifts of snow. But beyond the middle where springs flowed from the Black Bank, a gap in the ice yawned sombre and menacing out of the corroded whiteness. The water was freckled with the wild duck that were wintering there.

Pantelei drove off first with the old bullocks, leaving his sons to follow later. On the slope down to the river-crossing Pyotr and Grigory caught up with Anikushka. With a new axe handle sticking out of his sledge, and wearing a broad green sash he was walking at the side of his bullocks, while his wife, a stunted sickly woman, held the reins.

"Hullo, neighbour, surely you're not taking your woman with you?" Pyotr shouted to him.

Anikushka, hopping up and down to keep warm, grinned and went over to the brothers.

"Yes, I am, to keep me warm."

"You'll get no warmth from her, she's too lean."

"That's true; and I feed her with oats, but still she doesn't fatten!"

"Shall we be cutting in the same strip?" Grigory asked, jumping off the sledge.

"Yes, if you'll give me a smoke."

"You've always been a scrounger, Anikushka."

"The sweetest things in life are begged and stolen," Anikushka chuckled, wrinkling his hairless womanish face in a smile.

249

The three drove on together. The forest was laced with rime, and of a virgin whiteness. Anikushka rode in front, lashing his whip against the branches overhead. The needle-sharp snow crystals showered down on his wife.

"Don't play about, you devil!" she shouted at him, as she shook the snow off.

"Drop her into the snow head first," Pyotr advised trying to get his whip under the bullock's belly to speed its pace.

At a turn of the road they met Stepan Astakhov driving two yoked bullocks back towards the village. The leather soles of his felt boots squeaked on the snow as he strode along. His curly forelock hung below his fur cap like a bunch of white grapes.

"Hey, Stepan, lost your way?" Anikushka shouted as he passed.

"Lost my way be damned! We swung over, and the sledge snapped its runner on a stump. So I've got to go back." Stepan cursed obscenely and his fierce light eyes narrowed insolently as he passed Pyotr.

"Left your sledge behind?" Anikushka asked, turning round.

Ignoring the remark, Stepan cracked his whip at the bullocks that were heading away from the track and gave Grigory a long hard stare as he passed on. A little farther on the group came to a sledge abandoned in the middle of the road. Aksinya was standing by it. Holding down the edge of her sheepskin with her left hand, she was gazing along the road in their direction.

"Out of the way or I'll run you over. Oho, you're the wife for me!" Anikushka roared. Aksinya stepped aside with a smile, and sat down on the overturned sledge.

"You've got your own wife with you."

"Yes, she sticks to me like a burr on a pig's tail, otherwise I'd give you a lift."

"Thank you kindly."

As Pyotr came up to her he gave a quick glance back at Grigory. Grigory was smiling uncertainly, anxiety and expectation expressed in all his movements.

"Good health to you, neighbour," Pyotr greeted her, touching his cap with his mitten.

"Praise be."

"What, sledge broken?" Pyotr asked.

"Yes, it is," she replied slowly without looking at Pyotr, and rising to her feet, turned towards Grigory. "Grigory Panteleyevich, I'd like a word with you," she said as he came up.

Asking Pyotr to look after his bullocks for a moment, Grigory turned to her. Pyotr laughed suggestively, and drove on.

The two stood silently regarding each other. Aksinya glanced cautiously around, then turned her liquid black eyes again to Grigory's face. Shame and joy flamed in her cheeks and dried her lips. Her breath came in sharp gasps.

At a turn in the road Anikushka and Pyotr disappeared behind the brown oak trunks.

Grigory looked straight into Aksinya's eyes and saw in them a spark of stubborn recklessness.

"Well, Grisha, do as you please, but I can't live without you," she said firmly, and pressed her lips together waiting for his answer.

Grigory made no reply. The forest was locked in silence. A glassy emptiness rang in his ears. The surface of the road, polished smooth by sledge-runners, the grey rag of sky, the forest, dumb, deathly drowsy.... A sudden cry of a raven near by seemed to rouse Grigory from his momentary lethargy. He raised his head and watched the bird winging away in silent flight. He was surprised when he heard himself say:

"It's going to be warm. He's making for the warm." He seemed to shake himself and laughed hoarsely. "Well...." He turned his intoxicated eyes furtively on Aksinya, and suddenly snatched her to him.

## IX

During the winter evenings a little group
of villagers gathered in Stockman's room at Lukeshka's house. There were Christonya, and
Knave from the mill, a greasy jacket draped
over his shoulders, the ever-smiling David (now
three months a loafer), the engineman, Ivan
Alexeyevich Kotlyarov, sometimes Filka the
cobbler, and always Misha Koshevoi, a young
Cossack who had not yet done his regular army
service.

At first the group played cards. Then Stockman casually brought out a book of Nekrasov's
poetry. They began to read the volume aloud,
and liked it. Then they went on to Nikitin, and
about Christmas-time Stockman suggested the
reading of a dog-eared, unbound booklet.
Koshevoi, who had been to the church school
and could read aloud, glanced contemptuously
at the greasy pages.

"You could make noodles of it, it's so
greasy," he said in disgust.

Christonya roared with laughter; David
smiled dazzlingly. But Stockman waited for
the merriment to die away, and then said:

"Read it, Misha. It's interesting. It's all
about the Cossacks."

Bending his head over the table, Koshevoi spelt out laboriously:

"*A Short History of the Don Cossacks*," and then glanced around expectantly.

"Read it!" Kotlyarov said.

They laboured through the book for three evenings, reading about the free life of the past, about Pugachov, Stenka Razin and Kondraty Bulavin. Finally they came down to recent times. The unknown author poured scorn on the Cossacks' miserable existence; scoffed at the authorities and the system, the tsar's government and the Cossackry itself which had hired itself out to the monarchs as their henchmen. The listeners grew excited and began to quarrel among themselves. Christonya, his head touching the roof-beam, spoke up in his booming voice. Stockman sat at the door, smoking a pipe, his eyes smiling.

"He's right! It's all true!" Christonya burst out.

"It's not our fault such shame was brought upon the Cossacks." Koshevoi spread his arms in perplexity and puckered up his handsome face.

He was thick-set, broad in the shoulders and hips, almost square. From the cast-iron foundation of his body rose a firm brick-red neck on which his small, gracefully set head looked strange, with its effeminately soft cheeks, small obstinate mouth and dark eyes under the golden slab of curly hair.

The engineman Kotlyarov, a tall thin Cossack, was steeped to the bone in Cossack traditions, and his round protruding eyes flashed as he vigorously defended the Cossacks:

"You're a muzhik, Christonya, you've only got a drop of Cossack blood in you to a bucketful of water. Your mother was mated with a muzhik from Voronezh."

"You're a fool, you're a fool, brother!" Christonya boomed. "I stand for the truth."

"I wasn't in the Lifeguards," Kotlyarov said slyly. "They're all fools there."

"There are some pretty hopeless cases in the rest of the army too."

"Shut up, muzhik!"

"And aren't the muzhiks just as much men as you?"

"They're muzhiks, they're made of bast and stuffed with brushwood."

"When I was serving in Petersburg, brother, I saw many things," Christonya said, his southern accent coming out strongly. "Once it happened that we were on guard at the tsar's palace, inside and outside. We used to ride round the walls on horseback, two this way and two that. When we met we used to ask:

'All quiet, no disorders anywhere?' and then we'd ride on. We weren't allowed to stop and talk. And they chose us for our looks. When we had to take our turn on guard at the doors they'd choose each pair so as they should be alike in their faces and their figures. Once the barber even had to dye my beard because of this stupidity. I had to take a turn at guard with a Cossack in our squadron with hair that was a kind of bay colour. Plagued if I know how he got like it, must have been scorched by a fire or something. They searched all through the regiment and there wasn't another like him. So the troop commander sent me to the barber to have my beard dyed. When I looked in the glass afterwards my heart almost broke. I looked as if I was on fire. Honestly I did. Made my fingers sizzle to touch the thing!"

"Now he's off, the old windbag. But what were we talking about?" Kotlyarov interrupted him.

"About the people."

"Well, tell us about them. What the blithering hell do we want to hear about your beard for!"

"Well, as I was saying—I once had to take a turn on guard outside. We were riding along, me and my comrade, when a mob of students came running round the corner. Thick as flies they were! As soon as they saw us they roared: Hah!' and then again: 'Hah!' And before we knew where we were they had surrounded us. 'What are you riding about for, Cossacks?' they asked. And I said: 'We're keeping guard, and you let go those reins, young fella'' and clapped my hands on my sword. 'Don't get me wrong, Cossack, I'm from Kamenskaya District myself, and I'm studying in the uniservity, or the univorsity, or whatever you call it, one said. We make to ride on, and one fellow with a big nose pulls out a ten-ruble piece and says: 'Drink to the health of my dead father.' And then he pulls a picture out of his pocket. 'Look, that's my father,' he says, 'take it as a keepsake.' Well, we took it, we couldn't refuse. And they went off again. Just then a lieutenant comes riding out of the back gates of the palace with a troop of men. 'What's happened?' he shouts. And I tell him students had come and begun talking to us, and we had wanted to sabre them according to instructions, but as they had set us free we had ridden off. When we went off duty later, we told the corporal we'd earned ten rubles and wanted to drink them to the memory of the old man, showing him the picture. In the evening the corporal brought some vodka, and we had a good time

for a couple of days. But afterwards we found
out what the trick was. It turned out that this
student, the young bastard, had given us a
picture of the biggest trouble-maker in Germany. I had hung it over my bed; he had a
grey beard and looked a decent sort of chap.
But the lieutenant saw it and asked: 'Where
did you get that picture from, you son of a
gun?' So I told him, and he began swearing
at me and punching me in the face: 'Do you
know who that is? He's their ataman Karl. . . .'
Drat it, I've forgotten his name. Now, what
was it. . . ?"

"Karl Marx?" Stockman suggested with a
broad smile.

"That's it, Karl Mars," Christonya exclaimed
joyfully. "He got me into trouble all right.
Why, sometimes the tsarevich Alexei and his
tutors used to come into the guardroom. They
might have seen it. What would have happened
then?"

"And you keep praising the muzhiks. What
a trick they played on you," Kotlyarov
chuckled.

"But we drank the ten rubles. It was the
bearded Karl we drank to, but we drank all
the same!"

"He deserves to be drunk to," Stockman
smiled, playing with his cigarette-holder.

"Why, what good did he do?" Koshevoi queried.

"I'll tell you another time, it's getting late now." Stockman held the holder between his fingers, and ejected the dead cigarette-end with a slap from the other hand.

After long sifting and testing, a little group of ten Cossacks began to meet regularly in Stockman's workshop. Stockman was the heart and soul of the group and he worked straight towards a goal that only he fully understood. He ate into the simple understandings and conceptions like a worm into wood, instilling repugnance and hatred towards the existing system. At first he found himself confronted with the cold steel of distrust, but he was not to be repulsed. Even that could be worn away.

## X

On the sandy slope of the left bank of the Don lies Vyeshenskaya stanitsa, the most ancient stanitsa of the upper Don. Originally called Chigonaki, it was moved to a new site after being sacked during the reign of Peter the First, and renamed Vyeshenskaya. It was formerly an important link along the great water-way from Voronezh to Azov.

Opposite Vyeshenskaya the Don bends like

a Tatar bow, turns sharply to the right, and by the little village of Bazki majestically straightens again, carries its greenish-blue waters over the chalky base of the hills on the west bank, then, with thickly-clustered villages on the right and occasional stanitsas on the left, down to the sea, to the blue Sea of Azov.

At Ust-Khoperskaya it joins with its tributary the Khoper, and at Ust-Medveditskaya, with the Medveditsa, and then it flows on deep and full-watered amid a riotous growth of populous villages and stanitsas.

The stanitsa of Vyeshenskaya stands among yellow sand-drifts. It is a bald cheerless place without orchards. In the square stands an old church, grey with age, and six streets run out of the square in lines parallel with the river. Where the Don bends towards Bazki, a lake, about as wide as the Don in the dry season, branches off into a thicket of poplars. The far end of Vyeshenskaya slopes down to this lake, and in a smaller square, overgrown with golden prickly thorn, is a second church, with green cupolas and green roof, matching the green of the poplars on the other side of the lake.

Beyond the village to the north stretches a saffron waste of sands, a stunted pine plantation, and creeks whose water is pink from the red-clay soil. Here and there in the sandy wilderness are rare oases of villages, meadow-land, and a rusty scrub of willows.

One Sunday in December a dense crowd of five hundred young Cossacks from all the villages in the district was assembled in the square outside the old church. Mass ended, the senior sergeant, a gallant old Cossack with long-service decorations, gave an order, and the youngsters drew up in two long straggling ranks. Sergeants rushed to and fro to get them dressed off.

"Ranks!" the sergeant boomed and making a vague gesture with his hand, snapped: "Form fours."

The ataman entered the churchyard, dressed according to form and wearing a new officer's greatcoat, his spurs jingling, and followed by the military policeman.

Grigory Melekhov who was standing next to Mitka Korshunov heard him whisper:

"My boot pinches like hell."

"Stick it out, they'll make you an ata-man."

"We'll be going inside soon."

As if to confirm this, the senior sergeant fell back a pace or two, turned sharply on his heels and shouted:

"Right turn. Forward march!"

The column filed through the wide-open

gate, and the church dome rang with the sound of tramping feet.

Grigory paid no attention to the words of the oath of allegiance being read by the priest. By his side stood Mitka Korshunov, his face contorted with the pain of his tight new boots. Grigory's upraised arm grew numb, an aching jumble of thoughts was running through his mind. As he came up to the crucifix and kissed the silver, damp with the moisture of many lips, he thought of Aksinya, and of his wife With the suddenness of a flash of forked lightning he had a vision of the forest, its brown trunks and branches fluffed with white down, and the humid gleam of Aksinya's black eyes under her kerchief. . . .

When the ceremony was ended they were marched out into the square and were again drawn up in ranks. Blowing his nose and stealthily wiping his fingers on the lining of his coat, the sergeant addressed them:

"You're not boys any longer now, you're Cossacks. You've taken the oath and you ought to understand what's what. You've grown up into Cossacks and you've got to guard your honour, obey your fathers and mothers and all the rest of it. You were boys once, you've had your fun and games—used to play tipcat in the road, I expect—but now you must think about

your future service. In a year's time they'll be
calling you up into the army. . . ." Here the
sergeant blew his nose again, shook his hand
clean and, drawing on his rabbit's down gloves,
ended: "And your fathers and mothers must
think about getting you your equipment. They
must fit you out with an army horse, and . . .
in general. . . . And now, home you go and God
be with you, my lads.'

Grigory and Mitka joined up with the rest
of the lads from their village, and they set off
together for home.

They walked back along the Don. The smoke
of cottage stoves hung in wisps over the village
of Bazki, and bells were ringing faintly. Mitka
limped along behind the others, leaning on a
knotty stake that he had broken out of a fence.

"Take your boot off," one of the lads advised.

"I'll get my foot frost-bitten," Mitka replied
hesitantly.

"You can keep your sock on."

Mitka sat down on the snow and tugged off
his boot. Then he walked on, stepping heavily
on his stockinged foot. The thick knitted stocking made a sharp imprint in the crisp snow.

"What road shall we take?" the stumpy
shock-headed Alexei Beshnyak asked.

"Along the Don," Grigory answered for
them all.

They walked on, talking and jostling one another off the road. Each of them was pulled over by the others, who piled on top of him. Between Bazki and Gromkovsky Mitka was the first to spot a wolf crossing the Don.

"Look, lads, there's a wolf!"

The young Cossacks started shouting and catcalling and the wolf loped off, then halted, standing sideways, not far from the opposite bank.

"Catch him!"

"Yah!"

"It's you he's looking at, Mitka, walking in your sock."

"What a fat neck he's got!"

"Look, there he goes!"

The grey form stood stiffly for a moment, as though carved out of granite, then took a hurried leap and slunk away into the willows girding the bank.

It was dusk when they reached the village. Grigory made his way along the ice to the path that led up to his home. A disused sledge stood in the yard; in a heap of brushwood piled near the fence the sparrows were twittering. He felt the smell of habitation, of charred soot, and the steamy odour of the stables.

Grigory went up the steps of the house and glanced in at the window. The hanging lamp

shed a dim yellow glow through the room.
Pyotr was standing in its light with his back
to the window. Grigory brushed the snow off
his boots with the besom at the door, and
entered the kitchen amid a flurry of steam.

"Well, I'm back."

"You've been quick. You got frozen, I expect," Pyotr replied in an anxious and hurried
tone.

Pantelei was sitting with his head bowed in
his hands, his elbows on his knees. Darya was
spinning at the droning spinning-wheel. Natalya was standing at the table with her back to
Grigory, and did not turn round on his entry.
Glancing hastily around the kitchen Grigory
rested his eyes on Pyotr. His brother's agitatedly expectant face told him that something
was amiss.

"Taken the oath?"

"Uh-huh."

Grigory took off his outdoor clothes slowly,
playing for time, and turning over in his mind
all the possibilities which might have led to
this chilly and silent welcome. Ilyinichna came
out of the best room, her face expressing her
agitation.

"It's Natalya!" Grigory thought, as he sat
down on the bench beside his father.

"Get him some supper," his mother said to

Darya, indicating Grigory with her eyes. Darya stopped in the middle of her spinning-song, and went to the stove, her girlish figure swaying from the waist. The kitchen was engulfed in a silence broken only by the heavy breathing of a goat and its newly-born kid.

As Grigory sipped his soup he glanced at Natalya. But he could not see her face. She was sitting sideways to him, her head bent over her knitting-needles. Pantelei was the first to be provoked into speech by the general silence. Coughing artificially, he said:

"Natalya is talking about going back to her parents."

Grigory pressed some bread-crumbs into a ball, and said nothing.

"And why's that?" his father asked, his lower lip quivering: the first sign of a coming outburst of frenzy.

"I don't know," Grigory replied as he rose and crossed himself.

"But I know!" his father raised his voice.

"Don't shout, don't shout!" Ilyinichna interposed.

"Yes, there's no cause for shouting." Pyotr moved from the window to the middle of the room. "It's up to her. If she wants to stay, she can stay; if she doesn't, well ... God be with her!"

"I'm not blaming her. Of course it's a disgrace and a sin before God to leave your husband, but I don't blame her. It's not her fault, but that son of a bitch's." Pantelei pointed to Grigory who was warming himself at the stove.

"Who have I done wrong?" Grigory asked.

"You don't know? You don't know, you devil?"

"No, I don't."

Pantelei jumped up, overturning the bench, and went close up to Grigory. Natalya dropped her stocking and the needles clattered to the floor. At the sound a kitten jumped down from the stove and, with its head on one side and paw curved, began to pat the ball of wool towards the chest.

"What I say to you is this," the old man began slowly and deliberately. "If you won't live with Natalya, you can clear out of this house and go wherever your feet will carry you. That's what I say to you. Go where your feet will carry you," he repeated in a calm voice, and turned and picked up the bench.

Dunya sat on the bed, her round frightened eyes darting from one to the other.

"I don't say this in anger, Dad," Grigory's voice was jarringly hollow. "I didn't marry of my own choice, it was you who married me off. As for Natalya, I'm not stopping her. She can go to her father, if she wants to."

"You clear out yourself."

"I will!"

"Go to the devil!"

"I'm going. I'm going, don't be in a hurry." Grigory reached for the sleeve of his short fur coat lying on the bed, his nostrils dilated, his whole body quivering with a boiling anger that was just like his father's. The same mingled Turkish and Cossack blood flowed in their veins, and at that moment their resemblance to each other was extraordinary.

"Where are you going?" Ilyinichna groaned, seizing Grigory's arm. But he pushed her away forcibly and snatched up his fur cap.

"Let him go, the sinful swine! Let him go, curse him! Go on, go! Clear out!" the old man thundered throwing the door wide open.

Grigory ran out on to the steps, and the last sound he heard was Natalya's loud uncontrollable weeping.

The frosty night held the village in its grip, prickly snow was falling from the black sky, the cracking of the ice on the Don resounded like cannon shots. Grigory ran panting out of the gate. At the far end of the village dogs were barking discordantly, and yellow points of light shone through the frosty haze.

He walked aimlessly down the street. The blackness of the Astakhovs' windows gleamed with the brilliance of a diamond.

"Grisha!" he heard Natalya's yearning cry from the gate.

"You go to hell!" Grigory grated his teeth and hastened his steps.

"Grisha, come back!"

He stumbled drunkenly into the first cross-lane, and for the last time heard her distant, anguished cry:

"Grisha, darling...."

He swiftly crossed the square and stopped at a fork in the road, wondering where to spend the night. He decided on Misha Koshevoi. Misha lived with his mother, sister and two little brothers in a lonely straw-thatched house right by the hill. Grigory entered their yard and knocked at the tiny window.

"Who is it?"

"Is Misha there?"

"Yes, who is it wants him?"

"It's me, Grigory Melekhov."

After a moment, Misha, awakened from his first sleep, opened the door.

"You, Grisha?"

"Me."

"What do you want at this time of night?"

"Let me in, we'll talk inside."

In the passage, Grigory gripped Misha's elbow and cursing himself for being unable to find the right words, whispered: "I want to spend the night with you. I've fallen out with my people. Have you got room for me? Anywhere will do."

"We'll fix you up somewhere. What's the row about?"

"I'll tell you later.... Where's the door here? I can't see it."

They made Grigory a bed on the bench. He lay thinking, his head tucked under his sheepskin so as not to hear the whispering of Misha's mother, who slept in the same bed as her daughter. What was happening at home now, he wondered. Would Natalya go back to her father or not? Well, life had taken a new turn. Where should he go? And the answer came swiftly. He would send for Aksinya tomorrow, and go with her to the Kuban, far away from here ... far, far away....

Rolling steppeland, villages, stanitsas, unknown, unloved, floated before Grigory's closed eyes. And beyond the rolling hills, beyond the long grey road lay a welcoming land of blue skies, a fairy-tale land with Aksinya's love, in all its rebellious late-flowering strength, to make it the more attractive.

His sleep was troubled by the approaching unknown. Before he finally dozed off he tried hard to recall what it was that oppressed him. In his drowsy state his thoughts would flow easily and smoothly, like a boat going downstream, then suddenly they would come up against something, as though the boat had struck a sandbank. He wrestled with the baffling obstacle. What was it that lay in his path?

In the morning he awoke and at once remembered what it was—his army service! How could he go away with Aksinya? In the spring there was the training camp, and in the autumn the army draft.

He had some breakfast, and called Misha out into the passage.

"Misha, go to the Astakhovs for me, will you?" he said. "Tell Aksinya to come to the windmill this evening after dark."

"But what about Stepan?" Misha said hesitantly.

"Say you've come on some business or other."

"All right, I'll go."

"Tell her to be sure to come."

"Oh, all right."

In the evening Grigory went to the mill and sat there smoking, hiding the cigarette in his cuff. Beyond the mill the wind was stumbling over withered maize stalks. A scrap of torn canvas flapped on the chained and motionless sail. It sounded like a great bird flapping round the mill, unable to fly away. Aksinya did not appear. The sun had set in the west in a fading, gilded lilac, from the east the wind began to blow freshly; darkness was overtaking the moon stranded among the willows. Above the windmill the ruddy, blue-streaked sky was deathly dark; the last sounds of busy day hovered over the village.

He smoked three cigarettes in succession, thrust the last end into the trodden snow, and gazed round in anxious irritation. Half-thawed cart-tracks from the mill to the village showed darkly in the snow. There was no one in sight. He rose, stretched himself, and moved towards the light twinkling invitingly in Misha's window. He was approaching the yard, whistling through his teeth, when he stumbled into Aksinya. She had evidently been running: she was out of breath, and the faint scent of the winter wind, or perhaps of fresh steppe hay, came from her fresh cold mouth.

"I waited and waited, I thought you weren't coming."

"I had to get rid of Stepan."

"You've made me frozen, you wretch!"

"I'm hot, I'll warm you." She flung open her wool-lined coat and wrapped herself round Grigory like hops round an oak.

"Why did you send for me?"

"Take your arms away, somebody may pass."

"You haven't quarrelled with your people, have you?"

"I've left them. I spent the night with Misha. I'm a homeless dog now."

"What will you do now?" Aksinya relaxed the grip of her arms and drew her coat tight with a shiver. "Let's go over to the fence, Grisha. We can't stand here in the middle of the road."

They turned off the road, and Grigory, sweeping away the drift-snow, leaned against the frosty crackling wattle fence.

"You don't know whether Natalya has gone home, do you?"

"I don't. . . . She'll go, I expect. How can she stay here?"

Grigory slipped Aksinya's frozen hand up the sleeve of his coat, and squeezing her slender wrist, he said:

"And what about us?"

"I don't know, dear. Whatever you think best."

"Will you leave Stepan?"

"Without a sigh. This evening, if you like."

"And we'll find work somewhere, and live somehow."

"They can put me in the shafts as long as I'm with you, Grisha. Anything to be with you."

They stood close together, each warming the other. Grigory did not want to stir; he stood facing into the wind, his nostrils quivering, his eyelids closed. Aksinya, her face pressed into his armpit, breathed in the familiar, intoxicating scent of his sweat; and on her shamelessly avid lips, hidden from Grigory's eyes, trembled a joyous smile of happiness fulfilled.

"Tomorrow I'll go and see Mokhov. He may be able to give me work," Grigory said, shifting his grip on Aksinya's wrist, which had grown damp with perspiration under his fingers. Aksinya did not speak, nor did she raise her head. The smile slipped like a dying wind from her face, and the anxiety and fear lurking in her dilated eyes gave them the look of a frightened animal. "Shall I tell him or not?" she thought, as she remembered that she was pregnant. "I must tell him," she decided, but immediately, trembling with fear, she drove away the terrible thought. With a woman's instinct she sensed that this was not the moment to tell him; she realized that she might lose Grigory for ever; and uncertain whether the child leaping beneath her heart was Grigory's or Stepan's, she deceived her conscience, and did not tell him.

"Why are you trembling? Are you cold?" Grigory asked, wrapping his coat about her.

"I am a little. . . . I must go, Grisha. Stepan will come back and find me away."

"Where's he gone?"

"To Anikei's to play cards."

They parted. The agitating scent of her lips remained on Grigory's lips; the scent of the winter wind, or perhaps that faint, faraway scent that comes from the hay after a spring shower in the steppe.

Aksinya turned into a by-way; bending low, she almost ran. By a well, where the cattle had churned up the autumn mud, she stumbled awkwardly, her foot slipping on a frozen clod; and feeling a lacerating pain in her belly she caught at the fence. The pain died away, but in her side something living, moving, beat angrily and strongly time and again.

## XI

Next morning Grigory went to see Mokhov. Mokhov had just returned from the shop and was sitting with Atyopin in the dining-room with its rich oak-coloured wall-paper, sipping strong, claret-coloured tea. Grigory left his cap in the hall and went in.

"I'd like to have a word with you, Sergei Platonovich."

"Ah, Pantelei Melekhov's son, isn't it? What do you want?"

"I've come to ask whether you could give me a job."

As Grigory spoke the door creaked, and a young officer in a khaki tunic with a lieutenant's epaulettes entered. Grigory recognized him as the young Listnitsky whom Mitka Korshunov had outraced the previous summer. Mokhov moved a chair up for the officer, and turned back to Grigory.

"Has your father come down in the world, that he is putting his son out to work?" he inquired.

"I'm not living with him any more."

"Left him?"

"Yes."

"Well, I'd gladly take you on. I know your family to be a hard-working lot, but I'm afraid I haven't any work for you to do."

"What's the matter?" Listnitsky inquired, pulling his chair up to the table.

"This lad is looking for work."

"Can you look after horses? Can you drive a team?" the officer asked as he stirred his tea.

"I can. I've had the care of our own six horses."

"I want a coachman. What are your terms?"

"I'm not asking for much."

"In that case come to my father at our estate tomorrow. You know the house? At Yagodnoye, about twelve versts from here."

"Yes, I know it."

"Then come tomorrow morning and we shall settle the matter."

Grigory went to the door. As he turned the handle he hesitated, and said: "I'd like to have a word with you in private, Your Honour."

Listnitsky followed Grigory out into the semi-darkness of the passage. A rosy light filtered dimly through the Venetian glass of the door leading to the balcony.

"Well, what is it?"

"I'm not alone...." Grigory flushed darkly. "I've got a woman with me.... Perhaps you can find something for her to do?"

"Your wife?" Listnitsky inquired, smiling and raising his eyebrows.

"Someone else's."

"Oh, I see. All right, we'll fix her up as cook for the servants. But where is her husband?"

"Here in the village."

"So you've stolen another man's wife?"

"She wanted to come."

"A romantic affair! Well, come along tomorrow. You may go now."

Grigory arrived at Yagodnoye at about eight the next morning. The house was surrounded by a peeling brick and plaster wall. Outbuildings straggled over the big yard: a wing with a tiled roof, the date 1910 picked out with tiles of a different colour; the servants' quarters, a bath-house, stables, poultry-house and cattle-shed, a long barn and coach-house.

The house was large and old, and nestled in an orchard. Beyond it rose a grey wall of bare poplars and the meadow willows, empty rooks' nests swinging in their brown tops.

As he entered the yard Grigory was welcomed by a pack of Crimean borzois. An old bitch, rheumy-eyed and lame, was the first to sniff at him and follow him with drooping head. In the servants' quarters a cook was quarrelling with a young, freckled maid. A thick-lipped old gaffer was sitting in a cloud of tobacco smoke on the door-step. The maid conducted Grigory to the house. The hall reeked of dogs and uncured pelts. On a table lay the case of a double-barrelled gun and a game-bag with a frayed green silk fringe.

"The young master will see you," the maid called to Grigory through a side door.

Grigory glanced apprehensively at his muddy

boots, and entered. Listnitsky was lying on a bed next to the window. On the eider-down was a box containing tobacco and smoking utensils. The officer made himself a cigarette, buttoned up the collar of his white shirt, and remarked:

"You're in good time. Wait, my father will be here in a minute."

Grigory stood by the door. Presently he heard the sound of footsteps in the ante-room, and a deep bass voice asked through the door: "Are you asleep, Yevgeny?"

"Come in."

An old man wearing black Caucasian felt boots entered. Grigory gave him a sideways glance. He was immediately struck by the thin crooked nose and the white arch of his moustache, stained yellow by tobacco under the nose. Old Listnitsky was tall and broad-shouldered, but gaunt. He wore a long camel-hair tunic that hung loosely, the collar encircling his brown wrinkled neck like a noose. His faded eyes were set close to the bridge of his nose.

"Papa, here's the coachman I spoke to you about. The lad's from a decent family."

"Whose son is he?" the old man asked in a booming voice.

"Melekhov's."

"Which Melekhov's?"

"Pantelei Melekhov's."

279

"I knew Prokofy, I remember Pantelei too. Lame, isn't he?"

"Yes, Your Excellency," Grigory replied, coming stiffly to attention. He recalled his father's stories of the retired General Listnitsky, a hero of the Russo-Turkish war.

"Why are you seeking work?" the old man inquired.

"I'm not living with my father, Your Excellency."

"What sort of Cossack will you make if you hire yourself out? Didn't your father provide for you when you left him?"

"No, Your Excellency."

"Hm, that's another matter. You want work for your wife as well?"

The younger Listnitsky's bed creaked heavily. Grigory, glancing in his direction, saw the officer winking and nodding his head.

"That's right, Your Excellency."

"None of your 'excellencies.' I don't like them. Your wage will be eight rubles a month. For both of you. Your wife will cook for the servants and seasonal workers. Is that satisfactory?"

"Yes."

"Move in tomorrow morning. You'll occupy the previous coachman's quarters."

"How did the hunting go yesterday?" List-

280

nitsky asked his father, lowering his narrow feet on to the carpet.

"We started a fox out of the gully at Gremyachy and chased it as far as the woods, but it was an old one and fooled the dogs."

"Is Kazbek still limping?"

"He must have sprained his foot. Hurry up, Yevgeny, breakfast is getting cold."

The old man turned to Grigory and snapped his bony fingers.

"Quick march! Be here at eight."

Grigory went out. On the far side of the barn the borzois were sunning themselves on a patch of ground bare of snow. The old bitch with the rheumy eyes trotted up to Grigory, sniffed at him from behind and followed him a little way with head still drooping mournfully, then turned back.

## XII

Aksinya had finished her cooking early. She banked up the fire, washed the dishes, and glanced out of the window looking on to the yard. Stepan was standing by the wood-pile close to the fence bordering on the Melekhovs' yard. A half-smoked cigarette hung from the corner of his firm lips. The left-hand corner of the shed was tumbling down, and he was selecting posts suitable for its repair.

Aksinya had arisen with two rosy blushes in her cheeks and a youthful glitter in her eyes. Stepan noticed the change, and as he was having breakfast he could not forbear to ask: "What's happened to you?"

"What's happened?" Aksinya echoed him, flushing.

"Your face is shining as though you had smeared yourself with oil."

"It's the heat of the fire." And turning away she glanced stealthily out of the window to see whether Misha Koshevoi's sister was coming.

But the girl did not arrive until late in the afternoon. Tormented with waiting, Aksinya started up:

"Do you want me, Mashutka?"

"Come out for a moment."

Stepan was standing before a scrap of mirror fixed into the whitewashed stove, combing his forelock and chestnut moustache with a stumpy ox-horn comb. Aksinya looked at him nervously.

"You aren't going out, are you?"

He did not answer immediately, but put the comb into his trouser pocket, and picked up a pack of cards and his tobacco pouch which were lying on the stove ledge. Then he said: "I'm going along to Anikushka's for a while."

"And when are you ever at home? You spend every night at cards. And all night, too."

"All right, I've heard that before."

"Are you going to play pontoon again?"

"Oh, drop it, Aksinya. Look, there's someone coming to see you."

Aksinya sidled out into the passage. The freckled, rosy-faced Mashutka welcomed her with a smile.

"Grisha's back."

"Well?"

"He told me to tell you to come along to our house as soon as it's dark."

Seizing the girl's hand, Aksinya drew her towards the outer door.

"Softer, softer, dear! Did he tell you to say anything else?"

"He said you're to get your things together and take them along."

Burning and trembling, unable to keep her feet still, Aksinya turned and glanced at the kitchen door.

"Lord, how am I to. . . . So quickly? Well . . . wait. Tell him I'll be along as soon as I can. But where will he meet me?"

"You're to come to our house."

"Oh, no!"

"All right, I'll tell him to come out and wait for you."

Stepan was drawing on his coat as Aksinya went in.

"What did she want?" he asked between two puffs at a cigarette.

"Who?"

"The Koshevois' girl."

"Oh, she came to ask me to cut out a skirt for her."

Blowing the ash off his cigarette, Stepan went to the door.

"Don't wait up for me," he said as he went out.

Aksinya ran to the frosted  window  and dropped to her knees before the bench. Stepan's footsteps sounded along the path trodden out in the snow to the gate. The wind caught a spark from his cigarette and  carried it back  to the window. Through the melted circle of glass Aksinya caught a glimpse of his fur cap and the outline of his swarthy cheek.

Feverishly she turned jackets, skirts and kerchiefs—her dowry—out of the great chest and threw them into a large shawl. Panting and wild-eyed, she passed through the kitchen for the last time, and putting out the light, ran on to the steps. Someone emerged from the Melekhovs' house to see to the cattle. She waited until the footsteps had died away, fastened the door by the chain, then ran down to the Don. Strands of hair escaped from her kerchief and tickled her cheeks, and as she made her way by side lanes to the Koshevois' hut, clutching her bundle, her strength ebbed and her feet dragged leadenly. Grigory was waiting for her at the gate. He took the bundle and silently led the way into the steppe.

Beyond the threshing-floor Aksinya slowed her pace and caught at Grigory's sleeve. "Wait a moment," she said.

"What for? The moon will be late tonight, we must hurry."

"Wait, Grisha!" She halted, doubled up with pain.

"What's the matter?" Grigory turned back to her.

"Something ... inside me. I must have lifted something heavy." She licked her dry lips, screwing up her eyes in pain till she saw pinpoints of fire, and clutched at her belly. She stood a moment, bowed and miserable, and then, poking her hair under her kerchief, set off again.

"I'm all right now, come along."

"You haven't even asked where I'm taking you to. I might be leading you to the nearest cliff to push you over," Grigory said smiling in the darkness.

"It's all the same to me now. I can't go back." Her voice trembled with an unhappy laugh.

That night Stepan returned at midnight as

usual. He went first to the stable, threw the scattered hay back into the manger, removed the horse's halter, then went to the house. "She must have gone out for the evening," he thought, as he unfastened the chain. He entered the kitchen, closed the door fast, and struck a match. He had been in a winning vein that evening, and so was quiet and drowsy. He lit the lamp, and gaped at the disorder of the kitchen, not guessing the reason. A little astonished, he went into the best room. The open chest yawned blackly. On the floor lay an old jacket which Aksinya had forgotten in her hurry. Stepan tore off his sheepskin and ran back to the kitchen for the light. He stared around the best room, and at last he understood. He dropped the lamp, and, scarcely aware of what he was doing, tore his sabre from the wall, gripped the hilt until the veins swelled in his fingers, raised Aksinya's blue and yellow jacket on its point, threw the jacket up in the air and with a short swing of the sabre slashed it in two as it fell.

Grey, savage in his wolfish grief, he threw the pieces of the old jacket up to the ceiling again and again; the sharp steel whistled as it cut them in their flight.

Then, tearing off the sword-knot, he threw the sabre into a corner, went into the kitchen, and sat down at the table. His head bowed, with trembling iron fingers he sat stroking the unwashed table-top.

## XIII

Troubles never come singly. The morning after Grigory left home, through Het-Baba's carelessness Miron Korshunov's pedigree bull gored the throat of his finest mare. Het-Baba came running into the house, white, distracted and trembling:

"Trouble, master! The bull, curse him, the damned bull. . . ."

"Well, what about the bull?" Miron asked in alarm.

"He's done the mare in. Gored her. . . ."

Miron ran half-dressed into the yard. By the well Mitka was beating the red five-year-old bull with a stake. The bull, his head down and dewlap dragging over the ground, was churning up the snow with his hoofs and scattering a silvery powder around his tail. Instead of yielding before the drubbing, he bellowed huskily and stamped his hind-feet as though about to charge. Mitka beat him on his nose and sides, cursing the while and paying no heed to Mikhei, who was trying to drag him back by his belt.

"Keep back, Mitka ... for Lord's sake. He'll gore you! Master, why don't you tell him?"

Miron ran to the well. The mare was standing by the fence, her head drooping sadly. Her dark heaving flanks were wet with sweat, and blood was running down her chest. Her light-bay back and sides were quivering, causing great shivers in her groin.

Miron ran to look at her front. A rose-coloured wound, big enough to take a man's hand, and revealing the windpipe, gaped in her neck. Miron seized her by the forelock and raised her head. The mare fixed her glittering violet eyes on her master as though mutely asking: "What next?" And as if in answer to the question Miron shouted: "Run and tell someone to scald some oak bark. Hurry!"

Het-Baba, his Adam's apple trembling in his dirty neck, ran to strip some bark from a tree, and Mitka came across to his father, one eye fixed on the bull circling and bellowing about the yard.

"Hold the mare by her forelock," his father ordered. "Someone run for some twine. Quick! Or do you want a box on the ears?"

They tied the string tightly round the mare's velvety, slightly hairy upper lip so that she should not feel the pain.

Old Grishaka came hobbling up. An infusion, the colour of acorns, was brought out in a painted bowl.

"Cool it down," he croaked. "It's too hot, isn't it? Miron, do you hear me?"

"Go inside, Dad. You'll catch cold out here."

"I tell you to cool it down. Do you want to kill the mare?"

The wound was bathed. With freezing fingers Miron threaded raw twine through a darning needle and sewed up the edges, making a neat seam. He had hardly turned away to go back to the house when his wife came running from the kitchen, alarm written large on her flabby cheeks. She called her husband aside:

"Natalya's here, Miron...! Oh, my God!"

"Now what's the matter?" Miron demanded, his face paling.

"It's Grigory. He's left home!" Lukinichna flung out her arms like a rook preparing for flight, clapped her hands against her skirt, and broke into a wail:

"Disgraced before the whole village! Lord, what a blow! Oh...!"

Miron found Natalya in a shawl and short winter coat standing in the middle of the kitchen. Two tears welled in her eyes, and her cheeks were deeply flushed.

"What are you doing here?" her father blustered as he ran into the room. "Has your husband beaten you? Can't you get on together?"

"He's gone away!" Natalya groaned, swallowing dry tears, and she swayed and fell on her knees before her father. "Father, my life is ruined.... Take me back.... Grigory's gone away with that woman. He's left me. Father, I've been crushed into the dust!" she sobbed out the half-finished phrases, gazing imploringly up at her father's ruddy beard.

"Wait, wait now...."

"There's nothing for me to live for there! Take me back!" She crawled on her knees to the chest and dropped her head on to her arms. Her kerchief slipped off her head and her smooth straight black hair fell over her pale ears. Tears at such a time are like rain in a May drought. Her mother pressed Natalya's head against her sunken belly, whispering motherly foolish words of comfort; but Miron, infuriated, ran out to the steps.

"Harness up two sleighs!" he shouted.

On the steps a cock, perched busily on the back of a hen, took fright at the shout, jumped clear, and stalked off towards the barn, squawking indignantly.

"Harness up two sleighs!" Miron kicked again and again at the fretted balustrade of the steps until it was hopelessly ruined. He returned to the house only when Het-Baba hurried out from the stables with a pair of horses, harnessing them as he ran.

Mitka and Het-Baba drove to the Melekhovs' for Natalya's possessions. In his abstraction Het-Baba sent a young pig in the road flying. "Mebbe the master will forget all about the mare now," he was thinking, and rejoiced, letting the reins hang loose. "But he's such an old devil, he'll never forget," and sneering to himself, Het-Baba tried to get the whip lash under the tenderest part of the horse's belly.

## XIV

Yevgeny Listnitsky held a commission as lieutenant in the Ataman's Lifeguards Regiment. Having had a tumble during the officers' hurdle races and broken his left arm, he took furlough when he came out of hospital and went to stay with his father for six weeks.

The old general lived alone at Yagodnoye. He had lost his wife while driving in the suburbs of Warsaw in the 1880's. Shots fired at the Cossack general had missed him, but riddled the carriage, killing his wife and coachman. Listnitsky was left with his two-year-old son Yevgeny. Soon after this event the general retired, abandoned an estate of ten thousand acres in the Saratov Province which had been granted to his great-grandfather in recognition of his services during the war of 1812, and moved to Yagodnoye, where he lived an austere and rigorous life.

He sent his son Yevgeny to the cadets' corps as soon as the lad was old enough, and occupied himself with farming. He purchased blood stock from the imperial stables, crossed them with the finest mares from England and from the famous Provalsky stables, and reared a new breed. He raised cattle and livestock on his own, and bought land, sowed grain (with hired labour), hunted with his borzois in the autumn and winter, and occasionally locked himself in the dining hall and drank for weeks on end. He was troubled with a stomach complaint, and his doctor had strictly forbidden him to swallow anything solid; he had to extract the goodness from all his food by mastication, spitting out the residue on to a silver tray held by his personal servant Venyamin.

Venyamin was a half-witted, swarthy young peasant, with a shock of thick black hair. He had been in Listnitsky's service for six years. When he first had to wait on the general it made him feel sick to watch the old man spitting out the chewed food. But he got used to it.

The other inhabitants of the estate were the cook Lukerya, the ancient stableman Sashka, and the shepherd Tikhon. From the very first the flabby pock-marked Lukerya, who with her huge bottom looked like a yellow lump of un-risen dough, would not allow Aksinya near the stove.

"You can cook when the master takes on ex-tra workers in the summer. Now I can manage by myself."

Aksinya was set to work washing the floors of the house three times a week, feeding the innumerable fowls, and keeping the fowl-house clean. She worked with a will, trying to please everyone, even the cook. Grigory spent much of his time in the spacious log-built stables with Sashka the stableman. The old man was one mass of grey hair, but everybody still fa-miliarly called him "Sashka." Probably even old Listnitsky, for whom he had worked more than twenty years, had forgotten his surname. In his youth Sashka had been the coachman, but as he grew old and feeble and his sight began to fail he was made stableman. Stocky, covered with greenish-grey hair (even the hair on his hands was grey), with a nose that had been flattened by a club in his youth, he wore an everlasting childish smile and gazed out on the world with blinking artless eyes. The apostolic expression of his face was marred by his broken nose and his hanging scarred underlip.

In his army days Sashka had once got drunk and taken by mistake a swill of *aqua regia* instead of vodka. The fiery liquid had welded his lower lip to his chin, leaving a crooked glowing pink scar. Sashka was fond of vodka, and when he was in his cups he would strut about the yard as though he were master. Stamping his feet, he would stand under old Listnitsky's bedroom and call loudly and sternly:

"Mikolai 'Lexeyevich! Mikolai 'Lexeyevich!"

If old Listnitsky happened to be in his bedroom he would come to the window.

"You're drunk, you good-for-nothing!" he would thunder.

Sashka would hitch up his trousers, and wink and smile. His smile danced diagonally right across his face, from his puckered left eye to the pink scar trailing from the right corner of his mouth; it was a crooked smile but a pleasant one.

"Mikolai 'Lexeyevich, Your Excellency, I know you!" he would wag his lean, dirty finger threateningly.

"Go and sleep it off!" his master would smile pacifyingly, twisting his drooping moustache with all five nicotine-stained fingers.

"You can't take me in!" the stableman would laugh, going up to the railings of the fence. "Mikolai 'Lexeyevich, you're like me. You and me—we know each other like a fish knows water. You and me, we're rich. Ah!" Here he would fling his arms wide open to show how rich. "We're known by everybody, all over the Don District. We. . . ." Sashka's voice would suddenly grow mournful and ingratiating: "Me and you—Your Excellency, everything's all right, only we've both got rotting noses."

"Why is that?" his master would ask, turning purple with laughter and twitching his moustache.

"Through vodka!" Sashka would bark out the words, blinking rapidly and licking his lips. "Don't drink, Mikolai 'Lexeyevich, or we'll go broke—you and me. We'll drink everything away!"

"Go and drink this away!" old Listnitsky would throw out a twenty-kopeck piece, and Sashka would catch it and hide it in his cap, crying:

"Well, good-bye, General."

"Have you watered the horses yet?" his

master would ask with a smile, knowing what was coming.

"Oh, you lousy devil! You son of a swine!" Sashka would turn livid, and his voice would crack with anger. "Sashka forget to water the horses? Eh? Even if I was dead I'd still crawl for a pail to water the horses. And he thinks. . . ."

The old man would march off fuming at the undeserved reproach, cursing and shaking his fist. Everything he did was forgiven, even drinking and his familiarity with his master. He was indispensable as a stableman. Winter and summer he slept in the stables, in an empty stall. He was stableman and horse-doctor; he gathered herbs for the horses in the spring, and dug up medicinal roots in the steppe and in the valleys. Bunches of dried herbs hung high up on the stable walls: milfoil to cure heaves, snake-eye grass as an antidote for adder-bite, blackleaf for the feet, a small white herb that grows at the root of the willow to treat sores, and many other little-known remedies for all the various ailments and diseases of horses.

Winter and summer, a subtle throat-tickling aroma hung like a fine-spun web about the stall in which Sashka slept. Hay packed as hard as a board, covered with a horse-cloth, and his coat, smelling of horse sweat, served as mattress and bedding to his plank-bed. The coat and a sheepskin were all the old man's worldly goods.

Tikhon, a huge, dull-witted Cossack, lived with Lukerya, and secretly nursed a quite needless jealousy of her and Sashka. Once every month he would take the old man by the button of his greasy shirt and lead him round to the back of the house.

"Old man, don't you set your cap at my woman."

"That depends . . ." Sashka would wink significantly.

"Keep off her!" Tikhon begged.

"I like 'em pock-marked, lad. I don't need vodka if you can give me a pock-marked wench. The more pock-marked they are the fonder they are of us menfolk, the hussies."

"You ought to be ashamed of yourself at your age. . . . And you a doctor, too; you look after the horses, you know all the secrets."

"I can do all kinds of doctoring," Sashka persisted.

"Keep off her, grandad. It's wrong."

"I'll get that Lukerya one of these days, lad, I'll have her, my lad. You can say good-bye to Lukerya, I'll be taking her away from you.

She's like a currant pie, only with the currants picked out. That's the kind for me!"

"Don't let me catch you or I'll kill you!" Tikhon would say, sighing and drawing some copper coins out of his pocket.

And so it went on month after month.

Life mouldered away in a sleepy torpor at Yagodnoye. The estate lay in a valley remote from all frequented roads, and from the autumn onward all communication with the neighbouring villages was broken. In the winter nights the wolf packs emerged from their forest lairs and terrified the horses with their howling. Tikhon used to go to the meadow to frighten them off with his master's double-barrelled gun, and Lukerya, wrapping her ample bottom in her rough blanket, would wait in suspense for the sound of the shots, her little eyes disappearing into her greasy pockmarked cheeks. At such times her imagination transformed the ugly bald-headed Tikhon into a handsome and reckless youth, and when the door of the servants' quarters slammed and Tikhon entered in a cloud of steam, she made room for him on the bed and, cooing affectionately, warmly embraced her frozen mate.

In summer-time Yagodnoye hummed till late at night with the voices of labourers. The master sowed some forty dessiatines with various crops, and hired labourers to harvest them. Occasionally Yevgeny came home, and would stroll through the orchard and over the meadow, and feel bored. The mornings he spent fishing in the pond. Plump-chested and of medium height, he wore a forelock Cossack fashion on the right side of his head. His officer's tunic fitted him snugly.

During the first days of Grigory's life on the estate he was frequently in the young master's company. One day Venyamin came smiling into the servants' quarters and, bowing his fuzzy head, announced:

"The young master wants you, Grigory."

Grigory, as on many other occasions, went to Yevgeny's room and stood at the door. The master pointed to a chair. Grigory seated himself on the very edge.

"How do you like our horses?"

"They're good horses. The grey is fine."

"Give him plenty of exercise, but don't gallop him."

"So Grandad Sashka told me."

"What about Sturdy?"

"The bay? He's a fine horse. Shoe's loose though, I'll have to get him reshod."

Screwing up his piercing grey eyes, the young master said: "You have to go to the training camp in May, don't you?"

"Yes."

"I'll speak to the ataman about it. You won't have to go."

"Thank you, sir."

There was a momentary silence. Unbuttoning the collar of his uniform, Yevgeny scratched his womanishly white chest.

"Aren't you afraid of Aksinya's husband taking her from you?"

"He's thrown her over; he won't take her back."

"How do you know?"

"I saw one of the men from the village the other day when I went there for nails. He told me Stepan was drinking hard. Says he doesn't want Aksinya any more, thinks he'll find someone hotter."

"Aksinya's a fine-looking woman," Listnitsky remarked thoughtfully, staring over Grigory's head with something licentious in his smile.

"Not bad," Grigory agreed, and his face clouded.

Yevgeny's furlough was nearly over. He no longer wore a sling and could bend his arm freely.

During the last few days of his stay Yevgeny spent a great deal of his time in Grigory's room. Aksinya had whitewashed the dirt-caked walls, scrubbed the window-frames, and scoured the floor with broken brick. There was a feminine warmth and cosiness in the cheerful empty little room. The officer, his short, fashionably-out coat thrown over his shoulders, chose times for his visits when Grigory was occupied with the horses. He would first go into the kitchen, stand joking with Lukerya for a minute or two, then pass into the farther room. He would sit down on a stool, hunching his shoulders, and fix a shamelessly smiling gaze on Aksinya. She was embarrassed by his presence, and the knitting-needles trembled in her fingers.

"Well, Aksinya, how are you getting on?" he would ask, puffing at his cigarette until the room was filled with blue smoke.

"Very well, thank you." Aksinya would raise her eyes, and meeting the lieutenant's transparent gaze, silently telling of his desire, she turned crimson. That naked stare of his was unpleasant and annoying. She replied disconnectedly to his questions, avoiding his eyes and seeking an opportunity to leave the room.

"I must go and feed the ducks now."

"There's no hurry. The ducks can wait," he smiled, and his legs trembled in his tight riding breeches, and he continued to ply her with questions concerning her past life, using the

deep tones of his voice, which was like his father's and pleading lewdly with his crystal-
clear eyes.

When Grigory came in, the fire would die
out of Yevgeny's eyes and he would offer him
a cigarette, leaving soon after.

"What did he want?" Grigory would ask
Aksinya, not looking at her.

"How should I know?" Remembering the
officer's look, Aksinya would laugh forcedly.
"He came in and just sat there like this, Grisha," (she showed him how Yevgeny had sat
with hunched back) "and sat and sat until I
was sick of him."

"Did you ask him in?" Grigory's eyes would
narrow angrily.

"What do I need him for?"

"You watch out, or I'll kick him down the
steps one day."

Aksinya would gaze at Grigory with a smile
on her lips, and not be sure whether he was
speaking in jest or earnest.


## XV

The winter broke up during the fourth week
of Lent. Open water began to fringe the edges
of the Don; the ice, melting from the top, turned
grey and swelled  spongily. In  the  evening

a low murmur came from the hills, indicating frost according to the time-honoured saying, but in reality the thaw was already on its way. In the morning the air tingled with the light frost, but by noon the earth was bare in patches, and in the nostrils was the scent of March, of the frozen bark, of cherry-trees, and rotting straw.

Miron Korshunov took his time preparing for the ploughing season, spending the lengthening days in the shed sharpening the teeth of the harrows and repairing cartwheels. Old Grishaka usually fasted in the fourth week of Lent. He would come home from church, blue with cold, and complain to his daughter-in-law Lukinichna:

"That priest makes me sick. He's no good. He's as slow with the service as a carter with a load of eggs."

"You'd have been wiser to have fasted during Passion Week, it's warmer by then."

"Call Natalya," he replied. "I'll get her to make me a pair of warmer stockings."

Natalya still lived in the belief that Grigory would return to her; her heart longed and waited for him, and would not listen to the warning whisper of sober reason. She spent the nights in weary yearning, tossing on her bed, crushed by her undeserved and unexpected shame. Another woe was now added to the first, and she awaited its sequel in cold terror, fluttering about in her maiden room like a wounded lapwing in a forest glade. From the earliest days of her return home her brother Mitka had begun to give her odd glances, and one day, catching her in the porch, he asked frankly:

"Still hankering after Grisha?"

"What's it got to do with you?"

"I want to cheer you up."

Natalya glanced into his eyes and was terrified by what she saw there. Mitka's green cat's eyes glittered and their slits gleamed greasily in the dim light of the porch. Natalya slammed the door and ran to her grandfather's room, where she stood listening to the wild beating of her heart. The next day Mitka came up to her in the yard. He had been turning over fresh hay for the cattle, and green stalks of grass hung from his straight hair and his fur cap. Natalya was chasing the dogs away from the pigs' trough.

"Don't fret yourself, Natalya. . . ."

"I'll tell Father," she cried, raising her hands to protect herself.

"You're an idiot!"

"Keep away, you beast!"

"What are you shouting for?"

"Go away, Mitka! I'll go at once and tell Father. How dare you look at me like that? Have you no shame! It's a wonder the earth doesn't open and swallow you up."

"Well, it doesn't, does it?" Mitka stamped with his boots to confirm the statement and edged up to her.

"Don't come near me, Mitka!"

"I won't now, but I'll come at night. By God, I'll come!"

Trembling, Natalya left the yard. That evening she made her bed on the chest, and took her younger sister to sleep with her. All night she tossed and turned, her burning eyes seeking to pierce the darkness, her ears alert for the slightest sound, ready to scream the house down. But the silence was broken only by the snores of Grishaka sleeping in the next room, and an occasional grunt from her sister.

The thread of days unwound in that constant inconsolable grief that only women know.

Mitka had not got over the shame of his recent attempt at marriage, and he went about morose and ill-tempered. He went out every evening and rarely arrived home again before dawn. He carried on with women who liked to amuse themselves while their husbands were soldiering and went to Stepan Astakhov's to play cards for stakes. His father watched his behaviour, but said nothing for the time being.

Just before Easter, Natalya met Pantelei Prokofyevich outside Mokhov's shop. He called to her:

"Wait a moment!"

She halted. Her heart felt a pang of yearning as she saw her father-in-law's face, remotely reminding her of Grigory.

"Why don't you come and see us old folks, sometimes?" the old man asked her, giving her a quick look, as though he himself had been guilty of some offence against her. "The wife misses you. . . . Well, how are you getting on?"

Natalya recovered from her embarrassment. "Thank you . . ." she said, and after a moment's hesitation (she wanted to say "Father!"), she added: "Pantelei Prokofyevich, I've been very busy at home."

"Our Grisha . . . ah!" the old man shook his head bitterly. "He's let us down, the scoundrel. And we were getting on so well together."

"Oh well, Father," Natalya answered shrilly with a catch in her voice. "I suppose it wasn't to be."

Pantelei fidgeted in embarrassment as he saw Natalya's eyes fill. Her lips twisted in an effort to hold back her tears.

"Good-bye, my dear," he said. "Don't grieve

over him, the son of a bitch! He's not worth the nail on your little finger. Maybe he'll come back. I'd like to see him. I'd like to get at him."

Natalya walked away with her head sunk on her breast. Pantelei stood shifting from foot to foot as though about to break into a run. As she turned the corner Natalya glanced back; the old man was limping across the square, leaning heavily on his stick.

## XVI

As spring approached, the meetings in Stockman's workshop were held less frequently. The villagers were preparing for the field work, and only Ivan Alexeyevich the engineman and Knave came from the mill, bringing David with them. On Maundy Thursday they gathered at the workshop in the early evening. Stockman was sitting on his bench, filing a silver ring made from a fifty-kopeck piece. A sheaf of rays from the setting sun streamed through the window, forming a square of dusty yellowish-pink light on the floor. The engineman picked up a pair of pincers and turned them over in his hand.

"I had to go to the master the other day to ask about a piston," he remarked. "It will have to be taken to Millerovo, we can't mend it here. There's a crack in it this long." Ivan Alexeyevich measured the length of his little finger.

"There's a works at Millerovo, isn't there?" Stockman said, scattering a fine silver dust as he filed the coin.

"A steel foundry. I had to spend a few days there last year."

"Many workers?"

"I should say four hundred or thereabouts."

"And what are they like?" Stockman's tone was deliberate.

"They're well off. They're none of your proletariat, they're muck."

"Why is that?" asked Knave, who was sitting next to Stockman, his stubby fingers clasped under his knees.

David, the mill-hand, his hair grey with flour dust, padded about the workshop, listening with a smile to the dry rustle of the shavings that he stirred up with his boots. He felt as if he were walking along a ravine deep in fallen scarlet leaves with the leaves giving easily and the damp turf springing youthfully underfoot.

"Because they're too well off. Each has his own little house, his wife, and every comfort. And a good half of them are Baptists into the bargain. The master himself is their preacher, and they suck one another's noses, and the dirt on them is so thick you couldn't scrape it off with a hoe."

"Ivan Alexeyevich, what are these Baptists?" asked David, pouncing on the unfamiliar word.

"Baptists? They worship God in their own fashion. A kind of sect, like the Old Believers."

"Every fool goes crazy in his own fashion," added Knave.

"As I was saying, I went to see Sergei Platonovich," Ivan Alexeyevich continued his story, "and Atyopin was there, so he told me to wait outside. I sat down and waited and heard them talking through the door. Mokhov was saying there was going to be a war with the Germans very soon; he had read it in a book. But Atyopin said there couldn't be a war between Germany and Russia."

Ivan Alexeyevich so cleverly imitated Atyopin's lisp that David let out a short laugh, but, seeing Knave's sarcastic expression, immediately shut up.

" 'There can be no war with Germany because Germany's feeding on our grain,' " Ivan Alexeyevich continued to report the conversation he had overheard. "Then I heard a a third voice: I found out afterwards it was the officer, old Listnitsky's son. 'There will be a war,' he said, 'between Germany and France, over the vineyards, but it has nothing to do with us.' What do you think, Osip Davydovich?" Ivan asked, turning to Stockman.

"I'm no good at prophecies," Stockman replied, staring fixedly at the ring in his outstretched hand.

"Once they do start we'll have to be in it too. Like it or not, they'll drag us there by the hair," Knave declared.

"It's like this, boys," Stockman said, gently taking the pincers out of the engineman's hands. He spoke seriously, evidently intending to explain the matter thoroughly. Knave seated himself comfortably on the bench, and David's lips shaped into an "O," revealing his strong teeth. In his concise vivid way Stockman outlined the struggle of the capitalist states for markets and colonies. When he had finished Ivan Alexeyevich asked indignantly:

"Yes, but where do we come in?"

"Your heads will ache from the drunken orgies of others," Stockman smiled.

"Don't talk like a kid," Knave said sarcastically. "You know the saying: 'When masters quarrel, the peasants' forelocks shake.'"

"Humph," Ivan Alexeyevich frowned as if he were trying to break down some great unyielding lump of thought.

"What's that Listnitsky always calling on

Mokhov for? After his daughter, eh?" David asked.

"The Korshunov brat has had a go there already," Knave interposed maliciously.

"Ivan Alexeyevich, can't you hear? What's that officer nosing around there for?" David repeated.

Ivan Alexeyevich started as if he had been struck behind the knees with a whiplash.

"Eh? What were you saying?"

"He's been having a nap! We're talking about Listnitsky."

"He was on his way to the station. Yes, and here's some more news. When I went out of the house I saw ... who do you think? Grigory Melekhov! He was standing outside with a whip in his hand. 'What are you doing here, Grigory?' I says. 'Taking Lieutenant Listnitsky to Millerovo Station.'"

"He's Listnitsky's coachman," David explained.

"Picking the crumbs from the rich man's table."

"You're like a dog on a chain, Knave, you'd snarl at anyone."

The conversation flagged. Ivan Alexeyevich rose to go.

"Hurrying off to service?" Knave got in a last dig.

"I do plenty of serving every day."

Stockman accompanied his guests to the gate, then locked up the workshop and went into the house.

The night before Easter Sunday the sky was overcast with masses of black cloud, and rain began to fall. A raw darkness weighed on the village. At dusk the ice on the Don began to crack with a protracted, rolling groan, and squeezed by a mass of broken ice the first floe emerged from the water. The ice broke up all at once over a stretch of four versts, and drifted downstream. The floes crashed against one another and against the banks, while in the background the church bell rang measuredly for service. At the first bend, where the Don sweeps to the left, the ice was dammed up. The roar and clash of the bumping floes reached the village. A crowd of lads had gathered in the churchyard, which was already dotted with puddles. Through the open doors came the muffled tones of the service, and lights gleamed with festive brightness in the latticed windows, while in the darkness of the yard the lads tickled and kissed the girls, and whispered dirty stories to one another.

The churchwarden's lodge was crowded with Cossacks from villages all over the district. Weary with fatigue and the stuffiness of the room, people slept on benches, even on the floor.

Men were sitting on the rickety steps, smoking and talking about the weather and the winter crops.

"When will your lot be going out in the fields?"

"Should be moving about Thomas' day, I reckon."

"That's all right for you, the land round your way is sandy."

"Some of it is, this side of the gully there's a salt marsh."

"The earth'll get plenty of moisture now."

"When we ploughed last year it was like gristle, hard and sticky all the way over."

"Dunya, where are you?" a high-pitched voice called from the steps of the lodge.

From the churchyard gate a rough throaty voice could be heard blustering: "A fine place to be kissing, you.... Get out of here, you dirty young brats. What an idea!"

"Can't you find a partner for yourself? Go and kiss the bitch in our yard," a wobbly young voice retorted from the darkness.

"Bitch?! I'll learn you...."

A squelchy patter of running feet, a rustle of skirts.

Water dripped from the roof with a glassy tinkle; and again that slow voice, clinging as the muddy black earth:

"Been trying to buy a plough off Prokhor, offered him twelve rubles but he won't take it. He wouldn't let something go cheap, not him...."

From the Don came a smooth swishing, rustling and crunching, as though a buxom wench, dressed-up and tall as a poplar, were passing by, her great skirts rustling.

At midnight, Mitka Korshunov, riding a horse bareback, clattered through the sticky darkness up to the church. He tied the bridle rein to the horse's mane, and gave her a smack on her steaming flanks. He listened to the squelch of the hoofs for a moment, then, adjusting his belt, he went into the churchyard. In the porch he removed his cap, bent his head devoutly, and thrusting aside the women, pressed up to the altar. The Cossacks were crowded in a black mass on the left; on the right was a motley throng of women. Mitka found his father in the front row, and gripping him by the elbow, whispered into his ear: "Father, come outside for a moment."

As he pushed his way out of the church through the dense curtain of mingled odours, Mitka's nostrils quivered. He was overwhelmed by the vapour of burning wax, the odour of women's sweating bodies, the sepulchral stench of clothes brought out only at Christmas and Easter time, and the smell of damp leather, moth balls, and the windiness of fast-hungered bellies.

In the porch Mitka put his mouth close to his father's ear and said: "Natalya's dying."

## XVII

Grigory returned on Palm Sunday from his journey with Yevgeny to the station. He found the thaw had eaten away the snow; the road had broken up within a couple of days.

At a Ukrainian village some twenty-five versts from the station he all but lost his horses as he was crossing a stream. He had arrived at the village early in the evening. During the previous night the ice had broken up and started moving, and the stream, swollen and foaming with muddy brown water, threatened the streets. The inn at which he had stopped to feed the horses on the way out lay on the farther side of the stream. The water might easily rise still higher during the night, and Grigory decided to cross.

He drove to the point where he had crossed the ice on the outward journey, and found the stream had overflowed its banks. A piece of fencing and half a cartwheel were eddying in the middle. There were fresh traces of sledge runners on the bare sand at the edge. He halted the sweating foam-flecked horses and jumped down to look at the marks more closely. At the water's edge the tracks turned a little to the left and disappeared into the stream. He measured the distance to the other side with his eyes: fifty paces at the most. He went to the horses to check the harness. At that moment an aged Ukrainian came towards him from the nearest hut.

"Is there a good crossing here?" Grigory asked him, waving his reins at the seething brown flood.

"Some folk crossed there this morning."

"Is it deep?"

"No. But it might splash into your sleigh."

Grigory gathered up the reins, and holding his knout ready, urged on the horses with a curt, imperative command. They moved unwillingly, snorting and snuffing at the water. Grigory cracked his whip and stood up on the seat.

The bay on the left tossed its head and suddenly pulled on the traces. Grigory glanced down at his feet; the water was swirling over the front of the sledge. At first the horses were wading up to their knees, but suddenly the stream rose to their breasts. Grigory tried to turn them back, but they refused to answer the rein and began to swim for it. The tail of the sledge was swung round by the current, and the horses' heads were forced upstream. The water flowed in waves over their backs, and the sledge rocked and pulled them back strongly.

"Hey! Hey! To the right!" the Ukrainian shouted, running along the bank and waving his fur cap.

In a wild fury Grigory kept shouting and urging on the horses. The water foamed in eddies behind the dragging sledge. The runners struck against a jutting pile, the remains of the bridge which had been swept away overnight, and the sledge turned over with extraordinary ease. With a gasp Grigory plunged in head first, but he did not lose his grip of the reins. While he was tossed about by the rocking sledge, the water dragged at his legs and the skirts of his sheepskin with gentle insistence. He succeeded in clutching a runner, dropped the reins, and hauled himself along hand over hand, making his way to the swingle-tree. He was about to seize the iron-shod end of the swingle-tree when the bay, in its struggle against the current, lashed out with

317

its hindleg and struck him on the knee. Choking, Grigory threw out his hands and caught at the traces. He felt himself being dragged away from the horses, his grip weakened. Every fibre in his body tingling with the cold, he managed to reach the horse's head, and the animal fixed the maddened, mortally terrified gaze of its bloodshot eyes straight into his dilated pupils.

Again and again he grasped at the slippery leather reins, but they eluded his fingers. Somehow he managed at last to seize them. Abruptly his legs scraped along the ground. Dragging himself to the edge of the water, he stumbled forward and was knocked off his feet in the shallows by a horse's breast.

Trampling over him, the horses tugged the sledge violently out of the water and, exhausted, halted a few paces away, shuddering and steaming. Unconscious of any pain, Grigory jumped to his feet; the cold enveloped him as though in unbearably hot dough. He was trembling even more than the horses, and felt as weak on his legs as an unweaned infant. Slowly he gathered his wits, and turning the sledge on to its runners, drove the horses off at a gallop to get them warm. He flew into the street of the village as though attacking an enemy, and turned into the first open gate without slackening his pace.

The host turned out to be a hospitable Ukrainian; he sent his son to attend to the horses and himself helped Grigory to undress. In a tone that brooked no refusal he ordered his wife to light the stove. While his own clothes were drying Grigory stretched himself out on top of the stove in his host's trousers. After a supper of meatless cabbage soup he went to sleep.

He set off again long before dawn. A good hundred and thirty-five versts' driving lay before him, and every minute was precious. The untracked confusion of the flooded spring steppe was at hand; the melting snow had turned every little ravine or gully into a roaring torrent.

The black, bare road exhausted the horses. Over the hard surface created by the early morning frost he reached a village lying four versts off his route, and stopped at a crossroad. The horses were steaming with sweat; behind him lay the gleaming track of the sledge runners in the ground. He abandoned the sledge and set off again, riding one horse bareback and leading the other by the reins. He arrived at Yagodnoye in the morning on Palm Sunday.

Old Listnitsky listened attentively to his story of the journey, and went to look at the horses. Sashka was leading them up and down the yard, angrily eyeing their sunken flanks.

"How are they?" the master asked. "They haven't been overdriven, have they?"

"No. The bay's got a sore on his chest where his collar rubbed, but it's nothing," Sashka answered without stopping the horses.

"Go and get some rest," Listnitsky motioned to Grigory with his hand. Grigory went to his room but he had only one night's rest. The next morning Venyamin came into the room in a new sateen shirt, his fat face beaming, and called to him:

"Grigory, the master wants you. At once."

The general was shuffling about the hall in felt slippers. Only after Grigory had coughed twice did he look up.

"What do you want?"

"You sent for me."

"Ah, yes! Go and saddle the stallion and my horse. Tell Lukerya not to feed the dogs. They're going hunting."

Grigory turned to leave the room. His master stopped him with a shout: "D'you hear? And you're going with me."

Aksinya thrust a cake into the pocket of Grigory's coat and hissed: "He won't even let a man eat, the devil take him. Put on your scarf at least, Grisha."

Grigory led the saddled horses to the fence, and whistled to the dogs. Listnitsky came out, attired in a jerkin of blue cloth and girdled with an ornamental leather belt. A nickel-plated flask in a cork case was slung at his back; the whip hanging from his arm trailed behind him like a snake.

As he held the bridle for his master to mount Grigory was astonished at the ease with which old Listnitsky hoisted his bony body into the saddle. "Keep close behind me," the general curtly ordered, as he lovingly gathered the reins in his gloved hand.

Grigory rode the stallion. Its hind hoofs were not shod, and as it trod on the shards of ice it slipped and sat on its hind quarters. The old general sat hunched but firm in the saddle.

The horses moved on at a good pace. The stallion strained at the bit and arched its short neck, squinting round at its rider and trying to bite his knees. When they reached the top of the rise, Listnitsky put his horse into a fast trot. The chain of hounds followed Grigory; the old black bitch ran with her muzzle touching the end of the stallion's tail. The horse tried to reach her by falling back on its hind quarters, but the bitch dropped behind, looking up plaintively, like an old woman, at Grigory as he glanced round.

They reached their objective, the Olshansky ravine, in half an hour. Listnitsky rode through the undergrowth along the brow of the slope. Grigory dropped down into the rain-washed ravine, cautiously avoiding the numerous potholes. From time to time he looked up, and through the steely-blue of a straggling and naked elder grove he saw Listnitsky's clean-cut figure. As the old man leaned forward and rose in his stirrups, his blue, belted coat wrinkled at the back. Behind him the hounds were running in a bunch along the undulating ridge. As he rode across the steep watercourse Grigory leaned back in the saddle.

"I could do with a smoke," he thought, "I'll let go of the reins and get my pouch." Pulling off his glove, Grigory fumbled in his pocket for some cigarette paper.

"After him!" the shout came like a pistol shot from the other side of the ridge.

Grigory looked up sharply, and saw Listnitsky galloping up the slope with upraised whip. . . .

"After him!"

Slipping along with body close to the ground, a moulting dirty-brown wolf was running swiftly across the marshy rush and reedy-grown bottom of the ravine. Leaping a gully, it stopped and turned quickly, catching sight of the dogs. They were coming after it spread out in horseshoe formation, to cut it off from the wood at the end of the ravine.

With a springy stride the wolf leaped on to a small hillock and headed for the wood. The old bitch was cutting it off, husbanding her strength in short strides, another hound, one of the best and fiercest in the pack, was coming up from behind. The wolf hesitated for a moment, and as Grigory rode up out of the ravine he lost sight of it. When next he had a good view from the hillock the wolf was far away in the steppe, making for a neighbouring ravine. Grigory could see the hounds running through the undergrowth behind it, and old Listnitsky riding slightly to the side, belabouring his horse with the butt of his whip. As the wolf reached the ravine the hounds began to overtake it, and one, the grizzled hound known as Hawk, seemed to hang like a whitish rag from the wolf's loins.

"After him!" the shout was wafted back to Grigory.

Grigory put his horse into a gallop, vainly trying to see what was happening ahead of him. His eyes were streaming with tears and his ears were stuffed up with the whistling wind. He was suddenly fired by the excitement of the hunt. Bending over his horse's neck, he

flew along at a mad gallop. When he reached
the ravine neither wolf nor dogs were to be
seen. A moment or two later Listnitsky overtook him. Reining in his horse sharply he
shouted:

"Which way did they go?"

"Into the ravine, I think."

"You overtake them on the left. After them!"
The old man dug his heels into his horse's
flanks and rode off to the right. Grigory dropped
into a hollow, and with whip and shout
rode his horse hard for a verst and a half. The
damp, sticky earth flew up under the hoofs,
striking him on the face. The long ravine
curved to the right and branched into three.
Grigory crossed the first fork, and then caught
sight of the dark chain of hounds chasing the
wolf across the steppe. The animal had been
headed off from the heart of the ravine, which
was densely overgrown with oaks and alders,
and was now making for a dry brush and this-
tle-covered dell.

Rising in his stirrups, and wiping the tears
from his wind-lashed eyes with his sleeve,
Grigory watched them. Glancing momentarily
to the left, he realized that he was in the steppe
close to his native village. Near by lay the
irregular square of land which he and Natalya
had ploughed in the autumn. He deliberately

guided the stallion across the ploughed land, and during the few moments in which the animal was sliding and stumbling over the clods the zest for the hunt died to ashes within him. He now calmly urged on the heavily-sweating horse, and glancing round to see whether Listnitsky was looking, dropped into an easy trot.

Some distance away he could see the deserted camping quarters of the ploughmen; a little farther off three pairs of bullocks were dragging a plough across the fresh, velvety soil.

From our village, surely. Whose land is that? That's not Anikushka, is it? Grigory screwed up his eyes trying to recognize the man following the plough.

He saw two Cossacks drop the plough and run to head off the wolf from the near-by ravine. One, in a peaked, red-banded cap, the strap under his chin, was waving an iron bar. Suddenly the wolf squatted down in a deep furrow. The foremost hound flew right over it and fell with its forelegs doubled under it; the old bitch following tried to stop, her hind quarters scraping along the cloddy, ploughed ground; but unable to halt in time, she tumbled against the wolf. The hunted animal shook its head violently, and the bitch ricochetted off it. Now the mass of hounds fastened on the wolf, and they all dragged for some paces over the ploughed land. Grigory was off his horse half a minute before his master. He fell to his knees, drawing back his hunting knife.

"There! In the throat!" the Cossack with the iron bar cried in a voice which Grigory knew well. Panting heavily, he dropped down at Grigory's side, and dragging away the hound which had fastened on the hunted animal's belly, gripped the wolf's forelegs in one hand. Grigory felt under the animal's shaggy fur for its windpipe, and drew the knife across it.

"The dogs! The dogs! Drive them off," old Listnitsky croaked as he dropped from the saddle.

Grigory with difficulty managed to drive away the dogs, then glanced towards his master. Standing a little way off was Stepan Astakhov. His face working strangely, he was turning the iron bar over and over in his hands.

"Where are you from, my man?" Listnitsky turned to Stepan.

"From Tatarsky," Stepan answered after a momentary hesitation, and took a step in Grigory's direction.

"What's your name?" Listnitsky asked.

"Astakhov."

"When are you going home, my lad?"

"Tonight."

Listnitsky pointed to the wolf with his foot. The animal's jaws were snapping feebly in its death agony and one of its hindlegs, with a brownish tuft.of fur sticking to it, was stiffly raised.

"Bring us that carcass," he said. "I'll pay whatever it costs." He wiped the sweat from his purple face with his scarf, turned away, and slipped the flask off his back.

Grigory went to his stallion. As he set foot in the stirrup he glanced back. Trembling uncontrollably, Stepan was coming towards him, his great, heavy fists pressed against his chest.

## XVIII

On Good Friday night the women gathered in the house of Korshunov's neighbour, Pelageya Maidannikova, for a talk. Her husband Gavrila had written from Lodz that he was trying to get furlough for Easter. Pelageya had whitewashed the walls and tidied up the hut as early as the Monday before Easter, and from Thursday onward she waited expectantly, running to the gate and standing at the fence, bare-headed and gaunt, the signs of her pregnancy showing in her face. Shading her eyes with her palm she stared down the road to see whether he was coming. Gavrila had returned from his regiment the previous year, bringing his wife a present of Polish chintz. He had spent four nights with her, and on the fifth day had got drunk, cursed in Polish and German, and with tears in his eyes had sat singing an old Cossack song about Poland that dated from 1831. His friends and brothers had sat with him, singing and drinking vodka before dinner.

*They said of Poland, it's a very rich land,*
*But we found out it's as poor as the damned.*
*And in this said Poland there stands an inn,*
*A Polish inn, belongs to the Polish king.*
*And at this said inn three lads had a drink,*
*A Prussian, a Pole, and a Don Cossack*
*Russian.*
*The Prussian, he drinks vodka, and pays his*
*score.*
*The Pole, he drinks vodka, and pays some*
*more.*
*The Cossack, he drinks—and the inn's as*
*poor as before.*
*Then he walks around with clinking spur*
*And the barmaid sees his eye is on her.*
*"Oh, mistress, dear, come live with me,*
*"Come live with me, on the quiet Don,*
*"The folk on the Don, they don't live your*
*way,*

*"Don't weave, don't spin, don't sow, don't*
*mow,*
*"Don't sow, don't mow, but they dress very*
*gay."*

After dinner Gavrila had said good-bye to his family and ridden off. And from that day Pelageya had begun to watch the hem of her skirt.

She explained to Natalya Korshunova how she came to be with child. "A day or two before Gavrila arrived, I had a dream," she said. "I was going through the meadow, and I saw our old cow in front of me, the one we had sold last holiday. She was going along with the milk dripping from her teats. Lord, I thought, however did I come to milk her so badly? Next day old Drozdikha came for some hops, and I told her my dream. And she told me to break a bit of wax off a candle, roll it into a ball, and to take and bury it in some cowdung, for misfortune was watching at the window. I ran to do as she said, but I couldn't find the candle. I had had one, I knew, but the children must have taken it to catch tarantulas. Then Gavrila arrived, and trouble with him. Before that I had gone for three years without trouble, and now look at me!" She prodded her swollen belly.

Pelageya fretted while waiting for her

husband. She was bored with her own company, and so on the Friday she invited her women friends to come and spend the evening with her. Natalya came with an unfinished stocking she was knitting, for when spring came Grandad Grishaka felt the cold all the more. She was unnaturally full of high spirits, and laughed more than necessary at the others' jokes, trying to hide her yearning for her husband from them. Pelageya was sitting on the stove with her bare, violet-veined legs dangling, and bantering the young shrewish Frosya.

"How d'you come to beat your husband, Frosya?"

"Don't you know how? On the back, on the head, and wherever I could lay my hands on him."

"I didn't mean that, I meant how did it happen."

"It just happened," Frosya answered unwillingly.

"If you were to catch your husband with another woman would you keep your tongue quiet?" a tall gaunt woman asked deliberately.

"Tell us all about it, Frosya."

"There's nothing to tell. . . ."

"Oh, come on, we're all friends here."

Spitting the husk of a sunflower seed into her hand, Frosya smiled:

"Well, I'd noticed his goings-on for a long time, and then someone told me he'd been carrying on at the mill with a hussy from across the Don. I went out and found them by the mill."

"Any news of your husband, Natalya?" the gaunt woman interrupted, turning to Natalya.

"He's at Yagodnoye," she replied in a whisper.

"Do you think of living with him or not?"

"She might think of it, but he doesn't," their hostess intervened. Natalya felt the hot blood surging to her face. She bent her head over her stocking and glanced from under her brows at the women. Realizing that she could not hide her flush of shame from them, she deliberately, yet so clumsily that everybody noticed it, sent the ball of wool rolling from her knees, and then bent down and groped over the cold floor.

"Spit on him, woman! So long as you have a neck, you'll always find a yoke for it," one woman advised her with unconcealed pity in her voice.

Natalya's affected liveliness died away like a spark in the wind. The women's conversation turned to the latest scandal, to tittle-tattle and gossip. Natalya knitted in silence. She forced herself to sit on until the party broke up, and then went home, with a half-formed decision in her mind. Shame for her uncertain situation (for she still would not believe that Grigory had gone for ever, and was ready to forgive him and take him back) drove her on to a further step. She resolved to send a letter secretly to him, in order to learn whether he had gone for good or whether he might change his mind. When she reached home she found Grishaka sitting in his little room reading an old, greasy leather-bound copy of the Gospels. Her father was in the kitchen mending a fishing-net and listening to a story Mikhei was telling him about a recent murder. Her mother had put the children to bed and was asleep over the ledge above stove, the blackened soles of her feet facing the door. Natalya took off her jacket and wandered aimlessly about the rooms. In one corner of the front room there was a pile of hempreed and the mice could be heard scampering and squeaking.

She stopped for a moment in her grandfather's room, staring dully at the stack of devotional books under the icons.

"Grandad, have you any paper?"

"What sort of paper?" Grishaka asked, puckering his forehead into a frown.

"Paper to write on."

The old man fumbled in a psalter, and drew

out a crumpled sheet of paper that smelt strongly of incense.

"And a pencil?"

"Ask your father. Go away, my dear, and don't bother me."

She obtained a stump of pencil from her father, and sitting down at the table, struggled again with the thoughts that had tortured her for so long, thoughts that evoked a numb, gnawing pain in her heart.

She wrote:

*Grigory Panteleyevich,*

*Tell me how I am to live, and whether my life is quite lost or not. You left home and you didn't say a single word to me. I haven't done you any wrong, and I've waited for you to untie my hands, to say you've gone for good, but you've gone away and are as silent as the grave.*

*I thought you had gone off in the heat of the moment, and waited for you to come back, but I don't want to come between you. Better one should be trodden into the ground than two. Have pity for once and write. Then I shall know what to think, but now I stand in the middle of the road.*

*Don't be angry with me, Grisha, for the love of Christ.*

*Natalya.*

Next morning she promised vodka to Het-Baba and persuaded him to ride with the letter to Yagodnoye. Moody in expectation of his drinking spell, Het-Baba led a horse into the yard, and without informing his master went jogging off to Yagodnoye.

On his horse he looked awkward, as any stranger among Cossack riders does; his ragged elbows jerked as he trotted. The Cossack children playing in the street sent him off with jeering cries.

"Dirty Ukrainian!"

"Mind you don't fall off!"

"Looks like a dog on a fence!"

He returned in the afternoon. He brought with him a piece of blue sugar-bag paper, and as he drew it out of his pocket he winked at Natalya.

"The road was terrible. I got such a shaking it near brought my liver up."

Natalya read the note, and her face turned grey. The four words scribbled on the paper entered her heart like sharp teeth rending a weave.

*Live alone.–Grigory Melekhov.*

Hurriedly, as though not trusting her own strength, Natalya went into the house and lay down on her bed. Her mother was lighting the stove for the night, in order to have the place tidy early on Easter Sunday morning and to get the Easter cake ready in time.

"Natalya, come and give me a hand," she called to her daughter.

"I've got a headache, Mamma, I'll lie down for a bit."

Her mother put her head in at the door. "Drink some pickle juice, it'll put you right in no time."

Natalya licked her cold lips with her dry tongue and made no reply.

She lay until evening, her head covered with a warm woollen shawl, a light tremor shaking her huddled body. Miron and Grishaka were about to go off to church when she got up and went into the kitchen. Beads of perspiration shone on her temples under her smoothly-combed hair, and her eyes were dim with an unhealthy, oily film.

As Miron fastened his fly-buttons, he glanced at his daughter:

"A fine time to fall sick, Daughter. Come along with us to the service."

"You go, I'll come along later."

"In time to go home again, I expect?"

"No, I'll come when I've dressed."

The men went out. Lukinichna and Natalya were left in the kitchen. Natalya went listlessly backward and forward from the chest to the bed, stared with unseeing eyes at the jumbled heap of clothing in the chest, her lips whispering, the same agonizing thoughts in her mind. Lukinichna decided she could not make up her mind which clothes to wear, and with motherly kindness she suggested: "Wear my blue skirt, dear. It will just fit you. Shall I get it for you?"

Natalya had had no new clothes made for Easter, and Lukinichna, suddenly remembering how before she married her daughter had loved to wear her dark-blue hobble skirt, pressed Natalya to take it, thinking she was worried about what to wear.

"No, I'll go in this!" Natalya carefully drew out her green skirt, and suddenly remembered that she had been wearing it when Grigory first visited her as her future bridegroom, when he had shamed her with that first fleeting kiss by the barn. Shaking with sobs, she fell forward against the raised lid of the chest.

"Natalya, what is the matter?" her mother exclaimed, clapping her hands.

Natalya choked down her desire to scream and, mastering herself, gave a rasping, wooden laugh.

"I don't know what's come over me today."

"Oh, Natalya, I've noticed...."

"Well, and what have you noticed, Mamma?" she cried with unexpected irritation, crumpling the green skirt in her fingers.

"You can't go on like this; what you need is a husband."

"One was enough for me!"

She went to her room, and quickly returned to the kitchen, dressed, girlishly slender, a bluish mournful flush in her pallid cheeks.

"You go on, I'm not ready yet," her mother said.

Pushing a handkerchief into her sleeve, Natalya went out. The rumble of the floating ice and the bracing tang of thaw dampness was wafted to her on the wind. Holding up her skirt in her left hand, picking her way across the pearly-blue puddles, she reached the church. On the way she attempted to recover her former comparatively tranquil state of mind, thinking of the holiday, of everything vaguely and in snatches. But her thoughts returned stubbornly to the scrap of blue paper hidden at her breast, to Grigory and the happy woman who was now complacently laughing at her, perhaps even pitying her.

As she entered the churchyard some lads barred her way. She passed round them, and heard the whisper:

"Who is she? Did you see?"

"Natalya Korshunova."

"She's ruptured, they say. That's why her husband left her."

"That's not true. She got playing about with her father-in-law, lame Pantelei."

"Oh, so that's it! And is that why Grigory ran away from home?"

"That's right. And she's still at it. . . ."

Stumbling over the uneven stones, followed by the shameful, filthy whispering, she reached the church porch. The girls standing in the porch giggled as she turned and made her way to the farther gate. Swaying drunkenly, she ran home. At the gate of the yard she took a quick breath and then entered, stumbling over the hem of her skirt, biting her lips till the blood came. Through the lilac darkness the open doorway of the shed yawned blackly. With fierce determination she gathered her last strength, ran to the door and hastily stepped across the threshold. The shed was dry and cold, and smelled of leather harness and musty straw. Gropingly, without thought or feeling, in a sombre yearning which clawed at her shamed and despairing soul, she made her way to a corner. There she picked up a scythe by the handle, removed the blade (her movements were deliberately assured and precise), and,

338

throwing back her head, in a sudden joyous
fire of resolution slashed her throat with its
point. She fell as though struck down by the
burning, savage pain, and vaguely aware that
she had not completely carried out her inten-
tion, she struggled on to all fours, then on to
her knees. Hurriedly (she was terrified by the
blood pouring over her chest), with trembling
fingers she tore off the buttons of her jacket,
then with one hand she drew aside her taut, unyielding breast, and with the other she guided
the point of the scythe. She crawled on her
knees to the wall, thrust the blunt end of the
scythe blade into it, and throwing her arms
behind her head, pressed her chest firmly forward, forward. . . . She clearly heard and felt
the revolting cabbage-like scrunch of the rending flesh; a rising wave of intense pain flowed
over her breast to her throat, and pressed ringing needles into her ears. . . .

The kitchen door scraped. Lukinichna groped
her way down the steps. From the belfry came
the measured tolling of the church bell. With
an incessant grinding roar the giant upreared
floes were floating down the Don. The joyous,
full-flowing, liberated river was carrying its
icy fetters away down to the Sea of Azov.

# XIX

Stepan walked up to Grigory and, seizing the horse's stirrup, pressed hard against its sweating flank.

"Well, how are you, Grigory?"

"Praise be!"

"What are you thinking about? Huh?"

"What should I be thinking about?"

"You've carried off another man's wife. . . . Having your will of her?"

"Let go of the stirrup."

"Don't be scared! I won't hit you."

"I'm not afraid. Don't start that!" Grigory flushed and raised his voice.

"I shan't fight you today. I don't want to. . . . But mark my words, Grigory, sooner or later I'll kill you."

" 'We'll see,' the blind man said!"

"Mark my words well. You've wronged me. You've gelded my life like a hog's. You see there . . ." he stretched out his hands with their grimy palms upward. "I'm ploughing, and the Lord knows what for. Do I need it for myself? I could shift around a bit and get through the winter that way. It's only the loneliness of it all that gets me down. You've done me a great wrong, Grigory."

"It's no good complaining to me. The full man doesn't understand the hungry."

"That's true," Stepan agreed, staring up into Grigory's face. And suddenly he broke into a simple, boyish smile which splintered the corners of his eyes into tiny cracks. "I'm sorry only for one thing, lad, very sorry.... You remember the year before last, that village fight at Shrovetide?"

"No, I don't."

"The day they killed the fuller. When the single men fought the married, don't you remember? Remember how I chased after you? You were young and weak then, a green rush compared to me. I spared you that time, but if I'd hit you as you were running away, I'd have split you in two. You ran quickly, all springy-like; if I'd struck you hard in the ribs you wouldn't be living in the world today."

"Don't let it worry you, we'll have another go at each other yet."

Stepan rubbed his forehead as though trying to recall something. Old Listnitsky, leading his horse by the reins, called to Grigory. Still holding the stirrup with his left hand, Stepan walked alongside the stallion. Grigory watched his every movement. He noticed Stepan's drooping chestnut moustache, the heavy scrub on his long-unshaven chin, the cracked patent-leather strap of his military cap. His dirty face, marked with white runnels of sweat, was sad and strangely unfamiliar. As he looked Grigory felt that he might well be gazing from a hilltop at the distant steppe veiled in a rainy mist. A grey weariness and emptiness ashened Stepan's features. He dropped behind without a word of farewell. Grigory rode on at a walk.

"Wait a bit. And how is ... how is Aksinya?"

Knocking a lump of earth off his boot with the whip, Grigory replied: "Oh, she's all right."

He halted the stallion and glanced back. Stepan was standing with his feet planted wide apart, chewing a stalk between his teeth. For a moment Grigory suddenly felt unaccountably sorry for him, but jealousy rose uppermost. Turning in his saddle, he shouted:

"She doesn't miss you, don't worry!"

"Is that so?"

Grigory lashed his horse between the ears and galloped away without replying.

## XX

Aksinya confessed her pregnancy to Grigory only during the sixth month, when she was no longer able to conceal it from him. She had kept silent so long because she was afraid he would not believe it was his child she was carrying. During the first months of anxious expectation she had sometimes been sick without Grigory noticing it, or if he had noticed it, without his guessing the reason why.

Wrought up, she told him one evening, anxiously scanning his face the while for any change in its expression. But he turned away to the window and coughed with vexation.

"Why didn't you tell me before?"

"I was afraid to, Grisha. I thought you might throw me over. . . ."

Drumming his fingers on the back of the bed, he asked:

"Is it to be soon?"

"The beginning of August, I think."

"Is it Stepan's?"

"No, it's yours!"

"So you say."

"Reckon up for yourself. From the day of the wood-cutting it's. . . ."

"Don't make things up, Aksinya! Even if it was Stepan's, what could you do about it? I want an honest answer."

Weeping angry tears, Aksinya sat down on the bench and broke into a fierce whisper.

"I lived with him so many years and nothing ever happened! Think for yourself! I'm not an ailing woman. .... I must have got it from you. .... And you. ...."

Grigory talked no more about the matter. A new thread of wary aloofness and a light mocking pity was woven into his attitude to Aksinya. She withdrew into herself, asking for no favours. During the summer she lost her good looks, but pregnancy hardly affected her shapely figure; her general fullness concealed her condition, and although her face was thinner it gained a new beauty from her warmly-glowing eyes. She easily managed her work as cook, especially as that year fewer labourers were employed on the estate.

Old Sashka grew fond of Aksinya, with the capricious fondness of old age. Perhaps it was because she treated him with daughterly care: washed his linen, mended his shirts, gave him softer bits at the table. After seeing to his horses old Sashka would come into the kitchen, fetch water, mash potatoes for the pigs, do all kinds of odd jobs, and hopping about round her, expose the bare gums of his mouth as he said:

"You're good to me, and I'll repay you. I'll do anything for you, Aksinya. I'd have been done for without a woman's care. The lice were eating me up. If you ever want anything, just ask me."

Yevgeny had arranged for his coachman to be freed from the spring training camp, and Grigory worked at the mowing, occasionally drove old Listnitsky to the district centre, and spent the rest of the time hunting with him after bustards. The easy-going, comfortable life began to spoil him. He grew lazy and stout, and looked older than his years. The only thing that worried him was the thought of his forthcoming army service. He had neither horse nor equipment, and he could hope for nothing from his father. He saved the wages he received for himself and Aksinya, and even stinted himself on tobacco, hoping to be able to buy a horse without having to beg from his father. Old Listnitsky also promised to help him. Grigory's presentiment that his father would give him nothing was quickly confirmed. At the end of July Pyotr visited his brother, and in the course of conversation mentioned that his father was as angry with him as ever, and had declared that he wouldn't help him get a horse. "Let him go to the local command for one," he had said.

"He needn't worry, I'll go to do my service on my own horse," Grigory declared, stressing "my own."

"How'll you get it? Dance for it?" Pyotr asked, chewing his moustache.

"I'll dance for it, or beg for it, and if I can't get it that way I'll steal it."

"Good lad!"

"I'm going to buy a horse with my wages," Grigory said more seriously.

Pyotr sat on the steps, asking Grigory about his work, food, wages, and chewing the ends of his moustache, nodded his approval. Having completed his inquiries, as he turned to go, he said to his brother:

"You'd better come back, it's no good sticking on your high horse. Do you expect to earn more this way?"

"No, I don't."

"Are you thinking of staying with her?"

"With who?"

"With this one."

"Yes. Why not?"

"Oh, I just wondered."

As Grigory went to see his brother off he asked at last: "How's everything at home?"

Pyotr laughed as he untied his horse from the railing of the steps.

"You've got as many homes as a hare has holes! Everything's all right. Mother misses you. We've got in the hay, three loads of it."

Grigory worriedly scanned the old mare his brother was riding: "No foal this year?"

"No, Brother, she's barren. But the bay

which we got from Christonya has foaled. A stallion it is, a good one too. Long in the legs, sound pasterns, and a strong chest on him. It'll be a good horse."

Grigory sighed. "I miss the village, Pyotr," he said. "I miss the Don. You never see running water here. It's a dreary hole!"

"Come and see us," Pyotr replied as he hoisted his body on to the mare's bony spine.

"Some day."

"Well, good-bye."

"A good journey."

Pyotr had ridden out of the yard when, remembering something, he called to Grigory who was still standing on the steps:

"Natalya ... I'd forgotten ... a terrible thing. . . ."

The wind hovering vulture-like over the farm carried the end of the sentence away from Grigory's ears. Pyotr and the horse were enveloped in velvety dust, and Grigory shrugged his shoulders and went off to the stables.

The summer was bone-dry. Little rain fell and the corn ripened early. As soon as the rye was garnered the barley was ripe and yellow. The four day-labourers and Grigory went out to reap it.

Aksinya had finished work early that day, and she asked Grigory to take her with him.

Despite his attempt to dissuade her, she quickly threw a kerchief over her head, ran out, and caught up with the wagon in which the men were riding.

The event which Aksinya anticipated with yearning and joyous impatience, and Grigory with vague apprehension, happened during the harvesting. Feeling the symptoms, she threw down the rake and lay under a stook. Her travail came on quickly. Biting her blackened tongue, she lay flat on the ground. The labourers with the reaping machine passed her on the turn and shouted. One of them, a young man with a festering sore on his nose and numerous folds in his yellow face that looked as if it has been carved out of wood, called out to her:

"Hey, you! Get up, or you'll melt!"

Grigory got one of the men to take his place at the machine and went across to her.

"What's the matter?"

Her lips writhing uncontrollably, she said hoarsely:

"I'm in labour...."

"I told you not to come, you devil's bitch! Now what are we to do?"

"Don't be angry with me, Grisha...! Oh...! Oh...! Grisha, harness the horse to the wagon. I must get home.... How could I, here

". . . with the Cossacks . . ." she moaned, as the pain gripped her like an iron band.

Grigory ran for the horse. It was grazing in a hollow a little way off, and by the time he drove up, Aksinya had struggled on to all fours, thrust her head into a pile of dusty barley, and was spitting out the prickly ears she had chewed in her pain. She fixed her dilated eyes vacantly on Grigory, and set her teeth into her crumpled apron to prevent the labourers from hearing her horrible, rending cry.

Grigory lifted her into the wagon and drove the horse fast towards the estate.

"Oh! Don't hurry. . . . Oh, death! You're . . . shaking . . . me . . ." Aksinya screamed as her head knocked on the bottom of the wagon.

Grigory silently plied the whip and swung the reins around his head, without a glance back at her.

Pressing her cheeks with her palms, her staring, frenzied eyes rolling wildly, Aksinya bounced about in the wagon as it swung from side to side over the bumpy, little-used road. Grigory kept the horse at a gallop; the shaft-bow bobbed up and down before his eyes, obscuring a dazzling white cloud that hung like polished crystal in the sky. For a moment Aksinya ceased her shrieking howls. The wheels rattled, and her head thudded heavily against

the bottom-board. At first her silence did not
impress itself on Grigory, but then he glanced
back. Aksinya was lying with a horribly distorted face, her cheek pressed hard against the
side of the wagon, her jaws working like a
fish flung ashore. The sweat was pouring from
her brow into the deep sockets of her eyes.
Grigory turned and raised her head, putting
his crumpled cap under it. Glancing sidelong
at him, she said firmly:

"I shall die, Grisha. And that's all there is
to it!"

Grigory shuddered; a chill ran down his
body to his toes. He sought for words of en-
couragement, of comfort, but could not find
them. His lips twisted harshly and he burst
out: "Don't talk nonsense, you fool!" Then he
shook his head, and leaning over backwards,
squeezed her foot: "Aksinya, my little
pigeon. . . ."

The pain died away and left Aksinya for a
moment, then returned with redoubled force.
Feeling something rending her belly, she
arched her body and pierced Grigory's ears
with a terrifying, rising scream. Grigory frantically whipped up the horse.

Then above the rattle of the wheels Grigory
heard her thin, feeble voice:

"Grisha!"

He reined in the horse and turned his head. Aksinya lay in a pool of blood, her arms flung out. Between her legs a living thing was stirring and squealing. Grigory frenziedly jumped down from the wagon and stumbled to the back. Staring into Aksinya's panting, burning mouth, he guessed rather than heard the words:

"Bite through the cord ... tie it with cotton ... from your shirt. ..."

With trembling fingers he tore strands of threads from the sleeve of his cotton shirt, and screwing up his eyes till it hurt, he bit through the navel cord and carefully tied up the bleeding end with cotton.

## XXI

The estate of Yagodnoye clung to the side of the broad dry valley like a growth. The wind blew changeably from north or south; the sun floated in the bluish whiteness of the sky; autumn rustled in on the heels of summer, winter clamped down with its frost and snow, but Yagodnoye remained sunk in its wooden torpor. So the days passed one after the other, alike as twins, and always the estate was cut off from the rest of the world.

The black whisperer-ducks with red rings like spectacles round their eyes still waddled about the farmyard; the guinea-fowls were scattered about like beady rain; gawdy-feathered peacocks miaowed throatily like cats from the stable roof. The old general was fond of all kinds of birds, and even kept a maimed crane. In November, when it heard the faint call of the wild cranes flying to the south, it wrung the heart-strings with its copper-tongued cry of yearning. But it could not fly, for one wing hung uselessly at its side. As the general stood at the window and watched the bird stretching out its neck and jumping, fluttering off the ground, he laughed opening his big mouth under the grey awning of his moustache, and the deep tones of his laughter rocked through the empty white-walled hall.

Venyamin carried his fuzzy head as high as ever, and spent whole days alone in the anteroom, playing cards with himself. Tikhon was as jealous as ever of his pock-marked mistress and Sashka, the day-labourers, Grigory, the master and even the crane to whom Lukerya was devoting the tenderness which overflowed her widowed heart. Every now and then old Sashka would get drunk and beg for twenty-kopeck pieces under old Listnitsky's window.

During all the time of Grigory's stay only two events disturbed the mildewed torpor of the sleepy, monotonous life of Yagodnoye: the coming of Aksinya's child, and the loss of a prize gander. The inhabitants of Yagodnoye quickly grew accustomed to the baby girl, and finding some of the gander's feathers in the meadow, concluded that a fox had carried him off, and settled down again to their peaceful existence.

In the morning, when he awoke, the master would call in Venyamin.

"Did you dream of anything last night?"

"Why, of course, I had a wonderful dream."

"Tell it to me," Listnitsky would order curtly, rolling himself a cigarette.

And Venyamin would relate it. If the dream happened to be uninteresting or frightening, Listnitsky would get angry.

"You dolt! A fool is visited by foolish dreams."

Venyamin started to invent gay and amusing dreams. But it was difficult for him. He started to invent his gay dreams several days in advance, sitting on his trunk and shuffling the cards—puffy and oily as the cheeks of the player. His eyes staring fixedly, he exerted his brain until he reached a point where he stopped having proper dreams altogether. When he woke in the morning, he would strain his memory, trying to recall what he had dreamed, but darkness lay behind him, black darkness.

He had dreamed nothing, not even seen a face in his sleep.

Venyamin's store of artless inventions was soon exhausted, and the master grew angry when he caught him repeating himself.

"You told me that dream about a horse last Thursday, damn you!"

"I dreamed it again, Nikolai Alexeyevich! Honest to God, I dreamed it again!" Venyamin lied calmly.

In December Grigory was summoned to the district administration at Vyeshenskaya. There he was given a hundred rubles to buy a horse, and was instructed to report two days after Christmas at the village of Mankovo for the army draft.

He returned to Yagodnoye in considerable agitation. Christmas was approaching, and he had nothing ready. With the money he had received from the authorities plus his own savings he bought a horse for a hundred and forty rubles. He took Sashka with him and they purchased a presentable enough animal, a six-year-old bay with one hidden blemish. Old Sashka combed his beard with his fingers and said:

"You won't get one cheaper, and the authorities won't see the flaw! They haven't got enough gumption!"

Grigory rode the horse back to Yagodnoye, putting it through its paces.

A week before Christmas Pantelei arrived unexpectedly at Yagodnoye. He did not drive into the yard, but tied up his horse and basket sledge at the gate, and limped towards the servants' quarters, rubbing the icicles off his beard that hung like a black log over the collar of his coat. Grigory happened to be looking out of the window and saw his father approaching.

"Well I'm ... Father!"

For some reason Aksinya ran to the cradle and wrapped up the child. Pantelei stumped into the room, bringing a breath of cold air with him. He removed his fur cap and crossed himself facing the icon, then gazed slowly around the room.

"Good health!"

"Good-morning, Father!" Grigory replied, rising from the bench and striding to the centre of the room.

Pantelei offered Grigory an icy hand, and sat down on the edge of the bench, wrapping his sheepskin around him. He scarcely glanced at Aksinya, who stood very still by the cradle.

"Getting ready for your service?"

"Of course."

Pantelei was silent, staring long and questioningly at Grigory.

"Take your things off, Father, you must be frozen."

"It doesn't matter."

"We'll get the samovar going."

"Thank you." The old man scraped an old spot of mud off his coat with his finger-nail, and added: "I've brought your kit; two coats, a saddle, and trousers. You'll find them all there in the sledge."

Grigory went out and removed the two sacks of equipment from the sledge. When he returned his father rose from the bench.

"When are you going off?" he asked his son.

"The day after Christmas. You aren't going already, are you, Father?"

"I want to get back early."

He took leave of Grigory, and still avoiding Aksinya's eyes, went towards the door. As he lifted the latch he turned his eyes in the direction of the cradle, and said:

"Your mother sends her greetings. She's in bed with trouble in her legs." After a momentary pause, he said heavily: "I shall ride with you to Mankovo. Be ready when I come."

He went out thrusting his hands into warm, knitted gloves. Aksinya, pale with the humiliation she had suffered, said nothing. Grigory paced the room, glancing sideways at Aksinya as he passed her, and constantly stepping on a creaking board.

On Christmas Day Grigory drove his master to Vyeshenskaya. Listnitsky attended mass, had breakfast with his cousin, a local land-owner, and then ordered Grigory to get the sleigh ready for the return journey. Grigory had not finished his bowl of rich pork and cabbage soup, but he rose at once, went to the stable, and harnessed the dapple-grey trotting-horse to the light sleigh.

The wind was sifting the fine, tingling snow-flakes; a silvery froth hissed through the yard; a soft fringe of hoar-frost hung from the trees beyond the fence. The wind shook it down, and as it fell and scattered, it reflected a rainbow-rich variety of colours from the sun. On the roof close to the smoking chimney the chilly jackdaws·were chattering loudly. Startled by the sound of footsteps, they flew off, circled round the house like dove-coloured snow-flakes, then flew to the east, to the church clearly outlined against the violet morning sky.

"Tell the master we're ready," Grigory shouted to the maid that came to the steps of the house.

Listnitsky came out and climbed into the sleigh, his whiskers buried in the collar of his raccoon coat. Grigory wrapped up his legs and adjusted the velvet-lined wolf-skin.

"Warm him up," Listnitsky said glancing at the horse.

Leaning back in his seat, his hands tense on the quivering reins, Grigory watched the ruts, anxiously remembering the far from feeble box on the ears the master had given him for handling the sleigh awkwardly one day early in winter. As they drove down to the Don Grigory released his grip on the reins and rubbed his wind-seared cheeks with his glove.

They arrived at Yagodnoye within two hours. Listnitsky had been silent throughout the drive, occasionally tapping Grigory on the back with his finger as a signal to stop while he rolled and lit a cigarette. Only as they were descending the hill to the house did he ask:

"Early tomorrow morning?"

Grigory turned sideways in his seat, and dragged his frozen lips apart with difficulty. His tongue, stiff with cold, seemed to swell and stick to the back of his teeth.

"Yes," he managed to reply.

"Got all your money?"

"Yes."

"Don't worry about your wife, she'll be all right with us. Be a good soldier; your grandfather was a fine Cossack. And mind," Listnitsky's voice grew muffled as he hid his face from the wind in the collar of his coat, "and mind you conduct yourself in a manner worthy of your grandfather and father. Your father received the first prize for trick riding at the Imperial Review, didn't he?"

"Yes."

"Well then!" the old man ended with a stern note in his voice, as though admonishing Grigory, and buried his face once more in his fur coat.

At the yard Grigory handed over the horse to Sashka, and turned to go to the servants' quarters.

"Your father's arrived," Sashka shouted after him.

Grigory found Pantelei sitting at the table, eating meat jelly. "Tight!" Grigory decided, glancing at his father's flushed face.

"So you're back, soldier?"

"I'm frozen," Grigory answered, clapping his hands together. Turning to Aksinya, he added: "Untie my hood, my fingers are too stiff."

"You must have had the wind against you," his father grunted, chewing steadily.

This time his father was in a kindlier mood, and ordered Aksinya about as if he were in his own home. "Don't be so stingy with the bread, cut some more," he told her.

When he had finished he rose from the table and went towards the door to have a smoke in the yard. As he passed the cradle he rocked it once or twice, pretending that the action was accidental, and asked: "A Cossack?"

"A girl," Aksinya replied for Grigory; and catching the expression of dissatisfaction that passed over the old man's face, she hurriedly added: "She's the image of Grisha!"

Pantelei attentively examined the dark little head sticking out of the clothes, and declared, not without a touch of pride: "She's of our blood...! Well, I never!"

"How did you come, Father?" Grigory asked.

"With the mare and Pyotr's horse."

"You need only have used one, and we could have harnessed mine for the journey to Mankovo."

"Let him go light. He's not a bad horse, you know."

They were both troubled by the same thought, but they talked of various trivial matters. Aksinya took no part in the conversation, and sat on the bed. Her full breasts swelled tightly under her blouse. She had grown noticeably stouter since the birth of the child, and had a new, confidently happy air.

It was late when they went to bed. As she

nestled close at Grigory's side, Aksinya mois-
tened his shirt with her tears and the over-
abundant milk seeping from her breasts.

"I shall pine away. What shall I do without
you?"

"You'll be all right," Grigory murmured.

"The long nights ... the child awake. ...
Just think, Grisha! Four years!"

"In the old days service lasted twenty-five
years, they say."

"What do I care about the old days?"

"Come now, enough of that!"

"Curse your army service, I say."

"I shall come home on furlough."

"On furlough!" Aksinya moaned, sobbing
and wiping her nose on her shift. "A lot of
water will go down the Don before then."

"Not so much whimpering! You're like rain
in autumn, always drizzling."

"You should be in my shoes."

Grigory fell asleep a little before dawn. Aksinya got up and fed the child, then lay down
again. Leaning on her elbows she gazed unblinkingly into Grigory's face, and took a long
farewell of him. She recalled the night when
she had tried to persuade him to go away with
her to the Kuban; it had been the same as
now, except that there had been a moon flooding the yard outside the window with its white

light. The same, and Grigory was still the same, yet not the same. Behind them both lay a long track trodden out by the passing days.

He turned over, muttered something about Olshansky village, and then was silent. Aksinya tried to sleep, but her thoughts drove all sleep away, like wind scattering a haycock. Until daybreak she lay thinking over his disconnected phrase, seeking its meaning. Pantelei awoke as soon as daylight began to foam on the frosty windows.

"Grigory, get up, it's getting light."

Kneeling on the bed, Aksinya pulled on her skirt and with a sigh started looking for the matches.

By the time they had breakfasted and packed, dawn had fully come. The black stakes of the fence were clearly outlined and the stable roof loomed darkly against the misty lilac of the sky. Pantelei went to harness his horses while Grigory tore himself away from Aksinya's desperately passionate kisses and went to say good-bye to Sashka and the other servants.

Wrapping the child up warmly, Aksinya took her out with her to take a last farewell. Grigory lightly touched his daughter's damp little forehead with his lips, and went to his horse.

"Come in the sledge," his father called, as he touched up his horses.

"No, I'll ride my horse."

With deliberate slowness Grigory fastened the saddle-girths, mounted his horse, and gathered the reins in his hand. Aksinya touched the stirrup with her hand and kept repeating:

"Grisha, wait.... There's something I wanted to say....," And puckering her brow, trembling and bewildered, she tried to remember what it was.

"Well, good-bye.... Look after the child.... I must be off; see how far Father's got already."

"Wait, dearest!" With her left hand Aksinya seized the icy iron stirrup; her right arm pressed the baby to her breast; and she had no free hand with which to wipe away the tears streaming from her wide staring eyes.

Venyamin came to the steps of the house.

"Grigory, the master wants you!"

Grigory cursed, waved his whip, and dashed out of the yard. Aksinya ran after him, stumbling in the drifted snow.

He overtook his father at the top of the hill. With an effort of will, he turned and looked back. Aksinya was standing at the gate, the child still pressed to her breast, the ends of her crimson shawl fluttering in the wind.

He rode his horse alongside his father's sledge. After a few moments the old man turned his back to his horses and asked:

"So you're not thinking of living with your wife?"

"That old story again? We've had that out already...."

"So you're not."

"No, I'm not!"

"You haven't heard that she laid hands on herself?"

"Yes, I've heard. I happened to meet a man from the village."

"And in the sight of God?"

"Why, Father, after all ... it's no use crying over spilt milk."

"Don't use that devil's talk to me. What I'm saying to you, I'm saying for your own good," Pantelei flared up.

"I've a child back there. What's the use of talking? You can't push the other on to me now...."

"Are you sure you're not rearing another man's child?"

Grigory turned pale; his father had touched a sore spot. Ever since the child was born he had tormentedly nursed the suspicion in his mind, while concealing it from Aksinya and from himself. At night, when Aksinya was asleep, he had more than once gone to the cradle and stared down at the child, seeking his own features in its swarthily rosy face, and had turned back to bed as uncertain as before. Stepan was dark-chestnut, almost as dark as he, and how was he to know whose blood flowed in the child's veins? At times he thought the child resembled him, at other times she was painfully like Stepan. Grigory had no feeling for her, except perhaps hostility as he recalled the moments he had lived through when he had driven Aksinya back from the steppes in the throes of childbirth. Once when Aksinya was busy in the kitchen, he had had to change the child's wet napkin. As he did so he had felt a sharp, burning emotion. He had bent stealthily over the cradle and pressed the baby's pink stiff toe between his teeth.

His father probed mercilessly at the wound, and Grigory, his palm resting on the saddle-bow, numbly replied:

"Whoever it belongs to, I won't leave the child."

Pantelei waved his whip at the horses without turning round:

"Natalya's spoilt her good looks. She carries her head on one side like a paralytic. It seems she cut a tendon." He lapsed into silence.

The runners creaked as they cut through the snow; the hoofs of Grigory's horse clicked as they knocked together.

"And how is she now?" Grigory asked, studiously picking a burr out of his horse's mane.

"She got over it somehow or other. She was laid up seven months. On Trinity Sunday she was all but gone. Father Pankraty came to say prayers. And then she began to pick up. She'd tried to stab herself with a scythe but her hand shook and she just missed her heart. It would have been the end of her otherwise...."

"Quicker down the hill!" Grigory said, standing in his stirrups and using his whip; the horse leaped forward, sending a shower of snow from its hoofs over the sledge, and broke into a trot.

"We're taking Natalya in," Pantelei shouted, coming up with him. "The woman doesn't want to live with her own folk. I saw her the other day and told her to come to us."

Grigory made no reply. They drove as far as the first village without exchanging a word, and his father made no further reference to the subject.

That day they covered seventy versts. They arrived at Mankovo the following evening as dusk was falling, and spent the night in the quarters allotted to the Vyeshenskaya recruits.

Next morning the district ataman took the Vyeshenskaya recruits before the medical commission. Grigory fell in with the other lads from his own village. In the morning Mitka Korshunov, riding a tall bay horse equipped with a new and gaily-ornamented saddle and harness, had passed Grigory standing at the door of his quarters, but had gone by without a word of greeting.

The men undressed in turn in the cold room of the local civil administration. Military clerks bustled around, and the adjutant to the provincial ataman hurried past in short patent-leather boots. From an inner room came the sound of the doctors' orders, and snatches of talk.

"Sixty-nine."

"Pavel Ivanovich, pass me an indelible pencil," croaked a drink-sodden voice near the door.

"Chest measurement...."

"Yes, obviously hereditary...."

"Put down syphilis."

"Take your hand away. You're not a girl."

"Fine physique."

"... Infects the whole village. Special measures must be taken. I have already reported the matter to His Excellency."

"Pavel Ivanovich, look at this fellow's physique."

"Oho!"

Grigory got undressed beside a tall redhaired lad from another village. A clerk came out and, straightening his shoulders so that his tunic creased at the back, curtly called Grigory and the other lad into the examination room.

"Hurry up!" gasped the red-head, blushing and pulling off a sock.

Grigory went in, his back all goose-flesh with the cold. His swarthy body was the colour of oak. He felt embarrassed as he glanced down at his hairy legs. In the corner a square-limbed lad was standing naked on the scales. Someone, evidently the doctor's assistant, flicked the weights to and fro, called out a figure and told him to get down.

The humiliating procedure of the medical examination irritated Grigory. A grey-haired doctor in a white coat sounded him with the aid of a stethoscope. A younger doctor turned up his eyelids and looked at his tongue. Behind him a third in horn-rimmed spectacles bustled about, rubbing his hands.

"On the scales!" an officer ordered.

Grigory stepped on to the cold platform.

"Five poods ... six and a half pounds."

"Wha-a-at! He's not particularly tall, either," the grey-haired doctor exclaimed, turning Grigory round by the arm.

"Astonishing!" the younger man coughed.

"How much?" an officer sitting at the table asked in surprise.

"Five poods, six and a half pounds," the grey-haired doctor replied.

"How about the Lifeguards for him?" the district military commissary asked, bending a black sleek head towards his neighbour at the table.

"He has the face of a brigand. . . . Very savage-looking. . . ."

"Hey, turn round! What's that on your back?" an officer wearing colonel's epaulettes shouted, impatiently tapping his finger on the table. The grey-haired doctor mumbled something and Grigory, trying to restrain the trembling of his body, turned his back to the table and replied:

"I caught cold in the spring. It's a boil."

By the end of the examination the officers at the table had decided that Grigory would have to be drafted into an ordinary regiment.

"The Twelfth Regiment, Melekhov. D'you hear?" he was told. And as he went towards the door he heard a shocked whispering:

"It's impossible. Just imagine it, if the emperor saw a face like that? His eyes alone...."

"He's a cross-breed. From the East, no doubt."

"And his body isn't clean. Those boils...."

Other men from his village who were waiting their turn crowded round Grigory:

"How did it go, Grisha?"

"What regiment?"

"The Lifeguards, eh?"

"How much did you go on the scales?"

Hopping on one foot while he pushed his legs into his trousers, Grigory snapped: "Oh, go to hell! What regiment? The Twelfth."

"Korshunov, Dmitry; Kargin, Ivan," shouted the clerk, poking his head round the door.

Buttoning up his coat as he went, Grigory ran down the steps.

The warm wind breathed of thaw; the road was bare of snow in places, and steaming. Clucking hens fluttered across the street, geese were splashing in a puddle; their feet looked orange-pink in the water, like frost-nipped autumn leaves.

The examination of the horses took place the following day. They were all drawn up on the square in a long line against the church wall. Officers bustled to and fro; a veterinary surgeon and his assistant passed down the long line of animals. The Vyeshenskaya ataman went running from the scales to the table in the middle of the square, where the results of the examination were being recorded. A military police officer went by, deep in conversation with a young captain.

When his turn came, Grigory led his horse to the scales. The surgeon and his assistant measured every part of the animal's body, then weighed it. Before it could be led from the platform the surgeon had deftly taken it by the upper lip, looked at its teeth, felt its chest muscles and, running his strong fingers over its body, like a spider, reached its legs. He felt the knee joints, tapped the tendons, squeezed the bone above the fetlocks. When he had finished his examination he passed on, his white apron flapping in the wind and scattering the scent of carbolic acid.

Grigory's horse was rejected. Sashka's hopes had proved unjustified, and the experienced surgeon had been shrewd enough to discover the secret blemish of which the old man had spoken. Grigory at once held an agitated consultation with his father, and before half an hour had elapsed he led Pyotr's horse on to the scales. The surgeon passed it almost without examination.

Grigory led the horse a little way off, found a comparatively dry spot, and spread out his saddle-cloth on the ground. His father held his horse, talking to another old man who was also seeing off his son. Past them strode a tall, grey-haired general in a light-grey cloak and a silver astrakhan cap, followed by a group of officers.

"That's the provincial ataman," Pantelei whispered, nudging Grigory from behind.

"Looks like a general."

"Major-General Makeyev. He's a strict devil!"

A crowd of officers from various regiments and batteries followed in the wake of the ataman. An artillery major, broad in the hips and shoulders, was talking loudly to a tall handsome Guards officer of the Ataman's Regiment:

"... What the devil! Such an amazing contrast, you know! An Estonian village, the majority of the people blonde, and this girl such a contrast! And she wasn't the only one! We had all sorts of guesses about it, and then we learned that twenty years ago...." The officers walked past the spot where Grigory was arranging his equipment on his saddle-cloth and the wind brought him the final words amid a burst of laughter from the officers: "...Apparently a squadron of your Guards used to be stationed in the village."

A clerk ran past buttoning his jacket with trembling ink-stained fingers and the district assistant chief of police bellowed after him: "I told you three copies. Confound you!"

Grigory stared curiously at the unfamiliar faces of the officers and officials. An adjutant fixed a bored gaze on him, and turned away as he met Grigory's attentive eyes. An old captain went by almost at a run, looking agitated by something and biting his upper lip with his yellow teeth. Grigory noticed a vein beating over the captain's ginger eyebrow.

On his new saddle-cloth Grigory had set out his saddle, with its green pommel and saddle-bags at back and front; two army coats, two pairs of trousers. a tunic, two pairs of top-boots, a pound and a half of biscuit, a tin of corned beef, groats, and other food in the regulation quantities. In the open saddle-bags were four horseshoes, shoe-nails wrapped in a greasy rag, a soldier's hussif with a couple of needles and thread, and towels.

He gave a last glance over his accoutrements, and squatted down to rub some mud off the ends of the packstrings with his sleeve. From the end of the square the army commission slowly passed along the rows of Cossacks drawn up behind their saddle-cloths. The officers and the ataman examined the equipment closely, holding up the edges of their light-coloured greatcoats as they stooped to rummage in the saddle-bags, turned out the contents of the hussifs, and weighed the bags of biscuits in their hands.

"Look at that tall one over there, lads," said a young Cossack standing next to Grigory, pointing towards the provincial chief of military police, "scratching like a dog after a polecat."

"Just look at the devil. Turning the bag inside out!"

"Something wrong there, or he wouldn't do that."

"Surely he isn't counting the shoe-nails."

"Just like a dog!"

The talk gradually died away as the commission approached. Only a few more men and it would be Grigory's turn. The provincial ataman was carrying a glove in his left hand and swinging his right, keeping the elbow straight. Grigory drew himself up. Behind him his father coughed. The wind carried the smell of horse piss and melted snow over the square. The sun looked unhappy, as though after a drinking bout.

The group of officers halted by the man next to Grigory, then came on to him one by one.

"Your surname, Christian name?"

"Melekhov, Grigory."

The police officer picked up the greatcoat by its belt, smelled the lining, and hurriedly counted the fastenings; another officer, wearing a cornet's epaulettes, felt the good cloth of the trousers between his fingers. A third stopped and rummaged in the saddle-bags, stooping so low that the wind threw the skirts of his greatcoat on to his back. With his thumb and forefinger the police officer cautiously poked at the rag containing shoe-nails as though afraid it might be hot, and counted the nails in a whisper.

"Why are there only twenty-three nails? What is this?" he angrily pulled at the corner of the rag.

"Not at all, Your Honour. Twenty-four."

"What, am I blind?"

Grigory hastily turned back a folded corner, revealing the twenty-fourth nail. As he did so his rough swarthy fingers lightly touched the officer's sugar-white hand. The officer snatched his hand away as though struck, rubbed it on the edge of his greatcoat, frowning fastidiously, and drew on his glove.

Grigory noticed his action and straightened up with a bitter smile. Their eyes met, and the officer flushed and raised his voice.

"What's all this, what's all this, Cossack? Why aren't your packstrings in order? Why aren't your snaffles right? And what does this mean? Are you a Cossack or a muzhik? Where's your father?"

Pantelei pulled on the horse's rein and stepped forward a pace, clicking his lame leg.

"Don't you know the Cossack regulations?" the officer, who was ill-tempered after losing at cards that morning, poured out his wrath upon him.

The provincial ataman came up, and the officer subsided. The ataman thrust the toe of his boot into the padding of the saddle, hiccupped and passed on to the next man. The draft officer of the regiment to which Grigory had been drafted politely turned out all his belongings down to the contents of the hussif, and passed on last of all, walking backwards to shield a match from the wind as he lit a cigarette.

A day later a train of red railway trucks loaded with horses, Cossacks and forage left for Voronezh. In one of them stood Grigory. Past the open door crawled an unfamiliar, flat landscape; a blue and tender thread of forest whirled by in the distance. Behind him the horses were munching hay and stepping from hoof to hoof as they felt the unsteady floor beneath them. The wagon smelled of wormwood, horses' sweat, and the spring thaw; a distant thread of forest lurked on the horizon, blue, pensive, and as inaccessible as the faintly-shining evening-star.

# PART THREE

## I

It was on a warm and cheerful spring day in March, 1914 that Natalya returned to her father-in-law's house. Pantelei was mending the broken wattle fence with fluffy dove-coloured twigs. The silvery icicles hanging from the roofs were dripping, and the traces of former runnels showed like black tar stains under the eaves. A ruddier, warmer sun caressed the melting hills, and the earth was swelling; the early grass looked like green malachite on the bare chalky headlands that bulged from the hill beyond the Don.

Natalya, thinner and much changed, approached her father-in-law from behind and bowed her scarred, slightly crooked neck:

"Good health, Father!"

"Natalyushka! Welcome, my dear, welcome!" Pantelei exclaimed fussing over her. The twigs dropped out of his hand. "Why haven't you been to see us? Come in, Mother will be right glad to see you."

"Father, I've come. . . ." Natalya stretched out her hand uncertainly, and turned away. "If you don't drive me away, I'd like to stay with you always," she added.

"And why shouldn't you, my dear? Are you a stranger to us? Look, Grigory has written about you in his letter. He's told us to ask about you."

They went into the kitchen. Pantelei limped about in joyful agitation. Ilyinichna wept as she embraced Natalya.

"You want a child," she whispered. "That would win him. Sit down. I'll get you some pancakes, shall I?"

Dunya, flushed and smiling, came running into the kitchen and embraced Natalya round the knees. "You shameless thing! You forgot all about us!" she reproached her.

"Now then, you madcap!" her father shouted at her with feigned severity.

"How you've grown!" Natalya murmured, pulling Dunya's arms apart and looking into her eyes.

They all talked together, interrupting one another. Ilyinichna, supporting her cheek on her palm, grieved as she looked at Natalya, so changed from what she had been.

"You've come for good?" Dunya asked, clasping Natalya's hands.

"Who knows...?"

"Why, where else should my own daughter-in-law live? You'll stay with us," Ilyinichna decided, as she pushed a platter of pancakes across the table.

Natalya had come to her husband's parents only after long vacillation. At first her father would not let her go. He shouted at her in indignation when she suggested it, and attempted to persuade her against such a step. But it was difficult for her to look her own people in the face; since her attempted suicide she felt that with her own family she was almost a stranger. For his part, after he had seen Grigory off to the army Pantelei was continually wheedling her to come, for he was determined to have her back and to reconcile Grigory to her.

From that day in March Natalya lived with the Melekhovs. Pyotr was friendly and brotherly; Darya gave little outward sign of her dissatisfaction, but her occasional sidelong glances were more than compensated by Dunya's attachment and the parental attitude of the old people.

The very day after Natalya came to them Pantelei ordered Dunya to write a letter to Grigory:

*Greetings, our own son, Grigory Panteleye-vich! We send you a deep bow, and from all my fatherly heart, with your mother Vasilisa Ilyinichna, a parental blessing. Your brother Pyotr Panteleyevich and his wife Darya Mat-veyevna greet you and wish you health and well-being; also your sister Dunya and all at home greet you. We received your letter, sent in February, the fifth day, and heartily thank you for it. And as you wrote that the horse is knocking his legs smear him with some lard, you know how, and don't shoe his hind hoofs so long as there is no slipperiness or bare ice about. Your wife Natalya Mironovna is living with us and is well and comfortable. Your mother sends you some dried cherries and a pair of woollen socks, and some bacon and other things. We are all alive and well, but Darya's baby has died. The other day Pyotr and I roofed the shed, and he orders you to look after the horse and keep it well. The cows have calved, the old mare seems to be in foal, we put a stallion from the district stables to her. We are glad to hear about your service and that your officers are pleased with you.*

*Serve as you should. Service for the Tsar will not be in vain. And Natalya will live with us now, and you think that over. And one other trouble, just before Lent a wolf killed three sheep. Now, keep well, and in God's keeping. Don't forget your wife, that is my order to you. She is a good woman and your legal wife. Don't break the furrow, and listen to your father.*

*Your father, Senior Sergeant*

*Pantelei Melekhov.*

Grigory's regiment was stationed at a little place called Radzivillovo some four versts from the Russo-Austrian frontier. He rarely wrote home. To the letter informing him that Natalya was living with his father he wrote a cautiously worded reply, and asked his father to greet her in his name. All his letters were non-committal and obscure in their meaning. Pantelei made Dunya or Pyotr read them to him several times, pondering over the thought concealed between the lines. Just before Easter he wrote and asked Grigory definitely whether on his return from the army he would live with his wife or with Aksinya as before.

Grigory delayed his reply. Only after Trinity Sunday did they receive a brief letter from

382

him. Dunya read it quickly, swallowing the ends of her words, and Pantelei had difficulty in grasping the essential thought among the numerous greetings and inquiries. At the end of the letter Grigory dealt with the question of Natalya:

*You asked me to say whether I shall live with Natalya or not, but I tell you, Father, once a thing's been cut off, you can't stick it on again. And how shall I make it up with Natalya, when you know yourself that I have a child. And I can't promise anything, it is painful for me to talk about it. The other day a fellow was caught smuggling goods across the frontier and we happened to see him. He said there would be war with the Austrians soon, that their tsar has come to the frontier to see where to begin the war from and which land to grab for himself. If war begins maybe I shan't be left alive, and nothing can be settled beforehand.*

Natalya worked for her foster-parents and lived in continual hope of her husband's return. She never wrote to Grigory, but nobody in the family yearned with more pain and desire to receive a letter from him.

Life in the village continued in its inviolable order, Cossacks who had served their term in the army returned home, on workdays dull labour imperceptibly consumed the time, on Sunday mornings the village poured in family droves into the church: the Cossacks in tunics and holiday trousers, the women in long, coloured skirts that swept the dust, and embroidered blouses with puff sleeves.

In the square stood empty wagons, their shafts high in the air, horses whinnied and all kinds of people went to and fro; by the fireshed the Bulgar settlers traded in vegetables set out in long rows; behind them the children ran about in bands and stared at the unharnessed camels superciliously surveying the market square. Everywhere were crowds of men wearing red-banded caps, and women in bright kerchiefs. The camels, their eyes glazed with a torpid green, chewed the cud as they rested from their constant toil on the water-wheels.

In the evening the streets groaned with the tramp of feet, with song, and dancing to the accordions; and only late at night did the last voices die away on the outskirts of the village.

Natalya, who never went to the evening gatherings, sat listening gladly to Dunya's artless stories. Imperceptibly Dunya was growing into a shapely and, in her way, good-looking girl. She matured early, like an early apple.

That year her elder girl-friends forgot that they had reached adolescence before her and took her into their circle. Dunya was like her father, dark and sturdy. She was fifteen now, her figure still girlish and angular. She was an artless, almost pitiful mixture of childhood and blossoming youth; her small breasts grew and pressed noticeably against her blouse; and her black eyes in their long, rather slanting sockets, still sparkled bashfully and mischievously. She would come back after an evening out and tell only Natalya her innocent secrets.

"Natalya, I want to tell you something. . . ."

"Well, tell on!"

"Yesterday Misha Koshevoi sat the whole evening with me on the stump by the village granaries."

"Why are you blushing?"

"Oh, I'm not!"

"Look in the glass; you're all one great flame."

"Well, you made me."

"All right, go on, I won't say a thing."

Dunya rubbed her burning cheeks with her brown palms, pressed her fingers to her temples, and her laughter tinkled out youthfully and without cause.

"He said I was like a little azure flower."

"Well, go on!" Natalya encouraged her, rejoicing in another's joy, forgetting her own past and downtrodden happiness.

"And I said: 'Don't tell lies, Misha!' And he swore it was true."

Shaking her head, Dunya sent her laughter pealing through the room. The black, heavy plaits of her hair slipped like lizards over her shoulders and back.

"What else did he say?"

"He asked me to give him my hanky for a keepsake."

"And did you?"

"No. I said I wouldn't. 'Go and ask your woman,' I told him. He's been seen with Yerofeyev's daughter-in-law, and she's a bad woman, she plays about with the men."

"You'd better keep away from him."

"I'm going to!" Dunya continued her story, trying to hide the smile that came to her lips. "And then, as the three of us, two other girls and me, were coming home, drunken old Grandpa Mikhei came after us. 'Kiss me, my dears, and I'll pay you two kopecks apiece,' he shouted. And Nyura hit him on the face with a twig and we ran away."

The summer was dry. By the village the Don grew shallow, and where the surging current had run swiftly a ford was made, and bullocks could cross to the other bank without wetting their backs. At night a sultry stuffiness flowed down into the village from the range of hills, and the wind filled the air with the spicy scent of scorched grass. The dry growth of the steppe was afire, and a sickly-smelling haze hung over the Don-side slopes. At night the clouds deepened over the river and ominous peals of thunder were heard; but no rain came to refresh the parched earth, although the lightning rent the sky into jagged, livid fragments.

Night after night an owl screeched from the belfry. The cries surged terrifyingly over the village, and the owl flew from the belfry to the cemetery and moaned over the brownish grassy mounds of the graves.

"There's trouble brewing," the old men prophesied, as they listened to the owl screeching from the cemetery.

"There's war coming. An owl called just like that before the Turkish campaign."

"Perhaps there will be cholera again."

"Expect no good when it flies from the church to the dead."

For two nights Martin Shamil, who lived close to the cemetery, lay in wait by the cemetery fence for the accursed owl, but the invisible, mysterious bird flew noiselessly over him, alighted on a cross at the other end of the cemetery, and sent its alarming cries over the sleepy village. Martin swore indecently, shot at the black, hanging belly of a cloud, and went home. On his return his wife, a timorous, ailing woman as fertile as a doe rabbit, greated him with reproaches.

"You're a fool, a hopeless fool!" she declared. "The bird doesn't interfere with you, does it? What if God should punish you? Here I am in my last month and suppose I don't give birth because of you."

"Shut up, woman!" Martin ordered her. "You'll be all right, never fear! What's that bird doing here, giving us all the cold shivers? It's calling down woe on us, the devil! If war breaks out they'll take me off, and look at the litter you've given me!" He waved at the corner where the children were sleeping.

Talking with the old men in the market place, Pantelei solemnly announced:

"Our Grigory writes that the Austrian tsar has come to the frontier, and has given orders to collect all his troops in one place and to march on Moscow and Petersburg."

The old men remembered past wars, and shared their apprehensions with one another.

"But there won't be any war," one objected. "Look at the harvest."

"The harvest has nothing to do with it. It's the students giving trouble, I expect."

"In any case we shall be the last to hear of it. But who will the war be with?"

"With the Turks, about the sea. They can't come to an agreement on how to divide the sea."

"Is it so difficult? Let them divide it into two strips, like we do the meadowland."

The talk turned to jest, and the old men went about their business.

The early meadow hay was waiting to be mown. The fading grass beyond the Don, which was not a patch on the grass of the steppe, was sickly and scentless. It was the same earth, yet the grass drank in different juices. In the steppe there was black soil, so heavy and firm that the herd left no traces where they passed over it. The grass there was strong and fragrant. But along the Don banks the soil was damp and rotten, growing a poor and scrubby grass which even the cattle would not always look at.

Haymaking was about to begin when an event occurred which shook the village from one end to the other. The district chief of police arrived with an inspector and a little black-toothed officer in a uniform never seen before in the village. They sent for the ataman, collected witnesses, and then went straight to cross-eyed Lukeshka's house. They walked along the path on the sunlit side of the street, the village ataman running ahead like a cockerel. The inspector, his dusty boots stamping on the blobs of sunlight, questioned him:

"Is Stockman at home?"

"Yes, Your Honour."

"What does he do for a living?"

"He's just a craftsman. Works with his plane. . . ."

"You haven't noticed anything suspicious about him?"

"Not at all."

As the police chief walked along, hat in hand, he squeezed a pimple on the bridge of his nose and panted in his thick uniform. The little officer picked his black teeth with a straw and puckered his red-rimmed eyes.

"Does he ever have visitors?" the inspector asked, pulling the ataman back.

"Yes, they play cards sometimes."

"Who?"

"Chiefly labourers from the mill."

"Who exactly?"

"The engineman, the scalesman, the roller-man David, and sometimes some of our Cossacks."

The inspector halted and waited for the of-

ficer, who had lagged behind. He said something to him, twisting a button on his tunic,
then beckoned to the ataman. The ataman
ran up on tiptoe, holding his breath. Knotted
veins throbbed and quivered in his neck.

"Take two of those on duty and arrest the
men you mentioned. Bring them to the administration, and we'll be along in a minute or
two. Do you understand?"

The ataman drew himself up so that the
veins bulged over his high collar, uttered a
kind of grunt and turned away to execute his
instructions.

Stockman, his vest unbuttoned, was sitting
with his back to the door, cutting out a plywood pattern with a fret-saw.

"Kindly stand up; you're under arrest."

"What for?"

"You occupy two rooms?"

"Yes."

"We shall search them."

The officer caught his spur on the doormat,
walked across to the table and with a frown
picked up the first book that came to hand.

"I want the key of that trunk."

"To what do I owe this visit?"

"There'll be time to talk to you afterwards."

Stockman's wife looked through the doorway from the other room and drew back. The

inspector and his clerk followed her into the other room.

"What's this?" the officer asked Stockman quietly, holding up a book in a yellow cover.

"A book," Stockman replied with a shrug.

"You can keep your witticisms for a more suitable occasion. Answer the question properly."

Suppressing a wry smile Stockman leaned his back against the stove. The district chief of police glanced over the officer's shoulder at the book, and then turned to Stockman:

"Are you studying this?"

"I'm interested in the subject," Stockman replied drily, parting his black beard into two equal strands with a small comb.

"I see!"

The officer glanced through the pages of the book and threw it back on the table. He looked through a second, put it aside, and having read the cover of the third, turned to Stockman again.

"Where do you keep the rest of this type of literature?"

Stockman screwed up one eye as though taking aim, and replied:

"You see all that I have."

"You're lying," the officer retorted, waving the book at him.

"I demand. . . ."

"Search the rooms!"

Gripping the hilt of his sabre, the chief of police went across to the trunk, where a pock-marked Cossack guard, obviously terrified by the circumstances in which he found himself, had begun to rummage among the clothing and linen.

"I demand polite treatment," Stockman managed to say at last, screwing up his eye and aiming at the bridge of the officer's nose.

"Be quiet, fellow."

The men turned out everything that it was possible to turn out. The search was conducted in the workshop also. The zealous inspector even knocked on the walls with his knuckles.

When the search was over, Stockman was taken to the administration office. He walked along the middle of the road in front of the Cossack guard, one hand tucked into the lapel of his old coat, the other swinging as though he were shaking mud off his fingers. The others walked along the sunlit path by the walls; and again the inspector trod on the blobs of sunlight with his boots that were now green from the grass. He was no longer carrying his hat in his hand, but had clamped it down firmly over his gristly ears.

Stockman was the last of the prisoners to be examined. Ivan Alexeyevich, with hands still oily, the smiling David, Knave with his jacket over his shoulders, and Misha Koshevoi, who had already been questioned, were herded together in the ante-room, guarded by Cossacks.

Rummaging in his portfolio the inspector questioned Stockman:

"When I examined you in regard to the manslaughter at the mill why did you conceal the fact that you are a member of the Russian Social-Democratic Labour Party?"

Stockman stared silently over the investigator's head.

"That much is established. You will receive a suitable reward for your work," the inspector shouted, annoyed by the prisoner's silence.

"Please begin your examination," Stockman said in a bored tone, and glancing at a stool, he asked for permission to sit down. The inspector did not reply, but glared as Stockman calmly seated himself.

"When did you come here?"

"Last year."

"On the instructions of your organization?"

"Without any instructions."

"How long have you been a member of your party?"

"What are you talking about?"

"I ask you, how long have you been a member of the Russian Social-Democratic Labour Party?"

"I think that. . . ."

"I don't care what you think. Answer the question. Denial is useless, even dangerous." The inspector drew a document out of his portfolio and pinned it to the table with his forefinger. "I have here a report from Rostov, confirming your membership in the party I mentioned."

Stockman turned his eyes quickly to the document, rested his gaze on it for a moment, and then, stroking his knee, replied firmly:

"Since 1907."

"I see! You deny that you have been sent here by your party?"

"Yes."

"In that case why did you come here?"

"There seemed to be a shortage of mechanics here."

"But why did you choose this particular district?"

"For the same reason."

"Have you now, or have you at any time had any contact with your organization during the period of your stay here?"

"No."

"Do they know you have come here?"

"I expect so."

The inspector sharpened his pencil with a pearl-handled penknife, and pursed his lips:

"Are you in correspondence with any members of your party?"

"No."

"Then what about the letter which was discovered during the search?"

"That is from a friend who has no connection whatever with any revolutionary organization."

"Have you received any instructions from Rostov?"

"No."

"What did the labourers at the mill gather in your rooms for?"

Stockman shrugged his shoulders as though astonished at the stupidity of the question.

"They used to come along in the winter evenings, to pass the time away. We played cards. . . ."

"And read books prohibited by law?" the inspector suggested.

"No. Everyone of them was almost illiterate."

"Nonetheless the engineman from the mill, and the others also do not deny this fact."

"That is untrue."

"It seems to me you haven't even an elementary understanding of ..." Stockman smiled at this, and the inspector, forgetting what he had been going to say, concluded: "You simply have no sense. You persist in denials that are to your own disadvantage. It is quite clear that you've been sent here by your party in order to carry on demoralizing activities among the Cossacks, in order to turn them against the government. I fail to understand why you're playing this game of pretence. It can't diminish your offence...."

"Those are all guesses on your part. May I smoke? Thank you. And they are guesses entirely without foundation."

"Did you read this book to the workers who visited your rooms?" the inspector put his hand on a small book and covered the title. Above his hand the name "Plekhanov" was visible.

"We read poetry," Stockman replied, and puffed at his cigarette, gripping the bone holder tightly between his fingers.

The next morning the postal tarantass drove out of the village with Stockman dozing on the back seat, his beard buried in his coat collar. On each side of him a Cossack armed with a sabre was squeezed on the seat. One of them, a curly-headed pock-marked fellow, gripped Stockman's elbow firmly in his knotty, dirty fingers, casting timorous sidelong glances at him, and keeping his other hand on his battered scabbard. The tarantass rattled briskly down the street. By the Melekhovs' farmyard a little woman wrapped in a shawl stood waiting for it, her back against the wattle fence.

The tarantass sped past, and the woman, pressing her hands to her breast, flung herself after it.

"Osip! Osip Davydovich! Oh, what shall I do...."

Stockman attempted to wave his hand to her, but the pock-marked Cossack jumped up and clutched his arm, and in a hoarse, savage voice shouted:

"Sit down, or I'll cut you down!"

For the first time in all his simple life he had seen a man who dared to act against the tsar himself.

## II

The long road from Mankovo to the little town of Radzivillovo lay somewhere behind him in a grey, intangible mist. Grigory tried occasionally to recall the road, but could only dimly remember station buildings, the train wheels clattering beneath the shaking floor, the scent of horses and hay, endless threads of railway line flowing under them, the smoke that billowed from the engine, and the bearded face of a gendarme on the station platform either at Voronezh or at Kiev, he was not sure which.

At the place where they detrained were crowds of officers, and clean-shaven men in grey overcoats, talking a language he could not understand. It took a long time for the horses to be unloaded, but when this had been accomplished the assistant echelon commander led three hundred or more Cossacks to the veterinary hospital. A long procedure in connection with the examination of the horses. Then allotment to troops. N.C.O.'s bustling about. The First Troop was formed of light-brown horses, the Second of bay and dun, the Third of dark-brown. Grigory was allotted to the Fourth, which consisted of plain brown and golden horses. The Fifth was composed entirely of sorrel, and the Sixth of black horses. The troops were put under the command of sergeants-major, who took them out to the various cavalry squadrons stationed at villages and estates in the neighbourhood.

The debonair pop-eyed sergeant-major wearing long-service badges rode past Grigory and asked:

"What stanitsa are you from?"

"Vyeshenskaya."

"Are you bob-tailed*?"

The Cossacks from other stanitsas chuckled and Grigory swallowed the insult in silence.

The road taken by Grigory's troop led them along the highway. The Don horses, which had never seen proper highways before, at first stepped along gingerly, as if on an ice-bound river, setting their ears back and snorting; but after a while they got the feel of the road and their fresh-shod hoofs clattered sharply as they moved on. The unfamiliar Polish land was criss-crossed with slices of straggling forest. The day was warm and overcast, and the sun hovering behind a dense curtain of cloud also seemed alien and unfamiliar.

The estate of Radzivillovo was some four versts from the station, and they reached it in half an hour.

"What village is this, uncle?" a young Cossack asked the sergeant-major, pointing to the naked tree tops in a garden.

"What village? You forget about your Cossack villages here, my lad, this isn't the Don Province."

"What is it then, uncle?"

---

* Each stanitsa had a nickname. Vyeshenskaya was known as Dogs.

"I, your uncle? A fine nephew you make! That, my lad, is the estate of Princess Urusova. Our Fourth Company is quartered here."

Despondently stroking his horse's neck, Grigory stared at the neatly-built, two-storied house, the wooden fence, and the unfamiliar style of the farm buildings. But as they rode past the orchard the bare trees whispered the same language as those in the distant Don country.

Life now showed its most tedious, stupefying side to the Cossacks. Deprived of work, the young men quickly grew homesick, and spent most of their free time talking. Grigory's troop was quartered in a great tile-roofed wing of the house, sleeping on pallet beds under the windows. At night the paper pasted over the chinks of the window sounded in the breeze like a distant shepherd's horn, and as he listened to it amid the snoring Grigory was seized with a well-nigh irresistible desire to get up, go to the stables, saddle his horse and ride and ride until he reached home again.

Reveille was sounded at five o'clock, and the first duty of the day was to clean and groom the horses. During the brief half-hour when the horses were feeding there was opportunity for desultory conversation.

"This is a hell of a life, boys!"

"I can't stick it."

"And the sergeant-major! What a swine! Making us wash the horses' hoofs!"

"They're making the pancakes at home now . . . today is Shrove-Tuesday."

"I could just do with a spot of necking."

"I had a dream last night, lads, I dreamed that Father and me were mowing hay in the meadow and the village folk were all scattered round like daisies on a threshing-floor," said Prokhor Zykov, a quiet lad with gentle calf-like eyes. "And we just went on mowing and mowing. . . . Made me feel right cheerful!"

"I bet my wife is saying: 'I wonder what my Nikolai is doing?' "

"Ho-ho-ho! She'll be belly-rubbing with your father most likely!"

"Well, that's. . . ."

"There isn't a woman in the world who won't try another man when her husband's away."

"Why worry? A woman's not a jug of milk. There'll be enough left for us when we get back."

Yegor Zharkov, the gayest, lewdest man in the company, who had little respect for anyone and still less shame, broke into the conversation, winking and smiling suggestively:

"It's a sure thing: your father won't leave your wife alone. He's a fine he-dog. I'll tell you a story," he added, sweeping his listeners with his glittering glance.

"One old grumble kept running after his daughter-in-law, gave her no rest, but his son was always in the way. So what did the old man do? At night he went into the yard and opened the gate. And all the cattle got out. So he says to his son: 'What have you done, you lazy so-and-so? Why didn't you shut the gate? Look, all the cattle have wandered out. Go and drive them back.' You see, he thought when his son had gone he'd have time to get at his daughter-in-law. But his son was lazy and whispered to his wife: 'You go and drive them back.' So she went out, and he lay there, listening. The father slipped down from the stove and crawled over on his hands and knees towards the bed. But his son was no fool. He took a rolling-pin from the shelf and waited. As soon as his father crawled up to the bed and put his hand on him, he gave him such a whack with the pin right across his bold head. 'Go away,' he shouted, 'don't you chew my blanket, curse you.'

"You see, they had a calf in the house which had a habit of chewing things, so the son pretended he had struck the calf. The old man managed to crawl back to his stove and lay there, tenderly fingering the bump which was as big as a goose egg. 'Ivan,' says he at last, 'who did you strike just now?' 'Only the calf,' Ivan answers. 'What kind of a master will you make,' says the old man almost in tears, 'if you knock the cattle about like that?' "

"You're a mighty good liar!"

"What's this, the market-place? Break it up!" shouted the sergeant-major, coming up to them. The Cossacks went to their horses, laughing and joking.

During exercise the officers stood smoking at the side of the yard, occasionally intervening. As Grigory glanced at the polished, well-groomed officers in their handsome grey greatcoats and closely-fitting uniforms, he felt that there was an impassable wall between them and himself. Their very different, comfortable, well-ordered existence, so unlike that of the Cossacks, flowed on peacefully, untroubled by mud, lice, or fear of the sergeant-major's fists.

An incident which occurred on the third day after their arrival at Radzivillovo made a painful impression on Grigory, and indeed on all the young Cossacks. They were being instructed in cavalry drill, and the horse ridden by Prokhor Zykov, the lad with gentle eyes, who often dreamed of his faraway Cossack village, was a wild, spirited animal and happened to kick the sergeant-major's mount as it passed.

The blow was not very hard and it only grazed the skin on the horse's left leg. But the sergeant-major struck Prokhor across the face with his whip, and riding straight at him, shouted:

"Why the hell don't you look where you're going, you son of a bitch? I'll show you. . . . You'll spend the next three days on duty!"

The squadron commander happened to witness the scene, but he turned his back, fingering the sword-knot of his sabre and yawning with boredom. His lips trembling, Prokhor rubbed a streak of blood from his swollen cheek.

Pulling his horse into line, Grigory looked at the officers, but they continued their conversation as if nothing untoward had occurred. Five days later Grigory dropped a bucket into the well. The sergeant-major swooped on him like a hawk, and raised his fist.

"Don't you touch me," Grigory said huskily, looking into the rippling water below.

"What? Climb down and get it, you bastard! I'll smash your face in for this!"

"I'll get it, but don't you touch me," Grigory said slowly, without raising his head.

If there had been any Cossacks at the well, the sergeant-major would undoubtedly have beaten Grigory, but they were attending to their horses at the fence and could not hear what was going on. The sergeant-major approached Grigory, glancing back at the Cossacks, his bulging eyes insane with rage as he hissed:

"Who do you think you are? How dare you speak to your superior in this way?"

"Don't look for trouble, Semyon Yegorov."

"Are you threatening me? I'll. . . ."

"Look here," Grigory said, raising his head from the well. "If you strike me—I'll kill you. Understand?"

The sergeant-major's great carp-like mouth gaped in amazement but no answer came. The moment for punishment had been missed. Grigory's greyish face boded nothing good. The sergeant-major was nonplussed. He walked away from the well, slipping in the mud, and when some distance away, turned and shook his huge fist.

"I'll report you to the squadron commander," he shouted. "Yes, I'll report you."

However, for some unknown reason, he did not report Grigory. But for about a fortnight afterwards he was always finding fault with him and appointing him for sentry duty out of turn.

The dreary, monotonous order of existence crushed the spirit out of the young Cossacks.

Until sundown they were kept continually at foot and horse exercises, and in the evening the horses had to be groomed and fed. At ten o'clock, after roll call and stationing of guards, they were drawn up for prayers, and the sergeant-major, his eyes wandering over the ranks before him, intoned the Lord's prayer.

In the morning the same routine began again, and the days were as like one another as peas.

In the whole of the estate there were only two women: the old wife of the steward, and the steward's pretty young housemaid, a Polish girl Franya. Franya often ran from the house to the kitchen where the old, browless army cook was in charge. Winking and heaving exaggeratedly loud sighs, the troops drilling on the parade ground watched every movement of the girl's grey skirt as she ran across the yard. Feeling the gaze of Cossacks and officers fixed upon her, she bathed in the streams of lasciviousness that came from three hundred pairs of eyes, and swung her hips provocatively as she ran backward and forward between the kitchen and the house, smiling at each troop in turn, and at the officers in particular. Although all fought for her attentions, rumour had it that only the squadron commander had won them.

One day in early spring Grigory was on
duty in the stables. He spent most of his time
at one end, where the officers' horses were excited by the presence of a mare. He had just
given the squadron commander's horse a taste
of the whip and was attending to his own.
With a sidelong glance at its master the horse
went on champing the hay, its grazed hindfoot lifted off the ground. As he adjusted the
halter, Grigory heard a sound of struggling
and a muffled cry coming from the dark corner at the far end of the stable. Startled by
the unusual noise, he hurried past the stalls.
His eyes were suddenly blinded as someone
slammed the stable door, and he heard a suppressed voice calling:

"Hurry up, boys!"

Grigory hastened his steps, and called out:
"Who's there?"

The next moment he bumped into one of the
sergeants, who was groping his way to the
door. "That you, Melekhov?" the sergeant whispered, putting his hand on Grigory's shoulder.

"Stop! What's up?"

The sergeant burst into a guilty snigger and
seized Grigory's sleeve. "We. . . . Hey, where're
you going?" Tearing his arm away, Grigory
ran and threw open the door. In the deserted
yard a draggle-tailed hen, unaware that the

cook already had designs on her for the steward's soup the next day, was scratching some
dung in search of a place to lay her egg.

The light momentarily blinded Grigory; he
shaded his eyes with his hand and turned
round, hearing the noise in the dark corner of
the stable growing louder. He ran towards the
sound, and was met by Zharkov, buttoning up
his trousers.

"What the ... what are you doing here?"

"Hurry up!" Zharkov whispered, breathing
bad breath in Grigory's face. "It's wonderful. . . . They've dragged the girl Franya in
there ... laid her out!" His snigger suddenly
broke off as Grigory sent him flying against
the log wall of the stable. Grigory's eyes grew
accustomed to the darkness and there was fear
in them as he ran towards the noise. In the
corner, Grigory found a crowd of Cossacks of
the First Troop. He silently pushed his way
through them, and saw Franya lying motionless on the floor, her head wrapped in horse-
cloths, her dress torn and pulled back above
her breasts, her legs, white in the darkness,
flung out shamelessly and horribly. A Cossack
had just risen from her; grinning sheepishly,
he was stepping back to make way for the
next. Grigory tore his way back through the
crowd and ran to the door, shouting for the

sergeant-major. But the other Cossacks ran after him and caught him at the door. They dragged him back, putting their hands over his mouth. He tore one man's tunic from hem to collar and gave another a kick in the stomach, but the others pinned him down. As they had done to Franya, they wound a horsecloth round his head and tied his hands behind him, then, keeping quiet so that he should not recognize their voices, threw him into an empty manger. Choking in the stinking horse-cloth, he tried to shout, and kicked furiously at the partition. He heard whispering in the corner, and the door creaking as the Cossacks went in and out. He was set free some twenty minutes later. The sergeant-major and two Cossacks from another troop were standing at the door.

"You just keep your mouth shut!" the sergeant-major said to him, winking hard and glancing over his shoulder.

"Don't blab or we'll tear your ears off," Dubok, a Cossack from another troop, said with a grin.

The two Cossacks went in and lifted up the motionless bundle that was Franya (her legs were parted stiffly under her skirt), and climbing on to a manger, thrust it through a hole left in the wall by a lose plank. The wall bordered on the orchard. Above each stall was a tiny, grimy window. Some of the Cossacks clambered on to the stall partitions to watch what Franya would do, others hastened out of the stables. Grigory, too, was seized by a bestial curiosity, and gripping a cross-beam, he drew himself up to one of the windows and looked down. Dozens of eyes stared through the dirty windows at the girl lying under the wall. She lay on her back, her legs crossing and uncrossing like scissor blades, her fingers scrabbling in the snow by the wall. Grigory could not see her face but he heard the suppressed breathing of other Cossacks at the windows, and the soft and pleasant crunch of hay under their feet.

She lay there a long time, and at last struggled on to her hands and knees. Her arms trembled, hardly able to bear her. Grigory saw that clearly. Swaying, she scrambled to her feet, and, dishevelled, unfamiliar, hostile, she passed her eyes in a long, slow stare over the windows.

Then she staggered away, one hand clinging to the woodbine bushes, the other groping along the wall.

Grigory jumped down from the partition and rubbed his throat, feeling that he was about to choke. At the door someone, afterwards he could not even remember who, said to him in distinct and unequivocal tones:

"Breathe a word ... and by Christ, we'll kill you!"

On the parade ground the troop commander noticed that a button had been torn from Grigory's greatcoat, and asked:

"Who have you been wrestling with? What style d'you call this?"

Grigory glanced down at the little round hole left by the missing button; overwhelmed by the memory, for the first time in years he felt like crying.

### III

A sultry, sunny July haze lay over the steppe. The ripe unharvested floods of wheat smoked with yellow dust. The metal of the reapers was too hot to touch. It was painful to look up at the flaming, bluish-yellow sky. Where the wheat ended, a saffron sweep of clover began.

The entire village had moved out into the steppe to cut the rye. The horses choked in the heat and the pungent dust, and were restive as they dragged the reapers. Now and then a wave of air from the river raised a fringe of dust over the steppe, and the sun was enveloped in a tingling haze.

Since early morning Pyotr, who was forking the wheat off the reaper platform, had drunk half a bucketful of water. Within a minute of his drinking the warm, unpleasant liquid his throat was dry again. His shirt was wet through, the sweat streamed from his face, there was a continual trilling ring in his ears. Darya, her head and face wrapped in her kerchief, her shirt unbuttoned, was gathering the corn into stooks. Big grey beads of sweat ran down between her dusky breasts. Natalya was leading the horses. Her cheeks were burned the colour of beetroot, and the glaring sun brought tears to her eyes. Pantelei was walking up and down the swaths of corn, his wet shirt scalding his body. His beard looked like a stream of melting black cart-grease flowing over his chest.

"Make you sweat?" Christonya shouted from a passing cart.

"Wet through!" Pantelei stumped on, wiping his perspiring belly with the tail of his shirt.

"Pyotr!" Darya called. "Let's stop."

"Wait a bit; we'll finish this row."

"Let's wait till it's cooler. I've had enough."

Natalya halted the horses; her chest was heaving as though it were she who had been pulling the reaper. Darya went across to them,

413

picking her way carefully over the cut corn on her dark blistered feet.

"Pyotr, it's not far from the pond here."

"Not far! Only three versts or so!"

"What wouldn't I give for a dip!"

"While you're getting there and back . . ." Natalya began with a sigh.

"Why the devil should we walk! We'll unharness the horses and ride."

Pyotr glanced uneasily at his father tying up a sheaf, and shrugged.

"All right, unharness the horses."

Darya unfastened the traces and jumped agilely on to the mare's back. Natalya, smiling with cracked lips, led her horse to the reaper and tried to mount from the driver's seat. Pyotr went to her aid and gave her a leg up on to the horse. They rode off. Darya, sitting her horse Cossack fashion, trotted in front, her skirt tucked up above her bare knees, her kerchief pushed on to the back of the head.

"Mind you don't get sore!" Pyotr could not help shouting after her.

"You needn't worry!" Darya shouted back carelessly.

As they crossed the field track Pyotr glanced to his left and noticed a tiny cloud of dust moving swiftly along the distant highroad from the village.

"Someone riding there!" he remarked to Natalya, screwing up his eyes.

"And fast, too! Look at the dust!" Natalya replied in surprise.

"Who on earth can it be! Darya!" Pyotr called to his wife. "Rein in for a minute, and let's watch that rider!"

The cloud of dust dropped down into a hollow and disappeared, then came up again on the other side. Now the figure of the rider could be seen through the dust. Pyotr sat gazing with his dirty palm set against the edge of his straw hat.

"No horse can stand that pace for long. He'll kill it!" He frowned and took his hand away; an agitated expression passed across his face.

Now the horseman could be seen quite plainly. He was riding his horse at a furious gallop, his left hand holding on his cap, a dusty red flag fluttering in his right. He rode along the track so close to them that Pyotr heard his horse's panting breath. As he passed, the man shouted:

"Alarm!"

A flake of yellow soapy foam flew from his horse and fell into a hoof-print. Pyotr followed the rider with his eyes. The heavy snort of the horse, and, as he stared after the retreating figure, the sight of the horse's croup, wet and glittering like steel, remained impressed in his memory.

Still not realizing the nature of the misfortune that had come upon them, Pyotr gazed stupidly at the foam flying in the dust, then glanced around the rolling steppe. From all sides the Cossacks were running over the yellow strips of stubble towards the village; across the steppe, as far as the distant upland, little clouds of dust indicating horsemen were to be seen. A long trail of dust moved along the road to the village. The Cossacks who were on the active service list abandoned their work, took their horses out of the shafts and galloped off to the village. Pyotr saw Christonya unharness his Guards charger from a wagon and ride off at a wild pace, glancing back over his shoulder.

"What's it all about?" Natalya half groaned, with a frightened look at Pyotr. Her gaze, the gaze of a trapped hare, startled him to action. He galloped back to the reaper, jumped off his horse before it had halted, hustled into the trousers he had flung off while working, and waving his hand to his father, tore off to add one more cloud of dust to those which had already blossomed over the sultry steppe.

# IV

He found a dense grey crowd assembled on the square. Many were already wearing their army uniform and equipment. The blue military caps of the men belonging to the Ataman's Regiment rose a head higher than the rest, like Dutch ganders among the small fry of the farmyard.

The village tavern was closed. The military police officer had a gloomy and care-worn look. The women, attired in their holiday clothes, lined the fences along the streets. One word was on everybody's lips: "Mobilization." Intoxicated, excited faces. The general anxiety had been communicated to the horses, and they were kicking and plunging and snorting angrily. The square was strewn with empty bottles and wrappers from cheap sweets. A cloud of dust hung low in the air.

Pyotr led his saddled horse by the rein. Close to the church fence a big swarthy Cossack of the Ataman's Regiment stood buttoning up his blue *sharovari*, with his mouth gaping in a white-toothed smile, while a stocky little woman, his wife or sweetheart, stormed at him.

"I'll give it you for going with that hussy!" the little woman promised.

She was drunk, her dishevelled hair was scattered with the husks of sunflower seed, her flowered kerchief hung loose. The guardsman tightened his belt and, grinning widely, dropped to his haunches, leaving enough room for a year-old calf to pass under the voluminous folds of his *sharovari*.

"Keep off, Mashka."

"You great shameless brute! Woman-chaser!"

"What about it?"

"I'll give it you!"

Near him a red-bearded sergeant-major was arguing with an artilleryman.

"Nothing will come of it, never fear!" he was assuring him. "We'll be mobilized for a few days, and then back home again."

"But suppose there's a war?"

"Pah, my friend! What country could stand up to us?"

In a neighbouring group a handsome, elderly Cossack was arguing heatedly.

"It's nothing to do with us. Let them do their own fighting, we haven't got our corn in yet."

"It's a shame! Here we are standing here, and on a day like this we could harvest enough for a whole year."

"The cattle will get among the stooks!"

"And we'd just begun to reap the barley!"

418

"They say the Austrian tsar's been murdered."

"No, his heir."

"But the ataman says they've called us up just in case."

"We're in for it now, lads."

"Another twelve months and I'd have been out of the third line of reserves," an elderly Cossack said regretfully.

"What do they want you for, Grandad?"

"Don't you worry, as soon as they start killing the men off, they'll be taking the old ones, too."

"The tavern's closed!"

"What about going to Marfutka's? She'd sell us a barrel!"

The inspection started. Three Cossacks led a fourth, blood-stained and completely drunk, into the village administration. He threw himself back, tore his shirt open, and rolling his eyes, shouted:

"I'll show the muzhiks! I'll have their blood! They'll know the Don Cossack!"

The circle around him laughed approvingly.

"That's right, give it to them!"

"What have they grabbed him for?"

"He went for some muzhik!"

"Well, they deserve it."

"We'll give them some more!"

"I took a hand when they put them down in 1905. That was a sight worth seeing!"

"There's going to be war. They'll be sending us again to put them down."

"Enough of that. Let them hire people for that, or let the police do it. It's a shame for us to."

Mokhov's shop was surging with people. In the middle Ivan Tomilin was arguing drunkenly with the owners. Mokhov was trying to pacify him. Atyopin, his partner, had retired to the doorway. "What's all this?" he expostulated. "My word, this is an outrage! Boy, run for the ataman!"

Rubbing his sweaty hands on his trousers, Tomilin pressed against the frowning merchant and sneered:

"You've squeezed us and squeezed us with your interest, you swine, and now you've got the wind up. I'll smash your face in! Stealing our Cossack rights, you fat slug!"

The village ataman was busily pouring out soothing words for the benefit of the Cossacks surrounding him: "War? No, there won't be any war. His Honour the chief of the military police said the mobilization was only a drill. There's no need for alarm."

"Good! Back to the fields as soon as we're home!"

"What are the authorities thinking about? I have over a hundred dessiatines of harvesting to do."

"Timoshka! Tell our folk we'll be home again tomorrow."

"Looks as if they've put a notice up. Let's go and have a look."

Until late at night the square was alive and noisy with excited crowds.

Some four days later the red trucks of the troop trains were carrying the Cossack regiments and batteries towards the Russo-Austrian frontier.

"War. . . ."

From the stalls came the snorting of horses and the damp stench of dung.

The same kind of talk in the wagons, the songs mostly of this kind:

> The Don's awake and stirring,
> The quiet and Christian Don,
> In obedience to the call,
> The monarch's call, it marches on.

At the stations the Cossacks were eyed with inquisitive, benevolent looks. People stared curiously at the stripes on the Cossacks' trousers, at their faces, still dark from their recent labour in the fields.

"War. . . ."

Newspapers screamed out the news. At the stations the women waved their handkerchiefs, smiled, threw cigarettes and sweets. Only once, just before the train reached Voronezh, did an old railway worker, half drunk, thrust his head into the truck where Pyotr Melekhov was crowded with twenty-nine other Cossacks, and ask:

"You going?"

"Yes. Get in and come with us, Grandad," one of the Cossacks replied.

"My boy. . . . Bullocks for slaughter!" the old man responded and shook his head reproachfully.

V

During the fourth week of June, 1914, the divisional staff transferred Grigory Melekhov's regiment to the town of Rovno, to take part in manoeuvres. Two infantry divisions were located in the neighbourhood as well as cavalry units. The Fourth Squadron was stationed in the village of Vladislavka. A fortnight later, tired out with continual manoeuvring, Grigory and the other Cossacks of the Fourth Squadron were lying in their tents, when the squadron commander, Junior Captain Polkovnikov, galloped furiously back from the regiment staff.

"We'll be on the move again I suppose," Prokhor Zykov suggested tentatively, and fell silent waiting for the sound of the bugle.

The troop sergeant thrust the needle with which he had been mending his trousers into the lining of his cap, and remarked:

"Looks like it; they won't let us rest for a moment."

"Sergeant-major said the brigade commander will be visiting us."

A minute or two later the bugler sounded the alarm. The Cossacks jumped to their feet.

"What have I done with my pouch?" Prokhor exclaimed, searching frantically.

"Boot and saddle!"

"Your pouch can go to hell," Grigory shouted as he ran out.

The sergeant-major ran into the yard and, holding the hilt of his sword, made for the hitching posts. They had their horses saddled well within regulation time. As Grigory was tearing up the tent-pegs the sergeant managed to mutter to him:

"It's war this time, my boy!"

"You're fooling!"

"God's truth! The sergeant-major told me."

The squadron formed up in the street, the commander at its head. "In troop columns!" his command flew over the ranks.

Hoofs clattered as the horses trotted out of the village on to the highway. From a neighbouring village the First and Fifth squadrons could be seen riding towards the station.

A day later the regiment was detrained at a station some thirty-five versts from the Austrian frontier. Dawn was breaking behind the station birch-trees. The morning promised to be fine. The engine fussed and rumbled over the tracks. The lines glittered under a varnish of dew. The Cossacks of the Fourth Squadron led their horses by the bridles out of the wagons and over the level-crossing, mounted, and moved off in column formation. Their voices sounded eerily in the crumbling, lilac darkness. Faces and the contours of horses emerged uncertainly out of the gloom.

"What squadron is that?"

"And who are you? Where've you come from?"

"I'll show you who I am! How dare you speak to an officer in that way?"

"Sorry, Your Honour, didn't recognize you."

"Ride on! Ride on!"

"What are you dawdling about for? Get moving."

"Where's your Third Troop, sergeant-major?"

"Squadron, bring up the rear!"

Muttered whispers in the column:

"Bring up the rear, blast him, when we haven't slept for two nights."

"Give me a puff, Syomka, haven't had a smoke since yesterday."

"Hold your horse...."

"He's bitten through his saddle-strap, the devil."

"Mine's lost a hoof in front."

A little farther on the Fourth Squadron was held up for a while by the first, which had detrained before it. Against the bluish grey of the sky the silhouettes of the horsemen ahead stood out clearly, as though drawn with Indian ink. Their lances swung like bare sunflower stalks. Occasionally a stirrup jingled or a saddle creaked.

Prokhor Zykov was riding at Grigory's side. Prokhor stared into his face and whispered:

"Melekhov, you're not afraid, are you?"

"What is there to be afraid of?"

"We may be in action today."

"Well, what of it?"

"But I'm afraid," Prokhor admitted, his fingers playing nervously with the dewy reins. "I didn't sleep a wink all night."

Once more the squadron advanced; the horses moved at a measured pace, the lances swayed and flowed rhythmically. Dropping the reins, Grigory dozed. And it seemed to him that it was not the horse that put its legs forward springily, rocking him in the saddle, but he himself who was walking along a warm, dark road, and walking with unusual ease, with irresistible joy. Prokhor chattered away at his side, but his voice mingled with the creak of the saddle and the clatter of hoofs, and did not disturb his thoughtless doze.

The squadron turned into a by-road. The silence rang in their ears. Ripe oats hung over the wayside, their tops smoking with dew. The horses tried to reach the low ears and dragged the reins out of their riders' hands. The gracious daylight crept under Grigory's puffy eyelids. He raised his head and heard Prokhor's monotonous voice, like the creak of a cartwheel.

He was abruptly aroused by a heavy, rumbling roar that billowed across the oatfields.

"Gun-fire!" Prokhor almost shouted, and fright clouded his calf-like eyes. Grigory lifted his head. In front of him the troop-sergeant's grey greatcoat rose and fell in time with the horse's back; on each side stretched fields of unreaped corn; a skylark danced in the sky at the height of a telegraph pole. The entire squadron was aroused, the sound of the firing ran through it like an electric current. Lashed into activity, Junior Captain Polkovnikov put the squadron into a fast trot. Beyond a cross-road, where a deserted tavern stood, they began to meet with carts of refugees. A squadron of smart-looking dragoons went by. Their captain, riding a sorrel thoroughbred, stared at the Cossacks ironically and spurred on his horse. They came upon a howitzer battery stranded in a muddy and swampy hollow. The riders were lashing at their horses, while the gunners struggled with the carriage wheels. A great, pock-marked artilleryman passed carrying an armful of boards probably torn from the fence of the tavern.

A little farther on they overtook an infantry regiment. The soldiers were marching fast, their greatcoats rolled on their backs. The sun glittered on their polished mess-tins and streamed from their bayonets. A lively little corporal in the last company threw a lump of mud at Grigory:

"Here, catch! Chuck it at the Austrians!"

"Don't play about, grasshopper!" Grigory replied, and cut the lump of mud in its flight with his whip.

"Say hullo to 'em from us, Cossacks!"

"You'll have a chance yourselves."

At the head of the column someone struck up a bawdy song; a soldier with fat womanish

427

buttocks marched beside the column slapping his stumpy calves. The officers laughed. The keen sense of approaching danger had brought them closer to the men and made them more tolerant.

From now on the column was continually passing foot regiments crawling like caterpillars, batteries, baggage-wagons, Red Cross wagons. The deathly breath of fighting close at hand was in the air.

A little later, as it was entering a village, the Fourth Squadron was overtaken by the commander of the regiment, Lieutenant-Colonel Kaledin, accompanied by his second in command. As they passed, Grigory heard the latter say agitatedly to Kaledin: "This village isn't marked on the map, Vasily Maximovich! We may find ourselves in an awkward position."

Grigory did not catch the colonel's reply.

The adjutant galloped past overtaking them. His horse was stepping heavily on its left hindfoot. Grigory mechanically noted its fine points.

The regiment was continually changing its pace, and the horses began to sweat. The cottages of a small village lying under a gentle slope appeared in the distance. On the other side of the village was a wood, its green treetops piercing the azure dome of the sky. From beyond the wood splashes of gunfire mingled

with the frequent rattle of rifle-shots. The horses
pricked up their ears. The smoke of bursting shrapnel hovered in the sky a long way off;
the rifle-fire moved slowly to the right of the
company, now dying away, now growing
louder.

Grigory listened tensely to every sound, his
nerves tautened into little bundles of sensation.
Prokhor Zykov fidgeted in his saddle, talking
incessantly:

"Grigory, those shots sound just like boys
rattling sticks along railings, don't they?"

"Shut up, magpie!"

The squadron entered the village. Soldiers
were milling about in the yards. The inhabitants of the cottages, alarm and confusion written on their faces, were packing their belongings
to flee. As Grigory passed he noticed that soldiers were firing the roof of a shed, but its
owner, a tall, grey-haired Byelorussian, crushed
by his sudden misfortune, went past them
without paying the slightest attention. Grigory
saw the man's family loading a cart with red-
covered pillows and ramshackle furniture, and
the man himself was carefully carrying a broken wheel-rim, which was of no value to anybody, and had probably lain in the yard for
years. Grigory was amazed at the stupidity
of the women, who were piling the carts with

flower pots and icons and were leaving necessary and valuable articles behind in their houses.
Down the street the feathers from a feath-
er-bed blew like a miniature snow-storm and
there was a pungent smell of burning soot and
musty cellars in the air.

At the end of the village they met a Jew running towards them. The narrow slit of his
mouth was torn apart in a cry!

"Mister Cossack, Mister Cossack! Oh, my
God!"

A short, round-headed Cossack rode ahead
of him at a trot, waving his whip and ignoring
him completely.

"Stop!" a junior captain from the Second
Squadron shouted to the Cossack.

The Cossack bent over the pommel of his
saddle and galloped into a side street.

"Stop, you scoundrel. What regiment are
you?"

The Cossack's round head pressed closer to
the horse's neck. He galloped madly towards
a tall fence, reared his horse, and took the
jump neatly.

"The Ninth Regiment is stationed here, Your
Honour. That's where he's from," said the sergeant.

"Let him go to the devil," the junior captain frowned, and turned to the Jew who was

clutching at his stirrup. "What did he take from you?"

"Mister Officer ... my watch, Mister Officer." The Jew blinked, turning his handsome face towards the approaching officers.

The junior captain, freeing the stirrup with his foot, started forward.

"The Germans would have taken it anyhow, when they came," he said smiling into his moustache.

The Jew stood confusedly in the middle of the road. His face twitched.

"Make way, master Sheeny," shouted the squadron commander sternly, raising his whip.

The Fourth Squadron rode by, hoofs clattering, saddles creaking. The Cossacks jeered at the disconcerted Jew, and spoke among themselves:

"The likes of us can't help stealing."

"Everything sticks to a Cossack's hand."

"Let them be more careful about their things!"

"A nimble fellow, that!"

"The way he took that fence, like a borzoi."

Sergeant-Major Kargin dropped behind the squadron, and to the accompaniment of laughter from the Cossacks lowered his lance and shouted:

"Run, Sheeny, before I. . . ."

The Jew gasped and ran. The sergeant-major overtook him and struck him with his whip. Grigory saw the Jew stumble and, covering his face with his palms, turn to the sergeant-major. Through his thin fingers the blood was trickling.

"What for?" he sobbed.

The sergeant-major, his sharp button-like eyes smiling greasily as he rode away, shouted:

"Don't go barefoot, you fool!"

Beyond the village a group of engineers was completing a broad trestle bridge across a hollow overgrown with sedge and yellow water-lilies. Close by a motor car stood rattling and humming with a chauffeur fussing round it. A stout grey-haired general with a Spanish beard and baggy cheeks was half-sitting, half-lying on the back seat. Lieutenant-Colonel Kaledin and the commander of the engineers' battalion stood at attention by the car. The general, clutching the strap of his map case, bawled furiously at the engineer:

"You were ordered to finish this work yesterday. Silence! You should have arranged the supply of materials beforehand. Silence!" he roared again, although the officer had made no attempt to open his trembling lips. "How do you expect me to cross over? Answer me, Captain, how am I to cross?"

A young black-moustached general also sitting in the car smoked a cigar and smiled. The engineer captain bent forward and pointed to one side of the bridge.

At the bridge the squadron rode down into the hollow. The horses sank into the brownish-black mud up to their knees, and feathery white shavings scattered down on them from the bridge.

The squadron crossed the Austrian frontier at noon. The horses leaped the broken black-and-white pole of the frontier post. From the right came the rumble of gunfire. In the distance the red-tiled roofs of a farm showed up in the perpendicular rays of the sun. A bitter-tasting cloud of dust settled thickly on everything. The regimental commander issued orders for advance patrols to be detached and sent ahead. The Third Troop under Lieutenant Semyonov was sent out from the Fourth Squadron. The regiment, split up into squadrons, was left behind in a grey haze. A detachment of some twenty Cossacks rode past the farm along the rutted road.

The lieutenant led the reconnaissance patrol about three versts, then halted to study his map. The Cossacks gathered in a group to smoke. Grigory dismounted to ease his saddle-girth, but the sergeant-major shouted:

"What do you think you're doing? Get back on your horse!"

The lieutenant lit a cigarette, and carefully wiped his binoculars. A valley lay before them in the midday heat. To the right rose the jagged outline of a wood pierced by a pointed spear of railway tracks. About a verst and a half away was a little village, beyond it the gouged clay banks of a stream and the cool glassy surface of the water. The officer stared intently through his binoculars, studying the deathly stillness of the village streets, but they were as deserted as a graveyard. Only the blue ribbon of water beckoned challengingly.

"That must be Korolyovka!" the officer indicated the village with his eyes.

The sergeant-major took his horse nearer the lieutenant; he made no reply, but the expression of his face said eloquently: "You know better than I! I'm concerned only with minor questions."

"We'll go there," the officer said irresolutely, putting away his binoculars and frowning as though he had a toothache.

"We may run into them, Your Honour?"

"We'll be careful."

Prokhor Zykov kept close to Grigory. They rode cautiously down into the deserted street. Every window suggested an ambush, every open cellar door evoked a feeling of loneliness and sent a sickening shudder down the back. All eyes were drawn as though by magnets to the fences and ditches. They rode in like beasts of prey, like wolves approaching human habitations in the blue winter night—but the streets were empty. The silence was stupefying. From the open window of one house came the innocent sound of a clock striking. The chimes rang out like pistol shots, and Grigory saw the officer tremble and his hand flash to his revolver.

There was not a soul in the village. The patrol forded the river. The water reached the horses' bellies, they entered willingly and tried to drink, but their riders pulled at the reins and urged them on. Grigory stared thirstily down at the turbid water, close yet inaccessible; it drew him almost irresistibly. Had it been possible he would have jumped out of his saddle and lain without undressing with the stream murmuring over him until his sweating chest and back were shivering with cold.

From the rise beyond the village they saw a distant town: square blocks of houses, brick buildings, gardens, and church spires. The officer rode to the top of the hill and put his binoculars to his eyes.

"There they are," he shouted, the fingers of his left hand playing nervously.

The sergeant-major rode to the sun-baked crest followed by the other Cossacks in single file, and stared. They saw tiny figures scurrying about the town. Wagons dammed up the side streets; horsemen were galloping to and fro. With eyes screwed up, gazing from under his palm, Grigory was able to distinguish even the grey, unfamiliar colour of the uniforms. Before the town stretched the brown lines of freshly-dug trenches, with men swarming about them.

"What a lot of them!" Prokhor said with a gasp.

The others, all gripped by the same feeling, were silent. Grigory listened to the quickening throb of his heart and realized that the feeling he was experiencing at the sight of these foreigners was something quite different from what he had felt in the face of "the enemy" on manoeuvres.

The sergeant-major drove the Cossacks hurriedly back down the rise. The lieutenant made some pencil notes in his field notebook, and then beckoned to Grigory:

"Melekhov!"

"Sir!"

Grigory dismounted and went to the officer, his legs feeling like stone after the long ride. The officer handed him a folded paper.

"You've got the best horse. Deliver this to the regimental commander. At a gallop!"

Grigory put the paper in his breast-pocket and went back to his horse, slipping his chin-strap under his chin as he went. The officer watched him until he had mounted, then glanced at his wrist-watch.

The regiment had nearly reached the village of Korolyovka when Grigory rode up with the report. After reading it the colonel gave an order to his adjutant, who galloped off to the First Squadron.

The Fourth Squadron streamed through Korolyovka and, as quickly as though on the parade ground, spread out in formation over the fields beyond. Lieutenant Semyonov rode up with his men. The horses tossed their heads to shake off the horse-flies, and there was a continual jingle of bridles. The noise of the First Squadron passing through the village sounded heavily in the midday silence.

Junior Captain Polkovnikov rode on his prancing horse to the front of the ranks. Gathering the reins tightly in one hand, he dropped the other to his sword-knot. Grigory held his breath and awaited the word of command.

There was a rumble of hoofs on the left flank as the First Squadron got into position.

The officer wrenched his sabre from its sheath; the blade gleamed like blue light.

"Squadron!" He swung his sabre to the right, then to the left, and finally lowered it in front of him, holding it poised above the horse's ears. Grigory tried to think what the next order would be. "Lances at the ready! Sabres out! Into the attack ... gallop!" The officer snapped, and gave his horse the rein.

The earth groaned dully under the crushing impact of a thousand hoofs. Grigory, who was in the front ranks, had hardly brought his lance to the ready when his horse, carried away by a lashing flood of other horses, broke into a gallop and went off at full speed. Ahead of him the figure of the commanding officer bobbed up and down against the grey background of the field. A black wedge of ploughed land sped irresistibly towards him. The First Squadron raised a surging quivering shout, the Fourth Squadron took it up. The ground streaked past close under the horses' straining bellies. Through the roaring whistle in his ears Grigory caught the sound of distant firing. The first bullet whined high above them, furrowing the glassy vault of the sky. Grigory pressed the hot shaft of his lance against his side until it hurt him and his palm sweated. The whistle of flying bullets made him duck his head down to the wet neck of his horse, and the pungent scent of the animal's sweat penetrated his nostrils. As though through the misty glass of binoculars he saw the brown ridges of trenches, and men in grey running back to the town. A machine-gun hurled a fan of whistling bullets tirelessly at the Cossacks; in front of them and under the horses' feet the bullets tore up woolly spurts of dust.

The part of Grigory that before the attack had sent the blood coursing faster through his veins now turned to stone within him; he felt nothing except the ringing in his ears and a pain in the toes of his left foot. His thoughts, emasculated by fear, congealed in a heavy mass in his head.

Cornet Lyakhovsky was the first to drop from his horse. Prokhor rode over him. Grigory glanced back, and a fragment of what he saw was impressed on his memory as though cut with a diamond on glass. As Prokhor's horse leaped over the fallen cornet, it bared its teeth and stumbled. Prokhor was catapulted out of the saddle and, falling headlong, was crushed under the hoofs of the horse behind him. Grigory heard no cry, but from Prokhor's face, with its distorted mouth and its calf-like eyes bulging out of their sockets, he realized that he must be screaming inhumanly. Others fell, both horses and Cossacks. Through the film of tears caused by the wind in his eyes Grigory stared ahead at the grey, seething mass of Austrians fleeing from the trenches.

The squadron, which had torn away from the village in an orderly stream, now scattered and broke into fragments. Those in front, Grigory among them, had nearly reached the trenches, others were lagging behind.

A tall, white-eyebrowed Austrian, his cap drawn over his eyes, fired almost point-blank at Grigory. The heat of the bullet scorched his cheek. He struck with his lance, at the same time pulling on the reins with all his strength. The blow was so powerful that it plunged for half a shaft length into the Austrian's body. Grigory was not quick enough to withdraw the lance. He felt a quivering convulsion in his hand, and saw the Austrian, bent right back so that only the point of his unshaven chin was visible, clutching the shaft and clawing at it with his nails. Grigory dropped the lance and felt with numbed fingers for his sabre-hilt.

The Austrians fled into the streets of the town. Cossack horses reared up over the grey clots of their uniforms.

In the first moment after dropping his lance

Grigory, without knowing why, turned his horse and saw the sergeant-major gallop past him, his lips parted in a snarl. Grigory struck at his horse with the flat of his sabre; arching its neck, it carried him away down the street.

An Austrian was running along by the railings of a garden, swaying, without a rifle, his cap clutched in his hand. Grigory saw the back of his head and the damp collar of his tunic. He overtook him and, lashed on by the frenzy of the moment, whirled his sabre above his head. The Austrian was running close to the railings on the left-hand side, and it was awkward for Grigory to hew him down. But, leaning over his saddle, holding his sabre aslant, he struck at the man's temple. Without a cry the Austrian pressed his hand to the wound and spun around with his back to the railings. Grigory rode past reining in his horse, turned round, and rode back at a trot. The square fear-contorted face of the Austrian was black as cast iron. His arms hung at his sides, his ashen lips were quivering. The sabre had struck him a glancing blow on the temple, and the flesh was hanging over his cheek like a crimson rag. The blood streamed on to his uniform. Grigory's eyes met the terror-stricken eyes of the Austrian. The man was sagging at the knees; a gurgling groan came from his throat. Screwing up his eyes, Grigory swept his sabre down. The blow split the cranium in two. The man flung out his arms and fell; his shattered skull knocked heavily against the stone of the road. At the sound Grigory's horse reared and, snorting, carried him into the middle of the street.

Ragged firing sounded in the streets. A foaming horse carried a dead Cossack past Grigory. One foot was caught in the stirrup, and the horse was dragging the bruised and battered body over the stones. Grigory saw only the red stripe on the trousers and the torn green tunic drawn in a bundle over the head.

Grigory felt a leaden heaviness in his head. He slipped from his horse and shook his head vigorously. Cossacks of the Third Squadron galloped by. A wounded man was carried past on a greatcoat. A crowd of Austrian prisoners were driven past at a trot. The men ran in a huddled grey herd, their iron-shod boots clattering joylessly on the stones. Grigory saw them as a jellied blob, the colour of clay. He dropped his horse's reins and went across to the Austrian soldier he had cut down. The man lay where he had fallen, by the fanciful wrought-iron work of the railings, his dirty brown palm stretched out as though begging. Grigory glanced at his face. It seemed small, almost childlike, despite the hanging moustache and the tortured expression (was it from physical suffering or a joyless past?) of the harsh, distorted mouth.

"Hey, you!" a strange Cossack officer shouted as he rode down the middle of the street.

Grigory looked up and stumbled across to his horse. His steps were heavy and tottering, as though he were carrying an unbearable weight on his back. Loathing and bewilderment crushed his spirit. He took the stirrup in his hand, but for a long time could not lift his heavy foot into it.

## VI

The first reserve Cossacks from Tatarsky and the neighbouring villages spent the second night after their departure from home in a little village. The men from the lower end of Tatarsky drew into a separate group from those of the upper end, so Pyotr Melekhov, Anikushka, Christonya, Stepan Astakhov, Ivan Tomilin and others were all billeted in one house. The Cossacks had lain down to sleep, spreading out their blankets in the kitchen and the front room, and were having a last smoke for the night. The master of the house, a tall, decrepit old man who had served in the Turkish war, sat talking with them.

"So you're off to war, soldiers?"

"Yes, Grandad, off to war."

"It won't be anything like the Turkish war was, I don't suppose. They've got different weapons now!"

"It'll be just the same. Just as devilish. Just as they killed people then, so it'll be now," Tomilin grunted, angry with no one knew whom.

"That's stupid talk, young fellow. It'll be a different kind of war."

" 'Course it will," Christonya affirmed, yawning lazily, and stubbing out a cigarette with his finger-nail.

"We'll do a bit of fighting," Pyotr Melekhov yawned and, making the sign of the cross over his mouth, covered his head with his greatcoat.

"My sons, I ask you one thing. I ask you seriously, and you mark what I say," the old man said. "Remember this! If you want to come back from the mortal struggle alive and with a whole skin, you must keep the law of humanity."

"Which one?" Stepan Astakhov asked, smiling distrustfully. He had begun to smile again from the day he heard of the war. The war called him, and the general anxiety and pain assuaged his own.

"This law: don't take other men's goods.

That's one. As you fear God, don't do wrong to any woman. That's the second. And then you must know certain prayers."

The Cossacks sat up, and all spoke at once:

"More likely to lose our own stuff than get other people's!"

"And why mustn't we touch a woman? You can't make her, but suppose she's willing?"

"It's hard to be without a woman."

"You bet!"

"What about the prayer?"

The old man fixed his eyes sternly on them and answered:

"You must not touch a woman. Never! If you can't restrain yourselves you'll lose your heads, or you'll be wounded. You'll be sorry after, but then it will be too late. I'll tell you the prayers. I went right through the Turkish war, death at my heels like a saddle-bag, but I came through alive because of these prayers."

He went into the other room, rummaged under the icon and brought back a crumbling, faded scrap of paper.

"Get up now and write them down!" he commanded. "You'll be off again before cock-crow tomorrow, won't you?"

He spread the paper out on the table and left it. Anikushka was the first to get up; the shadows cast by the flickering light played on his smooth, womanish face. All except Stepan sat down and wrote out the prayers. Anikushka rolled up the paper he had used and fastened it to the string of the crucifix at his breast. Stepan jeered at him:

"That's a nice nest you've made for the lice, wasn't the cross cosy enough?"

"Young man, if you don't believe, hold your tongue!" the old man interrupted him sternly. "Don't be a stumbling block to others and don't laugh at faith. It's a sin."

Stepan grinned, but he lapsed into silence.

The prayers which the Cossacks wrote down were three, one could take one's choice.

### THE PRAYER AGAINST ARMS

God bless us. On the mountain there lies a white stone like a horse. As water enters not the stone, so may not bullet and arrow enter into me, the slave of God, nor my comrades, nor my horse. As the hammer flies back from the anvil, so may the bullet fly back from me. As millstones turn, so may the arrow turn and not touch me. As the sun and moon are bright, so may I, the slave of God, be strong. Behind this mountain there is a fortress, I shall lock this fortress, and throw the key into the sea. I shall put it under the white stone called Altor which can be seen by neither sorcerers nor witches, by neither monks nor nuns. Even as the waters flow not from the ocean and the yellow grains of sand cannot be counted, so may I, the slave of God, suffer no harm. In the name of the Father, the Son and the Holy Ghost. Amen.

## THE PRAYER IN BATTLE

There is a great ocean, and in this great ocean there is a white stone, Altor. On that stone there is a stone man of mighty stature. Cover me, the slave of God, and my comrades, with stone from east to west, from earth to sky. Protect me from sharp sabre and sword; from steel blade and bear-spear; from dagger tempered and untempered; from knife and axe, and from cannon-fire; from lead bullets and mortal weapons; from all arrows feathered with the feathers of eagles, swans, geese, cranes, or ravens; from all battles with Turks, Crimeans, Austrians, Tatars, Lithuanians, Germans and Kalmyks. Holy Fathers and Heavenly Powers, protect me, the slave of God. Amen.

## THE PRAYER IN TIME OF ATTACK

Supreme Ruler, Holy Mother of God and our Lord Jesus Christ. Bless, Lord, thy servant entering battle, and my comrades who are with me. Wrap them in cloud, with thy heavenly, stony hail protect them. Holy Dmitry of Salonica, defend me, the slave of God, and my comrades on all four sides; suffer not evil men to shoot, nor with spear to pierce, nor with pole-axe to strike, nor with butt-end of axe to smite, nor with axe to hew down, nor with sword to cut down or pierce, nor with knife to stab or cut; neither old nor young, neither brown nor black; neither heretic nor sorcerer, nor any magic-worker. All is before me now, the slave of God, orphaned and judged. In the sea, in the ocean, on the island of Buyan stands an iron post; on the post is an iron man resting on an iron staff, and he biddeth iron, steel, lead, zinc and all manner of bolt: "Go, iron, into your mother-earth away from the slave of God and past my comrades and my horse. The

447

arrow-shafts into the forest, and the feather to its mother-bird, and the glue to the fish." Defend me, the slave of God, with a golden buckler from steel and from bullet, from cannon-fire and ball, from spear and knife. May my body be stronger than armour. Amen.

The Cossacks concealed the prayers under their shirts, tying them to the little icons with which their mothers had blessed them, and to the little bundles of their native earth. But death came upon all alike, upon those who did not carry prayers and upon those who did. Their bodies rotted on the fields of Galicia and East Prussia, in the Carpathians and Rumania, wherever the ruddy flames of war flickered and the hoof-marks of Cossack horses were imprinted on the earth.

VII

It was usual for the Cossacks of the upper stanitsas of the Don, including Vyeshenskaya, to be drafted into the Eleventh and Twelfth Cossack regiments and the Ataman's Life-guards. But for some reason part of the enrolment of 1914 was assigned to the Third Don Cossack Regiment, which was composed mainly of Cossacks from the Ust-Medveditskaya stanitsa. Among those so drafted was Mitka Korshunov.

The Third Don Cossack Regiment was stationed at Vilno, together with certain units of the Third Cavalry Division. One day in June the various squadrons rode out from the city to take up country quarters.

The day was dull but warm. The flowing clouds herded together in the sky and concealed the sun. The regiment was marching in column of route. The regimental band blared at the head of the column, and the officers in their light summer caps and drill uniforms rode in a bunch at the back, a cloud of cigarette smoke rising above them.

On each side of the road the peasants and their gaily-dressed womenfolk were cutting the hay, stopping to gaze at the columns of Cossacks as they passed. The horses sweated in the heat, a yellowish foam appeared between their legs, and the light breeze blowing from the south-east did not cool, but rather intensified the steaming swelter.

They had gone about half way and were not far from a small village when a young yearling colt trotted out from behind a fence and, seeing the great mass of horses, whinnied and came prancing up in front of the Fifth Squadron. Its bushy young tail waved to one side and the dust from its shapely hoofs scattered on the trampled grass. It pranced up to the First

Troop and poked its muzzle stupidly into the groin of the sergeant-major's stallion. The stallion jibbed but took pity on the youngster and did not kick.

"Out of the way, daft-head!" the sergeant-major shouted, waving his whip. But the colt looked so friendly and homely that the other Cossacks laughed. Then something unexpected happened. The colt cheekily pushed its way in between the ranks and the platoon broke up and lost its neat formation. The horses jibbed and refused to obey their riders. Squeezing between them, the colt tried to bite the horse next to it.

Up galloped the squadron commander:

"What's going on here?"

The horses were snorting and casting sidelong glances at the scatter-brained young colt while the grinning Cossacks tried to drive it off with their whips. The troop was in complete disorder with others pressing up from behind, and the furious troop officer could be seen galloping up from the rear of the column.

"What's all this?" boomed the squadron commander, steering his horse into the thick of the mob.

"It's a colt...."

"He's got between us."

"You can't get rid of him, the devil!"

"Give him the whip, don't pamper him!"

Grinning sheepishly, the Cossacks tried to hold in their excited mounts.

"Sergeant-major! Squadron commander, what the devil is happening? Get your troops in order! I've never heard of such a thing!"

The squadron commander retired from the confusion and his horse's hindlegs slipped into the roadside ditch. He spurred it on and the horse scrambled out on to a bank overgrown with goosefoot and yellow daisies. In the distance the party of officers had stopped. The lieutenant-colonel had his head thrown back and was drinking from a flask, his hand resting with fatherly affection on his saddle pommel.

The sergeant-major broke up the troop and, swearing furiously, drove the colt off the road. The troop formed up again and a hundred and fifty pairs of eyes watched the sergeant-major standing in his stirrups as he chased after the colt. But the colt kept stopping and edging up to the sergeant-major's giant stallion, then prancing away so that the sergeant-major could not land a single blow, except on its brush-like tail, which fell under the lash only to rise again the next moment and wave bravely in the wind.

The whole squadron laughed, including the officers. Even the captain's gloomy face twisted into a crooked semblance of a smile.

Mitka Korshunov was riding in the third rank of the leading troop with Mikhail Ivankov and Kozma Kruchkov, both from stanitsas on the Don. Ivankov, broad in the shoulders and face, kept silent, and Kruchkov, a slightly pock-marked, round-shouldered Cossack, known as "the camel," constantly found fault with Mitka. Kruchkov was an "old" Cossack, that is, a Cossack in his last year of service, and according to the unwritten rules of the regiment, shared with all other "old" Cossacks the right of chasing up the youngsters, ordering them about and giving them "stripes" for every petty offence. The established punishment for a Cossack of the 1913 draft was thirteen "stripes" and for a Cossack drafted in 1914, fourteen "stripes." The sergeants and officers encouraged this system on the ground that it imbued a Cossack with respect not only for rank but for age as well.

Kruchkov, who had recently been made a corporal, sat hunched in his saddle like a bird. He screwed up his eyes at a paunchy grey cloud and, imitating the accent of the squadron commander Captain Popov, asked Mitka:

"Ah ... te-e-ll me, Korshunov, what do we ca-a-all our squadron comma-a-ander?"

Mitka, who had frequently had a taste of the

strap for his obstinacy and dislike of obedi-
ence, put on a respectful expression.

"Captain Popov, corporal!"

"What?"

"Captain Popov, corporal!"

"That's not what I want to know. You tell
me what we, Cossacks, call him 'mongst ourselves."

Ivankov gave Mitka a cautioning wink and
grinned widely. Mitka glanced round and saw
the captain riding up behind.

"Now then, answer up!"

"He is called Captain Popov, corporal."

"Fourteen stripes for you. Answer me, you
young bastard!"

"I don't know, corporal."

"When we get to camp," Kruchkov said,
speaking in his normal voice. "I'll belt the hide
off you. Answer my question!"

"I don't know."

"Don't you know the nickname we've got for
him, rat-face?"

Mitka heard the furtive tread of the captain's horse behind them and remained silent.

"Well?" Kruchkov scowled furiously.

A restrained titter broke out in the rear
ranks. Not realizing what the laughter was
about, and thinking that the Cossacks were
laughing at him, Kruchkov snarled:

"Be careful, Korshunov! I'll give you fifty of the best when we get to camp!"

Mitka shrugged resignedly.

"Black goose."

"That's it."

"Kruchkov!" came a voice from behind.

Corporal Kruchkov, the "old" Cossack, started in his saddle and sat at attention.

"What's your game, scoundrel?" burst out the captain, drawing level with Kruchkov. "What are you teaching this young Cossack?"

Kruchkov blinked. A purple flush flooded his cheeks. Laughter came from the rear ranks.

"Who did I teach a lesson to last year? Who did I break this nail on?" The captain held the long pointed nail of his little finger under Kruchkov's nose. "Never let me hear that again! Understand, my man?"

"Yes, Your Honour."

The captain backed out of line and let the squadron go past.

Kruchkov straightened his shoulder-strap and glanced round at the receding figure of the captain. Adjusting his lance, he shook his head crossly:

"Where did he spring from, the old goose?"

Perspiring with laughter, Ivankov told him:

"He was riding behind us. He heard everything. Must have guessed what you'd be talking about."

"You should have given me a wink, blockhead."

"Should I?"

"Think you shouldn't, eh? Fourteen of the best!"

On arriving at its destination, the regiment was broken up by squadrons among the estates in the district. During the day the Cossacks cut the clover and meadow grass for the landowners; at night they grazed their hobbled horses in the fields assigned to them, and played cards or told stories by the smoke of the campfires. The Sixth Squadron was billeted on the large estate of a Polish landowner. The officers lived in the house, played cards, got drunk, and paid attention to the steward's daughter; the Cossacks pitched their tents a couple of versts away from the house. Each morning the steward drove out in a drozhki to their camp. The corpulent, estimable gentleman would get out of the drozhki and invariably welcome the Cossacks with a wave of his white, glossy-peaked cap.

"Come and cut hay with us, sir; it'll shake your fat down a bit," the Cossacks called to him. The steward smiled phlegmatically, wiped his bald head with his handkerchief, and went with the sergeant-major to point out the next section of hay to be cut.

At midday the field-kitchen arrived. The Cossacks washed and went to get their food.

They ate in silence, but in the rest period after dinner made up for their lack of conversation.

"Rotten stuff, the grass here. Don't compare with the steppe."

"Not much quitch though."

"They've finished mowing by now back home."

"Will be finished soon. New moon yesterday, there'll be rain."

"That Pole's a mean old beggar. Might have stood us a bottle for our pains."

"Ho-ho! He'd rob the altar to get a bottle himself."

"See, lads, what do you make of that? The more a man's got, the more he wants, eh?"

"Ask the tsar about that."

"Who's seen the master's daughter?"

"What about her?"

"There's a wench with plenty of meat on her!"

"Aye. . . ."

"Don't know how true it is, but they say she's had proposals from the royal family."

"A juicy bit like her wouldn't go to a common man, would it?"

"I've heard a rumour, lads, that there's going to be a big review for us soon."

"What did I say, if a cat's got nothing to do, he'll. . . ."

"Put a sock in it, Taras!"

"Give us a puff of your fag, boy?"

"You scrounging devil, you've got an arm as long as a beggar's at the church door."

"Look, lads, old Fedot can pull all right."

"He's smoked it to ash already."

"Look again, man, it's as fiery as a woman."

They lay on their bellies, smoking. Their bare backs were scorched red in the sun. In a corner of the field about five "old" Cossacks were questioning a new recruit:

"Where d'ye come from?"

"Yelanskaya."

"From the salt mines, eh?"

"Yes, corporal."

"How do they cart salt down your way?"

Not far off, Kruchkov lay on a horse-cloth, idly twisting his scanty moustache round his finger.

"With horses."

"And what else?"

"Bullocks, corporal."

"And how do they bring fish from the Crimea?

You know, kind of bullock, with humps on
their backs, eat thistles. What are they called?"

"Camels."

"Haw-haw-haw!"

Kruchkov got up lazily and walked towards
the guilty recruit, hunching his camel-like
shoulders and stretching out his saffron-swarthy
neck with its big Adam's apple.

"Bend over!" he commanded, taking off his
belt.

In the hot dusk of the June evening the Cossacks sang around the camp-fires:

> *A Cossack went to a distant land,*
> *Riding his horse o'er the plain;*
> . *His native village he left for aye;*

A silvery tenor voice sobbed mournfully,
while the basses expressed deep, velvety sorrow:

> *He'll n'er come back again.*

Now the tenor rose to a higher pitch of grief:

> *In vain did his youthful Cossack bride*
> *Gaze northwards every morn and eve;*
> *Waiting in hope that her Cossack dear*
> *Would return from the land he ne'er will*
> *leave.*

Many voices tended the song, and it grew
rich and heady like home-brewed beer:

*But beyond the hills where the snow lies*
                                    *deep,*
*The ice-fields crack and the tempests blow,*
*Where grimly bow the pines and firs*
*The Cossack's bones lie beneath the snow.*

The voices told their simple tale of Cossack
life and the tenor supported them with its quivering notes, like a skylark soaring above the
thawed earth of April:

*As the Cossack lay dying he pleaded and*
                                    *begged*
*That above him a mound be piled on his*
                                    *grave,*
*Where a guelder-tree from his native land*
*Its blossoms bright should for ever wave.*

At another camp-fire, the group was smaller
and the song was in a different strain:

> *From the stormy Azov Sea,*
> *The ships are sailing up the Don,*
> *For back to his own country*
> *A young ataman has come.*

At yet another, the squadron's story-teller,
coughing from the smoke, was spinning tales.
The Cossacks listened with unflagging attention. Only occasionally, when the hero of the
story cleverly escaped from a plot laid against

him by the evil spirit, did someone's hand gleam white in the fire-light as it was slapped against the leg of his boot, or a thick smoky voice gasp delighted approval. Then the flowing, unbroken tones of the story-teller would continue.

A week or so after the regiment's arrival at its country quarters the squadron commander sent for the smith and the sergeant-major.

"What condition are the horses in?"

"Not so bad, Your Honour, in pretty good shape."

The captain twisted the black moustache that had earned him his nickname and said in his rasping voice:

"The regimental commander has issued instructions for all stirrups and bits to be tinned. There is to be an imperial review of the regiment. Let everything be polished until it gleams, the saddles and the rest of the equipment. The Cossacks must be a sight to gladden the eye. When can you be ready?"

The sergeant-major looked at the smith; the smith looked at the sergeant-major. Then both of them looked at the captain. The sergeant-major suggested:

"How about Sunday, Your Honour?" and respectfully touched the tip of his tobacco-mouldered moustache with his finger.

"Mind it is Sunday!" the captain added threateningly and dismissed them both.

The preparations for the review were put in hand the same day. Ivankov, son of the squadron blacksmith and a good smith himself, helped to tin the stirrups and bits. The Cossacks groomed their horses, cleaned the bridles, and rubbed the snaffles and other metal parts of the horses' equipment with bath-brick. By the end of the week the regiment was shining like a new twenty-kopeck piece. Everything glittered with polishing, from the horses' hoofs to the Cossacks' faces. On the Saturday the regimental commander inspected the regiment and thanked the officers and Cossacks for their zealous preparations and splendid appearance.

The azure thread of July days reeled past. The Cossack horses were in perfect condition; only the Cossacks themselves were uneasy and troubled with the maggot of uncertainty. Not a whisper was to be heard of the imperial review. The week passed in unending talk, continual preparation. Then like a bolt from the blue came an order for the regiment to return to Vilno.

They were back in the city by evening. A second order was at once issued to the squadrons. The Cossacks' boxes were to be collected and stored in the warehouse, and preparations made for a possible further removal.

"Your Honour, what's it all about?" the Cossacks implored their troop officers for the truth. The officers shrugged their shoulders. They themselves would have given a lot to know it.

"I don't know."

"Will there be manoeuvres in the presence of His Majesty?"

"No one has any idea yet."

But on the first of August the regimental commander's orderly managed to whisper to a friend:

"It's war, my boy!"

"You're lying!"

"God's truth! But not a word to anyone!"

Next morning the regiment was drawn up in squadrons outside the barracks, awaiting the commander.

At the head of the Sixth Squadron rode Captain Popov on a fine mount. His left hand, immaculately gloved, held the bridle. The horse, arching its neck, rubbed its muzzle on the corded muscles of its chest.

The colonel came round a corner of the barrack buildings and, riding his horse to the front of the regiment, turned the animal sideways. The adjutant, elegantly extending his little finger, drew out his handkerchief to wipe his nose, but had no time to accomplish the operation. The colonel threw his voice into the tense silence:

"Cossacks!"

"Now it's coming!" everyone thought. The tension held them like a steel spring. Mitka Korshunov's horse was stepping from hoof to hoof, and he irritatedly brought his heel against its flank. Beside him Ivankov sat his horse motionlessly, listening with his hare-lipped mouth open, exposing a dark line of uneven teeth. Kruchkov was behind him, hunching his shoulders and frowning, further on Lapin twitched his gristly ears like a horse, while behind him could be seen the jagged outline of Shchegolkov's clean-shaven Adam's apple.

"Germany has declared war on us. . . ."

Along the ranks ran a whisper as though a puff of wind had rippled across a field of ripe, heavy-eared oats. A horse's neigh slashed through it. Round eyes and gaping mouths turned in the direction of the First Squadron where the animal had dared to neigh.

The colonel said much more. He chose his words carefully, seeking to arouse a feeling of national pride. But the picture that rose before the thousand Cossacks was not of silken foreign banners falling rustling at their feet, but of their own everyday life thrown into confusion, of

their wives, children, sweethearts, of ungathered grain, and orphaned villages in distress.

"In two hours we entrain ..." was the only
thought that penetrated all minds.

The officers' wives, who were standing in
a bunch not far away, wept into their handkerchiefs. Lieutenant Khoprov had almost to carry
away in his arms his blonde pregnant Polish
wife.

The regiment rode singing to the station. The
Cossacks' voices drowned the band, and it
lapsed into confused silence. The officers' wives
rode in drozhkis, a colourful crowd foamed
along the pavements, the horses' hoofs raised
a cloud of dust. Laughing at his own and
others' sorrow, twitching his left shoulder so
that his blue shoulder-strap tossed hectically,
the leading singer struck up a bawdy Cossack
song. Deliberately running the words into one
another, to the accompaniment of newly shod
hoofs the squadron carried its song along to
the red trucks at the station. The adjutant, his
face purple with laughter and embarrassment,
galloped up to the singers. One of the Cossacks
winked cynically at the crowd of women seeing them off, and it was not sweat but a
bitter brew of wormwood that streamed
down his bronzed cheeks to the black tips of
his mouth.

On the track the engine gave a warning bellow as it got up steam.

Trains. . . . Trains. . . . Trains innumerable.

Along the country's arteries, over the railway lines to the western frontier, a seething, distracted Russia was pumping its grey-coated blood.

## VIII

At a little town on the line the regiment was broken up into its respective squadrons. On the instructions of the divisional staff the Sixth Squadron was put at the disposal of the Third Army Infantry Corps, and proceeded to Pelikaliye.

The border was still guarded by frontier troops. New infantry and cavalry units were being moved up. On July 27th the squadron commander sent for the sergeant-major and a Cossack named Astakhov, from the First Troop. Astakhov returned to the troop late in the afternoon, just as Mitka Korshunov was bringing his horse back after watering.

"Is that you, Astakhov?" he called.

"Yes, it's me. Where's Kruchkov and the lads?"

"Over there, in the hut."

Astakhov, a massive, swarthy Cossack, came into the hut screwing up his eyes as if he could

not see. At the table Shchegolkov was mending a broken rein by the light of a wick-lamp.
Kruchkov was standing by the stove with his
hands behind him, winking at Ivankov and
pointing to the owner of the hut, a Pole, who
lay on his bed, swollen with dropsy.

A joke had just passed between them, and
Ivankov's cheek was still twitching with laughter.

"Tomorrow, lads, we go out at daybreak to
an outpost at Lyubov."

"Who's going?" Mitka inquired, entering at
that moment and setting the pitcher down at
the door.

"Shchegolkov, Kruchkov, Rvachev, Popov
and Ivankov."

"And what about me?"

"You stay here, Mitka."

"Well, then the devil take the lot of you!"

Kruchkov wrenched himself away from the
stove and, stretching himself till his bones
cracked, asked the host: "How far is it to this
place?"

"Four versts."

"It's quite near," said Astakhov and, sitting
down on a bench, took off his boot. "Where
could I hang up a foot-cloth to dry?"

They set out at dawn. At the end of the village a bare-footed girl was drawing water from a well. Kruchkov reined in his horse.

"Give us a drink, lass!"

Holding up her homespun skirt, the girl splashed through a puddle with her bare feet. Her grey eyes smiling from under their thick lashes, she held out the bucket. Kruchkov drank, gripping the heavy bucket by the rim, his hand trembling with the weight of it; the water dripped and splashed on to the red stripes of his trousers.

"Christ save you, grey eyes!"

"The Lord be praised."

She took the bucket and stepped away, glancing round and smiling.

"What are you grinning at? Come for a ride!"

Kruchkov shifted in his saddle as if to make room for her.

"Get moving!" Astakhov shouted, riding away.

Rvachev grinned at Kruchkov:

"Can't take your eyes off her, eh?"

"Her legs are pink as a pigeon's," Kruchkov said with a laugh, and they all looked round, as if by word of command.

The girl bent over the well, showing the cleft of her bottom under her tight skirt, and the pink calves of her parted legs.

"If only we could marry," Popov sighed.

"Suppose I marry you with my whip," Astakhov suggested.

"That won't help. . . ."

"Want it as bad as that, do you?"

"We'll have to get hold of him and do him up like a bull."

The Cossacks cantered on, laughing among themselves. After riding steadily for some time, they topped a rise and saw the large village of Lyubov lying stretched along a river valley. The sun was rising behind them. Close by, a lark sang lustily, perched on a telegraph pole.

Astakhov, who had been put in charge of the group because he had just finished a section commander's course, chose the last farm in the village for their observation post, as it was nearest to the frontier. The master of the farm, a clean-shaven, bandy-legged Pole in a white felt hat, showed the Cossacks a shed in which they could stable their horses. Behind the shed was a green field of clover. Slopes rolled away to a neighbouring wood, and a white stretch of grain was intersected by a road, grassland lying beyond. They took turns to watch with binoculars from the ditch behind the shed. The others lay in the cool shed, which smelled of long-stored grain, dusty chaff, mice, and the sweetish, mouldering scent of damp earth.

Ivankov made himself comfortable in a dark

corner beside a plough and slept till evening. At sunset Kruchkov came to him and taking a pinch of skin on Ivankov's neck between his fingers said gently:

"Sleeping well on army grub, you hog! Get up and go and keep watch on the Germans!"

"Stop fooling, Kozma!"

"Up you get!"

"Stop it, will you! I'm just getting up."

He scrambled to his feet, his face red and puffy, worked his head from side to side on the stumpy neck that held it firmly to his broad shoulders, sniffed (he had caught cold from lying on the damp earth), adjusted his cartridge belt and went out of the shed, dragging his rifle by its sling. He relieved Shchegolkov, who had been on duty all the afternoon, and adjusting the binoculars, stared in the direction of the north-west, towards the wood.

He could see the snowy stretch of grain waving in the wind, and a ruddy flood of sunlight bathing the green headland of fir wood. Children were splashing and shouting in the stream that lay in a fine blue curve beyond the village. A woman's contralto voice called: "Stassya, Stassya! Come here!"

Shchegolkov lit a cigarette, and remarked as he went back to the shed: "Look at the glow of that sunset! We'll be having some wind."

"Reckon so," Ivankov agreed.

That night the horses stood unsaddled. In the village all lights were extinguished and all sound died away.

The next morning Kruchkov called Ivankov from the shed.

"Let's go to town."

"What for?"

"We can get something to eat and have a drink there."

"Can we?" Ivankov looked doubtful.

"Sure we can. I asked our host. It's over there in that house. See the tiled roof?" Kruchkov pointed with his black-nailed finger. "The Sheeny over there has beer. Let's go."

They started out. Astakhov called after them:

"Where are you going?"

Kruchkov, who was senior in rank to Astakhov, waved him aside.

"We'll be back soon."

"Come back, lads!"

"Stop barking!"

An old Jew with a wrinkled eyelid and long side-curls bowed them in.

"Got any beer?"

"None left, Mister Cossack."

"We'll pay for it."

"Jesus-Maria, as if I . . . Mister Cossack, believe an honest Jew, I have no more beer!"

"You're lying, Sheeny!"

"Mister Cossack, I'm telling you. . . ."

"Look here," Kruchkov vexedly interrupted, pulling a shabby purse from his trouser pocket. "Get us some beer or I'll get angry."

The Jew pressed the coin between his palm and little finger, lowered his twisted lid and went into the passage.

A minute later he brought a bottle of vodka, damp and plastered with barley-chaff.

"And you told us you didn't have any! You old. . .!"

"I said I had no beer."

"Get us something to eat."

Kruchkov slapped the bottom of the bottle to knock out the cork, and poured himself a cup of vodka.

They went out half drunk. Kruchkov pranced along, shaking his fist at the black empty sockets of the windows.

In the shed, Astakhov was yawning. Behind the wall horses were munching damp hay.

The day passed in idleness. In the afternoon Popov was sent back to the squadron with a report.

Evening. Night. The yellow rim of the young moon rose over the village. From time to time a ripe apple dropped with a soft squelching thud from the tree in the garden.

About midnight, while Ivankov was on guard, he heard the sound of horses along the village street. He crawled out of the ditch to look, but the moon was swathed in cloud, and he could see nothing through the impenetrable darkness. He went and awoke Kruchkov, who was sleeping at the door.

"Kozma! Horsemen coming! Get up!"

"Where from?"

"They're riding into the village."

They went out. The clatter of hoofs came clearly from the street, some hundred yards away.

"Let's go into the garden. We can hear better there."

They ran past the hut into the tiny front garden, and dropped down by the fence. The jingle of stirrups and creak of saddles came nearer. Now they could see the dim outline of the horsemen riding four abreast.

"Who goes there?"

"And what do you want?" a voice answered in Russian from the leading rank.

"Who goes there? I shall fire!" Kruchkov rattled the bolt of his rifle.

One of the riders reined in his horse and turned it towards the fence.

"We're the frontier guard," he said. "Are you an outpost?"

"Yes."

"What regiment?"

"The Third Cossack. . . ."

"Who are you talking to there, Trishin?" a voice called out of the darkness. The man by the fence replied:

"There's a Cossack outpost stationed here, Your Honour."

A second horseman rode up to the fence.

"Hullo there, Cossacks!"

"Hullo," Ivankov answered guardedly.

"Have you been here long?"

"Since yesterday."

The second rider struck a match and lighted a cigarette. By the momentary gleam Kruchkov saw an officer of the frontier guard.

"Our regiment is being withdrawn," the officer said. "You must bear well in mind that you're now the farthest outpost. The enemy may advance tomorrow." He turned and gave the order for his men to ride on.

"Where are you making for, Your Honour?" Kruchkov asked, keeping his finger on the trigger.

"We are to link up with our squadron two versts from here. Come on, lads, let's move. Good luck, Cossacks!"

"Good luck."

At that moment the wind pitilessly tore the

apron of cloud from the moon, and over the village, the gardens, the steep roof of the hut and the detachment of frontier guards riding up the hill, fell a flood of deathly yellow light.

Next morning Rvachev rode back to the squadron with a report. During the night the horses had stood saddled. The Cossacks were alarmed by the thought that they were now left to confront the enemy. They had experienced no feeling of isolation and loneliness so long as they knew the frontier guard was ahead of them, but the news that the frontier was open had had a marked effect upon them.

Astakhov had a talk with the Polish farmer, and for a small sum the man agreed to let them cut clover for their horses. The Pole's meadow lay not far from the shed. Astakhov sent Ivankov and Shchegolkov to mow. Shchegolkov mowed while Ivankov raked the dank, heavy grass together and tied it into bundles.

As they were thus occupied, Astakhov, who was gazing through the binoculars along the road leading to the frontier, noticed a boy running across the fields from the south-west. The lad ran down the hill like a brown hare; when still some distance off he shouted and waved the long sleeve of his coat. He ran up to Astakhov, gasping for breath and rolling his eyes, and panted:

"Cossack! Cossack! The Germans! The Germans are coming!"

He pointed with his hand. Holding the binoculars to his eyes, Astakhov saw a distant bunch of horsemen. Without removing the binoculars he shouted:

"Kruchkov!"

Kruchkov appeared from the shed, looking round.

"Run and call the lads. A German patrol is coming!"

He heard Kruchkov dash away and now he could clearly see the group of horsemen flowing along beyond the greyish streak of grassland. He could even make out the bay colour of their horses and the dark-blue tint of their uniforms. There were over twenty of them, and they were riding in a compact mass, coming from the south-west, whereas he had been expecting them from the north-west. They crossed the road and struck along the ridge above the valley in which the village lay.

Breathing hard, the tip of his tongue showing between his tight-pressed lips, Ivankov was stuffing an armful of grass into a forage sack. The bandy-legged Pole stood near by, sucking a pipe. With his hands tucked into his belt he stared from under the brim of his hat at Shchegolkov, who was mowing.

"Call this a scythe?" Shchegolkov grumbled, wielding the toy-like blade fiercely. "Do you mow with it?"

"I mow," the Pole replied and took one finger out of his belt.

"This scythe of yours is just about big enough to mow a woman in the right place!"

"Uh-huh," the Pole agreed.

Ivankov giggled. He was about to say something but, looking round, saw Kruchkov running across the rough ploughland with his hand on his sabre.

"Drop it!" he shouted as he came up.

"Now what's the matter?" Shchegolkov asked, thrusting the point of the scythe into the ground.

"The Germans!"

Ivankov threw down the bundle of grass. The Pole, bending double as if bullets were already whistling over his head, ran off to the house.

They had just reached the shed and jumped on their horses when they saw a company of Russian soldiers entering the village from the direction of Pelikaliye. The Cossacks galloped to meet them. Astakhov reported to the company commander that a German detachment was making its way round the village by way of the hill. The captain inspected the dust-sprinkled toes of his boots severely and asked:

"How many are there?"

"More than twenty."

"Cut them off and we'll fire on them from here." He turned to his company, ordered them to form up and led them away at a rapid march.

When the Cossacks reached the crest of the hill the Germans were already between them and the town of Pelikaliye. They were riding at a trot, led by an officer on a dock-tailed roan.

"After them! We'll drive them along to our second outpost," Astakhov ordered.

The mounted frontier guard who had joined up with them in the village lagged behind.

"What's up? Leaving us, brother?" Astakhov shouted, turning in his saddle.

The frontier guard waved carelessly and rode down into the village at a walking pace. The Cossacks put their horses into a swift trot. The blue uniforms of the German dragoons were clearly visible. They had caught sight of the Cossacks following them, and were cantering in the direction of the second Russian outpost, which was stationed at a farm some three versts back from the village of Lyubov. The distance between the two parties perceptibly diminished.

"We'll fire at them!" Astakhov shouted, jumping from his saddle.

Standing with the reins looped over their arms, the Cossacks fired. Ivankov's horse reared at the shot and sent him headlong. As he fell he saw one of the Germans first lean to one side, then, throwing out his arms, suddenly tumble from his saddle. The others did not stop or even unsling their carbines from their shoulders, but rode on at a gallop in open formation. The pennants on their lances fluttered in the wind. Astakhov was the first to remount his horse. The Cossacks plied their whips. The Germans swung to the left, and the Cossacks following them passed close to the fallen dragoon. Beyond, an undulating stretch of country was intersected with shallow ravines. As the Germans rode up the farther side of each ravine the Cossacks dismounted and sent shots after them. A little farther on another German went down.

"Our Cossacks should be coming from that farm in a minute. That's the second outpost," Astakhov muttered, thrusting a cartridge clip into the magazine of his rifle with his tobacco-stained finger. The Germans broke into a steady trot. As the Cossacks rode past the farm they glanced towards it, but it was deserted. The sun licked greedily at the tiled roof. Afterwards they learned that the outpost had withdrawn the previous night, having discovered that the telegraph wires about half a verst away had been cut.

Astakhov sent another shot after the Germans, firing from the saddle, and one of them who had been lagging slightly behind shook his head and spurred on his horse.

"We'll drive them along to the first outpost," Astakhov shouted, turning round to the others behind him. As he did so, Ivankov noticed that Astakhov's nose was peeling and a piece of skin was hanging from his nostril.

"Why don't they turn and defend themselves?" he asked anxiously, adjusting his rifle on his back.

"Wait and see," grunted Shchegolkov, panting like a broken-winded horse.

The Germans dropped into a ravine and disappeared. On the farther side was ploughed land. On this side, scrub and an occasional bush. Astakhov reined in his horse, pushed back his cap, and wiped the beads of sweat away with the back of his hand. He looked at the others, spat and said:

"Ivankov, you ride down and see where they've got to."

Ivankov, red in the face, his back damp with sweat, licked his crusted lips thirstily and rode off.

"Oh for a smoke!" Kruchkov muttered, driving the gadflies off with his whip.

Ivankov rode steadily down into the ravine, rising in his stirrups and gazing across the bottom. Suddenly he saw the glittering points of lances; then the Germans appeared; they had turned their horses and were galloping back up the slope to the attack. The officer was in front, his sword raised picturesquely. In the seconds that elapsed while Ivankov wheeled his horse, the moody clean-shaven face of the officer and the fine way he sat in the saddle engraved themselves on Ivankov's memory. The thunder of German horses' hoofs flailed his heart. His back felt the pinching chill of death almost painfully. Without a cry he wheeled his horse round and rode back towards the others.

Astakhov did not have time to put his tobacco pouch in his pocket. Seeing the Germans behind Ivankov, Kruchkov was the first to ride down to meet them. The dragoons on the right flank were sweeping round to cut Ivankov off, and were overtaking him at amazing speed. Ivankov was lashing at his horse, wry shudders passing over his face and his eyes starting out of his head. Bent to the saddle-bow, Astakhov took the lead. Brown dust boiled in the horses' wake.

"Any moment now they'll catch me!" The numbing thought gripped Ivankov's mind and it did not occur to him to show resistance. He gathered his great body into a ball, his head touching his horse's mane.

A big, ruddy-faced German overtook him and thrust his lance at his back. The point pierced Ivankov's leather belt and passed sideways for about an inch into his body.

"Brothers, turn back!" he shouted insanely, drawing his sabre. He parried a second thrust aimed at his side, and cut down a German riding at him from the left. The next moment he was surrounded. A burly German horse struck the side of his mount, almost knocking it off its feet, and Ivankov got a terrible blurred close-up of an enemy face.

Astakhov was the first to reach the group. He was driven off. He swung his sabre and twisted like an eel in his saddle, his teeth bared, his face changed and deathly. Ivankov was lashed across the neck with the point of a sword. A dragoon towered above him on the left, and the terrifying gleam of steel glittered in his eyes. He countered with his sabre; steel clashed against steel. From behind, a lance caught in his shoulder-strap and thrust insistently, tearing the strap away. Beyond his horse's head appeared the perspiring, fevered face

of a freckled elderly German, who tried to get
at Ivankov's chest with his sword. But the
sword would not reach, and dropping it, the
German tore his carbine from its yellow saddle-
holster, his blinking eyes fixed on Ivankov's
face. He did not succeed in freeing his carbine,
for Kruchkov reached at him across his horse
with a lance. The German, tearing the lance
away from his breast, threw himself back,
groaning in fear and astonishment.

Eight dragoons surrounded Kruchkov, trying
to capture him alive. But causing his horse to
rear, he fought until they succeeded in knocking the sabre out of his hand. He snatched a
lance from a German and wielded it as though
on the parade ground. Beaten back, the Germans hacked at the lance with their swords.
They bunched together over a small patch of
dismal, clayey ploughed land, seething and rocking in the struggle as though shaken by the
wind.

Maddened with terror, the Cossacks and Germans thrust and hacked at whatever came their
way: backs, arms, horses and weapons. The
horses jostled and kicked against one another
in a frenzy of mortal fear. Regaining some
measure of self-command, Ivankov tried several times to strike at the head of a long-faced,
flaxen-haired German who had fastened on him,

but his sabre fell on the man's helmet and slipped off.

Astakhov broke through the ring and galloped free, streaming with blood. The German officer chased after him. Tearing his rifle from his shoulder, Astakhov fired and killed him almost at point-blank range. This proved to be the turning-point in the struggle. Having lost their commander, the Germans, all of them wounded with clumsy blows, dispersed and retreated. The Cossacks did not pursue them. They did not fire after them. They rode straight back to their squadron at Pelikaliye, while the Germans picked up a wounded comrade and fled towards the frontier.

After riding perhaps half a verst Ivankov swayed in his saddle.

"I'm.... I shall drop ..." he halted his horse. But Astakhov pulled at his reins, crying:

"Come on!"

Kruchkov smeared the blood over his face and felt his chest. Crimson spots were showing damply on his shirt. Beyond the farm where the second outpost had been stationed the party disagreed as to the way.

"To the right!" Astakhov said, pointing towards the green, swampy ground of an alder wood.

"No, to the left!" Kruchkov insisted.

They separated. Astakhov and Ivankov arrived at the regimental headquarters after Kruchkov and Shchegolkov. They found the Cossacks of their squadron awaiting them. Ivankov dropped the reins, jumped from the saddle, swayed and fell. They had difficulty in freeing the sabre-hilt from his clutching fingers.

Within an hour almost the entire squadron rode out to where the German officer lay. The Cossacks removed his boots, clothing and weapons and crowded around to look at the young, frowning, yellow face of the dead man. One of them managed to capture the officer's watch with a silver face-guard, and sold it on the spot to his troop sergeant. In a wallet they found a few bank-notes, a letter, a lock of flaxen hair and a photograph of a girl with a proud, smiling mouth.

## IX

Afterwards this incident was transformed into a heroic exploit. Kruchkov, a favourite of the squadron commander, received the Cross of St. George. His comrades remained in shadow. The hero was sent to the divisional staff headquarters, where he lived in clover until the end of the war, receiving three more crosses because influential ladies and officers came from Petersburg and Moscow to look at him. The ladies "ah-ed" and "oh-ed," and regaled the Don Cossack with expensive cigarettes and chocolates. At first he cursed them by all the devils, but afterwards, under the benevolent influence of the staff toadies in officers' uniform, he made a remunerative business of it. He told the story of his "exploit," laying the colours on thick and lying without a twinge of conscience, while the ladies went into raptures, and stared admiringly at the pock-marked, brigand face of the Cossack hero. Everyone was pleased and happy.

The tsar visited headquarters, and Kruchkov was taken to be shown to him. The sleepy emperor looked Kruchkov over as if he were a horse, blinked his heavy eyelids, and patted the Cossack on the shoulder.

"A fine Cossack lad!" he remarked and, turning to his suite, asked for some Seltzer water.

Kruchkov's forelock figured constantly in the newspapers and magazines. There were Kruchkov brands of cigarettes. The merchants of Nizhny-Novgorod presented him with a gold-mounted sabre.

The uniform taken from the German officer Astakhov had killed was mailed to a plywood board and General von Rennenkampf put it in his car with Ivankov and his adjutant to hold it and drove before parading troops about to go to the front, making the customary fiery speeches in the official jargon.

And what had really happened? Men, who had not yet acquired the knack of killing their own kind, had clashed on the field of death, and in the mortal terror that embraced them, had charged, and struck, and battered blindly at each other, mutilating one another and their horses; then they had turned and fled, frightened by a shot which had killed one of their number. They had ridden away morally crippled.

And it was called a heroic exploit.

## X

The front was not yet the huge unyielding viper that it was to become. Cavalry skirmishes and battles flared up along the frontier. In the days immediately following the declaration of war the German command put out feelers in the shape of strong cavalry detachments that caused alarm among the Russian troops by slipping past the frontier posts and spying out the disposition and numbers of their forces. The Russian Eighth Army was screened by the 12th Cavalry Division under the command of General Kaledin. On its left flank the 11th Cavalry Division had advanced across the Austrian frontier, but having captured Leshnuv and Brodi, was brought to a halt when the Austrians were reinforced by Hungarian cavalry. The Hungarian cavalry hurled itself at the Russian units and forced them back towards Brodi.

Since his first battle Grigory Melekhov had been tormented by a dreary inward pain. He grew noticeably thinner and frequently, whether on the march or resting, sleeping or waking, he saw the features and form of the Austrian whom he had killed by the railings. In his sleep he lived again and again through that first battle, and even felt the shuddering convulsion of his right hand clutching the lance. He would awaken and drive the dream off violently, shading his painfully screwed-up eyes with his hand.

The cavalry trampled down the ripened corn and scarred the fields with hoofprints, and it was as though a pounding hailstorm had swept Galicia. The heavy soldiers' boots tramped the roads, scratched the macadam, churned up the August mud. The gloomy face of the earth was pock-marked with shells; fragments of iron and steel rusted there, yearning for human blood. At night ruddy flickerings lit up the horizon: trees, villages, towns blazed like summer lightning. In August—when fruits ripen and corn is ready for harvest—the sky was unsmilingly grey, the rare fine days were oppressive and sultry.

August was drawing to a close. The leaves turned yellow in the orchards, and a mournful purple spread from their stalks. From a distance it looked as though the trees were gashed with wounds and bleeding to death.

Grigory studied with interest the changes that occurred in his comrades. Prokhor Zykov returned from hospital with the marks of a horseshoe on his cheek, and pain and bewilderment lurking in the corners of his lips. His calfish eyes blinked more than ever. Yegor Zharkov lost no opportunity to curse and swear, was even bawdier than before, and riled against everything under the sun. Yemelyan Groshev, a serious and efficient Cossack from Grigory's own village, seemed to char; his face turned dark, and he laughed awkwardly and morosely. Changes were to be observed in every face; each was inwardly nursing and rearing the seeds of grief implanted by the war.

The regiment was withdrawn from the line for a three-day rest, and its complement was made up by reinforcements from the Don. The Cossacks of Grigory's squadron were about to go for a dip in a neighbouring lake, when a considerable force of cavalry rode into the village from the station some three versts away. By the time the men had reached the dam of the lake the force was riding down the hill. Prokhor Zykov was pulling off his shirt when, looking up, he stared and exclaimed:

"They're Cossacks, Don Cossacks!"

Grigory gazed after the column crawling into the estate where the Fourth Squadron was quartered.

"Reserves, most likely."

"Look boys; surely that's Stepan Astakhov? There in the third rank from the front," Groshev exclaimed, and gave a short grating laugh.

"And there's Anikushka."

"Grisha! Melekhov! There's your brother. D'you see him?"

Narrowing his eyes, Grigory stared, trying to recognize the horse Pyotr was riding. "Must have bought a new one!" he thought, turning his gaze to his brother's face. Deeply tanned, with moustache clipped and brows bleeched by the summer sun, it was strangely altered since their last meeting.

Grigory went to meet him, taking off his cap and waving mechanically. After him poured the half-dressed Cossacks, trampling underfoot the brittle undergrowth of angelica and burdock.

Led by an elderly, stocky captain with a wooden hardness in the lines of his authoritative clean-shaven mouth, the detachment swung

round the orchard into the estate. "A sticker!"
Grigory thought, as he smiled at his brother and
at the same time ran his eye over the captain's
sturdy figure and his hook-nosed mount,
evidently of an Eastern strain.

"Hullo, Brother!" he shouted.

"Glory be! We're going to be together.
How're things?"

"All right."

"So you're still alive?"

"So far."

"Regards from the family."

"How are they all?"

"All right."

Pyotr rested his palm on the croup of his sturdy reddish horse and, turning his whole body in
the saddle, surveyed Grigory smilingly. Then
he rode on, and was hidden by the oncoming
ranks of other Cossacks, familiar and unfamiliar.

"Hullo, Melekhov! Regards from the village."

"So you're joining us?" Grigory grinned, recognizing Mikhail Koshevoi by the golden slab
of his forelock.

"That's right. Like chickens after corn."

"Mind you don't get pecked yourself."

"We'll see about that!"

Yegor Zharkov came from the lake dressed
only in his shirt and hopping on one leg

trying to thrust the other into his *sharovari* as
he ran.

"Hey, here's Zharkov!" rose a shout from
the ranks.

"Hullo, stallion! Have they had to hobble you
then?"

"How's my mother?"

"Still alive. She sent her love, but we wouldn't
take any presents. We had enough to carry as
it was."

Yegor listened with an unusually serious expression to the reply, and then sat down bare-
bottomed in the grass, hiding his disappointed
face and struggling ineffectually to get his
trembling leg into his trousers.

Half-dressed Cossacks stood behind the blue-
painted fence; on the other side the reserve
squadron from the Don flowed along the chest-
nut-lined road into the yard.

"That you, Alexander?"

"Yes, it's me."

"Andreyan! Why, you lop-eared devil, don't
you know me?"

"Love from the wife. So this is life in the army, eh!"

"Christ save you."

"Where's Boris Belov?"

"What squadron was he in?"

"The Fourth, I think."

"Where was he from?"

"Vyeshenskaya stanitsa, Zaton."

"What do you want him for?" a third voice broke into the fragmentary conversation.

"I've got a letter for him, that's what."

"He was killed a few days back, at Raibrodi."

"Is that so?"

"Believe me. I saw it with my own eyes. Bullet in the chest, just under his left tit."

"Anyone here from Chornaya Rechka?"

"No. On you go."

The squadron was drawn up in the yard. The other Cossacks returned to their bathe and were joined soon after by the new arrivals. Grigory dropped down at his brother's side. The damp, crumbling clay of the dam had an unpleasant raw smell about it; the water was bright-green at the edges. Grigory sat killing the lice in the folds and seams of his shirt, and told his brother:

"Pyotr, I'm played out. I'm like a man who only needs one more blow to kill him. It's as though I'd been between millstones; they've crushed me and spat me out." His voice was cracked and complaining, and a dark furrow (only now, with a feeling of anxiety, did Pyotr notice it) slanting diagonally across his forehead, made a startling impression of change and alienation.

"Why, what's the matter?" Pyotr asked as he pulled off his shirt, revealing his bare white body with the clean-cut line of sunburn around the neck.

"It's like this," Grigory said hurriedly, and his voice grew strong in its bitterness. "They've set us fighting one another, worse than a pack of wolves. Hatred everywhere. Sometimes I think to myself if I bit a man he'd get the rabies."

"Have you had to ... kill anyone?"

"Yes," Grigory almost shouted, screwing up his shirt and throwing it down at his feet. Then he sat pressing his throat with his fingers, as though pushing down a word that was choking him, and turned his eyes away.

"Tell me," Pyotr ordered, avoiding his brother's eyes.

"My conscience is killing me. I sent my lance through one man ... in hot blood ... I couldn't have done it otherwise.... But why did I cut down the other?"

"Well?"

"It isn't 'well'! I cut down a man, and I'm sick at heart because of him, the swine! The bastard comes haunting me in my dreams. Was I to blame?"

"You're not used to it yet; you'll get over it."

"Are you stopping with our squadron?" Grigory asked abruptly.

"No, we're drafted to the 27th Regiment."

"I thought you had come to help us out."

"Our squadron's going to be tacked on to some infantry division or other. We're catching it up. But we've brought you some replacements, a batch of young fellows."

"Well, let's have a swim."

Grigory hastily pulled off his trousers and went to the edge of the dam, sunburnt and well-built in spite of his stooped shoulders; he was older than when they last saw each other, Pyotr thought. Raising his hands, he dived into the water; a heavy green wave closed over him and billowed away. He struck out towards the group of Cossacks larking about in the middle, his hands slapping the water affectionately, his shoulders moving lazily.

Pyotr was slow in removing from his neck the cross with the prayer sewn to it. He thrust the string under his pile of clothes, entered the water with timorous caution, wetted his chest and shoulders, then pressed forward with a groan and swam to overtake Grigory. They made for the opposite bank, which was sandy and covered with bushes. The movement through the water cooled and soothed, and Grigory spoke restrainedly and without his previous passion.

"I've been so fed up I've let the lice eat me!" he remarked. "If I were only at home now! I'd fly there if I had wings. Just to take one little peep! How are they all?"

"Natalya is living with us."

"How are Father and Mother?"

"All right. But Natalya's still waiting for you. She still believes you'll go back to her."

Grigory snorted and spat out water without answering. Pyotr turned his head and tried to look into his brother's eyes.

"You might send her a word in your letters. The woman lives only for you."

"What, does she still want to tie up the broken ends?"

"Well, she lives on hope. . . . She's a fine little woman. Strict too. She won't let anybody play about with her!"

"She ought to get a husband."

"Strange words from you!"

"Nothing strange about them. That's how it ought to be."

"Well, it's your business. I shan't interfere."

"And how's Dunya?"

"She's a woman, Brother! She's grown so much this year that you wouldn't know her."

"Is that so!" Grigory said, surprised and a little cheered.

"God's truth! She'll be getting married next, and we shan't even get our whiskers into the vodka. Or we may even get killed off, damn them!"

"Nothing simpler!"

They lay side by side on the sand, basking in the mild warmth of the sun.

Misha Koshevoi swam past. "Come on, Grisha, into the water."

"No, I'm resting."

Burying a beetle in the sand, Grigory asked: "Heard anything of Aksinya?"

"I saw her in the village just before war broke out."

"What was she doing there?"

"She'd come to get some things of hers from her husband."

Grigory coughed and buried the beetle with a sweep of his hand.

"Did you speak to her?"

"Only passed the time of day. She was looking well, and cheerful. She seems to have an easy time at the estate."

"And what about Stepan?"

"He gave her her odds and ends all right. Behaved decently enough. But you keep your eyes open! I've been told that when he was drunk he swore he'd put a bullet through you in the first battle. He can't forgive you."

"I know."

"I got myself a new horse," Pyotr changed the conversation.

"Sold the bullocks?"

"For a hundred and eighty. And the horse cost a hundred and fifty. Not a bad one, either."

"What's the grain like?"

"Good. They took us off before we could get it in."

The talk turned to domestic matters, and the intensity of feeling passed. Grigory drank in Pyotr's news of home. For a brief moment he was living there again, just an ordinary self-willed lad.

"Well, let's have another dip and get dressed," Pyotr suggested, brushing the sand off his damp belly. His back and arms were covered with gooseflesh.

They returned with a crowd of Cossacks to the yard. At the orchard fence Stepan Astakhov overtook them. He was combing his hair back under the peak of his cap as he walked. Drawing level with Grigory, he said:

"Hullo, friend!"

"Hullo!" Grigory halted and turned to him with a touch of embarrassment and guilt in his face.

"You haven't forgotten me, have you?"

"Almost."

"But I remember you!" Stepan smiled derisive-
ly and passed on, slipping his arm round the
shoulder of a corporal walking ahead of them.

After sundown a telephone message came
from the divisional staff for Grigory's regiment
to return to the front. The squadrons were assembled within fifteen minutes, and rode off
singing to close a breach made in the line by
the enemy cavalry.

As they said good-bye to each other Pyotr
thrust a folded paper into his brother's hand.

"What's this?" Grigory asked.

"I've copied down a prayer for you. Take
it. . . ."

"Is it any good?"

"Don't laugh, Grigory!"

"I'm not laughing."

"Well, good-bye, Brother. Don't dash away
in front of the rest. Death has a fancy for the
hot-blooded ones. Look after yourself," Pyotr
shouted.

"What's the prayer for then?"

Pyotr waved his hand.

For some time the squadrons rode without ob-
serving any precautions. Then the sergeants
gave orders for the utmost possible quiet, and
for all cigarettes to be put out. Flares, adorned
with tails of lilac smoke, soared high over a distant wood.

A small brown Morocco notebook. The corners were frayed and broken; it must have spent a long time in its owner's pocket. The pages were covered with rather elaborate sloping handwriting.

... For some time now I have felt this need for putting pen to paper. I want to keep a sort of "college diary." First of all, about her. In February (I don't remember the date) I got to know her through a neighbour of hers, a student called Boyaryshkin. I ran into them outside a cinema. When Boyaryshkin introduced her, he said: "Liza comes from the Vyeshenskaya stanitsa. Be nice to her, Timofei. She's an excellent girl." I remember uttering some incoherent remark and taking her soft sweaty hand in mine. That was how I met Yelizaveta Mokhova. I realized at once that she had been spoiled. Women like her have something in their eyes that tells you too much. The impression she created on me, I admit, was not very favourable. It must have been that clammy hand of hers. I have never met anyone whose hands perspired so much; then those eyes, very beautiful eyes actually, with a glorious hazel tint in them, and yet unpleasant.

Vasya, old friend, I find myself consciously touching up my style, even resorting to imagery, for when this "diary" reaches you in Semipalatinsk (I'm thinking of sending it to you after this affair I have started with Yelizaveta Mokhova is over; it may amuse you) I want you to have a clear idea of what happened. I shall describe things in chronological order. Well, as I have said, I was introduced to her and the three of us went in to see some sentimental cinema rubbish. Boyaryshkin kept quiet (he had toothache, "molar-ache," as he called it) and I found it difficult to make conversation. We turned out to be from the same neighbourhood, that is, from neighbouring stanitsas, but after we had shared a few reminiscences about the beauty of steppe scenery and so on, our talk petered out. I preserved an unconstrained silence, so to speak, and she suffered the lack of conversation without the slightest discomfort. I learned from her that she was a second-year medical student, that she came of a merchant family, and that she was fond of strong tea and Asmolov's snuff. Extremely scanty information, as you can imagine, for getting to know a girl with hazel eyes. When we said good-bye (we saw her off to the tramstop), she asked me to call on her. I made a note of her address. I think I shall drop in on April 28th.

Called on her today, she gave me tea and *halvah*. As a matter of fact, there is something in her. Sharp tongue, moderately clever, but she's got hold of that Artsibashev do-as-you-please theory, you can smell it a verst off. Came home late. Made myself cigarettes and thought of things completely unconnected with her, mainly money. My suit is in an appalling state, but I have no "capital." On the whole, things are rotten.

*May 1st*

Today was marked by an event of some importance. While passing the time quite harmlessly in Sokolniki Park, we got involved in an incident. The police and a detachment of Cossacks, about twenty of them, were dispersing a workers' May Day meeting. A drunk hit one of the Cossack's horses with a stick and the Cossack brought his whip into play. (I don't know why, but some people persist in calling a whip a switch. It has its own glorious title—why not use it?) I went up and decided to intervene impelled by the most noble feelings, I assure you. I told the Cossack he was a lout, and one or two other things besides. He was going to take a swing at me with his whip, but I told him pretty firmly that I was a Cossack of Kamenskaya stanitsa

myself and could knock hell out of him any day
of the week. The Cossack happened to be a
good-natured fellow, young; hadn't been in the
army long enough to get sour. He replied that
he was from the stanitsa of Ust-Khoperskaya
and a useful man with his fists. We parted peacefully. If he had started anything against me,
there would have been a fight; and something
rather worse would have happened to my own
person. My intervention is to be explained by
the fact that Liza was with us and when I am
in her presence I am carried away by a purely
childish desire to do something heroic. I can
actually see myself turning into a young cockerel and feel an invisible red comb sprouting
under my cap. . . . What am I coming to!

*May 3rd*

The only thing to do in my present mood is
get drunk. On top of everything I have no money. My trousers are hopelessly split just where it
matters most (in the crutch, to put it bluntly),
like an overripe water-melon down on the Don,
and the chances of my darn holding out are remote indeed. Might as well try to sew up a water-melon. Volodka Strezhnev has been round.
Tomorrow I shall attend lectures.

### May 7th

Money from Father. Rather a grumpy letter, but I don't feel a scrap of shame. What if Dad knew his son's moral supports are rotting like this. . . . Have bought a suit. My new tie attracts the attention even of the cabmen. After a shave at the best hairdresser's in town, came out as fresh as a draper's shop assistant. At the corner of the boulevard a policeman smiled at me. The old scoundrel! But what is past is past. . . . I saw Liza quite by chance through the window of a tram. She waved her glove and smiled. How do you like that!

### May 8th

"To love all ages are submissive. . . ." I can still see the mouth of Tatyana's husband gaping up at me like a gun barrel. From my seat in the gallery I had an irresistible desire to spit into it. Whenever I think of that phrase, particularly the "sub-miss-ive" at the end, my jaw aches to yawn. Probably a nervous tick.

But the point is that I, at my age, am in love. Though it makes my hair stand on end to write it. . . . Called on Liza. Began with a very long and high-flown introduction. She pretended not to understand and tried to change the subject. Is it too early yet? Devil take it, this new suit has mixed everything up. When I look at myself in the mirror I feel I am irresistible. Now is the time, I think! Actually, with me it is straightforward accounting that wins the day. If I don't propose now, in two months' time it will be too late; my trousers will be worn out and I won't be able to propose anyhow. As I write this I overflow with self-admiration. What a brilliant combination I am of all the best qualities of the best people of our time. Here you have gentle yet fiery passion as well as the "voice of reason firm." A Russian salad of all the virtues, not to mention a host of other admirable qualities.

Well, I got no further with her than my preliminary introduction. We were interrupted by her landlady, who called her out into the corridor and asked her for a loan. She refused although she had the money. I knew that for a fact and I pictured her face as she refused in that truthful voice of hers and with such sincerity in those hazel eyes. I didn't want to talk about love after that.

*May 13th*

I am well and truly in love. There can be no doubt about it. Everything tells me so. Tomorrow I shall propose. So far I have not yet worked out my part.

The thing came about in a most unexpected fashion. It was raining, a nice warm shower. We were walking along the Mokhovaya, the wind was sweeping rain across the pavement. I talked and she was quiet, with her head down as if she were thinking. A trickle of rain ran off the brim of her hat on to her cheek, and she was beautiful. I quote our conversation:

"Yelizaveta Sergeyevna, I have told you what I feel, now it is up to you."

"I doubt the sincerity of your feelings."

I shrugged my shoulders in an idiotic fashion and said icily that I was ready to take an oath, or something of the kind.

She said: "Look here, you are talking like a character out of Turgenev. Can't you make it simpler?"

"Nothing could be simpler. I love you."

"And now what?"

"Now it's up to you."

"You want me to say I love you too?"

"I want you to say something."

"You see, Timofei Ivanovich.... How shall I put it? I like you just a little bit.... You're very tall."

"I'll get taller," I promised.

"But we know each other so little, we...."

"In ten years' time we'll know each other a lot better."

She rubbed her wet cheeks with a pink hand and said: "Well, all right then, let's live together. Time will show. But you must let me break off my former attachment first."

"Who is he?" I inquired.

"You don't know him. He's a doctor, a venerologist."

"When will you be free?"

"By Friday, I hope."

"Shall we be living together? In the same flat, I mean?"

"Yes, I think it would be more convenient that way. You will move into my flat."

"Why?"

"I have a very comfortable room. It is quite clean and the landlady is a nice person."

I raised no objection. At the corner of the Tverskaya we parted. To the great astonishment of a lady who happened to be passing we kissed.

What does the future hold in store?

*May 22nd*

Living a life of honey. Today my "honey" mood was clouded by Liza's telling me I must change my underwear. Of course, my underwear is in a disgusting state. But the money, the money. . . . We are spending mine and there isn't much left. Shall have to find work.

### May 24th

Today I decided to buy some new underwear but Liza put me to unexpected expense. She suddenly had an irresistible desire to dine at a good restaurant and buy herself a pair of silk stockings. We have dined and bought, but I am in despair. No underwear for me!

### May 27th

She's sucking me dry. I am physically no more than a bare sunflower stalk. Not a woman but a smouldering fire!

### June 2nd

We woke up today at nine. My accursed habit of wriggling my toes led to the following results. She pulled back the bed-clothes and subjected my foot to a prolonged examination. Then she summed up her observations thus:

"You have a foot like a horse's hoof. Worse! And that hair on your toes—ugh!" She jerked her shoulders in a kind of feverish disgust, buried her head under the bed-clothes and turned away to the wall.

I was confused. I tucked my feet out of sight and touched her on the shoulder.

"Liza!"

"Leave me alone!"

"Liza, this won't do at all. I can't change the shape of my feet, they weren't made to order, you know. And as for the vegetation, you never know where hair will grow next. It grows everywhere. You're a medical student, you ought to know the laws of nature."

She turned over. There was a nasty glint in her hazel eyes.

"For goodness sake buy some deodorant powder. Your feet stink like a corpse."

I remarked judiciously that her hands were always clammy. She remained silent and, to put it in lofty terms, a murky cloud descended on my soul. . . .

*June 4th*

Today we went for a boat trip down the river Moskva. Recalled the Don countryside. Liza's conduct is unworthy of her. She keeps making cutting remarks at my expense, and sometimes they are very rude. To pay her back in her own coin would mean the breaking-off of our relations, and I don't want that. In spite of everything, I am getting more and more attached to her. She is simply spoiled. But I fear my influence will not be strong enough to produce any radical change in her character. A lovable, spoiled little girl. A little girl, moreover, who has seen things that I know of only by hearsay. On the way home she dragged me into a chemist's and, with a smile on her face, bought talcum powder and some other rubbish. "This'll keep the smell down."

I made a gallant bow and thanked her.

Absurd, but there it is.

*June 7th*

She has really very little intellect, but she knows all the other things.

Every night before going to bed I wash my feet in hot water, pour eau-de-Cologne over them and powder them with some other disgusting stuff.

*June 16th*

Every day she becomes more and more intolerable. Yesterday she had an attack of hysterics. It is very hard to live with such a woman.

*June 18th*

We have absolutely nothing in common! We are not even talking the same language.

This morning she went to my pocket for money before going to the baker's, and came across this little book. She looked at it.

"What's this you are carrying about?"

I felt hot all over. Suppose she glanced through it? I was surprised to hear myself answer in such a natural voice: "Just a notebook for calculations."

She pushed it back into my pocket quite indifferently and went out. I must be more careful. Direct impressions of this kind are only worth while when the other person knows nothing about them.

They shall be a source of entertainment to my friend Vasya.

*June 21st*

I am astounded at Liza. She is twenty-one. When did she have time to get so immoral? What kind of family has she got, who had a hand in her development? These are questions that interest me intensely. She is devilishly beautiful. She takes pride in the perfection of her figure. It is just a cult of self-adoration—nothing else exists for her. I have tried several times to talk to her seriously. . . . It would be easier to convince an Old Believer that God does not exist than to re-educate Liza.

Life together has become impossible and absurd. Yet I hesitate to break things off. I must confess that in spite of everything I like her. She has grown upon me.

*June 24th*

It all came out at once. We had a heart-to-heart talk today and she told me I could not satisfy her physically. The break is not yet official, in a few days probably.

*June 26th*

What she needs is a stallion! A real one!

*June 28th*

It is very difficult for me to give her up. She drags me down like mud. Today we took a ride out to the Vorobyovy Hills. She sat by the hotel window and the sun filtered under the carved roof on to her curls. Her hair is the colour of pure gold. And there's a piece of poetry for you!

*July 4th*

I have left my work. Liza has left me. Today I drank beer with Strezhnev. Yesterday we drank vodka. Liza and I parted as educated people should, in a practical manner. No nonsense. Today I saw her in Dmitrov Street with a young man in jockey boots. She acknowledged my greeting with restraint. It is about time I stopped writing these notes—the source has run dry.

*July 30th*

I am quite unexpectedly impelled to take up
the pen again. War. An explosion of bestial en-
thusiasm. Every top-hat stinks like a dead dog
of patriotism. The other fellows are in-
dignant, but I am gratified. I am eaten up with
longing for my ... "paradise lost." Last night
I had a quiet little dream about Liza. She has
left a deep mark of yearning. I should be glad
of some diversion.

*August 1st*

I'm fed up with all this noise and fuss. The
old feeling of longing has returned. I suck at
it as a child sucks a dummy.

*August 3rd*

A way out! I shall go to the war. Foolish?
Very. Shameful?
But what else can I do? Oh for a taste of
something different! Yet there was no such feeling of satiety two years ago. Surely I'm not
getting old?

*August 7th*

I am writing in the train. We have just left
Voronezh. Tomorrow I shall be home. I have
made up my mind. I shall fight for "the Faith,
the Tsar, and the Fatherland."

512

*August 12th*

What a send-off they gave me. The ataman had a drink or two and made an impassioned speech. Afterwards I told him in a whisper that he was a fool. He was flabbergasted and so offended his cheeks turned green. Then he hissed spitefully: "And you call yourself educated! You wouldn't be one of those we gave the lash in 1905, would you?" I replied that, to my regret, I was not "one of those." My father wept and tried to kiss me with a dewdrop dangling from the tip of his nose. Poor dear father! He ought to be in my shoes. I suggested jokingly that he should come with me, and he exclaimed in alarm: "But what about the farm?" Tomorrow I leave for the station.

*August 13th*

Here and there unharvested corn-fields. Sleak marmots on the hillocks. They bear a striking resemblance to the picture-postcard Germans we see impaled on Kozma Kruchkov's lance. Once upon a time when I was a student of mathematics and other exact sciences, little did I think I should live to become such a "jingoist." When I get into a regiment I shall have a talk with the Cossacks.

### August 22nd

At one of the stations along the line I saw the first group of prisoners. A fine-looking Austrian officer with a sportsman's bearing was being taken under guard to the station building. Two young ladies strolling along the platform smiled at him. He managed a very neat bow without stopping and blew them a kiss.

Even as a prisoner he was clean-shaven, gallant, his brown boots glistened. I watched him as he walked away. A young handsome fellow, a pleasant friendly face. If you met him in battle, your arm would not lift to strike.

### August 24th

Refugees, refugees, refugees.... Every line is crowded with trains of refugees and troops.

The first hospital train has just passed. When it stopped a young soldier jumped out. His face was bandaged. We got talking. He had been wounded with grape-shot. Awfully glad he probably won't have to do any more service; his eye was damaged. He was actually laughing.

### August 27th

I am in my regiment. The regimental commander is a very fine old man. A Cossack from the lower Don. One can feel the smell of blood

514

round here. There are rumours that we shall be in the front line the day after tomorrow. Mine is the Third Troop of the Third Squadron–Cossacks from Konstantinovskaya stanitsa. A dull lot. Only one wag and songster.

August 28th

We are going up. Today there is a lot of noise out there. Sounds like thunder rumbling in the distance. I even sniffed the air for rain. But the sky is like blue satin.

Yesterday my horse went lame, grazed its leg on the wheel of a field-kitchen. Everything is new and strange. I don't know what to start on, what to write about.

August 30th

Yesterday there was no time to write. Now I am writing in the saddle. The jolting makes my pencil perform some monstrous antics. There are three of us riding with a forage train for grass.

Now the lads are tying down the load and I am lying on my stomach making a belated record of what happened yesterday. Yesterday Sergeant Tolokonnikov (he addresses me contemptuously as "student." "Hi there, student, can't you see your horse has got a shoe coming off?") sent six of us out on reconnaissance. We drove through some burnt-out village or other. It was very hot. The horses were sweating and so were we. Cossacks should not have to wear serge trousers in summer. In a ditch outside the village I saw my first corpse. A German. Lying on his back with his legs in the ditch. One arm twisted under him, a rifle magazine clasped in the other. No rifle anywhere near. A ghastly sight. A cold shiver runs down my spine as I think of it.... He looked as if he had been sitting with his legs in the ditch, and had then lain back to rest. Grey uniform and helmet. You could see the leather lining. I was so dazed by this first experience that I don't remember his face. Only the big yellow ants crawling over the yellow forehead and glassy half-closed eyes. The Cossacks crossed themselves as they rode past. I looked at the small spot of blood on the right side of his uniform. The bullet had hit him in the right side and gone straight through. As I rode past I noticed that where the bullet had come out, the stain on the uniform and the clot of blood on the ground were much bigger and the uniform was torn raggedly.

I rode past shuddering. So that is how it happens.

The senior sergeant, whose nickname is "Teaser," tried to restore our spirits by telling us a dirty story, but his own lips were trembling.

About half a verst on from the village we came to a gutted factory, just brick walls blackened with smoke at the top. We were afraid to go straight along the road because it lay past this heap of ashes, so we decided to go round it. As soon as we struck off the road somebody started firing at us from the factory. The sound of that first shot, ashamed though I am to admit it, nearly toppled me out of my saddle. I grabbed the pommel and instinctively ducked down and tugged the reins. We galloped back to the village past the ditch where the dead German lay, and did not recover our wits until the village was behind us. Then we turned round and dismounted. We left two men with the horses and the other four of us made our way back to that ditch. We crouched down to go along it. From a distance I saw the legs of the dead German in short yellow boots dangling over the edge. When I passed him I held my breath, as if he were asleep and I were afraid of waking him. The grass under him was moist and green.

We lay down in the ditch and a few minutes later nine German uhlans rode out from behind the ruins of the gutted factory. I could tell they were uhlans by their uniforms. One of them, evidently an officer, shouted something in a gutteral voice and the whole detachment rode in our direction. The lads are calling for me to come and help them load the grass. I must go.

*August 30th*

I want to finish describing how I shot at a man for the first time. The German uhlans rode down on us and I can still see those lizard-green uniforms, the glistening bell-shapes of their helmets, their lances with the flags fluttering at the tips.

They were mounted on dark bay horses. For some reason I let my glance wander to the bank of the ditch and noticed a small emerald-green beetle. It grew larger and larger before my eyes until it seemed enormous. Brushing aside the blades of grass like a giant, it lumbered towards my elbow that I had propped on the dry crumbling clay of the bank; it climbed the sleeve of my tunic and crawled quickly on to the rifle, then from the rifle, on to the sling. I was still watching it on its journey when I heard the Teaser's voice bawling: "Fire, what's the matter with you?!"

I settled my elbow more firmly, screwed up my left eye and felt my heart swelling till it was as huge as that emerald beetle. My sights trembled against a background of grey-green uniform. I pressed the trigger and heard the moaning flight of my bullet. Next to me the Teaser fired. I must have had my sights too low because the bullet ricochetted off a tussock and kicked up a spurt of dust. It was the first shot I had ever fired at a man. I emptied the magazine without aiming. And it was only when I pulled the trigger and got no response that I had a look at the Germans. They were galloping back in the same good order as before, with the officer bringing up the rear. There were nine of them and I could see the dark bay croupe of the officer's horse and the metal plate on the top of his uhlan's helmet.

### September 2nd

In *War and Peace* Tolstoi has a passage in which he speaks of the line between opposing armies, the line of the unknown that seems to divide the living from the dead. The squadron in which Nikolai Rostov is serving goes into the attack and Rostov sees that line in his mind's eye. I remember that passage particularly vividly today, because today at dawn we attacked a unit of German hussars. Ever since early morning their troops, with excellent artillery support, had been harrassing our infantry. I saw some of our men—the 241st and 273rd infantry regiments, I think—fleeing in panic. They had been literally demoralized after being thrown into an attack with no artillery support. Enemy fire had accounted for nearly a third of their number and they were being pursued by German hussars. Then our regiment, which had been standing in reserve in a forest clearing, was thrown into action. This is how I remember the affair.

We left the village of Tishvichi between two and three in the morning. Dawn was coming and it was very dark. The air was heavy with the smell of oats and pine needles. The regiment proceeded in squadrons. We turned off the road and struck across the fields. The horses snorted as they sprinkled the heavy dew off the oats with their hoofs.

It was chilly even in a greatcoat. They kept the regiment tracking across the fields for a long time and an hour passed before an officer rode up and handed an order to the regimental commander. Our old man passed on the order in a dissatisfied tone and the regiment turned at right angles into the woods. Our columns were bunched closely on the narrow path. Fighting was going on somewhere to the left. Judging by the noise a large number of German batteries were in action. The sound of the gunfire vibrated in the air and it felt as if all that scented pinewood was on fire above us. Until sunrise we could only listen. A cheer went up, a limp, ragged sort of cheer, and then—stillness threaded with the clean hammering of machine-guns. At that moment my head was in a whirl; the only thing I could think of, and that picture* was utterly and painfully clear, were the faces of our infantry as they advanced.

In my mind's eye I could see the baggy grey figures in their flat army caps and clumsy soldier's top-boots pounding over the autumn earth, and I could hear the sharp hoarse chuckle of the German machine-guns as they set to work transforming those living sweating human bodies into corpses. The two regiments were mown down and fled, abandoning their arms. Then a regiment of German hussars charged down on them. We came out on their flank at a distance of about seven hundred yards or less. An order was given. We formed up instantly. I heard a single cold command. "Forward!" It seemed to hold us back for a moment like a bit, then we were flying ahead. My horse's ears were pressed so flat against its head you couldn't have prised them up with your fingers. I glanced round—behind me were the regimental commander and two officers. Yes, this was it, this was the line dividing the living from the dead. Here it was, the great moment of insanity!

The hussars wavered and turned back. Before my eyes our squadron commander Chernetsov cut down a German hussar. I saw a Cossack of the Sixth Squadron overtake a German and hack madly at his horse's croup. Ribbons of skin streamed from the sabre as it rose and fell. It was inconceivable! There was no name for it! On the way back I saw Chernetsov's face, intent and controlledly cheerful—he might have been sitting at the card table, instead of in the saddle, having just murdered a man. Squadron-Commander Chernetsov will go far. A capable fellow!

*September 4th*

We are resting. The Fourth Division of the Second Army Corps is being brought up to the front. We are stationed at the small town of Kobylino. This morning units of the 11th Cavalry Division and the Urals Cossacks went through the town at a fast pace. Fighting continues in the west. A constant rumble. After dinner I went to the field hospital. A train of wounded had just arrived. Stretcher-bearers were unloading a big wagon and laughing. I went up to them. A tall ginger-haired soldier had just climbed down with the help of an or-

derly. "What do you think of that, Cossack,"
he said, addressing me. "They've given me a
load of peas in the behind. It's full of grape-
shot." The orderly asked him if the shell had
burst behind him. "Behind me be damned, I
was advancing behind-first myself." A nurse
came out of one of the cottages. I glanced at
her and suddenly felt so weak I had to lean
against a cart. Her resemblance to Liza was extraordinary. The same eyes, the same oval face,
nose, hair. Even her voice was similar. Or was
I imagining things? Now, I suppose, I shall see
a resemblance to her in every woman I meet.

### September 5th

The horses have had a day's feeding in the
stalls and we are off to the front again. Physically I am a wreck. The bugler is playing the
order to mount. There's a man I should love
to put a bullet through!

The squadron commander had sent Grigory
Melekhov with a message to regimental headquarters. As he rode through the district where
the recent fighting had taken place Grigory noticed a dead Cossack lying at the side of the
highway. He lay with his fair curly head close
to the hoof-pitted road. Grigory dismounted
and, holding his nose (the dead man already

reeked of decay), searched the body. In the trousers pocket he found this notebook, a stub of indelible pencil and a purse. He removed the cartridge belt and glanced at the pale, moist face that was already beginning to decompose. The temples and the bridge of the nose were turning black, on the forehead a slantwise furrow fixed in mortal concentration was grimed with dust.

Grigory covered the face with a cambric handkerchief that he found in the dead man's pocket and rode on to headquarters, pausing now and then to glance round. He handed in the notebook to the headquarters clerks, who gathered round to read it and laugh over this other man's brief life and its earthly desires.

## XII

During August the 11th Cavalry Division took town after town by storm, and by the end of the month they were deployed around the town of Kamenka-Strumilovo. Behind them came the army; infantry units massed on important strategic sectors, staff units and baggage trains gathered at the railway junctions. The front stretched from the Baltic like a death-dealing whiplash. At staff headquarters a big offensive was being planned; generals pored over their maps, dispatch riders dashed to and fro with battle orders, hundreds of thousands of soldiers marched to their death.

The reconnaissance patrols reported that considerable forces of enemy cavalry were approaching the town. In the woods along the roads skirmishes were fought between Cossack detachments and the enemy advance guards.

Ever since seeing his brother, Grigory Melekhov had sought to put an end to his painful thoughts, and to recover his former tranquillity of spirit. But it was no use. Among the last reinforcements from the second line of reservists a Cossack, Alexei Uryupin, had been drafted into Grigory's troop. Uryupin was tall, rather round-shouldered with an aggressive lower jaw and drooping Kalmyk whiskers. His merry, fearless eyes were always smiling, and he was bald, with only scanty ruddy hair around the edges of his angular scull. On the very first day of his arrival he was nicknamed "Tufty."

After fighting around Brodi the regiment had a day's respite. Grigory and Uryupin were quartered in the same hut. They soon fell into conversation.

"You know, Melekhov, you must be moulting or something."

"What do you mean—moulting?" Grigory asked with a frown.

"You're all limp, as though you were ill," Uryupin explained.

They had been feeding their horses and they stood smoking with their backs against a rickety moss-grown fence. Hussars were riding four abreast down the road; dead bodies were lying about by the fences, for there had been fighting in the streets when the Austrians withdrew; a charred smell rose from the ruins of a gutted synagogue. In the rich colours of early evening the town was one immense picture of destruction and repelling emptiness.

"I'm all right," Grigory spat out, not looking at the other.

"You're lying! I've got eyes to see!"

"Well, and what can you see?"

"You're scared! Is it death you're scared of?"

"You're a fool!" Grigory said contemptuously, staring narrowly at his finger-nails.

"Tell me, have you killed anyone?" Uryupin went on with his probing.

"Yes. What of it?"

"Does it weigh on your mind?"

"Weigh on my mind?" Grigory smiled bitterly.

Uryupin drew his sabre from its scabbard. "Would you like me to slash your head off?"

"And then?"

"I'll kill you without a sigh of regret. I have

no pity." Uryupin's eyes were smiling, but by his voice and the rapacious quiver of his nostrils Grigory realized that he meant what he said.

"You're queer—you're a savage," said Grigory, studying Uryupin's face intently.

"Bah, your heart's made of water. Do you know this stroke? Watch!" Uryupin selected an old birch-tree in the hedge and went straight towards it, measuring the distance with his eyes. His long, sinewy arms with their unusually broad wrists hung motionless.

"Watch!"

He slowly raised his sabre, and suddenly swung it slantwise with terrible force. Completely severed four feet from the ground, the birch toppled over, its branches scraping at the window and clawing the walls of the hut.

"Did you see that? Learn it. There was an ataman called Baklanov, ever heard of him? The blade of his sabre was filled with quick silver. It was heavy to lift, but he could cut a horse in two with it. Like that!"

It took Grigory a long time to master the difficult technique of the new stroke. "You're strong, but you're a fool with your sabre. This is the way!" Uryupin instructed him, wielding his sabre slantwise with terrific force. "Cut a man down boldly! Man is as soft as dough." A smile came into his eyes. "Don't think about the why and wherefore. You're a Cossack, and it's your business to cut down without asking questions. To kill your enemy in battle is a holy work. For every man you kill God will wipe out one of your sins, just as he does for killing a serpent. You mustn't kill an animal unless it's necessary, but destroy man! He's a heathen, unclean; he poisons the earth, he lives like a toadstool!"

When Grigory raised objections he only frowned and lapsed into an obstinate silence.

Grigory noticed with surprise that all horses were afraid of Uryupin. When he went near them they would prick up their ears and bunch together as though an animal were approaching, and not a man. On one occasion the squadron had to attack on foot over a wooded and swampy district. The horses were led aside into a dell. Uryupin was among those assigned to take charge of the horses, but he flatly refused.

"Uryupin, why the devil don't you lead away your horses?" the troop sergeant barked at him.

"They're afraid of me. God's truth, they are!" he replied with the usual twinkle in his eyes.

He never took his turn at minding the horses. He was kind to his own mount, but Grigory observed that whenever he went up to it a shiver ran down the animal's back, and it fidgeted uneasily.

"Tell me, why are the horses afraid of you?"
Grigory once asked him.

"I don't know," he replied with a shrug of his
shoulders. "I'm kind enough to them."

"They know a drunken man and are afraid
of him, but you're always sober."

"I've a hard heart, and they seem to feel it."

"You have a wolf's heart. Or maybe it's just
a stone you've got and not a heart at all."

"Maybe!" Uryupin willingly agreed.

The troop was dispatched on reconnaissance
work. The previous evening a Czech deserter
from the Austrian army had informed the Russian command of a change in the disposition
of the enemy forces and a proposed counter-
attack, and there was need for continual observation over the road along which the hostile
regiments must pass.

The troop officer left four Cossacks with the
sergeant at the edge of a wood, and rode with
the others towards a town lying beyond the
next rise. Grigory, Uryupin, Misha Koshevoi
and another Cossack were left with the sergeant.

The sergeant ordered them to dismount and
told Koshevoi to take the horses behind a thick
bunch of pine-trees and mind them.

The Cossacks lay smoking by a fallen pine,
while the sergeant watched the country through
his binoculars. Half an hour they lay there, ex-

changing lazy remarks. From somewhere to the right came the incessant roar of gunfire. A few paces away a field of ungathered rye, its ears emptied of grain, was waving in the wind. Grigory crawled into the rye, selected some still full ears, husked them, and chewed the grain.

A group of horsemen rode out of a distant plantation and halted, surveying the open country, then set off again in the direction of the Cossacks.

"They must be Austrians," the sergeant exclaimed under his breath. "We'll let them get closer and send them a volley. Have your rifles ready, boys," he added feverishly.

The riders steadily drew closer. They were six Hungarian hussars, in handsome tunics ornamented with white braid and piping. The leader, on a big black horse, held his carbine in his hands and was quietly laughing.

"Fire!" the sergeant ordered. The volley went echoing through the trees.

"What's up?" Koshevoi's startled shout came from behind the pines. "Whoa, you devil! Keep still there!" His voice sounded prosaically loud. The hussars galloped in single file into the grain. One of them, the leader, fired into the air. The last hussar dropped behind, clinging to his horse's neck and holding his cap on with his left hand.

Uryupin was the first to leap to his feet. He sped off, stumbling through the rye, holding his rifle at the trail. Some hundred yards away he found a fallen horse kicking and struggling, and a Hungarian hussar standing close by, rubbing his knee, which he had hurt in the fall. He shouted something to Uryupin and raised his hands in token of surrender, staring after his retreating comrades.

All this happened so quickly that Grigory hardly had time to take in what was occurring before Uryupin had brought back his prisoner.

"Off with it!" Uryupin shouted at the Hungarian, roughly tearing at the hussar's sword.

The prisoner smiled apprehensively and fumbled with his belt, only too willing to hand over his sword. But his hands trembled, and he could not manage to unfasten the clasp. Grigory cautiously assisted him, and the hussar, a young, fat-cheeked boy with a tiny mole in the corner of his shaven upper lip, thanked him with a smile and a nod of the head. He seemed glad to be deprived of the weapon and, fumbling in his pocket, pulled out a leather pouch and muttered something, offering the Cossacks tobacco.

"He's treating us!" the sergeant smiled, and felt for his cigarette papers.

"Have a smoke on foreign baccy," Silantyev chuckled.

The Cossacks rolled cigarettes from the hussar's tobacco and smoked. The strong, black tobacco quickly went to their heads.

"Where's his rifle?" the sergeant asked, drawing greedily at his cigarette.

"Here it is," Uryupin showed the stitched yellow sling from behind his back.

"He'd better be taken to the squadron. They'll want to hear what he's got to say."

"Who'll take him, boys?" the sergeant asked, passing his eyes over his men.

"I will," Uryupin replied quickly.

"All right, off with you!"

The prisoner evidently realized what was to happen to him, for he smiled wryly, turned out his pockets, and offered the Cossacks some soft broken chocolate.

"Rusin ich . . . Rusin . . . nein Austrische . . ." he stammered, gesticulating absurdly and holding out the chocolate.

"Any weapons?" the sergeant asked. "Don't rattle away like that, we can't understand you. Got a revolver? A bang-bang?" The sergeant pulled an imaginary trigger. The prisoner shook his head furiously.

He willingly allowed himself to be searched, his fat cheeks quivering. Blood was streaming from his torn knee. Talking incessantly, he dabbed it with his handkerchief. He had left his cap by his horse, and he asked permission to go and fetch it and his blanket and notebook, in which were photographs of his family. The sergeant tried hard to understand what he wanted but at last waved his hand in despair:

"Off with him!"

Uryupin took his horse and mounted it. Adjusting his rifle across his back, he motioned to the prisoner. Encouraged by his smile, the Hungarian also smiled and set off at the horse's side. With an attempt at familiarity he patted Uryupin's knee, but the Cossack harshly flung off his hand and pulled on the reins.

"Get along. None of your tricks!"

The prisoner guiltily drew away from the horse and strode along with a serious face, frequently looking back at the other Cossacks. His fair hair stuck up gaily on the crown of his head. So he remained in Grigory's memory: his tunic flung over his shoulders, his flaxen tuft of hair, and his confident, debonair walk.

"Melekhov, go and unsaddle his horse!" the sergeant ordered, regretfully spitting out the end of his cigarette, which he had smoked till it burned his fingers. Grigory went to the fallen animal, removed the saddle, and then for some undefined reason picked up the cap lying close by. He smelled the lining and caught the scent of cheap soap and sweat. He carried the horse's equipment back to the trees, holding the hussar's cap carefully in his left hand. Squatting on their haunches, the Cossacks rummaged in the saddle-bags and examined the unfamiliar design of the saddle.

"That tobacco he had was good; we should have asked him for some more," the sergeant sighed at the memory and swallowed down his spittle.

Not many minutes had passed when a horse's head appeared through the pines, and Uryupin rode up.

"Why, where's the Austrian? You haven't let him go?" the sergeant exclaimed, jumping up in alarm. Uryupin rode up waving his whip, dismounted and stretched his shoulders.

"What have you done with the Austrian?" the sergeant asked again, going up to him.

"He tried to run away," Uryupin snarled.

"And so you let him?"

"We came to an open glade, and he.... So I cut him down."

"You're a liar!" Grigory shouted. "You killed him for nothing."

"What are you shouting about? What's it to do with you?" Uryupin fixed icy eyes on Grigory's face.

"What?" Grigory was slowly rising, his hand groping along the ground.

"Don't poke your nose in where it isn't wanted! Understand?" the other replied sternly. Grigory snatched up his rifle and threw it to his shoulder. His finger quivered as it felt for the trigger, and his ashen face worked angrily.

"Now then!" the sergeant exclaimed threateningly, running to him. He struck the rifle before it fired and the bullet cut a branch from a tree and went whistling away.

"What's going on?" Koshevoi gasped.

Silantyev's jaw dropped and he sat still with his mouth open.

The sergeant pushed Grigory in the chest and tore the rifle out of his hands. Uryupin stood without changing his position, his feet planted apart, his left hand on his belt.

"Fire again!"

"I'll kill you!" Grigory rushed towards him.

"Here, what's all this about? Do you want to be court-martialled and shot? Put your arms down!" the sergeant shouted.

Thrusting Grigory back, he placed himself with arms outstretched between the two men.

"You lie, you won't kill me!" Uryupin smiled.

As they were riding back in the dusk Grigory was the first to notice the body of the

hussar lying in the path. He rode up in front
of the others, and reining in his frightened
horse, stared down. The man lay with arms
flung out over the velvety moss, his face downward, his palms, yellow like autumn leaves,
turned upward and open. A terrible blow from
behind had cloven him in two from the shoulder to the belt.

"Cut him in two . . ." the sergeant muttered
as he rode past glancing in alarm at the dead
man's flaxen tuft of hair sticking up lop-sidedly
from the twisted head.

The Cossacks rode past the body and on to
the squadron headquarters in silence. The evening shadows deepened. A breeze was driving
up a black, feathery cloud from the west. From
a swamp near by came the stagnant scent of
marshgrass, of rusty dampness and rot. A bit-
tern boomed. The drowsy silence was broken
by the jingle of the horses' equipment, and the
occasional clank of sabre on stirrup, or the
scrunch of pine cones under the horses' hoofs.
Through the glade the dark ruddy gleam of
the departed sun streamed over the pine trunks.
Uryupin smoked incessantly, and the fleeting
spark of his cigarette lit up his thick fingers
with their blackened nails firmly gripping the
cigarette.

The cloud floated over the forest, emphasizing and deepening the fading, inexpressibly mournful hues of the evening shadows on the ground.

## XIII

The following morning an assault was begun on the town. Flanked by cavalry and with cavalry units in reserve, the infantry was to have advanced from the forest at dawn. But somewhere, someone blundered; the two infantry regiments did not arrive in time; the 211th Rifle Regiment was ordered to cross over to the left flank, and during the encircling movement initiated by another regiment it was raked with fire from its own batteries. The hopeless confusion upset the plans, and the attack threatened to end in failure, if not disaster. While the infantry was thus being shuffled about and the artillery hauled its guns out of a bog into which it had been sent on someone's instructions, the order came for the Eleventh Cavalry Division to advance. The wooded and marshy land in which they had been held in readiness did not permit of an extended frontal attack, and in some cases the Cossacks had to advance in troops. The Fourth and Fifth squadrons of the Twelfth Regiment were held in reserve in the forest, and within a few minutes of the general advance the roaring, rending sound of the battle reached their ears.

There was a long quivering cheer. Now and then a Cossack spoke:

"That's ours."

"They've started."

"What a row that machine-gun's making."

"Giving our chaps what for."

"They're not cheering now, are they?"

"Not there yet."

"We'll be at it in a minute."

The two squadrons were drawn up in a glade. The stout pine trunks hemmed them in and prevented them from following the course of the battle.

A company of infantry went by almost at a trot. A brisk, smart-looking N.C.O. dropped back to the rear ranks and shouted hoarsely:

"Order in the ranks!"

The company tramped past with their equipment jangling and disappeared into an alder thicket.

Far away now, faintly through the trees came that quivering cheer, suddenly breaking off. A deep silence fell.

"They've got there now."

"Aye, now they're at it ... killing each other."

The Cossacks strained their ears, but could hear nothing more; on the right flank the Austrian artillery thundered away at the attacking forces; the roar was interspersed with the rattle of machine-guns.

Grigory glanced around his troop. The Cossacks were fidgeting nervously, and the horses were restive as though troubled by gadflies. Uryupin had hung his cap on the saddle-bow and was wiping his bald head; at Grigory's side Misha Koshevoi puffed fiercely at his home-grown tobacco. All the objects around were distinct and exaggeratedly real, as they appear after a night of wakefulness.

The squadrons were held in reserve for three hours.

The firing now died, now rose to a still higher pitch. An aeroplane roared overhead. After circling a few times at a great height, it flew eastward, gaining altitude. Milky puffs of bursting shells dotted the blue as anti-aircraft guns opened fire.

All stocks of tobacco had been exhausted and the men were pining in expectation, when just before noon an orderly galloped up with instructions. The commander of the Fourth Squadron immediately led his men off to one side. To Grigory it seemed that they were retreating rather than advancing. His own squadron rode for some twenty minutes through the forest, the sound of the battle drawing nearer and nearer. Not far behind them a battery was firing rapidly; the shells tore through the resisting air with a shrieking roar. The narrow forest paths broke up the squadron's formation, and they emerged into the open in disorder. About half a verst away Hungarian hussars were sabring the crew of a Russian battery.

"Squadron, form!" the commander shouted.

The Cossacks had not completely carried out the order when the further command came:

"Squadron, draw sabres; into the attack, forward!"

A blue lightening flash of blades. From a swift trot the Cossacks broke into a gallop.

Six Hungarian hussars were busily occupied with the horses of the field-gun on the extreme right of the battery. One was dragging at the bits of the excited artillery horses, another was beating them with the flat of his sword, while the others were tugging and pulling at the spokes of the carriage wheels. An officer on a dock-tailed chocolate mare was giving orders. At the sight of the Cossacks the hussars leapt to their horses.

"Closer, closer," Grigory counted to the rhythm of his galloping horse. As he galloped, one foot momentarily lost its stirrup, and feeling himself insecure in his saddie, with inward alarm he bent over and fished with his toe for the dangling iron. When he had recovered his foothold he looked up and saw the six horses of the field-gun in front of him. The outrider on the foremost, in a blood- and brain-spattered shirt, was lying over the animal's neck, embracing it. Grigory's horse brought its hoof down with a sickening scrunch on the body of the dead gunner. Two more were lying by an overturned case of shells. A fourth was stretched face downward over the gun-carriage. Silantyev was just in front of Grigory. The Hungarian officer fired at almost point-blank range and the Cossack fell, his hands clutching and embracing the air. Grigory pulled on his reins and tried to approach the officer from the left, the better to use his sabre; but the officer saw through his manoeuvre and fired under his arm at him. Having discharged the contents of his revolver, he drew his sword. He parried three smashing blows with the skill of a trained fencer. Grigory gritted his teeth and lunged at him yet a fourth time, standing in his stirrups. Their horses were now galloping almost side by side, and he noticed the ashy clean-shaven cheek of the Hungarian and the regimental number sewn on his collar. With a feint he diverted the officer's attention, and changing the direction of his stroke, thrust the point of his sabre between the Hungarian's shoulder-blades. He aimed a second blow at the neck, just at the top of the spine. The officer dropped his sword and reins from his hands, and arched his back as if he had been bitten, then toppled over his saddle-bow. Feeling a terrible relief, Grigory lashed at his head, and saw the sabre smash into the bone above the ear.

A terrible blow on the head from behind tore consciousness away from Grigory. He felt a burning, salty taste of blood in his mouth, and realized that he was falling; from one side the stubbled earth came whirling and flying up at him. The heavy crash of his body against the ground brought him momentarily back to reality. He opened his eyes; blood poured into them. A trample past his ears, and the heavy breathing of horses. For the last time he opened his eyes and saw the pink dilated nostrils of a horse, and someone's foot in a stirrup. "The end!" the comforting thought crawled through his mind like a snake. A roar, and then black emptiness.

## XIV

In the middle of August Yevgeny Listnitsky decided to apply for a transfer from the Ataman's Lifeguard Regiment to one of the Cossack regular army regiments. He made his formal application, and within three weeks received the appointment he desired. Before leaving St. Petersburg he wrote to his father:

*Father, I have applied for a transfer from the Ataman's Regiment to the regular army. I received my appointment today, and am leaving for the front to report to the commander of the Second Corps. You will probably be surprised at my decision, but I want to explain my reasons. I am sick of my surroundings. Parades, escorts, sentry duty—all this palace service sets my teeth on edge. I am fed up with it. I want live work and—if you wish—heroic deeds. I suppose it's my Listnitsky blood that is beginning to tell, the honourable blood of those who ever since the War of 1812 have added laurels to the glory of Russian arms. I am leaving for the front. Please give me your blessing.*

*Last week I saw the Emperor before he left for headquarters. I worship the man. I was standing guard inside the palace, he smiled as he passed me and said in English to Rodzyanko, who was with him: 'My glorious Guard. I'll beat Wilhelm's hand with it.' I worship him like a schoolgirl. I am not ashamed to confess it, although I am over twenty-eight now. I am terribly upset by the palace gossip, besmirch-*

ing the Emperor's glorious name. I don't believe it, I can't believe it. The other day I nearly shot Captain Gromov for uttering disrespectful words about Her Imperial Majesty in my presence. It was vile, and I told him that only people who had the blood of serfs flowing in their veins could stoop to such filthy slander. The incident took place before several other officers. I was beside myself, I drew my revolver and was about to waste a bullet on the cad, but my comrades disarmed me. My life becomes more miserable with each day spent in this cesspool. In the guards' regiments—among the officers, in particular—there is no genuine patriotism, and—one is terrified to utter it—there is even no love for the dynasty. This isn't the nobility, it's the rabble. This is really the explanation of my break with the regiment. I cannot associate with people I don't respect.

Well, that's about all. Please forgive my incoherence, I am in a hurry, I must pack my things and leave. Keep well, Papa. I shall write you a long letter from the front.

Your Yevgeny.

The train for Warsaw left Petrograd* at 8 p.m. Listnitsky took a drozhki and drove to the

---

* St. Petersburg was renamed Petrograd in 1914.

station. Behind him lay Petrograd in a dove blue twinkle of lights.

The station was noisy and crowded with troops. The porter brought in Listnitsky's suit-case and, on receiving a few coins, wished the young gentleman a good journey. Listnitsky removed his swordbelt and coat, and spread a flowery silk Caucasian eiderdown on the seat. By the window sat a priest with the lean face of an ascetic, his provisions from home laid out on a small table. Brushing the crumbs from his hemp-like beard, he offered some curd-cake to a slim dark girl in school uniform sitting in the seat opposite him.

"Try something, my dear."

"No, thank you."

"Now don't be shy, a girl with your com-plexion needs plenty to eat."

"No, thank you."

"Try some of this curd-cake then. Perhaps you will take something, sir?"

Listnitsky glanced down.

"Are you addressing me?"

"Yes, indeed." The priest's sombre eyes stared piercingly and only the thin lips smiled un-der his thin drooping moustache.

"No, thank you. I don't feel like food now."

"You are making a mistake. It is no sin to eat. Are you in the army?"

"Yes."

"May the Lord help you."

As Yevgeny dozed off he heard the priest's fruity voice as though coming from a distance, and it seemed to him that it was the disloyal Captain Gromov speaking:

"It's a miserable income my family gets, you know. So I'm off as a chaplain to the forces. The Russian people can't fight without faith. And you know, from year to year the faith increases. Of course there are some who fall away, but they are among the intelligentsia, the peasant holds fast to God."

The priest's bass voice failed to penetrate further into Yevgeny's consciousness. After two wakeful nights a refreshing sleep came to him. He awoke when the train was a good forty versts outside Petrograd. The wheels clattered rhythmically, the carriage swayed and rocked, in a neighbouring compartment someone was singing. The lamp cast slanting lilac shadows.

The regiment to which Listnitsky was assigned had suffered considerable losses, and had been withdrawn from the front to be remounted and have its complement made up. The regimental staff headquarters was at a large market village called Bereznyagi. Listnitsky left the train at some nameless halt. At the same station a field hospital was detrained. He inquired the destination of the hospital from the doctor in charge, and learned that it had been transferred from the south-western front to the sector in which his own regiment was engaged. The doctor spoke very unfavourably of his immediate superiors, cursed the divisional staff officers and, tugging his beard, his eyes glowing behind his pince-nez, poured his jaundiced anger into the ears of his chance acquaintance.

"Can you take me to Bereznyagi?" Listnitsky interrupted him.

"Yes, get into the trap, Lieutenant," he agreed, and familiarly twisting the button on Listnitsky's coat, rumbled on with his complaints.

"Just imagine it, Lieutenant. We've travelled two hundred versts in cattle trucks only to loaf about here, with nothing to do at a time when a bloody battle has been going on for two days in the section from which my hospital was transferred. There were hundreds of wounded there who needed our help badly!"

The doctor repeated the words "bloody battle" with spiteful relish.

"How do you explain such an absurdity?" the lieutenant asked out of politeness.

"How?" The doctor raised his eyebrows ironically over his pince-nez and roared: "Disorder, chaos, stupidity of the commanding staff —that's the reason why. Scoundrels occupy high posts and mix things up. Inefficient, lacking even common sense. Do you remember Veresayev's memoirs of the Russo-Japanese war? Well, it's the same thing all over again, only twice as bad."

Listnitsky saluted him and went to the carts. The angry doctor, his puffy red cheeks trembling, was croaking behind him:

"We'll lose the war, Lieutenant. We lost one to the Japanese but didn't grow any the wiser. We can only brag, that's all." And he went along the rails, stepping over little puddles filmed with rainbow spangles of oil, and shaking his head despairingly.

Dusk was falling as the field hospital approached Bereznyagi. The wind ruffled the yellow stubble. Clouds were massing in the west. At their height they were a deep violet black, but below they shaded into a tender, smoky lilac. In the middle the formless mass, piled like ice-floes against a river dam, was drawn aside. Through the breach poured an orange flood of sunset rays, spreading in a spurtling fan of light and weaving a Bacchanalian spectrum of colours below.

A dead horse lay by the roadside ditch. On one of its hoofs, flung weirdly upward, the horseshoe gleamed. As the trap jogged past, Listnitsky stared at the carcass. The orderly with whom he was riding spat at the horse's belly and explained:

"Been guzzling grain ... been eating too much grain ..." he corrected himself; he was about to spit again but for politeness' sake swallowed his spittle and wiped his mouth with his sleeve. "There it lies, and no one troubles to bury it. That's just like the Russians. The Germans are different."

"What do you know about it?" Yevgeny asked with unreasoning anger. At that moment he was filled with hatred for the orderly's phlegmatic face with its suggestion of superiority and contempt. The man was grey and dreary like a stubble field in September; he was in no way different from the thousands of peasant soldiers whom Yevgeny had seen on his way to the front. They all seemed faded and drooping, dullness stared in their eyes, grey, blue, green or any other colour, and they strongly reminded him of ancient, well-worn copper coins.

"I lived in Germany for three years before the war," the orderly replied unhurriedly. In his voice was the same shade of superiority and contempt that showed in his face. "I worked at a cigar factory in Königsberg," the orderly continued lazily, flicking the horse with the knotted rein.

"Hold your tongue!" Listnitsky commanded

sternly, and turned to glance at the horse's head with its forelock tousled over its eyes and its bare sun-yellowed row of teeth.

One leg was raised and bent in an arch; the hoof was slightly cracked but the hollow had a smooth grey-blue gleam about it and the lieutenant could tell by the leg and by the finely chiselled pastern that the horse was young and of a good breed.

They drove on over the bumpy road. The colours faded in the west, a wind sprang up and scattered the clouds. Behind them the leg of the dead horse stuck up like a broken wayside cross. As Yevgeny stared back at it, a sheaf of rays fell suddenly on the horse, and in their orange light the leg with its sorrel hair blossomed unexpectedly like some marvellous leafless branch of legend.

As the field hospital drove into Bereznyagi it passed a transport of wounded soldiers. An elderly Byelorussian, the owner of the first wagon, strode along at his horse's head, the hempen reins gathered in his hands. On the wagon lay a Cossack with bandaged head. He was resting on his elbow, but his eyes were closed wearily as he chewed bread and spat out the black mess. At his side a soldier was stretched out; over his buttocks his torn trousers were horribly shrivelled and taut with congealed

blood. He was cursing savagely, without lifting his head. Listnitsky was horrified as he listened to the intonation of the man's voice, for
it sounded exactly like a believer fervently muttering prayers. On the second wagon five or six
soldiers were lying side by side. One of them,
possessed of a feverish gaiety, his eyes unnaturally bright and inflamed, was telling a story:

". . . It seems an ambassador from that emper-
or of theirs came here and made an offer about
having peace. The thing is it was an honest
man who told me. I'm hoping he wasn't just
spinning a yarn."

"I expect he was," one of the others rejoined
doubtfully, shaking his round head that bore
the scars of a recent attack of scrofula.

"But perhaps he did really come here," responded a third man who was sitting with his
back to the horses, in a soft Volga country
brogue.

On the fifth wagon three Cossacks were comfortably seated. As Listnitsky passed they
stared silently at him, their harsh dusty faces
showing no sign of respect for an officer.

"Good-day, Cossacks!" the lieutenant greeted
them.

"Good-day, Your Honour," the handsome sil-
ver-moustached Cossack sitting nearest the driver replied indifferently.

"What regiment are you?" Listnitsky continued, trying to make out the number on the Cossack's blue shoulder-strap.

"The Twelfth."

"Where is your regiment now?"

"We couldn't say."

"Well, where were you wounded?"

"By the village ... not far from here."

The Cossacks whispered among themselves and one of them, holding his roughly bandaged hand with his sound hand, jumped down from the wagon.

"Just a minute, Your Honour." He padded across the road on bare feet, carefully nursing his bullet-torn hand, which was already showing signs of inflammation.

"You wouldn't be from Vyeshenskaya, would you? You're not Listnitsky?"

"Yes, I am."

"That's what we thought. You haven't got anything to smoke, have you, Your Honour? Give us something, for Christ's sake, we're dying for a smoke."

He walked along by the trap, gripping its painted side. Listnitsky took out his cigarette case.

"Could you spare us a dozen? There are three of us, you know," the Cossack smiled appealingly.

Listnitsky emptied the contents of his case on to the man's broad brown palm and asked: "Many wounded in your regiment?"

"A couple of dozen."

"Heavy losses?"

"A lot of us have been killed. Light a match for me, Your Honour. Thank you kindly." The Cossack took the light and as he dropped behind he shouted: "Three Cossacks from Tatarsky, near your estate, have been killed. They've done in a lot of us Cossacks."

He waved his sound hand and went to catch up with the wagon. The wind flapped through his unbelted tunic.

The commander of Listnitsky's new regiment had his headquarters in the house of a priest. On the square Listnitsky took leave of the doctor, who had kindly offered him a seat in the hospital trap, and went off to find regimental headquarters, brushing the dust off his uniform as he walked. A vividly red-bearded sergeant-major, busy changing the guard, marched past him with a sentry. He saluted smartly and, in reply to Listnitsky's question, pointed out the house. The place was very quiet and slack, like all staff headquarters situated away from the front line. Clerks were bent over a table; an elderly captain was laughing into the mouthpiece of a field-telephone. The flies droned around the windows, and distant telephone bells buzzed like mosquitoes. An orderly conducted Yevgeny to the regimental commander's private room. They were met on the threshold by a tall colonel with a scar on his chin, who greeted him coldly, and with a gesture invited him into the room. As he closed the door the colonel passed his hand over his hair with a gesture of ineffable weariness, and said in a soft, monotonous voice:

"The brigade staff informed me yesterday that you were on your way. Sit down."

He questioned Yevgeny about his previous service, asked for the latest news from the capital, inquired about his journey, but not once during all their brief conversation did he raise his weary eyes to Listnitsky's face.

"He must have had a hard time at the front; he looks mortally tired," Yevgeny thought sympathetically. As though deliberately to disillusion him, the colonel scratched the bridge of his nose with his sword-hilt and remarked:

"Well, Lieutenant, you must make the acquaintance of your brother officers. You must excuse me, I haven't been to bed for three nights running. In this dead hole there's nothing to do except play cards and get drunk."

Listnitsky saluted and turned to the door, hiding his contempt with a smile. He went out

554

reflecting unfavourably on this first meeting
with his commanding officer, and ironically
amused at the respect which the colonel's tired
appearance and the scar on his chin had in-
stilled in him.

## XV

The division was allotted the task of forcing
the river Styr and taking the enemy in the rear.

In a few days Listnitsky got used to the officers of the regiment and was quickly drawn
into the atmosphere of battle, which drove out
the feeling of ease and complacency that had
crept into his soul.

The operations to force the river were carried through brilliantly. The division shattered a
considerable concentration of enemy forces on
their left flank, and came out in the rear of the
main forces. The Austrians attempted to initi-
ate a counter-offensive with the aid of Magyar
cavalry, but the Cossack batteries swept them
away with shrapnel, and the Magyar squadrons
retreated in disorder, cut to pieces by flanking
machine-gun fire and pursued by the Cossacks.

Listnitsky went into the counter-attack with
his regiment. The troop he commanded lost one
Cossack, and four were wounded. One of them,
a young, hook-nosed man was crushed under
his dead horse. Outwardly calm, the lieutenant

rode past trying not to hear the Cossack's low hoarse groaning. He was wounded in the shoulder and kept beseeching the Cossacks riding past:

"Brothers, don't leave me. Get me free of the horse, brothers. . . ."

His low, tortured voice could be heard calling faintly, but there was no spark of pity in the surging hearts of the other Cossacks, or if there was, it was crushed by the will that drove them on relentlessly, forbidding them to dismount. The troop rode on for five minutes at a trot, letting the horses recover their wind. Half a verst away the scattered Magyar squadrons were in full retreat; here and there among them appeared the grey-blue uniforms of the enemy infantry. An Austrian baggage train crawled along the crest of a hill with the farewell smoke of shell bursts hovering above it. From the left a battery was bombarding the train, and its dull thunder rolled over the fields and echoed through the forest.

The sergeant-major leading the battalion gave the command "canter" and the three squadrons broke into a flagging trot. The horses swayed under their riders and foam scattered from their flanks in yellowish pink blossoms.

The regiment halted for the night in a small village. The twelve officers were all crowded into one hut. Broken with fatigue and hunger, they lay down to sleep. The field-kitchen arrived only about midnight. Cornet Chubov brought in a pot of soup. The rich smell awakened the officers and within a few minutes, their faces still puffy with sleep, they were eating in greedy silence, making up for the two days lost in battle. After the late meal their previous sleepiness passed, and they lay on their cloaks on the straw talking and smoking.

Junior captain Kalmykov, a tubby little officer whose face as well as his name bore the traces of his Mongolian origin, gesticulated fiercely as he declared:

"This war is not for me. I was born four centuries too late. You know, I shan't live to see the end of the war."

"Oh, drop your fortune-telling!"

"It's not fortune-telling. It's my predestined end. I'm atavistic, and I'm superfluous here. When we were under fire today I trembled with frenzy; I can't stand not seeing the enemy. The horrible feeling I get is equivalent to fear. They fire at you from several versts away, and you ride like a bustard hunted over the steppe."

"I had a look at an Austrian howitzer in Kupalka. Have any of you seen one, gentlemen?" asked Captain Atamanchukov, licking the remains of tinned meat off his ginger moustache, which was clipped in the English style.

"A wonderful piece of work! Those sights, the whole mechanism—sheer perfection," the enthusiastic reply came from Cornet Chubov, who had by this time emptied a second mess-tin of soup.

"I have seen it, but I have nothing to say. I am a complete ignoramus where artillery is concerned. To me it was just a gun like any other, with a big barrel, that's all."

"I envy those who fought in the old-time, primitive fashion," Kalmykov continued, turning to Listnitsky. "To thrust at your opponent in honourable battle, and to split him in two with your sword—that's the sort of warfare I understand. But this is the devil knows what."

"In future wars cavalry will play no part. It will be abolished."

"It simply won't exist."

"Well, that I couldn't say."

"No doubt about it."

"But you can't replace men by machines. You're going too far."

"I'm not referring to men, but to horses. Motor cycles or motor cars will take their place."

"I can just imagine a motor squadron!"

"That's all nonsense!" Kalmykov interposed excitedly. "An absurd fantasy! Armies will use horses for a long time yet. We don't know what war will be like in two or three centuries' time, but today cavalry...."

"What will you do with the cavalry when there are trenches all along the front? Tell me that!"

"They'll break through the trenches, ride across them, and make sorties far to the rear of the enemy; that will be the cavalry's task."

"Nonsense!"

"Oh, shut up and let's get some sleep."

The argument tailed off, and snores took its place. Listnitsky lay on his back, breathing the pungent scent of the musty straw on which he had spread his cloak. Kalmykov lay down at his side.

"You should have a talk with the volunteer Bunchuk," he whispered to Yevgeny. "He's in your troop. A very interesting fellow!"

"In what way?" Listnitsky asked, as he turned his back to Kalmykov.

"He's a Russianized Cossack. Lived in Moscow. An ordinary worker, but interested in the question of machinery. He's a first-rate machine-gunner, too."

"Let's go to sleep," Listnitsky proposed.

"Perhaps we should," Kalmykov agreed, thinking of something else. He frowned sheepishly: "You must forgive me, Lieutenant, for

the way my feet smell. You know, I haven't
changed my socks for a fortnight, they are
simply rotting with sweat. . . . It's really foul.
I must get a pair of foot-cloths from one of the
men."

"Not at all," Listnitsky mumbled as he
dropped asleep.

Listnitsky completely forgot Kalmykov's reference to Bunchuk, but the very next day chance
brought him into contact with the volunteer. The
regimental commander ordered him to ride at
dawn on reconnaissance patrol, and if possible
to establish contact with the infantry regiment
which was continuing the advance on the left
flank. Stumbling about the yard in the half-light,
and falling over the bodies of sleeping Cossacks,
Listnitsky found the troop sergeant and roused
him:

"I want five men to go on a reconnaissance
with me. Have my horse got ready. Quickly!"

While he was waiting for the men to assem-
ble, a stocky Cossack came to the door of the
hut.

"Your Honour," the man said, "the sergeant
will not let me go with you because it isn't my
turn. Will you give me permission to go?"

"Are you out for promotion? Or have you
done something wrong?" Listnitsky asked, trying to make out the man's face in the darkness.

"I haven't done anything."

"All right, you can come," Listnitsky decided. As the Cossack turned to go, he shouted after him:

"Hey! Tell the sergeant. . . ."

"My name's Bunchuk," the Cossack interrupted.

"A volunteer?"

"Yes."

Recovering from his confusion, Listnitsky corrected his style of address: "Well, Bunchuk, please tell the sergeant to. . . . Oh, all right, I'll tell him myself."

The morning darkness thinned as Listnitsky led his men out of the village past sentries and outposts. When they had ridden some distance he called:

"Volunteer Bunchuk!"

"Sir!"

"Please bring your horse up beside me."

Bunchuk brought his commonplace mount alongside Listnitsky's thoroughbred.

"What village are you from?" Listnitsky asked him, studying the man's profile.

"Novocherkasskaya."

"May I be informed of the reason that compelled you to join up as a volunteer?"

"Certainly!" Bunchuk replied with the slightest trace of a smile. The unwinking gaze of his greenish eyes was harsh and fixed. "I'm interested in the art of war. I want to master it."

"There are military schools established for that purpose."

"There are."

"Well, what is your reason?"

"I want to study it in practice first. I can get the theory afterwards."

"What were you before the war broke out?"

"A worker."

"Where were you working?"

"In Petersburg, Rostov, and the armament works at Tula. I'm thinking of applying to be transferred to a machine-gun detachment."

"Do you know anything about machine-guns?"

"I can handle the Bertier, Madsen, Maxim, Hotchkiss, Vickers, Lewis, and several other makes."

"Oho! I'll have a word with the regimental commander about it!"

"Please do."

Listnitsky glanced again at Bunchuk's stocky figure. It reminded him of the Don-side corkelm. There was nothing remarkable about the man. Only the firmly pressed jaws and the direct challenging glance distinguished him from the mass of other rank-and-file Cossacks around him. He smiled but rarely, with only the corners

of his lips; and even then his eyes grew no softer, but still retained a faint gleam of aloofness.
Coldly restrained, he was exactly like the corkelm, the tree of a stern, iron hardness that grows
on the grey, loose soil of the inhospitable Don-
side earth.

They rode in silence for a while. Bunchuk
rested his broad palms on his blistered saddle-
bow. Listnitsky selected a cigarette, and as he
lit it from Bunchuk's match he smelled the
sweet resinous scent of horse's sweat on the
man's hand. The back of his hand was thickly
covered with brown hair, and Listnitsky felt an
involuntary desire to stroke it.

Swallowing down the pungent tobacco
smoke, he said:

"When we get to the wood, you and another
Cossack will take the track running off to the
left. Do you see it?"

"Yes."

"If you don't come across our infantry by
the time you have gone half a verst, turn
back."

"Very good."

They broke into a trot.

At a turn of the road into the forest stood
a clump of maidenly birches. Beyond them the
eye was wearied by the joyless yellow of stunted pines, the straggling forest undergrowth

and bushes crushed by Austrian baggage trains. On the right the earth trembled with the thunder of distant artillery, but by the birches it was inexpressibly quiet. The earth was drinking in the heavy dew; the pink-hued grasses were flooded with autumnal colours that cried of the speedy death of colour. Listnitsky halted by the birches and, taking out his binoculars, studied the rise beyond the forest. A bee settled on the honey-coloured hilt of his sabre.

"Stupid!" Bunchuk remarked quietly and compassionately.

"What is?" Listnitsky turned to him.

With his eyes Bunchuk indicated the bee, and Listnitsky smiled:

"Its honey will be bitter, don't you think?"

It was not Bunchuk that answered him. From a distant clump of pines a piercing magpie stutter shattered the silence, and a spurt of bullets tore through the birches, sending a branch crashing on to the neck of Listnitsky's horse.

They turned and galloped back towards the village, urging on their horses with shout and whip. The Austrian machine-gun flung the rest of its ammunition after them.

After this first encounter Listnitsky had more than one talk with the volunteer Bunchuk. On each occasion he was struck by the inflexible will that gleamed in the man's eyes, and could not discover what lay behind the intangible secrecy that veiled the face of one so ordinary-looking. Bunchuk always spoke with a smile compressed in his firm lips, and he gave Listnitsky the impression that he was applying a definite rule to trace a tortuous path. He was transferred to a machine-gun detachment. A few days later, while the regiment was resting behind the front, Listnitsky overtook him walking along by the wall of a burned-out shed.

"Ah! Volunteer Bunchuk!"

The Cossack turned his head and saluted.

"Where are you going?" Listnitsky asked.

"To my commander."

"Then we're going the same way."

For some time they walked along the street of the ruined village in silence.

People were moving about round the few outbuildings that remained intact, horsemen rode past, a field-kitchen was smoking in the middle of the street with a long queue of Cossacks waiting their turn beside it; there was a cold drizzle in the air.

"Well, are you learning the art of war?" Listnitsky asked, glancing sidelong at Bunchuk, who was slightly behind him.

"Yes, I am."

"What do you propose to do after the war?" asked the lieutenant, glancing for some reason at Bunchuk's hands.

"Some will reap what is sown . . . but I shall see," Bunchuk replied.

"How am I to interpret that remark?"

"You know the proverb, 'Those who sow the wind shall reap the whirlwind'? Well, that's how."

"But dropping the riddles?"

"It's quite clear as it is. Excuse me, I'm turning to the left here."

He put his fingers to the peak of his cap and turned off the road. Shrugging his shoulders, Listnitsky stood staring after him.

"Is the fellow trying to be original, or is he just someone with a bee in his bonnet?" he wondered in irritation, as he stepped into the squadron-commander's well-kept dug-out.

## XVI

The second and third lines of reserves were called up together. The villages of the Don were as deserted as though everybody had gone out to mow or reap at the busy time of harvest.

But a bitter harvest was reaped along the frontiers that year; death dogged the footsteps of the men, and many a Cossack's wife wailed bare-headed for her departed one: "Oh, my darling, who has taken you from me?" The dear heads were laid low on all sides, the Cossack blood was shed, and glassy-eyes, unwakeable, they rotted while the artillery thundered its funeral dirge in Austria, in Poland, in Prussia. ... For the eastern wind did not carry the weeping of their wives and mothers to their ears.

The flower of the Cossackry had left the villages and perished amid the lice and horror of the battle-fields.

One pleasant September day a milky gossamer web, fine and cottony, hung over the village of Tatarsky. The bloodless sun smiled like one bereft, the stern, virginal blue sky was repellently clear and proud. Beyond the Don the forest was a jaundiced yellow, the poplar gleamed pallidly, the oak dropped occasional figured leaves; only the alder remained gaudily green, gladdening the keen eye of the magpie with its hardiness.

That day Pantelei Prokofyevich received a letter from the army on active service. Dunya brought it back from the post. As the postmaster handed it to her he bowed, shook his old bald pate, and deprecatingly opened his arms.

"Forgive me for the love of God for opening the letter. Tell your father I opened it. I badly

wanted to know how the war was going....
Forgive me and tell Pantelei Prokofyevich what
I said." He seemed confused and, unaware of
the ink-smear on his nose, came out of his office with Dunya, muttering something unintel-
ligible. Filled with foreboding, she returned
home, and fumbled at her breast a long time
for the letter.

"Hurry up!" Pantelei shouted, plucking at
his beard.

As she drew it out she said breathlessly:

"The postmaster told me he had read the letter and that you mustn't be angry with him."

"The devil take him! Is it from Grigory?"
the old man asked, breathing agitatedly into
her face. "From Grigory? Or from Pyotr?"

"No, Father.... I don't know the writing."

"Read it!" Ilyinichna cried, tottering heavily
to the bench. Her legs were giving her much
trouble these days. Natalya ran in from the
yard and stood by the stove with her head on
one side, her elbows pressing into her breasts.
A smile trembled like sunlight on her lips. She
still hoped for a message from Grigory or the
slightest reference to her in his letters, in reward for her dog-like devotion and fidelity.

"Where's Darya?" Ilyinichna whispered.

"Shut up!" Pantelei shouted. "Read it!" he
added to Dunya.

" 'I have to inform you,' " she began, then, slipping off the bench where she had been sitting, she screamed:

"Father! Mother...! Oh, Mama.... Our Grisha...! Oh, oh...! Grisha's ... been killed."

Entangled among the leaves of a half-dead geranium, a wasp beat against the window, buzzing furiously. In the yard a hen clucked contentedly; through the open door came the sound of ringing, childish laughter.

A shudder ran across Natalya's face, though her lips still wore her quivering smile. Rising to his feet, his head twitching paralytically, Pantelei stared in frantic perplexity at Dunya.

The communication read:

*I have to inform you that your son Grigory Panteleyevich Melekhov, a Cossack in the Twelfth Don Cossack Regiment, was killed on the 16th of September near the town of Kamenka-Strumilovo. Your son died the death of the brave; may that be your consolation in your irreplaceable loss. His personal effects will be handed to his brother, Pyotr Melekhov. His horse will remain with the regiment.*

*Commander of the Fourth Squadron,*

*Junior Captain Polkovnikov.*
*Field Army*
*18th September, 1914.*

After the arrival of the letter Pantelei seemed suddenly to wilt. He grew noticeably older every day. His memory began to go and his mind lost its clarity. He walked about with bowed back, his face an iron hue; and the feverish gleam in his eyes betrayed his mental stress.

He put the letter away under the icon. Several times a day he went into the porch to beckon to Dunya. When she came in he would order her to get the letter and read it to him, fearfully glancing at the door of the best room where his wife was mourning. "Read it quietly, to yourself like," he would say, winking cunningly. Choking down her tears, Dunya would read the first sentence, and then Pantelei, squatting on his heels, would raise his huge, hoof-like brown hand:

"All right. I know the rest. Take the letter back and put it where you found it. Quietly, or Mother...." And he would wink repulsively, his whole face contorted like burnt tree-bark.

He began to go grey, and the dazzling grey hairs swiftly patched his head and wove threads into his beard. He grew gluttonous too, and gobbled his food.

Nine days after the requiem mass, the Melekhovs invited Father Vissarion and their relations to the repast in memory of the fallen Grigory. Pantelei ate fast and ravenously with the noodles hanging from his beard like ringlets. Ilyinichna, who had been anxiously watching him during the past few days, burst into tears:

"Father, what's the matter with you?"

"Eh?" the old man said with a start, raising his bleary eyes from his plate. Ilyinichna waved her hand and turned away, pressing her handkerchief to her eyes.

"Father, you eat as though you had fasted for three days," Darya said angrily, her eyes glittering.

"I eat...? All right, I won't," Pantelei replied, overcome with embarrassment. He glanced around the table, then, pressing his lips together, and sitting with knitted brows, he lapsed into silence, not even replying to questions.

"Have courage, Prokofyevich! What's the good of grieving so much?" Father Vissarion attempted to rally him when the meal was ended. "Grigory's death was a holy one; don't offend God, old man. Your son has received a crown of thorns for his tsar and his fatherland. And you ... it's a sin, and God won't pardon you."

"That's just it, Father! 'Died the death of the brave.' That's what his commander said."

Kissing the priest's hand, the old man leaned

against the door-post, and for the first time since the arrival of the letter he burst into tears, his body shaking violently.

From that day he regained his self-control and recovered a little from the blow.

Each licked the wound in his own way. When Natalya heard Dunya scream that Grigory was dead she ran into the yard. "I'll kill myself. It's all over for me," the thought drove her on like fire. She struggled in Darya's arms, and then with joyful relief she swooned, for at least it postponed the moment when consciousness would return and violently remind her of what had happened. She passed a week in dull oblivion, and returned to the world of reality changed, quieter, gnawed by a black impotence.

An invisible corpse haunted the Melekhovs' house and the living breathed in its mouldering scent.

## XVII

On the twelfth day after the news of Grigory's death the Melekhovs received two letters by the same post from Pyotr. Dunya read them at the post office, and went speeding home like a stalk caught up by the wind, then swayed and stopped, leaning against a fence. She caused a great fluster in the village, and carried an indescribable feeling of agitation into the house.

"Grisha's alive! Our dear one's alive!" she sobbed and cried when still some distance away. "Pyotr's written. Grisha's wounded, but he isn't dead. He's alive, alive!"

In his letter dated September 20th, Pyotr had written:

*Greetings, dear parents, I must tell you that our Grisha all but gave up the ghost, but now, glory be, he's alive and well, as we wish you in the name of the Lord God health and well-being. Close to the town of Kamenka-Strumilovo his regiment was in battle, and in the attack the Cossacks of his troop saw him cut down by a Hungarian hussar, and Grigory fell from his horse and after that nobody knew anything, and when I asked them they could tell me nothing. But afterwards I learned from Misha Koshevoi that Grigory lay till night-time, but that in the night he came round and started crawling away. He crawled along making his way by the stars, and came across one of our officers wounded in the belly and legs by a shell. He picked him up and dragged him for six versts. And for this Grigory has been given the Cross of St. George and has been raised to the rank of corporal. Think of that! His wound isn't serious, he only received a skin wound on the scalp, but he fell from his horse, and got stunned. Misha told me he is already back at the front. You must excuse this letter, I'm writing in the saddle.*

In his second letter Pyotr asked his family to send him some dried cherries from their own orchard, and told them not to forget him but to write more often. In the same letter he upbraided Grigory because, so he had been told, he was not looking after his horse properly, and Pyotr was angry, as the horse was really his. He asked his father to write to Grigory, and said he had sent a message to him that if he did not look after the horse he would give him one on the nose that would draw blood, even if he had got the Cross of St. George. The letter ended with an endless list of greetings and between the crumpled, rain-blotted lines it was not hard to detect a feeling of bitterness and grief. Evidently Pyotr was not having an easy time at the front either.

Old Pantelei was a pitiful sight to see. He was dazed with joy. He seized both letters and went into the village with them, stopping all who could read and forcing them to read the letters. It was not vanity but belated joy made him brag all through the village.

"Aha! What do you think of my Grisha?" he raised his hand when the stumbling reader came to the passage where Pyotr described Grigory's exploit. "He's the first to get the Cross in our village," he declared proudly. And jealously taking the letters, he would thrust them into the lining of his cap and go off in search of another reader.

Even Sergei Mokhov, who saw him through his shop window, came out, taking off his cap.

"Come in for a minute, Prokofyevich!"

Inside, he squeezed the old man's fist in his own puffy white hand and said:

"Well, I congratulate you; I congratulate you. You must be proud to have such a son. I've just been reading about his exploit in the newspapers."

"Is it in the papers?" Pantelei's throat went dry and he swallowed hard.

"Yes, I've just read it."

Mokhov took a packet of the finest Turkish tobacco down from a shelf, and poured out some expensive sweets into a bag without troubling to weigh them. Handing the tobacco and sweets to Pantelei, he said:

"When you send Grigory Panteleyevich a parcel, send him a greeting and these from me."

"My God! What an honour for Grisha! The whole village is talking about him. I've lived to see ..." the old man muttered, as he went down the steps of the shop. He blew his nose violently and wiped the tears from his cheek with his sleeve, thinking: "I'm getting old. Tears come too easily. Ah, Pantelei, what has life done to you? You were as hard as flint once, you could carry eight poods on your back as easily as a feather, but now.... Grisha's business has taken it out of you a bit!"

As he limped along the street, pressing the bag of sweets to his chest, his thoughts again fluttered around Grigory like a lapwing over a marsh, and the words of Pyotr's letter wandered through his mind. Grigory's father-in-law Korshunov was coming along the road, and he called to Pantelei:

"Hey, Pantelei, stop a minute!"

The two men had not met since the day war was declared. A cold, constrained relationship had arisen between them after Grigory left home. Miron was annoyed with Natalya for humbling herself to Grigory, and for forcing her father to endure a similar humiliation.

"The wandering bitch," he would rail against Natalya to his family. "Why can't she live at home instead of going to her in-laws. As if they

576

fed her better there. It's through her foolishness that her father has to bear such shame and can't hold up his head in the village."

Miron went straight up to Pantelei and thrust out his oak-coloured hand:

"How are you?"

"Thanks be to God...."

"Been shopping?"

Pantelei shook his head. "These are gifts to our hero. Sergei Platonovich read about his deed in the peapers and has sent him some sweets and tobacco. Do you know, the tears came to his eyes," the old man boasted, staring fixedly into Miron's face in the attempt to discover what impression his words had made.

The shadows gathered under Miron's blond eye-lashes, giving his face a condescending smile.

"I see!" he croaked, and turned to cross the street. Pantelei hurried after him, opening the bag and trembling with anger.

"Here, try these chocolates, they're as sweet as honey," he said spitefully. "Try them, I offer them in my son's name. Your life is none too sweet, so you can have one; and your son may earn such an honour some day, but then he may not."

"Don't pry into my life.... I know best what it's like."

"Just try one, do me the favour." Pantelei bowed with exaggerated affability, running in front of Miron and fumbling with the paper bag.

"We're not used to sweets," Miron pushed away his hand. "Gifts from strangers are bad for our teeth. It was hardly decent of you to go begging alms for your son. If you're in need, you can come to me. Our Natalya's eating your bread. We could have given to you in your poverty."

"Don't you tell those lies, no one has ever begged for alms in our family. You're too proud, much too proud. Maybe it's because you're so rich that your daughter came to us."

"Wait!" Miron said authoritatively. "There's no point in our quarrelling. I didn't stop you to have a quarrel. I've some business I want to talk over with you."

"We have no business to talk over."

"Yes, we have. Come on."

He seized Pantelei's sleeve and dragged him into a side-street. They walked out of the village into the steppe.

"Well, what's the business?" Pantelei asked in more amiable tones. He glanced sidelong at Korshunov's freckled face. Folding the tail of his long coat under him, Miron sat down on

the bank of a ditch and pulled out his old tobacco pouch.

"You know, Prokofyevich, the devil knows
why you went for me like a quarrelsome cock.
As it is, things aren't too good, are they? I
want to know," his voice changed to a hard,
rough tone, "how long your son's going to
make a laughing-stock of Natalya. Tell me
that!"

"You must ask him about it, not me."

"I've nothing to ask him; you're the head of
your house and I'm talking to you."

Pantelei squeezed the chocolate he still held
in his hand, and the sticky mess oozed through
his fingers. He wiped his palm on the
brown clay of the bank and silently began to
make a cigarette, opening the packet of Turkish
tobacco and taking a pinch. Then he offered
the packet to Miron. Korshunov took it without hesitation and made a cigarette from the
tobacco Mokhov had presented so generously.
Above them hung a sumptuous foaming white
cloud, and a tender thread stretched up towards it, wavering in the wind.

The day came to its close. The September
stillness was lulled in peace and inexpressible
sweetness. The sky had lost its full summer
gleam, and was a hazy dove colour. Apple-
leaves, brought from God knows where,

scattered the ditch with vivid purple. The road disappeared over the undulating ridge of the hill; in vain did it beckon towards the unknown regions beyond the emerald, dream-vague thread of the horizon. Held down to their huts and their daily round, the people pined in their labour, exhausted their strength on the threshing-floor; and the road, a deserted, yearning track, flowed across the horizon into the unseen. The wind trod along it, stirring up the dust.

"This is weak tobacco, it's like grass," Miron said, puffing out a cloud of smoke.

"It's weak, but it's pleasant," Pantelei half-agreed.

"Give me an answer, Pantelei," Korshunov asked in a quieter tone, putting out his cigarette.

"Grigory never says anything about it in his letters. He's wounded now."

"Yes, I've heard...."

"What will come after, I don't know. Maybe he'll be killed, and then what?"

"But how can it go on like this?" Miron blinked distractedly and miserably. "There she is, neither maid nor wife nor honest widow, and it's a disgrace. If I had known it was going to turn out like this I'd never have allowed the match-makers across my threshold. Ah, Pantelei ... Pantelei. ... Each is sorry for his own child. Blood is thicker than water."

"How can I help it?" Pantelei replied with restrained frenzy. "Tell me! Do you think I'm glad my son left home? Was it any gain to me? You people!"

"Write to him," Miron dictated, and the dust trickling from under his hands into the ditch kept time with his words. "Let him say once and for all."

"He's got a child by that. ..."

"And he'll have a child by this!" Korshunov shouted, turning livid. "Can you treat a human being like that? Huh? She's already tried to kill herself and is maimed for life. ... Do you want to trample her into the grave? Huh. ... His heart, his heart ..." Miron hissed, tearing at his breast with one hand, tugging at Pantelei's coat tails with the other. "Is it a wolf's heart he's got?"

Pantelei wheezed and turned away.

"The woman's devoted to him, and there's no other life for her without him. Is she a serf in your service?"

"She's more than a daughter to us! Hold your tongue!" Pantelei shouted, and he rose from the bank.

They parted without a word of farewell, and went off in different directions.

## XVIII

When swept out of its normal channel, life scatters into many streams. It is difficult to foresee which it will take in its treacherous and winding course. Where today it trickles, like a rivulet over sand-banks, so shallow that the shoals are visible, tomorrow it will flow rich and full.

Suddenly Natalya came to the decision to go to Aksinya at Yagodnoye, and to ask, to beseech her to return Grigory to her. For some reason it seemed to Natalya that everything depended on Aksinya, that she had only to ask her and Grigory would return, and with him, her own former happiness. She did not stop to consider whether this was possible, or how Aksinya would receive her strange request. Driven on by subconscious motives, she sought to act upon her decision as quickly as possible.

At the end of the month a letter arrived from Grigory. After messages to his father and mother he sent his greeting and regards to Natalya. Whatever the reason inciting him to this, it was the stimulus Natalya required, and she made ready to go to Yagodnoye the very next Sunday.

"Where are you off to, Natalya?" Dunya

asked, watching her as she attentively studied her features in the scrap of looking-glass.

"I'm going to visit my people," Natalya lied, and blushed as she realized for the first time that she was risking great humiliation, a terrible moral test.

"You might have an evening out with me just for once," Darya suggested. "Come this evening, won't you?"

"I don't know, but I don't think so."

"You little nun! Our turn only comes when our husbands are away," Darya said with a wink and stooped to examine the embroidered hem of her new pale-blue skirt. Darya had altered considerably since Pyotr's departure. Unrest showed in her eyes, her movements and carriage. She arrayed herself more diligently on Sundays, and came back late in the evening sombre-eyed and out of temper, to complain to Natalya:

"It's terrible, really it is! They've taken away all the decent Cossacks, and left only boys and old men in the village!"

"Well, what difference does that make to you?"

"Why, there's nobody to lark about with of an evening. If only I could go off alone to the mill one day. There's no fun to be had here with our father-in-law." And with cynical frankness she asked Natalya: "How can you bear it, dear; so long without a Cossack?"

"Shame on you! Haven't you any conscience?" Natalya blushed.

"Don't you feel any desire?"

"It's clear you do."

"Of course I do!" Darya flushed and laughed and the arches of her brows quivered. "Why should I hide it? I'd make even an old man hot and bothered this very minute! Just think, it's two months since Pyotr left."

"You're laying up sorrow for yourself, Darya."

"Shut up, you respectable old woman! We know you quiet ones! You would never admit it."

"I've nothing to admit."

Darya gave her an amused sidelong glance, and bit her lips with her small snappish teeth.

"The other day Timofei Manitsev, the ataman's son, sat down beside me. I could see he was afraid to begin. Then he quietly slipped his hand under my arm, and his hand was trembling. I just waited and said nothing, but I was getting angry. If he had been a lad now —but he's only a little snot. Sixteen years old, not a day more. I sat without speaking, and he pawed and pawed, and whispered: 'Come along to our shed.' Then I gave him something!"

She laughed merrily; her brows quivered and laughter spurted from her half-closed eyes.

"What a ticking off I gave him! I jumped up. 'Oh, you this and that! You yellow-necked whelp! Do you think you can wheedle me like that? When did you wet the bed last?' I gave him a fine talking to."

Darya's attitude to Natalya had changed of late, and their relations had grown simple and friendly. The dislike which she had felt for the younger woman was gone, and the two, different in every respect, lived together amicably.

Natalya finished dressing and went out. Darya overtook her in the porch.

"You'll open the door for me tonight?" she asked.

"I expect I shall stop the night with my people."

Darya thoughtfully scratched her nose with her comb and shook her head:

"Oh, all right. I didn't want to ask Dunya, but I see I shall have to."

Natalya told Ilyinichna she was going to visit her people, and went into the street. The wagons were rattling away from the market in the square, and the villagers were coming from church. She turned up a side lane and hurriedly climbed the hill. At the top she turned and

looked back. The village lay flooded in sunlight, the little limewashed houses looked dazzlingly white, and the sun glittered on the steep
roof of the mill, making the sheet-iron glitter like molten ore.

## XIX

Yagodnoye also had been plucked of its
menfolk by the war. Venyamin and Tikhon had
gone, and the place was even sleepier, drearier
and more isolated than before. Aksinya waited on the general in Venyamin's place, while
fat-bottomed Lukerya took over all the cooking and fed the fowls. Old Sashka tended the
horses and looked after the orchard. There was
only one new face, an old Cossack named Nikitich who had been taken on as coachman.

This year old Listnitsky sowed less, and supplied some twenty horses for army remounts,
leaving only three or four for the needs of the
estate. He passed his time shooting bustards
and hunting with the borzois.

Aksinya received only brief, infrequent letters from Grigory, informing her that so far he
was well and going through the grind. He had
grown stronger, or else he did not want to tell
her of his weakness, for he never let slip any
complaint that he found active service difficult

and dreary. There was a cold note in his let
ters, as though he had written them because he
felt he had to, and only in one did he write:
"All the time at the front, and I'm fed up with
fighting and carrying death on my back." In
every letter he asked after his daughter, telling
Aksinya to write about her.

Aksinya seemed to bear the separation bravely. All her love for Grigory was poured out
on her child, especially after she became con-
vinced that it was really his. Life gave irrefu-
table proofs of that: the girl's chestnut hair
was replaced by a black, curly growth; her
eyes changed to a dark tint, and grew elongated
in their slits. With every day she became more
and more like her father; even her smile was
Grigory's. Now Aksinya could see him beyond
all doubt in the child, and her feeling for it
deepened. No longer did she start back from the
cradle, as she sometimes had before, thinking
she discerned in the child's sleeping face some
likeness to the hated features of Stepan.

But the days crawled on, and at the end of
each a caustic bitterness settled in Aksinya's
breast. Anxiety for the life of her beloved
pierced her mind like a sharp needle; it left her
neither day nor night. Restrained during the
hours of labour, it burst all dams at night, and
she tossed and turned, weeping soundlessly

and biting her hand to avoid awakening the child with her sobs; she tried to kill her mental anguish with a physical pain. She wept the rest of her tears into the baby's napkins, thinking in her childish naiveté: "It's Grisha's child, he must feel in his heart how I yearn for him."

After nights such as this she arose in the morning as though she had been beaten unmercifully. All her body ached, little silver hammers knocked incessantly in her veins, and sorrow lurked in the corners of her lips. The nights of yearning aged Aksinya.

One Sunday she had given her master his breakfast, and was standing on the steps when she saw a woman approaching the gate. The eyes under the white kerchief seemed strangely familiar. The woman opened the gate and entered the yard. Aksinya turned pale as she recognized Natalya. She slowly went to meet her. A heavy layer of dust had settled on Natalya's shoes. She halted, her big, toil-roughened hands hanging lifelessly at her sides, and breathed heavily, trying to straighten her scarred neck and failing, so that it seemed she looked sideways. "I've come to see you, Aksinya," she said, running her dry tongue over her lips.

Aksinya gave a swift glance at the windows of the house and silently led Natalya into her room. Natalya followed her. To her straining ears the rustle of Aksinya's skirt seemed unnaturally loud. "There's something wrong with my ears, it must be the heat," the confused thought scratched at her brain with a host of others.

Aksinya closed the door, and standing in the middle of the room with her hands under her apron, took charge of the situation.

"What have you come for?" she asked stealthily, almost in a whisper.

"I'd like a drink," Natalya replied, staring heavily about the room.

Aksinya waited. Natalya began to speak, with difficulty raising her voice:

"You've taken my husband from me. . . . Give me my Grigory back. You've broken my life. You see how. . . ."

"You want your husband?" Aksinya clenched her teeth, and the words fell steadily like slow raindrops on stone. "You want your husband? Who are you asking? Why did you come? You've thought of it too late. Too late!"

Laughing caustically, her whole body swaying, Aksinya went close up to Natalya. She sneered as she stared in the face of her enemy. There she stood, the lawful but abandoned wife, humiliated, crushed with misery. She who had come between Aksinya and Grigory, separating them, causing a bloody pain in Aksinya's heart. And while she had been wearing herself out with mortal longing, this other one, this Natalya, had been caressing Grigory and no doubt laughing at her, the unsuccessful, forsaken mistress.

"And you've come to ask me to give him up?" Aksinya panted. "You creeping snake! You took Grisha away from me first! You knew he was living with me. Why did you marry him? I only took back my own. He's mine. I have a child by him, but you. . . ."

With stormy hatred she stared into Natalya's eyes, and, waving her arms wildly, poured out a boiling torrent of words.

"Grisha's mine, and I'll give him up to no one! He's mine, mine! D'you hear . . .? Mine! Clear out, you shameless bitch, you're not his wife. You want to rob a child of its father? And why didn't you come before? Well, why didn't you come before?"

Natalya went sideways to the bench and sat down, dropping her head and covering her face with her hands.

"You left your husband. Don't shout like that."

"I have no husband but Grisha. No one, nowhere in the whole world." Feeling an anger that could not find vent raging within her, Aksinya gazed at the strand of black hair that had slipped from under Natalya's kerchief.

"Does he need you?" she demanded. "Look at your twisted neck! And do you think he longs for you? He left you when you were well, and is he likely to look at a cripple? I won't give Grisha up! That's all I have to say. Clear out!"

Aksinya grew ferocious in defence of her nest, in revenge for all the suffering of the past. She could see that, despite the slightly crooked neck, Natalya was as good-looking as before. Natalya's cheeks and lips were fresh, untouched by time, while her own eyes were webbed with wrinkles, and all because of Natalya.

"Do you think I had any hope of getting him back by asking?" Natalya raised her eyes, drunk with suffering.

"Then why did you come?" Aksinya panted.

"My yearning drove me on."

Awakened by the voices, Aksinya's daughter stirred in the bed and broke into a cry. The mother took up the child, and sat down with her face to the window. Trembling in every limb, Natalya gazed at the infant. A dry spasm clutched her throat. Grigory's eyes stared at her inquisitively from the baby's face.

Weeping and swaying, she walked out into the porch. Aksinya did not see her off.

A minute or two later Sashka came into the room.

"Who was that woman?" he asked, evidently half-guessing.

"Someone from our village."

Natalya walked back about three versts, and then lay down under a wild thorn. Crushed by her yearning, she lay thinking of nothing. Grigory's gloomy black eyes staring cut of a child's face were continually before her.

## XX

So vivid that it was almost a blinding pain, the night after the battle remained for ever imprinted in Grigory's memory. He returned to consciousness some time before dawn; his hands stirred among the prickly stubble, and he groaned with the pain that filled his head. With an effort he raised his hand, drew it up to his brow, and felt his blood-clotted hair. When his finger touched the wound it was as if a red-hot ember had been placed there. Then, grinding his teeth, he rolled over. Above him the frost-nipped leaves of a tree rustled mournfully with a glassy tinkle. The black branches were clearly outlined against the deep blue background of the sky, and stars glittered among them. Grigory gazed unwinkingly, and the stars seemed to him like strange, bluish-yellow fruits hanging from the twigs.

Realizing what had happened to him, and conscious of an inescapable horror, he crawled away on all fours, grinding his teeth. The pain played with him, threw him down headlong. He seemed to be crawling for an eternity. He forced himself to look back; the tree stood out blackly some fifty paces away. Once he crawled across a corpse, resting his elbows on the dead man's hard, sunken belly. He was sick with loss of blood, and he wept like a babe, and chewed the dewy grass to avoid losing consciousness. By an overturned case of shells he managed to get on to his feet, and stood a long time swaying, then started to walk. His strength began to return; he stepped out more firmly, and was even able to take his bearings by the Great Bear, moving in an easterly direction.

At the edge of the forest he was halted by a sudden warning shout:

"Stop, or I'll fire!"

He heard the click of a revolver, and looked in the direction of the sound. A man was leaning against a pine-tree.

"Who are you?" he asked, listening to the sound of his voice as though it were another's.

"A Russian? My God! Come here!" the man by the pine slipped to the ground. Grigory went to him.

"Bend down!"

"I can't."

"Why not?"

"I shall fall and not be able to get up again. I'm wounded in the head."

"What regiment are you from?"

"The Twelfth Don Cossack."

"Help me, Cossack!"

"I shall fall, Your Honour," Grigory replied, recognizing the man as an officer by his shoulder-straps.

"Give me your hand at least."

Grigory helped the officer to rise, and they went off together. But with every step the officer hung more heavily on his arm. As they rose out of a dell he seized Grigory by the sleeve and said:

"Leave me, Cossack. I've got a wound ... right through the stomach."

His eyes were dull behind his pince-nez and the breath came from his open bearded mouth in hoarse gasps. He fainted, but Grigory dragged him along, falling and rising again and again. Twice he dropped his burden and left it; but each time he returned, lifted it, and stumbled on as if walking in his sleep.

At eleven o'clock they were picked up by a patrol and taken to a dressing station.

Grigory slipped away from the station the very next day. Once on the road he tore the bandage from his head, and walked along waving the blood-soaked bandage in his relief.

"Where have you come from?" his squadron commander asked him in amazement, when he turned up at regimental headquarters.

"I've returned to duty, Your Honour."

When he left the squadron commander, Grigory saw his troop sergeant.

"My horse ... the bay, where is it?"

"He's all right, lad. We caught him as soon as we had finished with the Austrians. But what about you? We were praying for you to go to heaven."

"You were in a hurry," Grigory said with a grim smile.

An extract from regimental orders read as follows:

"For saving the life of the commander of the 9th regiment of dragoons Lieutenant-Colonel Gustav Grozberg, Cossack of the 12th Don Cossack Regiment Melekhov Grigory is promoted to the rank of corporal and recommended for the St. George Cross, 4th class."

Grigory's squadron had halted in Kamenka-Strumilovo for two days, and were now preparing to advance again. Grigory found the house in which the Cossacks of his troop were quartered, and went to see to his horse. His towels and some underlinen were missing from his saddle-bags.

"Stolen before my very eyes, Grigory," Misha Koshevoi admitted guiltily. "There was a swarm of infantry quartered here, and they stole them."

"Well, they can keep them, damn them! Only I want to bandage my head."

"You can take my towel."

Uryupin came into the shed where they were standing. He held out his hand as though the quarrel between him and Grigory had never occurred.

"Hullo, Melekhov! So you're still alive!"

"More or less."

"Your head's all bleeding. Wipe yourself."

"I will in my own time."

"Let's have a look at what they've done to you."

He forced back Grigory's head, and snorted:

"Why did you let them cut your hair off? What a sight you are! The doctors won't help you any. Let me heal you."

Without waiting for Grigory's consent he drew a cartridge out of his cartridge-case, broke the bullet open and poured the black powder into his hand.

"Misha, find me a spider's web."

With the point of his sabre Koshevoi scraped a web from a beam and handed it to Uryupin. With the same sabre Uryupin dug up some earth and, mixing it with the web and the powder, chewed it between his teeth. Then he plastered the sticky mess over the bleeding wound and smiled:

"It'll be all right again in three days," he declared. "But here I am looking after you, and yet you would have killed me."

"Thanks for looking after me, but if I'd killed you I'd have had one sin the less on my conscience."

"What a simpleton you are, lad."

"Maybe. What's my head look like?"

"There's a cut half an inch deep. Something to remember them by."

"I shan't forget them."

"You couldn't if you wanted to; the Austrians don't sharpen their swords properly so you'll have a scar for the rest of your life."

"Lucky for you, Grigory, that he got you on the slant, or you'd have been buried on foreign soil," said Koshevoi with a smile.

"What shall I do with my cap?"

Grigory twisted his hacked and blood-stained cap confusedly in his hands.

"Throw it away, the dogs will eat it."

"The grub's arrived, lads. Come and get it!" came a shout from the door of the house.

The Cossacks left the shed. Grigory's bay horse whinnied after him, turning up the whites of his eyes.

"He pined after you, Grigory," Koshevoi nodded to the horse. "I was surprised, he wouldn't eat, and whinnied all the time."

"When I crawled away I kept calling him," Grigory said in a thick voice. "I was sure he wouldn't leave me, and I knew it wouldn't be easy for a stranger to catch him."

"That's true. We only just managed to get him with a lasso."

"He's a good horse. He's my brother Pyotr's." Grigory turned his back to hide his wet eyes.

They went into the house. Yegor Zharkov was lying asleep on a spring mattress in the front-room. An indescribable disorder silently bore witness to the haste with which the owners had left the place. Fragments of broken utensils, torn paper, books, scraps of material, children's toys, old boots, scattered flour were all tumbled in confusion about the floor.

Yemelyan Groshev and Prokhor Zykov had cleared a space in the middle of the room, and were eating their dinner. At the sight of Grigory, Prokhor's calf eyes nearly dropped out of his head.

"Grisha! Where did you spring from?"

"From the other world!"

"Run and get him some grub. Don't stare like that!" Uryupin shouted.

"Won't be a minute. The kitchen's just round the corner."

Prokhor ran to the door, chewing as he went. Grigory sat down wearily in his place. "I don't remember when I ate last," he smiled guiltily.

Units of the Third Corps were moving through the town. The narrow streets were choked with infantry, baggage trains and cavalry, the crossroads were jammed and the noise of the traffic penetrated even through the closed doors of the houses. Prokhor quickly returned with a pot of soup and a pan of buckwheat.

"What shall I pour the grub into?"

Not knowing its purpose, Groshev picked up a chamber-pot, remarking: "Here's a pot with a handle."

"Your pot stinks," Prokhor said with a frown.

"Never mind. Pour it out and we'll share it afterwards."

Zykov turned the basket upside down over the vessel, and the rich, thick gruel fell out in a mass, with an amber edge of fat round it. They ate and talked.

"There's a battery of a highland mounted artillery battalion next door," Prokhor related, dabbing spittle over a grease spot on the stripe of his trousers. "They're feeding up their horses. Their warrant officer read in the paper that the Germans' allies were doing a bunk."

"You should've been here this morning, Melekhov," Uryupin muttered through a mouthful of gruel: "We were thanked by the division commander himself. He reviewed us and thanked us for smashing the Hungarian hussars and saving the battery. 'Cossacks,' he said, 'the tsar and the fatherland will not forget you.'"

As he spoke there was the sound of a shot outside, and a machine-gun began to stutter. Dropping their spoons, the Cossacks ran out. Overhead an aeroplane was circling low with a menacing roar.

"Lie down under the fence. They'll be dropping a bomb in a minute. There's a battery billeted next door to us," Uryupin shouted. "Someone go and wake Yegor up. He'll get killed on his soft mattress!"

"Bring out the rifles."

Aiming carefully, Uryupin fired from the steps.

Soldiers ran along the street, for some rea-

son ducking their heads. From the next yard
came the neighing of horses and a curt order.
Grigory glanced over the fence; the gunners
were hurriedly wheeling a gun into a shed.
Screwing up his eyes at the prickly blue of the
sky, he stared at the roaring, swooping bird.
At that moment something fell away from it
and glittered sharply in the sunlight.

A shattering roar shook the house and the
Cossacks crouching round the steps; in the next
yard a horse neighed in mortal agony. A pungent
wave of powder smoke drifted over the fence.

"Lie flat," Uryupin shouted rushing down
the steps. Grigory sprang after him, and they
threw themselves down by the palings. One
wing of the aeroplane glittered as it turned.
From the street came irregular shots. Grigory
had just thrust a fresh clip of cartridges into
the magazine of his rifle when a shattering explosion threw him six feet away from the fence.
A lump of earth struck him heavily on the
head, filling his eyes with dust.

Uryupin lifted him to his feet. A sharp pain
in the left eye prevented Grigory from seeing.
With difficulty opening the right eyelid, he saw
that half the house was demolished; the bricks
lay in a misshapen heap, a pink cloud of dust
hovering over them.

As he stood staring, Yegor Zharkov crawled

from under the steps. His entire face was a cry; bloody tears were raining from his eyes that had been forced out of their sockets. With his head buried in his shoulders he crawled along, screaming without opening his blackening lips.

Behind him one leg, torn away at the thigh, was dragged along by a shred of skin and a strip of scorched trouser; the other leg was gone completely. He crawled slowly along on his hands, a thin, almost childish scream coming from his lips. Then the scream stopped and he fell over on his side, pressing his face to the harsh, unkind, brick- and dung-littered earth. No one attempted to go to him.

"Pick him up!" Grigory shouted, still pressing his hand to his left eye.

Infantrymen ran into the yard; a two-wheeled cart with telephone operators stopped at the gate.

"Keep moving!" an officer shouted at them as he galloped past. "Don't stand there gaping!" Two women, and an old man in a long black coat came up. Zharkov was quickly surrounded by a little crowd. Pressing through them, Grigory saw that he was still breathing, whimpering and violently trembling. Great beads of sweat stood out on his deathly yellow brow.

"Pick him up! What are you, men or devils?"

"What are you howling about?" a tall infantryman snapped. "Pick him up, pick him up! But where are we to take him to? Can't you see he's dying?"

"Both legs gone!"

"Look at the blood!"

"Where are the stretcher-bearers?"

"What good could they do!"

"And he's still conscious."

Uryupin touched Grigory on the shoulder from behind. "Don't move him," he whispered. "Come round the other side and look."

He drew Grigory along by the sleeve, and pushed the crowd aside. Grigory took one glance, then hunched his shoulders and turned away to the gate. Under Zharkov's belly the pink and blue intestines were steaming. The tangled mass lay on the sand, stirring and swelling. Beside it the dying man's hand scrabbled at the ground.

"Cover his face," someone proposed.

Zharkov suddenly raised himself on his hands and, throwing his head back until it hung between his shoulder-blades, shouted in a hoarse, inhuman voice:

"Brothers, kill me.... Brothers...! What are you standing looking for...? Oh.... Oh .... Brothers, kill me!"

## XXI

The railway carriage rocked gently and the knock of its wheels was lullingly drowsy. A yellow band of light streamed from the lantern. It was good to be stretched out at full length, with boots off, giving the feet their freedom, to feel no responsibility for oneself, to know that no danger threatened one's life, and that death was so far away. It was especially pleasant to listen to the varying chatter of the wheels, for with their every turn, with every tug of the engine, the front was farther and farther off. And Grigory lay listening, wriggling the toes of his bare feet, all his body rejoicing in the fresh, clean linen. He felt as though he had thrown off a dirty skin, and, spotlessly clean, was entering a new life.

His quiet, tranquil joy was disturbed only by the pain in his left eye. It died away occasionally, then would suddenly return, burning the eye and forcing involuntary tears under the bandage. In the field hospital a young Jewish doctor had examined his eye and had told him: "You'll have to go back. Your eye is in a very unsatisfactory state."

"Shall I lose it, doctor?"

"Why should you think that?" the doctor smiled, catching the unconcealed alarm in Grigory's voice. "But you must have it attended to, and an operation may be necessary. We shall send you to Petrograd or Moscow. Don't be afraid, your eye will be all right." He clapped Grigory on the shoulder and gently drew him outside into the corridor. As he turned back he rolled up his sleeves in readiness for an operation.

After much hanging about Grigory found himself in a hospital train. He lay for days on end, enjoying the blessed peace. The ancient engine exerted all its strength to haul the long line of carriages. They drew near to Moscow, and arrived at night. The serious cases were carried out on stretchers; those who could walk were assembled on the platform. The doctor accompanying the train called out Grigory's name and handed him over to a nurse, instructing her as to his destination.

"Have you got your luggage with you?"

"What luggage do you expect a Cossack to have? A greatcoat and a field-bag, that's all."

"Follow me."

The nurse led the way out of the station, her dress rustling. Grigory walked uncertainly behind her. They took a cab. The roar of the great city, the jangle of tram-bells, the bluish gleam of electric lights had a crushing effect upon him. He leaned against the back of the cab, staring inquisitively at the crowded streets, and it was strange for him to feel the agitating warmth of a woman's body at his side. Autumn had arrived in Moscow. Along the boulevards the leaves of the trees gleamed yellow in the lamplight, the night breathed a wintry chill, the pavements were shining, and above him the stars were autumnally clear and cold. From the centre of the town they turned into a deserted side-street. The horse's hoofs clattered over the cobbles; the driver in his long blue coat swayed on his high seat and waved the ends of the reins at his mare. Railway engines whistled in the distance. "Perhaps a train just off to the Don," Grigory thought, pricked with yearning.

"Feeling sleepy?" the nurse asked.

"No."

"We shall soon be there."

The waters of a pond gleamed oilily behind an iron railing. Grigory caught a glimpse of a railed-off landing stage with a boat tied to it. There was a smell of dampness in the air.

"They even keep water behind iron bars here, not like our Don..." Grigory thought vaguely. Leaves rustled under the rubber tyres of the cab.

They stopped outside a three-storied house. Grigory jumped out.

"Give me your hand," the nurse said, bending towards him. He took her small, soft hand in his and helped her to alight.

"You smell of soldiers' sweat," she laughed quietly, ringing the bell.

"You ought to spend some time out there, nurse, then you might stink of something else," Grigory replied with suppressed anger.

The door was opened by a porter. They went up a gilt balustraded staircase to the first floor. Passing into an ante-room, Grigory sat down at a round table while the nurse whispered something to a woman in a white smock.

Faces wearing spectacles of various colours appeared round the doors that lined both sides of the long narrow corridor.

After a few minutes an orderly, also dressed in white, led him to a bathroom.

"Strip!"

"What for?"

"You've got to have a bath."

While Grigory was undressing and looking round in astonishment at the bathroom with its frosted-glass windows the orderly filled the bath with water, measured the temperature, and told him to get in.

"This tub won't do for me," Grigory muttered, lifting a swarthy leg into the bath.

The orderly assisted him to wash himself

thoroughly, then gave him a towel, linen, house-shoes, and a grey, belted dressing-gown.

"What about my clothes?" Grigory asked in amazement.

"You'll wear these while you're here. Your clothes will be returned to you when you're discharged from the hospital."

As Grigory passed a wall mirror he did not recognize himself. Tall, dark of face, with patches of crimson on his cheeks and a growth of moustache and beard, in a dressing-gown, his black hair pressed down under a bandage, he bore only a distant resemblance to the former Grigory Melekhov. "I've grown younger," he thought, smiling wanly to himself.

"Ward six, third door on the right," the attendant told him.

As Grigory entered the large white room a priest in a hospital gown and dark glasses half rose.

"Ah, a neighbour? Glad to meet you, we shall keep each other company. I am from Zaraisk," he announced sociably, offering Grigory a chair.

A few minutes later a corpulent nurse with a large, plain face opened the door.

"Melekhov, we want to have a look at your eye," she said in a low, chesty voice, and stood aside to let him pass.

## XXII

The army command decided on a big cavalry attack on the south-west front with a view to breaking through the enemy lines, destroying their communications and disorganizing their forces with sudden assaults from the rear. The command set great store by the plan, and large forces of cavalry were concentrated in the area, Yevgeny Listnitsky's regiment among them. The attack was to have begun on August 28th, but a rain storm caused it to be postponed until the following day.

Early in the morning the division was deployed over a huge area in preparation for the offensive.

About eight versts away the infantry on the right flank made a demonstrative attack to draw the fire of the enemy. Also sections of one cavalry division were dispatched in a misleading direction.

In front of Listnitsky's regiment there was no sign whatever of the enemy. About a verst away Yevgeny could see deserted lines of trenches, and behind them rye fields billowing in a wind-driven, bluish early morning mist. The enemy must have learned of the attack in preparation, for during the night they had retired some six versts, leaving only machine-gun nests to harass the attackers.

Behind heavy rainclouds the sun was rising. The entire valley was flooded with a creamy yellow mist. The order came for the offensive to begin, and the regiments advanced. Thousands of horses' hoofs set up a rumbling roar that sounded as though it came from under the ground. Listnitsky reined in his horse to prevent it from breaking into a gallop. A verst was covered, and the level lines of attacking forces drew near to the fields of grain. The rye, higher than a man's waist and entangled with twining plants and grasses, rendered the cavalry's progress extremely difficult. Before them still waved the ruddy heads of rye, behind them it lay crushed and trampled down by hoofs. After four versts of such riding the horses began to stumble and sweat, but still there was no sign of the enemy. Listnitsky glanced at his squadron commander; the captain's face wore an expression of utter despair.

Six versts of terribly heavy going took all the strength out of the horses; some of them dropped under their riders, even the strongest stumbled, exerting all their strength to keep moving. Now the Austrian machine-guns began to work, spraying a hail of bullets. The rifle fire came in volleys. The murderous fire mowed down the leading ranks. A regiment of lancers was the first to falter and turn; a Cossack regiment broke. A rain of machine-gun bullets lashed them into panic-stricken flight. Owing to the criminal negligence of the High Command, this extraordinarily extensive attack was overwhelmed with complete defeat. Some of the regiments lost half their complement of men and horses. Four hundred Cossacks and sixteen officers were killed and wounded in Listnitsky's regiment alone.

Listnitsky's own horse was killed under him, and he himself was wounded in the head and the leg. A sergeant-major leaped from his horse and picked him up, flung him over his saddle-bow and galloped back with him.

The chief of staff of the division, Staff Colonel Golovachev, took several snap-shots of the attack, and afterwards showed them to some officers. A wounded lieutenant struck him in the face with his fist and burst into tears. Then Cossacks ran up and tore Golovachev to pieces, made game of his corpse, and finally threw it into the mud of a roadside ditch. So ended this brilliantly inglorious offensive.

From a hospital in Warsaw Yevgeny informed his father that he had been given leave and was coming down to Yagodnoye. The old man shut himself up in his room, and came out again only the next day. He ordered Nikitich, the coachman, to harness the trotting horse to the drozhki, had breakfast, and drove to Vyeshenskaya. There he telegraphed four hundred rubles to his son and sent him a short letter.

*I am very glad, my dear boy, that you have received your baptism of fire. The nobleman's place is out there, not in the palace. You are much too honest and clever to be able to cringe with a peaceful conscience. Nobody in our family has ever done that. For that reason, your grandfather lost favour and died in Yagodnoye, neither hoping for nor awaiting grace from the Emperor. Take care of yourself, Yevgeny, and get well. Remember, you are all I have in the world. Your aunt sends her love. She is well. As for myself, I have nothing to write. You know how I live. How can things at the front be as they are? Is it possible that we have no people with common sense? I don't believe the newspaper reports. They are all lies, as I know from past years. Is it possible, Yevgeny, that we shall lose the campaign? I am impatiently awaiting you at home.*

True, there was nothing in old Listnitsky's life to write about. It dragged on as before, without variation; only the cost of labour rose, and there was a shortage of liquor. The master drank more frequently, and grew more irritable and fault-finding. One day he summoned Aksinya to him and complained:

"You're not attending to your duties. Why was the breakfast cold yesterday? Why wasn't the glass properly cleaned? If it happens again I shall discharge you. I can't stand slovenliness. D'you hear?"

Aksinya pressed her lips together and burst into tears.

"Nikolai Alexeyevich! My daughter is ill. Let me have time to attend to her. I can't leave her."

"What's the matter with the child?"

"She seems to be choking."

"What? Scarlet fever? Why didn't you speak before, you fool? Run and tell Nikitich to drive to Vyeshenskaya for the doctor. Hurry!"

Aksinya ran out, the old man bombarding her the while, with his deep bass voice:

"You fool of a woman, fool!"

Nikitich brought the doctor back the next morning. He examined the unconscious, feverish child, and without replying to Aksinya's entreaties went straight to the master. The old man received him in the ante-room.

"Well, what's wrong with the child?" he asked, acknowledging the doctor's greeting with a careless nod.

"Scarlet fever, Your Excellency!"

"Will it get better? Any hope?"

"Very little. It's dying. Think of its age."

"You fool!" The old man turned livid. "What did you study medicine for? Cure her!" He slammed the door in the doctor's face and paced up and down the hall.

Aksinya knocked and entered. "The doctor wants horses to take him to Vyeshenskaya."

The old man turned on his heel. "Tell him he's a blockhead! Tell him he doesn't leave this place until the child is well. Give him a room and feed him to his heart's content. But he won't go away," he shouted, shaking his bony fist. He strode over to the window, drummed with his fingers for a minute, and then, turning to a photograph of his son as a baby in his nurse's arms, stepped back two paces and stared hard at it, as though unable to recognize the child.

As soon as her child had fallen ill Aksinya had decided that God was punishing her for taunting Natalya. Crushed with fear for the child's life, she lost control of herself, wandered aimlessly about, and could not work. "Surely God won't take her!" the feverish thought beat incessantly in her brain, and not believing, with all her might trying not to believe, that the child would die, she prayed frantically to God for his last mercy, that its life might be spared.

But the fever was choking the little life. The girl lay flat on her back, the breath coming in little hoarse gasps from her swollen throat. The doctor attended her four times a day, and stood of an evening smoking on the steps of the servants' quarters, gazing up at the cold sprinkling of autumn stars.

All night Aksinya remained on her knees by the bed. The child's gurgling rattle wrung her heart.

"Mama..." whispered the small parched lips.

"My little one, my little daughter," she groaned; "my flower, don't go away, Tanya. Look, my pretty one, open your little eyes, come back. My dark-eyed darling! Why, oh Lord...?"

Occasionally the child opened its inflamed lids, and the bloodshot eyes gave her a wavering glance. The mother caught at the glance greedily. It seemed to be withdrawn into itself, yearning, resigned.

She died in her mother's arms. For the last time the little mouth gaped, and the body was racked with a convulsion. The tiny head fell back on its mother's arm, and the little Melekhov eyes gazed with an astonished, sombre stare.

Old Sashka dug a small grave under an old poplar by the lake, carried the coffin to the grave and with unwonted haste covered it with earth, then waited long and patiently for Aksinya to rise from the clayey mound. When he could wait no longer, he blew his nose violently and went off to the stables. He drew a bottle of eau-de-Cologne and a little flagon of denatured alcohol out of a manger, mixed the spirits in a bottle, and muttered as he held the concoction up to the light:

"In memory! May the heavenly kingdom open its gates to the little one! The angel is dead." He drank and shook his head wildly as he bit into a soft pickled tomato; then staring tenderly at the bottle, he said:

"Don't forget me, dear, and I'll never forget you!" and burst into tears.

Three weeks later Yevgeny Listnitsky sent a telegram saying he was on his way home. A troika of horses was sent to meet him at the station, and everybody on the estate was on tiptoe with expectation. Turkeys and geese were killed, and old Sashka flayed a sheep. The preparations were elaborate enough for a grand ball. The young master arrived at night. A freezing rain was falling, and the lamps flung little fugitive beams of light into the puddles. The horses drew up at the steps, their bells jangling. Throwing his warm cloak to Sashka, Yevgeny, limping slightly and very agitated, walked up the steps. His father hastened to meet him, sending the chairs flying in his progress.

Aksinya served supper in the dining-room, and went to summon them to table. Looking through the keyhole, she saw the old man embracing and kissing his son on the shoulder; the loose flesh of the old man's neck was quivering. Waiting a few minutes, she looked again. This time Yevgeny was on his knees before a great map spread out on the floor. The old man, puffing clouds of smoke from his pipe, was knocking with his knuckles on the arm of a chair and roaring indignantly:

"Alexeyev? It can't be! I don't believe it!"

Yevgeny replied quietly, persuasively running his fingers over the map.

The old man answered in a deep steady voice: "In that case the commander-in-chief was in the wrong. Complete lack of vision. Look, Yevgeny, I'll give you a similar instance from the Russo-Japanese campaign. Let me! Let me!"

Aksinya knocked. The old man came out animated and gay, with his eyes glittering youthfully. With his son he drank a bottle of wine of 1879 vintage. As Aksinya waited on them and observed their cheerful faces, she felt her own loneliness all the more keenly. An unwept yearning tortured her. After the death of the child she had wanted to weep, but tears would not come. A cry came to her throat, but her eyes were dry, and so the stony grief oppressed her doubly. She slept a great deal, seeking relief in a drowsy oblivion, but the child's call reached her even in sleep. She imagined the infant was asleep at her side, and she turned over and groped about the bed, hearing the whispered: "Mama, mama." "My darling," she would answer with icy lips. Even in the oppressive light of day she sometimes imagined that the child was at her knee, and she caught herself reaching out her hand to stroke the curly head.

The third day after his arrival Yevgeny sat until late in the evening with old Sashka in the stables, listening to his artless stories of the free life the Don Cossacks had led in bygone days. He left him at nine o'clock. A sharp wind was blowing through the yard; the mud squelched slushily underfoot. A young, yellow-whiskered moon pranced among the clouds. By its light Yevgeny looked at his watch, and turned towards the servants' quarters. He stopped by the steps to light a cigarette, stood thinking for a moment, then, shrugging his shoulders, resolutely mounted the steps. He cautiously lifted the latch and opened the door, passed through into Aksinya's room, and struck a match.

"Who's there?" she asked, drawing the blanket around her.

"It's only me."

"I'll be dressed in a minute."

"Don't trouble. I shall only stop for a moment or two."

He threw off his overcoat and sat down on the edge of the bed.

"So your little girl died...."

"Yes, she died ..." Aksinya exclaimed echoingly.

"You've changed considerably. I can guess what the loss of the child meant to you. But I think you're torturing yourself uselessly; you can't bring her back, and you're still young enough to have children. Take yourself in hand and be reconciled to the loss. After all, you haven't lost everything. All your life is still before you."

He pressed her hand and stroked her caressingly yet authoritatively, playing on the low tones of his voice. He dropped his voice to a whisper and, hearing Aksinya's stifled weeping, began to kiss her wet cheeks and eyes.

Woman's heart is susceptible to pity and kindness. Burdened with her despair, not realizing what she was doing, Aksinya yielded herself to him with all her strong, long dormant passion. But as the devastating, maddening wave of delight abated she came to her senses and cried out sharply; losing all sense of reason or shame she ran out half-naked, in only her shift, on to the steps. Yevgeny hastily followed her out, leaving the door open, pulling on his overcoat as he went. As he mounted the steps to the terrace of the house he smiled joyfully and contentedly.

Lying in his bed, rubbing his soft plump chest, he thought: "From the point of view of an honest man, what I have done is shameful, immoral. Grigory. . . . I have robbed my neighbour; but after all, I have risked my life at the front. If the bullet had been a little more to the right it would have gone through my head and I should have been feeding the worms now. These days one has to live passionately for each moment as it comes. I am allowed to do anything." He was momentarily horrified by his own thoughts; but his imagination again conjured up the terrible moment of attack, and how he had raised himself from his dead horse only to fall again, shot down by bullets. As he dropped off to sleep he decided: "Time enough for this tomorrow, but now to rest."

Next morning, finding himself alone with Aksinya in the dining-room, he went towards her, a guilty smile on his face. But she pressed against the wall and stretched out her hands, scorching him with her frenzied whisper:

"Keep away, you devil!"

Life dictates its own unwritten laws to man. Within three days Yevgeny went again to Aksinya at night, and she did not refuse him.


## XXIII

A small garden was attached to the eye hospital. There are many such clipped, uninviting gardens on the outskirts of Moscow, where the eye finds no rest from the stony, heavy dreariness of the city, and as one looks at them the memory recalls still more sharply and painfully the wild freedom of the forest. Autumn reigned in the hospital garden. The paths were covered with leaves of orange and bronze, a morning frost crumpled the flowers and flooded the patches of grass with a watery green. On fine days the patients wandered along the paths, listening to the church bells of pious Moscow. When the weather was bad (and such days were frequent that year) they wandered from room to room or lay silently on their beds, boring themselves and one another.

The civilian patients were in the majority in the hospital, and the wounded soldiers were accommodated in one room. There were five of them: Jan Vareikis, a tall, ruddy-faced, blue-eyed Latvian; Ivan Vrublevsky, a handsome young dragoon from the Vladimir Province; a Siberian rifleman named Kosykh; a restless little yellow soldier called Burdin, and Grigory. At the end of September another was added to the number.

While they were drinking their evening tea they heard a long ring at the bell. Grigory looked out into the corridor. Three people had entered the hall, a nurse and a man in a long Caucasian coat holding a third man under the armpits. The man's dirty soldier's tunic with dark blood-stains on the chest indicated that he had only just arrived from the station. He was operated on the same evening. A few minutes after he had been taken into the operating theatre, the other patients heard the muffled sound of singing. While he was under chloroform and the surgeon was removing the remains of one eye, which had been shattered by

a shell splinter, he sang and uttered unintel-
ligible curses. After the operation he was
brought into the ward. When the effects of the
chloroform passed, he informed the others
that he had been wounded on the German
front, that his name was Garanzha, and that
he was a machine-gunner, a Ukrainian from
Chernigov Province. He made a particular
friend of Grigory, whose bed was next to his,
and after the evening inspection they would
talk a long time in undertones.

"Well, Cossack, how goes it?" he opened
their first conversation.

"Rotten."

"Going to lose your eye?"

"I'm having injections."

"How many have you had?"

"Eighteen so far."

"Does it hurt?"

"No, I enjoy it."

"Ask them to cut the eye right out."

"What for? Not everybody has to be one-
eyed."

"That's so."

Grigory's jaundiced, venomous neighbour
was discontented with everything. He cursed
the government, the war, his own lot, the
hospital food, the cook, the doctors, everything
he could lay his tongue to.

"What did we, you and I, go to war for, that's what I want to know?"

"For the same reason everybody else did."

"Hah! You're a fool! I've got to chew it all over for you! It's the bourgeoisie we're fighting for, don't you see? What are the bourgeoisie? They're birds among the fruit-trees."

He explained the difficult words to Grigory, peppering his speech with invective. "Don't talk so fast. I can't understand your Ukrainian lingo. Speak slower," Grigory would interrupt him.

"I'm not talking so quick as that, my boy. You think you're fighting for the tsar, but what is the tsar? The tsar's a grabber, and the tsaritsa's a whore, and they're both a weight on our backs. Don't you see? The factory-owner drinks vodka, while the soldier kills the lice. The factory-owner takes the profit, the worker goes bare. That's the system we've got. Serve on, Cossack, serve on! You'll earn another cross, a good one, made of oak."

He spoke in Ukrainian, but on the rare occasions when he grew excited, he would break into pure Russian generously sprinkled with invective.

Day after day he revealed truths hitherto unknown to Grigory, explaining the real causes of war, and jesting bitterly at the autocratic government. Grigory tried to raise objections, but Garanzha silenced him with simple, murderously simple questions, and he was forced to agree.

Most terrible of all, Grigory began to think Garanzha was right, and that he was impotent to oppose him. He realized with horror that the intelligent and bitter Ukrainian was gradually but surely destroying all his former ideas about the tsar, the country, and his own military duty as a Cossack. Within a month of the Ukrainian's arrival the whole system on which Grigory's life had been based was a smoking ruin. It had already grown rotten, eaten up with the canker of the monstrous absurdity of the war, and it needed only a jolt. That jolt was given, and Grigory's artless straightforward mind awoke. He tossed about seeking a way out, a solution to his predicament, and gladly found it in Garanzha's answers.

Late one night Grigory rose from his bed and awoke Garanzha. He sat on the edge of the Ukrainian's bed. The greenish light of the September moon streamed through the window. Garanzha's cheeks were dark with furrows, the black sockets of his eyes gleamed humidly. He yawned and wrapped his legs in the blanket.

"Why aren't you asleep?"

"I can't sleep," Grigory replied. "Tell me this one thing. War is good for one and bad for another, isn't it?"

"Well?" the Ukrainian yawned.

"Wait!" Grigory whispered, blazing with anger. "You say we are being driven to death for the benefit of the rich. But what about the people? Don't they understand? Aren't there any who could tell them, who could go and say: 'Brothers, this is what you are dying for'?"

"How could they? Tell me that! Supposing you did. Here we are whispering like geese in the reeds, but talk out loud, and they'll have a bullet ready for you. The people are deep in ignorance. The war will wake them up. After the thunder comes the storm."

"But what's to be done about it? Tell me, you snake! You've stirred up my heart."

"And what does your heart tell you?"

"I can't understand what it's saying," Grigory confessed.

"The man who tries to push me over the brink will get pushed over himself. We mustn't be afraid to turn our rifles against them. We must shoot the ones who're sending the people into hell." Garanzha rose in his bed and, grinding his teeth, stretched out his hand:

"A great wave will rise and sweep them all away."

"So you think everything has to be turned upside down?"

"Yes! The government must be thrown aside like an old rag. The lords must be stripped of their fleece, for they've been murdering the people too long already."

"And what will you do with the war when you've got the new government? We'll still go on scrapping, and if we don't, then our children will. How are you going to root out war, when men have fought for ages?"

"It's true, war has gone on since the beginning of time, and will go on so long as we don't sweep away the evil government. But when every government is a workers' government they won't fight any more. That's what's got to be done. And it shall be done, may the devil bury them! It shall be. And when the Germans, and the French and all the others have got a workers' and peasants' government, what shall we have to fight about then? Away with frontiers, away with anger! One beautiful life all over the world. Ah... !" Garanzha sighed, and, twisting the ends of his whiskers, his one eye glittering, smiled dreamily. "Grisha, I'd pour out my blood drop by drop to live to see that day."

They talked on until the dawn came. In the grey shadows Grigory fell into a troubled sleep.

In the morning they were awakened by the sound of talking and a voice crying. Ivan Vrublevsky was lying face downwards on the bed sobbing, while round him stood the nurse, Jan Vareikis and Kosykh.

"What's he howling for?" Burdin grunted, poking his head out from under the bedclothes.

"He's broken his eye. He was just taking it out of the glass and it dropped on the floor," Kosykh answered with more malice than sympathy.

A Russified German, a seller of false eyes, had been moved by patriotic feelings to supply the army with his products free of charge. The day before, Vrublevsky had been fitted out with a glass eye made so skilfully that it looked just as blue and handsome as the real one. The work was so perfect that even close examination could not distinguish the imitation from the genuine. Vrublevsky had been laughing and happy as a child over it.

"I'll go home," he said in his broad Volga accent, "and catch any girl I like. I'll get married, then I'll confess that my eye's a glass one."

"He will, too, the devil!" chuckled Burdin.

And now an accident had happened and the handsome young man would return to his village a one-eyed cripple.

"They'll give you a new one, don't howl," Grigory consoled him.

Vrublevsky raised his tear-stained face from the pillow, revealing the empty socket.

"No, they won't. That eye cost three hundred rubles. They'll never give me a new one."

"And what an eye it was! Every little line was there!" Kosykh gloated.

After breakfast Vrublevsky went off with the nurse to the German's shop and the German gave him a new eye.

"Why, the Germans are better than the Russians!" Vrublevsky exclaimed, wild with joy. "A Russian merchant wouldn't give you a kopeck, but this one gives me a new eye without a murmur."

September passed. The days dragged by interminably, filled with deadly boredom. In the morning at nine o'clock the patients were served tea—two miserable, transparent slices of French bread, and a knob of butter the size of a finger-nail. After dinner they were still hungry. In the evening they had tea again, sipping cold water with it to break the monotony. The patients in the military ward changed. First the Siberian went, then the Latvian. At the end of October Grigory was discharged.

The hospital surgeon examined Grigory's eyes and pronounced their sight satisfactory. But he was transferred to another hospital, as the wound in his head had unexpectedly opened and was suppurating slightly. As he said good-bye to Garanzha, Grigory remarked:

"Shall we be meeting again?"

"Two mountains never meet, but...."

"Well, khokhol, thank you for opening my eyes. I can see now, and I'm not good to know."

"When you get back to your regiment tell the Cossacks what I've told you."

"I will."

"And if you ever happen to be in Chernigov District, in Gorokhovka, ask for the smith Andrei Garanzha, I'll be glad to see you. So long, boy."

They embraced. The picture of the Ukrainian, with his one eye, and pleasant lines running from his mouth across his sandy cheeks, remained long in Grigory's memory.

Grigory spent ten days in the second hospital. He nursed unformulated decisions in his mind. The jaundice of Garanzha's teaching was working within him. He talked but little with his neighbours in the ward, and a certain confusion and alarm was manifest in all his movements.

"A restless fellow," was the appraisal the head doctor gave him, glancing hurriedly at his non-Russian face during the first examination.

For the first few days Grigory was feverish, and lay in his bed listening to the ringing in his ears.

Then an incident occurred.

A high personage, one of the imperial family, came to pay a visit to the hospital. Informed of this in the morning, the staff of the hospital scurried about like mice in a burning granary. They redressed the wounded, changed the bed-clothes before the time appointed, and one young doctor even tried to instruct the men how to reply to the personage and how to conduct themselves in conversation with him. The anxiety was communicated to the patients also, and some of them began to talk in whispers long before the time fixed for the visit. At noon a motor horn sounded at the front door, and accompanied by the usual number of officials and officers, the personage passed through the hospital portals.

One of the wounded, a gay fellow and a joker, assured his fellow patients afterwards

that at the moment of the distinguished
visitors' entry the Red Cross flag hanging
outside the hospital suddenly began to flutter
furiously, although the weather was unusually
fine and still, while on the other side of the
street the dandy with elegant curls portrayed
on a hairdresser's signboard actually made a
low bow.

The distinguished personage went the round
of the wards, asking the usual absurd questions befitting one of his position and circumstances. The wounded, their eyes staring out of
their heads, replied in accordance with the instructions of the junior surgeon. "Just so, Your
Imperial Highness," and "Not at all, Your
Imperial Highness." The chief surgeon supplied
commentaries to their answers, squirming like
a grass-snake pierced by a fork; he was a
pitiful sight even from afar. The regal personage distributed little icons to the soldiers.
The throng of brilliant uniforms and the heavy
wave of expensive perfumes rolled towards
Grigory. He stood by his bed, unshaven, gaunt,
with feverish eyes. The slight tremor of the
brown skin over his angular cheek-bones revealed his agitation.

"There they are!" he was thinking. "There
are the people who get pleasure out of driving us from our native villages and flinging us

to death. Ah! The swine! Curse them! There are the lice on our backs. Was it for them we trampled other people's grain with our horses and killed strangers? And I crawled over the stubble and shouted? And our fear? They dragged us away from our families, starved us in barracks." The burning thoughts choked his brain. His lips quivered with fury. "Look at their fat shining faces! I'd send you out there, curse you. Put you on a horse, with a rifle on your back, load you with lice, feed you on rotten bread and maggoty meat!"

Grigory's eyes bored into the sleek-faced officers of the retinue, and rested on the marsupial cheeks of the royal personage.

"A Don Cossack, Cross of St. George," the chief surgeon smirked as he pointed to Grigory, and from the tone of his voice one would have thought it was he who had won the cross.

"From what district?" the personage inquired, holding an icon ready.

"Vyeshenskaya, Your Imperial Highness."

"How did you win the cross?"

Boredom and satiety lurked in the clear, empty eyes of the royal personage. His left eyebrow was artificially raised, in a manner intended to give his face greater expression. For a moment Grigory felt cold, and a queer chopping sensation went on inside him. He had felt a similar sensation when going into attack. His lips twisted and quivered irresistibly.

"Excuse me.... I badly want to.... Your Imperial.... Just a little need." Grigory swayed as though his back were broken, and pointed under the bed.

The personage's left eyebrow rose still higher. The hand holding the icon half-extended towards Grigory froze stiffly. His flabby lips gaping with astonishment, the personage turned to a grey-haired general at his side and asked him something in English. A hardly perceptible embarrassment troubled the members of his suite. A tall officer with epaulettes touched his eye with his white gloved hand; a second bowed his head; a third glanced inquiringly at his neighbour. The grey-haired general smiled respectfully and replied in English to His Imperial Highness, and His Highness was pleased to thrust the icon into Grigory's hand, and even to bestow on him the highest of honours, a touch on the shoulder.

After the guests had departed Grigory dropped on to his bed and, burying his face in his pillow, lay for some minutes, his shoulders shaking. It was impossible to tell whether he was crying or laughing. Certain it is that he rose with dry eyes. He was immediately summoned to the room of the chief surgeon.

"You common lout!" the doctor began, crushing his mousy-coloured beard in his fingers.

"I'm not a lout, you snake!" Grigory replied, striding towards the doctor. "I never saw you at the front." Then, recovering his self-control, he said quietly: "Send me home."

The doctor retreated behind his writing table, saying more gently: "We'll send you! You can go to the devil!"

Grigory went out, his lips trembling with a smile, his eyes glaring. For his monstrous, un-pardonable behaviour in the presence of the royal personage he was deprived of his food for three days. But his comrades in the ward, and the cook, a soft-hearted man who suffered from rupture, kept him supplied.

## XXIV

It was evening of November the fourth when Grigory on his way from the station arrived at the first village in his own district. Yagodnoye was only a few versts distant. As he passed down the street children were singing a Cossack song under the river willows:

*With shining swords the Cossacks ride....*

As he listened to the familiar words a chill gripped his heart and hardened his eyes. Avidly sniffing in the scent of the smoke coming from the chimneys, he strode through the village, the song following him.

"And I used to sing that song, but now my voice is gone and life has broken off the song. Here am I going to stay with another man's wife, no corner of my own, no home, like a wolf," he thought, walking along at a steady, tired pace, and bitterly smiling at his own queerly twisted life. He climbed out of the village, and at the top of the hill turned to look back. The yellow light of a hanging-lamp shone through the window of the last house, and in its light he saw an elderly woman sitting at a spinning-wheel.

He went on, walking through the damp, frosty grass at the side of the road. He spent the night in a little village, and set out again as soon as day was dawning. He reached Yagodnoye in the evening. Jumping across the fence, he went past the stables. The sound of Sashka's coughing arrested him.

"Grandad Sashka, you asleep?" he shouted.

"Wait, who is that? I know the voice. Who is it?"

Sashka came out, throwing his old coat around his shoulders. "Holy fathers...!

Grisha! Where the devil have you come from?"

They embraced. Gazing up into Grigory's face, Sashka said: "Come in and have a smoke."

"No, not now. I will tomorrow. I. . . ."

"Come in, I tell you."

Grigory unwillingly followed him in, and sat down on the wooden bunk while the old man recovered from a fit of coughing.

"Well, Grandad, so you're still alive. Still walking the earth?"

"Ah, I'm like a flint. There'll be no wear with me."

"And how's Aksinya?"

"Aksinya? Praise be, she's all right."

The old man coughed violently. Grigory guessed it was a pretence to hide his embarrassment.

"Where did you bury Tanya?"

"In the orchard under a poplar."

"Well, tell me all the news."

"My cough's been troubling me a lot, Grisha."

"Well?"

"We're all alive and well. The master drinks beyond all sense, the fool."

"How's Aksinya?"

"She's a housemaid now. You might have a smoke. Try my tobacco, it's first-rate."

"I don't want to smoke. Talk, or I'm leaving! I feel. . . ." Grigory turned heavily, and the wooden bunk creaked under him. "I feel you're keeping something from me, like a stone under your coat. Strike!"

"And I will strike! I can't keep silent, Grisha, and silence would be shameful."

"Tell me, then," Grigory said, letting his hand drop caressingly on the old man's shoulder. He waited, bowing his back.

"You've been nursing a snake," Sashka suddenly exclaimed in a harsh, shrill voice. "You've been feeding a serpent. She's been playing about with Yevgeny."

A stream of sticky spittle ran down over the old man's scarred chin. He wiped it away and dried his hand on his trousers.

"Are you telling the truth?"

"I've seen them with my own eyes. Every night he goes to her. I expect he's with her now."

"So that's how it is!" Grigory cracked his knuckles and sat with hunched shoulders for a long time, the muscles of his face working. There was a great vibrant ringing in his ears.

"A woman's like a cat," Sashka said. "She

makes up to anyone who strokes her. Don't you trust them, don't give them your trust."

He rolled a cigarette and thrust it into Grigory's hand. "Smoke!"

Grigory took a couple of pulls at the cigarette, then stubbed it out with his fingers. He went out without a word. He stopped by the window of the servants' quarters, panting heavily, and raised his hand several times to knock. But each time his hand fell as though struck away. When at last he did knock he tapped at first with his finger; but then, losing patience, he threw himself against the wall and beat at the window furiously with his fist. The frame rang with the blows, and the blue, nocturnal light shimmered on the pane.

Aksinya's frightened face appeared at the window for an instant, then she opened the door and gave a little scream. He embraced her, peering into her eyes.

"You knocked so hard you terrified me. I wasn't expecting you. My dear. . . ."

"I'm frozen."

Aksinya felt his big body shivering violently although his hands were feverishly hot. She fussed about unnecessarily, lighted the lamp and ran about the room, a downy shawl around her plump, white shoulders. Finally she lit a fire in the stove.

"I wasn't expecting you. It's so long since you wrote. I thought you'd never come. Did you get my last letter? I was going to send you a parcel, but then I thought I'd wait to see if I received a letter...."

She cast sidelong glances at Grigory, her red lips frozen in a smile.

Grigory sat down on the bench without taking off his greatcoat. His unshaven cheeks burned, and his lowered eyes were heavily shadowed by the cowl of his coat. He began to unfasten the cowl, but suddenly turned to fidget with his tobacco pouch, and searched his pockets for paper. With measureless yearning he ran his eyes over Aksinya's face.

She had devilishly improved during his absence, he thought. Her beautiful head was carried with a new, authoritative poise, and only her eyes and the large, fluffy ringlets of her hair were the same. But her destructive, fiery beauty did not belong to him. How could it, when she was the mistress of the master's son!

"You don't look like a housemaid, you're more like a housekeeper."

She gave him a startled look, and laughed forcedly.

Dragging his pack behind him, Grigory went towards the door.

"Where are you going?"

"To have a smoke."

"I've fried you some eggs."

"I won't be long."

On the steps Grigory opened his pack, and from the bottom drew out a hand-painted kerchief carefully wrapped in a clean shirt. He had bought it from a Jewish trader in Zhitomir for two rubles and had guarded it as the apple of his eye, occasionally pulling it out and enjoying its wealth of rainbow colours, foretasting the rapture with which Aksinya would be possessed when he should spread it open before her. A miserable gift! Could he compete in presents with the son of a rich landowner? Choking down a spasm of dry sobbing, he tore the kerchief into little pieces and pushed them under the step. He threw the pack on to the bench in the passage and went back to the room.

"Sit down and I'll pull your boots off, Grisha."

With white hands long divorced from hard work she struggled with Grigory's heavy army boots. Falling at his knees, she wept long and silently. Grigory let her weep to her heart's content, then asked:

"What's the matter? Aren't you glad to see me?"

In bed, he quickly fell asleep. Aksinya went
out to the steps in only her shift. She stood
there in the cold, piercing wind, with her arms
round the damp pillar, listening to the funeral
dirge of the northern blast, and did not change
her position until dawn came.

In the morning Grigory threw his greatcoat
across his shoulders and went to the house.
The old master was standing on the steps,
dressed in a fur jacket and a yellow Astrakhan
cap.

"Why, there he is, the Cavalier of St. George!
But you're a man, my friend!" He saluted
Grigory and stretched out his hand.

"Staying long?"

"Two weeks, Your Excellency."

"We buried your daughter. A pity ... a
pity. ..."

Grigory was silent. Yevgeny came on to the
steps, drawing on his gloves.

"Why, it's Grigory. Where have you arrived
from?"

Grigory's eyes darkened, but he smiled.

"Back on leave, from Moscow."

"You were wounded in the eye, weren't you?
I heard about it. What a fine lad he's grown,
hasn't he, Papa?"

He nodded to Grigory and turned towards
the stables, calling to the coachman:

"The horse, Nikitich!"

With a dignified air Nikitich finished harness-ing the horse and, giving Grigory an un-friendly look, led the old grey trotting horse to the steps. The frost-bound earth rustled under the wheels of the light droshki.

"Your Honour, let me drive you for the sake of old times," Grigory turned to Yevgeny with an ingratiating smile.

"The poor chap doesn't guess," Yevgeny thought, smiling with satisfaction, and his eyes glittered behind his pince-nez.

"All right, jump up."

"What, hardly arrived and you're already leaving your young wife? Didn't you miss her?" Old Listnitsky smiled benevolently.

Grigory laughed. "A wife isn't a bear. She won't run off into the forest."

He mounted the driver's seat, thrust the knout under it and gathered up the reins.

"Ah, I'll give you a drive, Yevgeny Nikolayevich!"

"Drive well and I'll stand you a tip."

"Haven't I already got enough to be thank-ful for.... I'm grateful to you for feeding ... my Aksinya ... for giving her ... a piece...."

Grigory's voice suddenly broke, and a vague, unpleasant suspicion troubled the lieutenant. "Surely he doesn't know? Of course

not! How could he?" He leaned back in his
seat and lit a cigarette.

"Don't be long," old Listnitsky called after
them.

Needle-sharp snow dust flew from under the
wheels.

Grigory pulled with the reins at the horse's
mouth and urged it to its topmost speed. Within
fifteen minutes they had crossed the rise, and
the house was out of sight. In the very first
dell they came to, Grigory jumped down and
pulled the knout from under the seat.

"What's the matter?" the lieutenant frowned.

"I'll show you!"

Grigory swung the knout and brought it
down with terrible force across the lieutenant's
face. Then, seizing it by the lash, he beat the
officer with the butt on the face and arms,
giving him no time to get up. A fragment of
the glass from his pince-nez cut Listnitsky
above the brow, and a little stream of blood
flowed into his eyes. At first he covered his face
with his hands, but the blows grew more
frequent. He jumped up, his face disfigured
with blood and fury, and attempted to defend
himself; but Grigory fell back and paralyzed
his arm with a blow on the wrist.

"That's for Aksinya! That's for me! For
Aksinya! Another for Aksinya! For me!"

The knout whistled, the blows slapped softly. At last Grigory threw Yevgeny down on the hard ruts of the road and rolled him on the ground, kicking him savagely with the iron-shod heels of his boots. When he had no strength to do more he got on to the drozhki seat, and sawing at the horse's mouth, galloped it back. He left the droshki by the gate, and, seizing the knout, stumbling over the flaps of his open greatcoat, he rushed into the servants' quarters.

As the door crashed open, Aksinya glanced round.

"You snake! You bitch!" The knout whistled and curled around her face.

Gasping for breath, Grigory ran into the yard, and heedless of Sashka's questionings, left the estate. When he had covered a verst he was overtaken by Aksinya. Panting violently, she walked along silently at his side, occasionally pulling at his sleeve. At a fork in the road, by a brown wayside cross, she said in a strange, distant voice:

"Grisha, forgive me!"

He bared his teeth, and hunching his shoulders, turned up the collar of his greatcoat. Aksinya was left standing by the cross. He did not look back once, and did not see her hand stretched out to him.

At the crest of the hill above Tatarsky he noticed in astonishment that he was still carrying the knout; he threw it away, then strode down into the village. Faces were pressed against the windows, amazed to see him, and the women he met bowed low as he passed.

At the gate of his own yard a slim, black-eyed beauty ran to meet him, flung her arms around his neck and buried her face on his breast. Pressing her cheeks with his hands, he raised her head and recognized Dunya.

Pantelei Prokofyevich limped down the steps, and Grigory heard his mother start weeping aloud in the house. With his left hand he embraced his father; Dunya was kissing his right hand.

The almost painfully familiar creak of the steps, and Grigory was in the porch. His ageing mother ran to him light-footed as a girl, wetted the lapels of his greatcoat with her tears, and embraced her son closely, muttering something disconnected in her own mother-language that could not be put into words; while by the door, clinging to it to save herself from falling, stood Natalya, a tortured smile on her pale face. Cut down by Grigory's hurried, distracted glance, she dropped to the floor.

That night in bed, Pantelei gave his wife a dig in the ribs and whispered:

"Go quietly and see whether they're lying together or not."

"I made up their bed on the bedstead."

"But go on and look, look!"

Ilyinichna got up and peeped through a crack in the door leading to the best room.

"They're together."

"Well, God be praised! God be praised!" the old man whimpered, raising himself on his elbow and crossing himself.

CPSIA information can be obtained
at www.ICGtesting.com
Printed in the USA
BVHW030810170620
581538BV00006B/436